KING OF THE ROAD

BOOKS BY R. S. BELCHER

The Six-Gun Tarot
The Shotgun Arcana
Nightwise
The Brotherhood of the Wheel
The Queen of Swords
The Night Dahlia
King of the Road

R. S. BELCHER

KING OF THE ROAD

A TOM DOHERTY ASSOCIATES BOOK ▲ TOR NEW YORK

KING OF THE ROAD

Copyright © 2018 by Rod Belcher

All rights reserved.

A Tor Book
Published by Tom Doherty Associates
175 Fifth Avenue
New York, NY 10010

www.tor-forge.com

Tor® is a registered trademark of Macmillan Publishing Group, LLC.

The Library of Congress Cataloging-in-Publication Data is available upon request.

ISBN 978-0-7653-9015-8 (hardcover)
ISBN 978-0-7653-9017-2 (ebook)

Our books may be purchased in bulk for promotional, educational, or business use. Please contact your local bookseller or the Macmillan Corporate and Premium Sales Department at 1-800-221-7945, extension 5442, or by email at MacmillanSpecialMarkets@macmillan.com.

First Edition: December 2018

Printed in the United States of America

0 9 8 7 6 5 4 3 2 1

I am indebted beyond words to the wonderful friends and family who stood with Emily, Jon, and me during a very challenging time in our lives that corresponded with the writing of this book. Thanks to Susan and David Lystlund, Faye and Jestin Jefferies, and to Justin Curtis, Robert Flack, and Matt Hazelgrove. I will never be able to fully express to you all, or repay, how much your love, support, and belief meant to my family and to me.

Also I wanted to dedicate this book to the members of Truckers Against Trafficking (TAT), who are real-life examples of the ideal of the Brotherhood of the Wheel. TAT are regular men and women working out on the roads of America, combating a silent, invisible evil that destroys innocent lives. You can find out more about TAT and their mission at http://truckersagainsttrafficking.org/. Thank you for your efforts and for your example. The wheel turns.

And for Jon and Emily, as always. Dad loves you.

I've rode a million miles or more, the rambling fever burns
deep inside.
I've been in almost every town, but I could never settle down.
I've got that one more train to ride.

AN OLD HOBO SONG

—*LIBERTY JUSTICE (retired trucker and hobo)*

KING OF THE ROAD

The coyote knew the devil was behind the headlights. The beams sprang out of the desert night, halogen blades stabbing his eyes in the rearview. It was an 18-wheeler, like his own, coming up fast, seemingly out of nowhere. This section of I-10 was like driving on the lunar surface, desolate desert, a sky burning with the ghost-light of a million stars. Traffic had been sparse on the highway since they'd left Lobo bound for Houston, and there were no signs of the Texas Highway Patrol along the road past Fort Stockton thanks to 'Dillo's friends. It should be a milk run, drop off the cargo and collect the cash. Now, he could see, feel, the other big rig closing behind him like a storm of diesel and chrome.

The driver didn't think of himself as a "coyote" any more than he considered himself a "human trafficker." He was just a swinging dick trying to make a living, doing a shit job that fulfilled an ever-growing demand. He felt he was overworked and underpaid. He had bills, a few little bastards he had to pay child support for, but he hadn't paid in years. He had a parole officer up his ass every few weeks, shylocks too. If he didn't piss in a cup or pay the fucking vig they both made his life miserable.

He was just trying to get by like everybody else. It wasn't like he fucked the cargo or something. He left that sick shit for the customers. He was strictly transportation, pick up and drop off. His name was Blue, and he'd never considered himself a slaver, never thought of the cargo chained up in the trailer of his rig—roasting in the desert sun, freezing in the unforgiving desert night—as children, as human. They were product, like lettuce or roosters, and he was taking them to market. Hopefully, not too much of the crop spoiled getting there.

"Shit," Blue muttered, seeing the 18-wheeler's cool, halogen headlights grow closer, brighter. Motherfucker wasn't slowing down.

"Wha?" Swifty, his partner on this run, grunted as he pushed his cowboy hat back on his head. A cold, half-smoked Black & Mild cigarillo dangled from Swifty's mouth. He cradled an AA-12 automatic shotgun against his chest. As far as Blue could tell from their association, Swifty didn't think about much, he just fucked people up and got paid for it. He didn't give a whore's damn what anyone thought. "Wha th' fuck you say, 'shit' fer?"

"Got a rig coming up on us," Blue said; the toothpick in his mouth was moving around in a furious circle. "Didn't see them, then, boom, they there are. I don't like it."

"Well, hell," Swifty said, straightening up in his seat, "probably just some joker that snuck in your back door, you paranoid fucker."

"It ain't," Blue said, getting a little pissed. "I don't like it."

"Let 'em roll on by," Swifty said. "Jist another gear-jammer. This load is protected; ain't no cop or no competition goin' to fuck with 'Dillo, you know that."

Blue relaxed a little. Swifty was right. They were carrying product branded with 'Dillo's mark—a crude jailhouse cartoon of a coiled armadillo—burned onto the back of the neck of every child in the trailer. Anyone tried to jack them, 'Dillo would make sure his crew of assassins, many with badges, explained how bad that was for their business. 'Dillo owned the Houston pipeline and no one was stupid enough to fuck with him or his people. The truck approached. It stayed in their lane; its brights were irritating now.

Blue grabbed his CB's mic. He was running with it on channel 19, the trucker's channel. "Break 1-9, Break 1-9, this is the Blue Boy to that bumper sticker up on my back pocket, you got your ears on?" Blue said into the hand mic. "You need to either put the pedal down, crackerhead, or kill those blinders you're hitting me with, come on?"

It was quiet, and Blue glanced over to Swifty, who was squinting into the side mirror and frowning. After a moment, there was a hiss on the radio, and then a voice thick with a southern twang cut through the silence. "Pull your rig over, Blue Boy, right now," the voice said. "Your run's over, son. You ain't taking those poor kids nowhere, and your ass is headed to the pokey. You can go in walking or they can carry you in a bag, don't make me no-never-mind."

"Who the fuck is this?" Blue said, panic swelling inside him like a balloon. Swifty flicked the safety off the shotgun and pulled out a burner cell phone. He hit a button for a saved number.

"The handle's Paladin," the voice said, "and you pull over right now. Don't try running, you won't make it."

"Paladin," Blue said, in a full panic now, "Paladin! Holy shit, it's *him*, it's fucking *them*!"

"Calm your ass down," Swifty said. "I'm calling our boys; they'll deal with this."

"Shit, they can't deal with *them*," Blue said, almost shouting. "You can't outrun *them*! They're fucking everywhere!"

"Shut your mouth and drive," Swifty said, waiting for someone to pick up on the other end of the burner. "*They* are a load of bullshit, a truck stop fairy tale. They ain't real." Someone answered the phone. "Yo, chief, it's me, we got some cowboy in a big ole pete on our tail. He knows about the cargo and he's ordering us off the road! I thought you mutherfuckers got paid to keep that shit from happening! Git your asses up here and earn your god-damn pay! We jist passed mile marker 263. You deal with him or you can explain to 'Dillo why the run didn't git through!" Swifty hung up and looked over to Blue, who was wiping perspiration off his upper lip and forehead with damp hands. "It's handled, ya pussy," he said. "Keep driving."

. . .

The truck pursuing Blue's beat-up old Mack was a Peterbilt 379 with no trailer. The cab of the truck was white with a red Jerusalem cross pattern on the hood and doors. The truck's chrome grille also bore the mark of the Crusader's cross. On the driver-side door was the CB handle of the truck's driver and owner, PALADIN, a scarlet signature.

The interior of the Peterbilt's cab looked more like the cockpit of a space-ship than a truck. There were illuminated instrument panels, a laptop com-puter mounted on a swivel base, GPS systems, police scanners, radar detectors, and an excellent stereo system. The Highwaymen's "American Remains" was playing on the system at present, accompanied by the deep, throaty hum of the rig's powerful engine.

The gear shift was shaped like a sawed-off shotgun, the barrel sunk into the transmission well, with the red Crusader's cross inlaid on the pearl handle pistol grip. Swaying beneath the rearview mirror were numerous charms and totems dedicated to gods and saints, patrons and protectors of travelers and roads: Hermes, the Egyptian god Min, St. Christopher, the Dōsojin, Meili, Legba—the loa of the crossroads—and others.

The driver, Jimmie Aussapile, was lanky except for his solid beer gut. Jimmie was in his early fifties with a scrub of beard from too many days on the road without a razor. His teeth were yellow and a little uneven, a chaw of tobacco nested in his swollen cheek. Jimmie's surviving blond hair resided in a fringe along the sides of his head and in a long, braided ponytail, Willie Nelson–style. He wore a gray mesh baseball cap adorned with a grotesque character from the *Squidbillies* cartoon show; it was a cherished gift from his little girl. He was dressed in a black T-shirt, a well-worn, red and black, unbuttoned flannel, and a black Air Force–style crew jacket with an American flag patch on the shoulder. He wore grease-stained, faded jeans, a wallet on a chain in his back pocket, and steel-toed work boots, a straight razor tucked away in one of them.

Jimmie switched the CB channel from 19 to 23; his bright green eyes never left Blue's truck as he did, nor as he keyed the Bluetooth wireless mic headset he wore.

"Bandit One to Bandit Two, do you copy, over?"

. . .

Ten miles further down I-10, Lovina Marcou watched the lonely highway and waited. The Louisiana State Police investigator held a walkie-talkie-like CB unit and answered Jimmie. "This is Bandit Two," she replied, "I'm reading you 5 by 5, Bandit One, over."

Lovina was a dark-complected black woman. Her hazel eyes were flecked with green and gold and she had prominent, angular cheekbones and a haughty, aristocratic nose. Her long, straight, black hair normally fell to her shoulders with straight bangs, but she had her hair pulled up into a simple ponytail trailing out from a dark blue LSU baseball cap. She wore jeans and a black sweater. Her dark blue windbreaker bore the Louisiana State Police seal on the breast and STATE POLICE in large yellow letters on the back. She leaned against her car and kept scanning the road.

Her car was a beauty, a 1968 matte black Dodge Charger with a 440 V-8 engine. Lovina and her Pops had built the car together when she was a girl. The Charger was pulled over to the side of I-10, which was dark and silent in the cold desert night, except for the crimson glow of the hissing road flares Lovina had dropped in a line across the highway. She keyed her radio's mic again.

"Where's our backup, Jimmie? Where's Cecil?" she asked.

"On his way," Jimmie said. "Something about warrants, jurisdictions, and some fool judge. We are headed at you, Lovina, ready or not. Bandit Three, you in position, come on?"

"Yeah, I am," a young man's voice replied from the CB. The voice had an odd accent, a mix of Scottish brogue and southern drawl. "And who the fuck came up with this Bandit Three shit?"

. . .

Roughly 150 miles to the west, on a low hill overlooking the town of Lobo, Texas, Hector "Heck" Sinclair sat on his T5 Blackie motorcycle and watched the compound below him through a pair of military night vision binoculars. Heck spoke over a wireless CB headset with the transmitter clipped to his belt.

"Burt Reynolds was Bandit One," Heck said into his headset mic, "Jerry Reed was Bandit Two, and there never was any fucking Bandit Three in the movies!"

The young biker's hair was an angry explosion of red—often likened to an anime cartoon superhero—with long red sideburns. Heck wore riding leather pants and military boots, an old, faded Dropkick Murphys T-shirt, a leather riding jacket with an MC cut for his club, the Blue Jocks, over the jacket as well as a military harness covered in weapons and grenades.

"Wasn't Bandit Three the orangutan?" Lovina offered over the radio. Heck shook his head and rolled his eyes.

"No—fuck—no—that was *Every Which Way but Loose*," Heck said into his mic, "and that wasn't even a fucking Burt Reynolds movie for fuck's sake! That was Clint Eastwood, Lovina." He sighed. "What should I expect from a dog-face?"

"You secure that shit right now, Jarhead," Lovina replied, smiling. "Maybe the one with the elephant, then?"

"Okay," Heck said, "Let's get this straight, right here, right now. There was only *one Smokey and the Bandit* movie—*one*. Just like there was only one *Highlander* movie . . . and the TV show."

"Great, I'm so glad we got that all cleared up," Jimmie said, noticing a pair of cars coming up on him from behind quickly. "I love our tactical chatter. Heck, be ready as soon as your backup gets there. Y'all are going to hit the whole town."

Lobo wasn't even a speck on most maps of Texas. It had been a small town once, but over long years the desert had devoured most of it. Lobo was a gas station, a Dollar General, some rotting clapboard houses left over from the last century, a few trailers, and even more ghosts.

Two years ago, a group of trucks and cars had driven into Lobo just as the sun bled out and died on the floor of the desert. A small army descended upon the less-than-a-hundred remaining citizens of the town. By dawn the human trafficker Emile Orlando Dia, better known to the Houston underworld as "Armadillo," or "'Dillo" outside of earshot, owned Lobo lock, stock, and barrel.

"Ready, willing, and able," Heck said, scanning the storage container the traffickers had converted into barracks. Many of the newly arrived children were locked inside them, forced to endure conditions that would be considered cruel for animals. Heck shifted his gaze to the "orphanage" the slavers had built. People came to Lobo and "adopted" children from the vaguely churchlike building. It had been in business for almost eighteen months. Heck's guts were vibrating in anticipation of the raid, of getting to strike out at these men. "They damn well better hurry up."

"Be cool," Jimmie said. "We've been setting this up and coordinating it with Cecil for months now. We want everything to go . . ." The blue LED rollers of a Texas state trooper and the red and blue lights of a county deputy's patrol car suddenly flared to life in Jimmie's rearview mirror. ". . . straight to hell," Aussapile finished. "Damn it, I got two Texas bubblegum machines on my back door. Let me switch over and see if I can smooth this out."

"Burt Reynolds, the real Bandit One, would know how to handle that," Heck said. Jimmie could hear the grin in the biker's voice. His only response was to switch back over to channel 19.

"Break 1-9 to the county mounties on my back door, how can I help you gentlemen?"

"You can pull your ass on over," one of the cops replied. "You're speeding, boy."

"The wheel turns," Jimmie said.

"Well they goddamned better stop turning pronto, gear-jammer," one of the cops replied into the radio.

"Officer, the truck I'm chasing is carrying abducted children bound for Houston!" Jimmie said. "I'm working with Major Hammer with the—" A gunshot shattered Jimmie's driver-side mirror. It was fired from one of the patrol cars chasing him. "Damn it!" Jimmie muttered to himself, "why is it always the mirror? Those things cost!"

"Shots fired, I repeat, shots fired!" one of the cop's voices shouted over the radio. "All units, we are under fire from the truck driver, I repeat, shots fired! All units respond!"

"What?" Jimmie said. "I didn't fire no—" A quick pattern of booms from the trafficker's truck ahead of him shattered his windshield and blew a hole in the neck rest of his seat, inches from his head. One of the talismans to a road god sacrificed itself to stop the shot pellets headed straight for Jimmie's face, but it couldn't stop the stinging rain of glass that sprayed him. A man was out on the running board on the passenger side of the slaver's cab. He held on to the bar by the door and cradled a still smoking automatic scatter gun. Jimmie was caught in a kill box between the cops behind him and the trafficker in front of him.

"Awww, hell." Jimmie began to swerve to avoid more shots coming from the police and to try to not give the man with the shotgun another clear shot. Jimmie flipped a switch, and a powerful spotlight flashed to life, blinding the shotgunner.

"Shit!" Swifty said, blinking and trying to focus. He got a mouthful of road dust for his trouble.

Jimmie flipped his CB back over to channel 23, "Lovina, Heck, we got dirty cops in this. I have two on my tail, one state and the other a county deputy. Watch yourselves!"

"So we may have no backup coming," Lovina said as she walked to the back of the Charger and opened the trunk. "I'm betting this Armadillo has paid off cops all the way along the pipeline to run interference for his shipments."

"We know we can trust Cecil," Jimmie said. "They can't buy him."

"I'm glad Cecil and Major Hammer kept this all as quiet as they could, or the traffickers would have been tipped off already." Over the radio, Lovina heard the whine of a bullet and a horrible crashing sound. "Jimmie, you okay?"

"Jimmie?" Heck said, straightening in the seat of his bike, as he too heard the ruckus over his headset.

"I'm good," Aussipile said, hunched over his wheel trying to present as little of a target as he could. His cap was on the floor alongside thousands of tiny cubes of broken windshield glass. "I feel like a squirrel run up a tree." The stereo was still blaring. Now it was "Under my Wheels" by Alice Cooper. "We're less than two miles from you, Lovina. Whatever you're going to do, get ready to do it."

▪ ▪ ▪

Lovina rummaged through the trunk's well-ordered contents. Among the survival, forensic science, and automotive repair gear stored was an aluminum gun case. Lovina opened the case to reveal a massive revolver with a 13-inch-long barrel. The gun had custom grips and sights and extensive port venting along the barrel. Lovina lifted the Pfeifer Zeliska revolver from its foam cradle and quickly loaded the massive .600 Nitro Express bullets through a gate opening in the side of the cylinder, rotating the cylinder until all five of the monstrous rounds were in the gun.

Lovina snapped the breach loader shut and hefted the pistol, which was the size of a sawed-off shotgun. She stepped onto the asphalt. In the distance, she saw the headlights of the approaching semis and the pulsing blue lights of the pursuing police cars. The red glare of the road flares painted Lovina's face as she planted herself square in the middle of the road.

Lovina turned, centered her feet evenly, and held the huge pistol in a modified point-shooting stance; her arms were low and bent in anticipation of the massive recoil. The trafficker's truck was barreling down on her, its air horn bellowing. The grille of the coyote's truck became Lovina's universe. The hurtling rig rumbled forward, straight toward her.

In Lobo, Heck was frantic to be back east, helping his friends. The lights all came on in the orphanage compound and there was a lot of shouting, most of it in Spanish. Music started blaring from a big PA speaker on a pole. It was "Ace of Spades" by Motörhead, probably intended to wake the whole compound up.

Gunmen, at least a dozen, poured out of the building, brandishing flashlights and rifles. Streams of sleepy Latino children also began to pour from the buildings. Most of them were naked and malnourished, shivering in the cold desert air.

"Uh, guys," Heck said, leaning closer, lowering his binoculars, "they're doing something with the kids." The traffickers ordered the children to move quickly toward a long scar of a trench that curled around the perimeter of the encampment. Some of the men carried gasoline cans. A sick realization twisted Heck's gut.

"No," Heck muttered to himself, "don't you do it, don't you fucking do it."

"Heck," Jimmie said, a reassuring voice in the middle of the chaos over the headset, "you have to wait for the backup. There are too damn many of them to handle alone. Wait, hold."

. . .

The cops were right on Jimmie's tail. The officers on the passenger sides of the two patrol cars were firing their 9mm sidearms at Jimmie's truck and had come damn close to hitting him several times. There were bullet holes and debris all over the cab. The guy with the combat shotgun on the running board of Blue Boy's truck had put a couple of holes in Jimmie's radiator, and steam was pouring out in angry plumes. Everything smelled of burning rubber and coolant.

Jimmie saw the light of Lovina's flares come into view ahead. It was now or never. He slowed his rig and let the cops do exactly what he expected them to do. The highway patrolman took the lead and accelerated up on Jimmie's truck until his car's rear bumper was at about the one o'clock position from Jimmie's front bumper. He was going to try a PIT maneuver to force Jimmie off the road. Jimmie knew he had to time his response perfectly or else this would end up an ugly mess.

. . .

Lovina closed her eyes and felt the unyielding blacktop under her feet, felt the white and yellow lines of paint, began to see them flare in her mind's eye, begin to glow behind her lids. She felt herself anchored to the highway, to the Road, the mysterious, ancient power burning though its asphalt arteries, moving up her legs, filling her, connecting her to endless energy. Lovina opened her eyes, and, impossibly, the truck was *further away* from her than it had been a second ago.

The lines of the Road burned in her vision, neon streamers, channels of velocity and inertia running like a river of secret fire from coast to coast. The power of the Road filled her, yielded to her will. The truck moved backward, moved forward slowly, slowly, then backward again.

Lovina took a sip of breath and slowly, evenly exhaled as she pulled the trigger of the .600 Nitro. The universe exploded in a bloom of cordite and flame. The force of the discharge made her wrists, her arms, her spine ache. It nearly knocked her off her feet, but Lovina dug her heels in and held her ground, letting the Road anchor her. The long hours of practice with this gun at the range, at the junkyard blowing holes in old engine blocks, paid off, and she endured the first shot. The grille of Blue's truck vaporized in an eruption of splinted steel and hemorrhaging steam, but the truck kept moving. Lovina blinked, and it was further away from her again, trailing steam, but now a good eighth of a mile further back than it had been a second before.

Blue was horrified as he jammed on the gas, trying to run over the cop in the road with the hand cannon, but with each shot, it was as if he was somehow being moved back just a little bit more on the highway, like a video game with the reset button being punched again, and again. It was impossible, but the highway seemed to be expanding outward, growing, stretching. He couldn't reach the woman, couldn't get past her.

Lovina was surprised and relieved that her attempt was working. She didn't trust road magic and still didn't fully understand how she had managed to be gifted with it, but like it or not, trust it or not, she had to meet it halfway, look it in the eye, and master it. She braced for another shot, ready for the bone-shaking impact of the gun. Lovina fired again and again and again.

■ ■ ■

Another bullet whined by Jimmie's ear. For a second, he thought he saw Lovina in the middle of the highway; then she was obscured by an explosion. It was the only spare second Jimmie had. He saw the troopers' car maintain his speed, and then he saw the hint of his brake lights coming on, and he slammed on the truck's brakes with a noisy shush of the air lines.

The deputy's patrol car behind Jimmie smashed into the back of his cab. It was crushed as it ran up onto the trailer coupling behind the cab. The patrolman swerved left to perform the PIT just as Jimmie braked hard. The patrolman's car shot in front of Jimmie's rig, swerved to stabilize, and failed as Jimmie's semi T-boned him, knocking him out of control. The dirty patrolman on the passenger side of the car that had been shooting at Jimmie flew free of the passenger-side window. The car began a series of vicious rolls that crushed the ejected patrolman under it and continued until the crumpled cruiser was on its roof at the bottom of a hill beside the highway, a fog of dust and steam cloaking it.

■ ■ ■

Lovina moved to the side, missing being hit by the trafficker's rig by inches, as the dying truck rolled to a stop on the road, its radiator and engine block demolished by the powerful nitro rounds. Swifty, still on the running board, still armed with his auto shotgun, began to bring it to bear on Lovina as the truck passed. Lovina was quicker on the draw than the coyote, and the final round from the massive gun tore through what had been Swifty's chest a second earlier and continued through the cab's door ending deep in Blue's now shattered right arm. The driver passed out in shock from the impact. The truck sputtered and died as what was left of Swifty slid down the door and plopped onto the cold asphalt of the highway, like a sacrifice to the Road itself. Lovina lowered the empty pistol and hurried to see if Jimmie was okay.

■ ■ ■

Jimmie brought his battered rig to a stop, dragging the crumpled deputy's car behind him. The trucker's face was a scarlet road map of glass cuts. Jimmie slipped the secret catch on his gear shift, and the fully functional, sawed-off shotgun slipped free of the transmission well. He pulled it out by the pistol grip and jumped from the truck. Both deputies in the car smashed into the back of Jimmie's truck were hidden by the expanded airbags but were still, either dead or badly injured from the crash. Down the hill, the surviving dirty trooper struggled from the wrecked car, and Jimmie hurried toward him.

. . .

"Guys . . ." Heck said, his whole body full of adrenaline burning like acid. "Jesus, they're getting ready to kill the kids, Jimmie? You there, man, you fucking read me?"

The traffickers were lining the kids up on one side of the pit. A half-dozen men with AK-47s were lined up on the opposite side. There were rows of kids after the first, waiting to be shot, to fall into the mass grave. The children were crying, moaning in terror. Some prayed in Spanish, some called upon mommy or daddy to save them. Stolen, abused, sold into slavery, and then murdered and burned in the desert, like trash. A great fucking life for a kid. Over the open channel, Heck heard distant sirens and Jimmie's labored breath.

. . .

Jimmie huffed and gasped for air as he tried not to fall down the side of the hill. He struggled to summon air to respond and wished for the millionth time he'd use that damn gym membership. "Heck, cavalry almost here! They must almost be to you too. Hang on!"

. . .

Heck felt the terrible thing that had spoken to him in the Afghan desert whisper in his churning blood. It was chanting in an alien language, just as it had when it burned, devoured, the rest of his squad, his friends. He didn't know the language, but it felt old, tasted like ancient dust in his mouth, but his heart knew the chant, knew what it was saying. Heck didn't listen to the calm voice of reason—Jimmie Aussapile—in his ear, he listened to the laughing fire in his veins, and he began to grin. Below, the first row of children were assembled, and the gunmen raised their rifles to fire.

"There are too damn many of them, Heck! You can't do this alone, son!" Jimmie's voice said over the headset.

"Can't?" Heck said, as he slipped his polished stainless steel facemask down. It was fashioned to resemble a grinning, tusked, Japanese demon with small horns, an Oni. "Well, that's a fucking bleak attitude, old-timer." He kicked the T5 in the guts and the motorcycle snarled like a primal thing. The slavers paused at the sound, turned toward the hill at their backs. The children looked up too. There was the low growl of an engine and then laughter, like a maniac's, that rose above the engine noise and carried on the wind.

"Too many? Let's fucking see, yeah?" Heck said. He jammed the accelerator as the bike's tires spit dirt. The machine and rider hurtled forward, launching off the hill into the air, a laughing demon with a steel face. In midair, Heck grabbed the MP9 machine guns strapped to his harness and opened up on the surprised executioners, guns clattering in either hand. The six men on his side of the trench twisted—spun by the bullets—and died. Heck let the smoking guns drop to his chest again; he grabbed the handlebars just as the bike's front wheel touched down.

. . .

"Heck," Jimmie shouted over the radio as he heard the laughter and the sound of machine gun fire. "Heck? No, wait! Damn it!"

The crooked trooper was out of the car and aiming his pistol at Jimmie. Aussapile brought his shotgun up. His lungs burned, and he couldn't gulp enough air, but he ignored it. The fear and the adrenaline helped with that.

"Drop the gun," the trooper and Jimmie said at the same time.

"You first," Jimmie said. "Your people know you're working for 'Dillo!"

"They don't know shit," the trooper said. His face was bleeding from a deep gash on his left cheek, and a dark stain was growing from a nasty wound under his gun arm. "You failed to pull over and started shooting at me and the deputy. I blow your cracker ass away, and I get to tell the story any damn way I please. Who they gonna believe, some anonymous shit-kicker or a brother officer with fifteen years on the job?"

"I have to say," a voice called out, "I'm leaning toward the shit-kicker." Lovina, from the crest of the hill, aimed her Glock at the dirty cop. "Lay down your sidearm, officer." The trooper looked widely from Jimmie to Lovina. "Put it down now, and you get to live, get to make some deal you don't deserve. Keep that gun in your hand and I'll send you on your way."

Lovina's gun didn't waver. The steel in her voice reached the last rational part of the patrolman's brain. He placed his gun on the ground with trembling hands, then placed his palms on the overturned police car. Jimmie stopped holding his breath and sighed, lowering the shotgun. Lovina made her way down the hill, shouting orders to the dirty cop, who struggled to his knees and then on his belly as she cuffed him.

"Thanks," Jimmie said with a sigh.

. . .

The town of Lobo burned. The bodies of traffickers littered the blood-soaked sand. The children had jumped into the pit that was supposed to be their grave but was now their salvation. The kids shrieked as bullets whined all about them.

Heck rode through a gauntlet of gunmen, a dozen still standing. Many of the shooters had taken cover and continued firing on the biker with shotguns, pistols, a few Uzis and MAC-10s. Heck kept moving, kept them off-kilter by lobbing grenades at the trucks and utility shacks they were hiding behind. Explosions lit the night.

Heck jammed a leg down and shifted the bike in a sharp turn toward a concentration of men clustered behind and under a beat-up old farm truck. He was out of ammo for one of the MP9s and the other was close to empty. He accelerated toward the truck; an angry, hot rain of gunfire whined around him. At the last possible second, he jerked the handlebar hard to the left and extended a leg off the pegs to slide the T5 under the truck. Heck dropped a grenade a foot from the face of a wide-eyed, horrified gunman and slid out the other side of the truck, pushed up with his road-rashed leg, righting the motorcycle, and accelerating up and out of the slide.

The truck was lifted off the ground by the force of the explosion as Heck sped away. The screams of slavers around the truck were lost in the blast, and the truck's exploding fuel tank rained flame onto the "orphanage" and the house trailers that the coyotes used for quarters. Black smoke rose into the night. Far off, there was a chorus of sirens, growing slowly closer.

The brutal, inexact math of the firefight tumbled and tabulated in Heck's head. He was pretty sure he'd taken out over a dozen men, but he knew there was at least half that number still up and trying to kill him. He turned the bike again, sharply, to keep them from getting a bead on him. He heard the *whoosh* of a rocket-propelled grenade sail past him and felt the pressure and the heat of the deafening explosion as it detonated, crumpling another trailer like it was a tin can.

Heck struggled to keep the bike up and stabilize himself after the blast; as he slowed to get control, a trafficker with a shotgun popped out from behind a brick wall and fired. The 12-gauge, solid slug felt like a speeding car had just hit him square in the chest. The biker grunted and flew off the bike, skidding about ten yards before he came to a stop on his back, unmoving. The ghost town grew quiet except for the cracking of the flames and foreboding howl of approaching intruders.

"¿Qué carajo fue eso?" one of the surviving gunman said, stepping out from cover. Another Hispanic man, large and heavily muscled with long black hair, dressed in camouflage BDU fatigues, boots, and a black T-shirt, raised a fist in a silent "hold" gesture to the gunman and his companions. Emile "Armadillo" Dia cautioned his remaining soldiers as he cautiously approached Heck's body.

The circle of slavers and killers tightened, all their guns leveled on the motionless body, the still mocking demon mask. Armadillo slid a heavy machete out of a back sheath and moved closer to Heck's body. The trafficker's Glock .44 stayed trained on the man who had slaughtered most of his army. Armadillo stood only a few feet from Heck, his gun trained on the biker's heart. The sirens of the American *federales* grew louder as they raced across the wasteland. Armadillo had lost everything because of this stranger. Five million in cash had gone up in the orphanage. The radio and phone were buzzing with frantic reports of how his fronts, his other operations across Texas were being raided, shut down. He would have to head south to Mexico and begin again. The anger made the tendons in his neck tighten. There was still time to get away, but first he was going to make sure this man was well and truly dead for the grief he had caused.

In the trenches, the children all watched, wide-eyed in terror as their tormentor, their nightmare, aimed his gun at their would-be savior.

"I don't know who you were," Armadillo said in English to the body, "but you fucked with the wrong man."

"The wheel turns, asshole," the corpse said.

Heck's leg kicked up and out with a speed and strength that didn't seem human. There was a crunch from one of Armadillo's kneecaps, and the hulking crime boss fell backward, his legs falling out from under him. The Glock thundered as Dia fell. The bullet hit Heck in the chest. The force of the gun was fierce, but after having already endured the shotgun round, Heck could hack it.

Under his now ruined Dropkick Murphys T-shirt was a ballistic T-shirt that included a chest trauma plate made of Ultra High Molecular Weight Polyethylene, or UHMWPE for short, but it really wasn't very short. Heck had little clue what most of that meant, but the little plastic plate had saved his ass twice now in one night. Science was cool.

Heck scrambled onto Armadillo's chest. The biker pinned Dia's arms under his knees. The slave lord's remaining men hesitated for a second for fear of hitting their boss. By the time they realized they had better start shooting, two of them were dead from Armadillo's .44. A bullet whined by Heck's ear and another struck Dia in the leg. Heck fired, swiveling his torso even as the torn muscles and broken bones in his rib cage screamed in protest. The desert was quiet again as the last of the army of traffickers fell to cool in the desert sand.

Heck's ears were ringing from the gunfire. Through the whining hum he heard the submerged sound of sirens nearing the edge of Lobo. Heck looked down at Dia. The giant said something Heck couldn't hear over the humming, invisible cotton stuffing his ears, but he understood just fine when the trafficker spit at him and tried to raise his machete to strike Heck.

Heck growled, drew his combat knife, and sunk it into Dia's biceps with a wet thud. Armadillo howled at the pain. Heck ripped his knife free with a roar of rage and a spray of blood. The slaver lost consciousness, convulsing as he began to bleed out.

Heck looked down at the monster who had robbed these children of part of their souls. The burning thing inside him snarled, hissed in his veins. Heck felt weightless with bright, hot anger, like he was made of light, an angel of rage. His awareness narrowed, tunneled, to this miserable piece of human garbage. He put the knife to Dia's throat.

"Heck? You okay? It's Jimmie! You need any help, son? Is the backup there yet? Heck, talk to me!" The voice in his ear, the headset, cut through the fog of his deafness and his anger. Heck paused and looked around. Rows of bright, frightened eyes were looking at him from the edge of the shadowed trench. The children were watching.

Heck Sinclair did what he had often done over the last year since meeting Aussapile, since becoming Jimmie's squire and his friend. Heck asked himself silently, once again, "What would Jimmie do?" The answer came without doubt or hesitation.

He put the knife away, told the thing snarling inside him to shut the fuck up, and climbed off Armadillo's chest. He looked over at the kids and nodded before picking up his bike and tearing off across the desert, sirens, lights, and flame at his back.

When the police arrived at the inferno that had been the ghost town of Lobo, when they asked the seventy-eight children saved and freed from slavery that night what had happened in the moments before they arrived, the children all told the same story—the Devil had come for the bad men and had saved them.

. . .

The children had crouched in swaying darkness for what seemed a roasting, freezing eternity. The interior of the semi's trailer did little to hold back the wrath of the desert, day or night. There was no light, no water, no toilet. Many of them had passed out from the stench, from the heat, and then, later, the bone-numbing cold. The oldest of them was fourteen, the youngest, five. The only thing worse than the trip in the trailer was what they feared waited for them at its end. Some, having lost all hope, prayed for death. The truck had swayed wildly and they heard the sound of sirens and gunshots, when the truck suddenly came to a stop, they huddled together, not sure if this was salvation or something worse about to be heaped upon them.

After a long time in the darkness, there had been the metallic clack of the trailer door's locks and then the groan of the doors thrown wide. Moonlight fell into the long, dark trailer, and then the beams of flashlights crossed their faces.

Lovina looked at the small, dirty, frightened faces in the light of her flashlight. She saw her sister, Delphine, in every face. Jimmie saw Lovina's eyes take her to another place, another time for just a second. Missing people, missing children had become the Louisiana investigator's life since her own sister had been abducted and murdered by a bloody cult in the middle of Hurricane Katrina. Jimmie knew these victories were fleeting for Lovina, her mind already imagining all the children still out there, victims of the twenty-first century's high-tech slave trade.

"Hey," Lovina said softly. "I know you're scared and that's okay. All this has been really scary. My name's Lovina, and this is Jimmie."

Jimmie stood beside her and translated her words into broken but adequate Spanish. Lovina thought Jimmie was going to cry for a moment, but the moment passed.

"You're safe, now," Jimmie said. "They can't hurt you anymore. We got y'all something . . ."

. . .

Lovina and Jimmie took off ten minutes before the cops arrived, Lovina in her Charger, and Jimmie nursing his battered, bleeding, steaming Peterbilt truck down the road. A horde of flashing, howling police cars—local and state—federal tactical teams, ambulances, social workers, descended on the trafficker's truck and the wreckage of the two police cars. Trailing the howling parade were several news trucks.

Helicopters thudded loudly above the scene, pinning spotlights on Blue's unmoving tractor trailer and the wrecked police cars. FBI Assistant Special Agent in Charge Cecil Dann climbed out of the passenger side of a Texas Ranger Ford pickup as it crunched to a halt on the side of the highway. Dann drew his weapon, a Springfield 1911-A1 .45, and sprinted toward the open trailer of the truck on long, lanky legs. Cecil's hair was salt-and-pepper, and he still had the loose, fluid movements of a baseball pitcher from his days of playing CIAA ball at North Carolina A&T.

Instead of going to the major leagues, Dann had joined the FBI. Since 2014, he had been in charge of a division of the FBI's VICAP program called the Highway Serial Killings Initiative. The initiative tracked violent crime occurring along America's highways, searching for patterns that might be the horrific signature of a serial killer or rapist. Most men Dann's age and in his position wouldn't be sprinting across a two-lane blacktop in the dead of night, ducking, sweeping his weapon side to side, making sure each shadow didn't hold an assailant with a gun. He reached the cover of the big rig's trailer and slammed his back against it. Major Bill Hammer of the legendary Texas Rangers reached the cover of the truck a second after Dann. Then a half dozen other agents and tactical officers did the same, sweeping the desert night on both sides of the wrecked truck.

"Ready?" Hammer asked Cecil. Dann nodded. "In!" Hammer called out. The FBI tac team, the highway patrolmen, the county deputies, and the rangers all moved as one well-trained, heavily armed organism and moved to and controlled the yawning doors of the trailer and the cab of the rig in a single breath.

The flashlights found children in the already opened trailer, dozens of children with wide eyes and gaunt faces staring back into their guns and lights.

"Kids! We got kids in here!" Cecil called out. "Guns down! We're clear! Clear!"

The hardened, battle-ready policemen, all around the door, lowered their weapons. Many began to climb up into the trailer, calling for medics and blankets.

"Sweet Jesus," Hammer said to Dann. "No matter how many times I see it, it breaks my heart, Cecil. How could anyone do this to a kid? This bastard, Armadillo, he snatched kids off the streets during and right after Hurricane Harvey. Everyone thought they were dead. That's sick."

"We're taking him off the streets tonight, Bill," Dann said. "He goes down, hard, and we smash his pipeline."

The tactical radios squawked to life. "We got two at the cab . . . make that one and a half," the voice of an FBI agent reported. "Both were armed. Guy outside the cab looks like he was shot with a cannon, no joke. The guy driving is in shock; he may lose his arm but he's still pumping, barely."

"I got a dead local cop in the road," another voice reported in. "Looks like Highway Patrol. His partner is pretty badly injured and cuffed to what's left of his car down that ravine on the side of the road."

"We got two county cops with broken bones and multiple lacerations in their cruiser as well," another voice reported. "What the hell chewed these guys up?"

Cecil watched the cops lift the kids off the back of the trailer. EMTs were taking the half-naked, starving children and wrapping them in blankets before leading them over to other ambulances to be checked out. Some of the kids didn't want to let go of the cops, and Dann saw a few of the troopers putting on a brave face behind eyes that begged to cry.

Bill Hammer and a disheveled-looking young blond man in a wrinkled suit, talking a mile a minute into a cell phone, approached Dann. The rumpled man was carrying a clipboard holding a bunch of file folders rubber-banded together.

"Special Agent in Charge Dann," Hammer said, "this is Texas DPS attorney Zachary Foose. He's with CID." Cecil extended his hand to Foose, who took it grudgingly. Foose had a large class ring on one finger, and this close up he smelled of Axe body spray. Cecil took his measure pretty quickly. Pains in the ass were often accompanied by clipboards.

"Zach," Dann said. "Pleasure."

Foose's face folded into a compact and practiced scowl, "Zachary," he said. "Agent, I need—"

"Special Agent," Dann corrected, letting go of Foose's hand, "in Charge." Foose's scowl got deeper.

"I need a face-to-face with your CIs, so I can ascertain their role in this massive clusterfuck."

"Are you shitting me?" Dann said. "No way. That's why they're called confidential informers, Zach. No."

"There are sixteen dead and eight more wounded human traffickers back at the Lobo compound, which is now a big pile of hot ash, by the way, and we've got one dead cop and three injured here. Someone is responsible for all that, Dann."

Dann's phone gave a chirp indicating he had received an email. He looked down at the screen and saw that a now familiar symbol, a wheel with three equidistant spokes, had replaced his FBI seal wallpaper on his phone. Two lines of text appeared below the symbol: *Evidence of dirty cops emailed to you, Cecil. Thank you.* The line under it said, *"The wheel turns."* The screen went blank for a second as the message and symbol vanished from his phone.

"Am I boring you?" Foose asked.

"Dirty cops," Dann replied, looking up at the DA. "We have three breathing and one dead. All of them dirty. All of them on Armadillo's payroll. I got the bank records to prove it."

"How they fuck did you get those?" Foose asked.

Dann lived for moment like this. "You're not cleared for that, Zach," he said. "Sorry. I'll make sure the U.S. attorney doesn't forget to send a copy over to you."

Foose muttered an obscenity and walked away. Hammer burst out laughing. "You know that little mouse turd is going to make your life miserable, Cecil," the Texas ranger said. "Especially if you catch any more cases down this way."

"Yeah." Cecil shrugged. "I probably shouldn't go out of my way to piss him off, but I deal with too many assholes like that back in D.C. I don't need 'em on the road." Hammer nodded.

"Well, whoever your CIs are, you tell them thank you," Hammer said. "Close to a hundred kids saved, Armadillo and his crew off the streets, and we just shut down a major route in the human trafficking pipeline at the national level. We couldn't have done this without the intel your people provided, Cecil. That's a damn good night."

Dann nodded. "Yeah, it sure is." He couldn't tell Bill Hammer that even he didn't know that much about the people, the group, who had set this whole operation up and handed it to him wrapped with a neat little bow. Dann still didn't know who the "Brotherhood of the Wheel" were exactly—a cult? Some kind of secret society? Really intense NASCAR fans? Whoever they were, they were in the business of saving lives on the highways and shutting down criminals using those roads. Dann only knew the Brotherhood existed at all because of a trucker, Jimmie Aussapile, he had crossed paths with several years back.

Hammer ambled over toward a cluster of other law enforcement personnel who were being interviewed on TV about the operation. Cecil liked to avoid the press. He didn't do this for kudos; he did it because it was dirty work that needed doing.

A little girl, maybe nine, at the ledge of the trailer looked over and saw Cecil. He smiled and waved to her. A quick smile fluttered across the little girl's face. The smile reminded him of his daughter, Janeice, at that age. She was nineteen now, in college. The little girl was wrapped in a warm blanket. Cecil noticed that most of blanket-garbed children were munching on packets of Teddy Grahams and sipping on juice boxes. As they lowered the little girl off the truck, Cecil walked over. He looked to the county cop holding her.

"Can you ask her where she got the snacks from?" he asked the deputy, a young woman with her blond hair tied back in a bun. The deputy asked in fluent Spanish, and the little girl, her voice small and raspy from neglect and thirst, whispered a reply. The deputy frowned, and then kissed the little girl on the forehead and helped her onto a stretcher. "What'd she say?" Cecil asked.

"She said, 'the nice people,'" the deputy replied. "Then she said 'the wheel turns,' whatever that means."

Cecil shook his head and smiled. "Yeah, I'm still working on that one myself," he said.

. . .

About a mile away on a curve of road in the middle of nowhere, Jimmie sat on the bumper of his truck and watched the bright, distant lights surrounding the coyote's truck. It was lit up like a carnival on the dark desert highway. This patch of desert was flat, and the lights gave him a pretty good view of the crime scene. Jimmie's face, neck, and scalp all ached from the cuts, and his whole body felt like he had been worked over with a pipe wrench. He was talking on his cell phone with Heck.

"You are the luckiest son of a gun alive," Jimmie said. "You took out how many of them?"

"About twenty," Heck said, "a small army, but who counts? And I'm not lucky, thank you very much. I'm the solidest son of a bitch you're ever gonna meet."

Jimmie laughed, winced, and hissed in pain. Heck laughed at that, and then he winced and groaned too. "You?" Jimmie asked.

"Broke a few ribs, tore some muscles. Maybe a cracked sternum," Heck said. "Nips like a bitch. You?"

"Cuts on my face," Jimmie said. "Windshield blew out. Ain't nothing."

"You okay?" Heck asked. He was driving along I-10 nearing Baton Rouge. His headset speakers and microphone were good enough to diminish some of the snarl of his engine and the noise of the highway traffic blurring by him.

"Had worse by my own hand shaving," Jimmie said. "Stop your naggin', Nanna Worry-Pants. Still, stings a bit."

"Wuss," Heck replied, chuckling. "Twelve-gauge and then a .44 slug in the chest. That little trauma plate you got me saved my ass. Why we do this shit again, boss?"

"The pay stinks, but it's worth it," Jimmie said to the biker.

"Lovina good?" Heck asked.

"Yeah," Jimmie said. "I think she did some road magic to help stop the truck."

"Shit," Heck muttered. "Jimmie, man, you and I both know how fucked up every road witch we've ever met has been. Whatever's on the Road that they tap into, it eats them up eventually."

"And then they disappear," Jimmie said. He knew where they all ended up, but he didn't say that. It felt obscene to even utter the name of that damned city. He remembered the howling spires of Metropolis-Utopia. The city shrieking like a wounded animal, mad road witches hanging out of every building window as the whole city had rumbled along, like a great beast, chasing them across the plains. He sighed and tried to push the memory away. "I know. She seems to have a decent handle on it so far. I think Max may have helped her some." Max was Dr. Mackenzie Leher, a brilliant specialist in the occult, a member of the Builders—one of the secret societies the Brethren were partnered with—and a good friend to Jimmie, Heck, and Lovina.

"We'll just have to see, won't we?"

"Not much choice," Heck answered. "That shit picks you. You don't get a say in it."

"I assume you're headed back home?" the trucker asked, trying to change the subject.

"Not straightaway," Heck replied. "I'm supposed to meet Roadkill at Nags Head. We've got a jumper to collect for the Jocks."

"Watch yourself. You just got banged up pretty good and then what, a day and night of riding to get back to North Carolina? You need to get some rest 'fore you dive straight into another scrap."

"Now who's being Nanna Worry-Pants," Heck said. "After the shit I was just in, picking up a bail-jumping check-kiter *is* a fucking vacation."

"Oh," Jimmie said, "about this getting shot at, Layla never hears a word about that, you got me?"

"Jimmie, she's gonna know when she sees your face, man! You shouldn't keep things from your wife," Heck said. Jimmie could hear the grin on his face across the line. "She's gonna know, and then you're gonna be in deeper trouble. Women have scary powers."

"I like to live dangerously," Jimmie said. "Not a word to Layla, squire, that's an order from your knight."

"Pulling rank," Heck said. "That's cheap, but okay. You headed home too?"

"Got a load to pick up in Corpus Christi first," Jimmie said. "Got diapers to pay for."

"Ah, the life of adventure you lead," Heck said. "Smugglers and smelly diapers."

"Wouldn't trade it," Jimmie said. "You'll see one of these days."

"Shit," Heck said. "Give me machine-gun-toting coyotes or creepy-ass shadow people any day of the week. I'd rather stare down a loaded fucking shotgun than a loaded diaper. See you on the other side, man. The wheel turns."

"You did good, kid," Jimmie said. "Take 'er slow and keep the shiny side up. The wheel turns." He hung up and stood with a groan. Lovina, looking tired and limping a bit, approached him.

"How we doing?" she asked Jimmie.

"'Bout same as usual," Jimmie said, patting the dented and scored grille of his truck. "There is no way in hell I'm going to be able to drive her to Corpus Christi in this condition. No windshield? It will cost an arm and a leg to get her street legal again. So I'm going to spend money we can't afford and still miss hitting the loading dock on time." He sighed. Lovina handed Jimmie his crumpled baseball cap. Jimmie slipped his lucky *Squidbillies* cap on his head, wincing at the pain from the cuts along his bare scalp. Just another chorus of the Brethren Blues.

The Brethren were one of three secret societies, one of the three "spokes in the wheel" of the modern reformation of the ancient order known, in vulgar parlance, as the Knights Templar.

When the Poor Fellow-Soldiers of Christ and the Temple of Solomon had begun in AD 1119 they were easily as poor as Jimmie Aussapile, not even having enough gold for each knight to have his own horse. In time they grew rich in power and in influence over the material and spiritual worlds.

In 1312, the Templars most well-known enemies, Pope Clement V and King Philip IV of France, plotted their downfall. Luckily for the Templars, their enemies underestimated the depth and scope of the order's spy network. Knowing the end was coming, the Templars held a secret meeting to discuss how they could survive.

From that conclave came the Tri-form Reformation and the plot to stage their own public demise. Several key members of the order offered themselves up as martyrs for the torture and the trials to follow, deliberately sowing misinformation about the Templars to the public for the greater good of the survival of the new orders.

To continue unhindered, the Templars went underground and split into three separate groups, each independent of the others and each dedicated to its own pursuits in the name of advancing civilization and the betterment of all humanity. While separate entities with their own satellite organizations spun out from them, the three orders all swore the most serious of oaths to work together, to share resources and knowledge, and to defend one another in times of crisis.

Of the three secret orders, the Brethren were sworn to the original centuries-old vow of the Templars, the protection of the roads and all who traveled upon them.

"The wheel turns," Lovina said.

"Yeah," Jimmie sighed, "the wheel turns, right over top of me." The trucker slumped a little against his bullet-riddled rig. He was tired, and he was in pain, and the lost money on this job combined with the repair work on the truck was going to hurt his family.

Lovina smiled and gave him a gentle hug as she led him toward her car. Her muscles and bones ached from firing the .600 Nitro to stop the truck, and she leaned a little on the trucker as well. "Come on," she said, nodding toward her Dodge. "Let's go find you a garage that will come out here and get your truck street legal."

Jimmie watched the tiny, distant line of children being loaded on board old school buses. They were so small in all this churning chaos, tiny flickers of light in a wasteland of darkness. He thought of little Jimmie—who they had taken to calling JJ—over a year old now, and of Peyton, so grown up, so quickly, back home in Lenore, of how lucky he was to have them. How privileged he was to get to protect them from the monsters. He shook off the gloom. *Suck it up, buttercup,* he thought to himself, summoning the ghost of his old drill instructor.

"Who knows," Lovina offered as they helped each other limp to her car, "maybe you'll still make that run with a little luck and some help from your friends."

"Yeah," Jimmie said, a crooked smile coming to his cut and bloodied face, as he opened the passenger door, "maybe I will at that."

Heck's eyeballs felt like deep-fried sandpaper as he glided on his bike down South Croatan Highway on the tiny sliver of island that was Nags Head, North Carolina. The sun was sinking in the west, and the sky above the Atlantic was a curtain of purple and indigo, paving a way for the moon's ascendance. Nags Head was a different kind of beach town, less rowdy and noisy. This was the kind of place where you could pull off to the side of the road, climb a dune, and find yourself the only person for miles on a long, pristine stretch of white beach.

Heck yawned and turned right onto Dune Street. There was a strip mall to his right with a deli, a sports bar, a vape shop, and a souvenir shop with inflatable float toys and beach balls hanging in front of a faux fisherman's net adorned with seashells and the husks of dead starfish. The parking lot was about half-empty. It was late April, and the tourists hadn't descended on the town yet.

Heck pulled into the lot and parked next to a beat-up old red and white Ford pickup with North Carolina tags. The truck was idling, the driver-side window down. The shitty factory radio was playing "Tuesday's Gone" by Lynyrd Skynyrd through the one working speaker in the dash while the driver dozed, his hand hanging out the open window, half of a cold cigarette dangling between his fingers. The driver grumbled and sat up as Heck shut off the T5 Blackie and dropped the kickstand. He was in his twenties, a small and slight man. His face had odd proportions; his nose was prominent, as were his ears. He had big eyes and they were so brown they almost looked black. His face was marked with acne scars and he had an unruly mop of greasy brown hair.

"Shit, Heck, you look half in the bag," Jethro Hume said. Most folks knew Jethro by his club name, the same nickname he'd had since he was a kid,

Roadkill. He had been Heck's best friend since they were both nine years old and they were both second-generation members of the one-percenter, or out-law, motorcycle club called the Blue Jocks. Roadkill wore a Blue Jocks MC cut over his gray hoodie. His cut had a patch that said "Sergeant At Arms" over the right breast.

"Feelin' it," Heck muttered. He didn't tell Roadkill that the only way he had made it from Texas in twenty-four hours was all the laws he broke, which included buying some speed off a guy at a truck stop off I-10 in Mis-sissippi. He grunted as he climbed off his bike for the first time in about ten hours.

"Tough day at the job, sweetheart?" Roadkill asked as he got out of the truck. "What the fuck were you doing in Texas anyway, man?"

"You remember that thing I told you about that I wasn't supposed to tell anyone about?" Heck said, stretching. His joints popped and cracked as he did.

"Of course I don't," Roadkill said, nodding. "What the fuck happened to your shirt and your jacket, man? You get tagged by a shotgun?" Heck gave a curt nod as he bent at the waist, trying to touch his toes. There were more snapping and crackling sounds than a campfire as he stretched. Heck gasped a little in pain as he did. "Your ribs fucked up?"

"Felt like some broke," Heck said, matter-of-factly. "You got a piece for me? I had to ditch all my leftover hardware in some lake."

"Shit, man, you need a doc?" Roadkill asked.

"Naw," Heck said, "I think they healed up on the drive back. I'm fucking starving, though."

"You're fucking lucky you heal so scary fast," Roadkill said. Heck pulled off his leather jacket and cut and grimaced with the exertion. A flattened slug from the 12-gauge fell to the floor of the parking lot.

"I feel lucky," he said, flatly, through gritted teeth. "Blessed even. Piece and a smoke?" Roadkill handed him a pistol, a Taurus 24/7 .45, butt first. Heck ejected the magazine and saw it was loaded with blue-tipped Glaser Safety Slugs. He nodded, slapped the clip back in, jacked a round into the pipe, snapped on the safety, and tucked it away at the back of his waistband. Road-kill handed him a fresh pack of unfiltered Lucky Strikes. Heck tapped the pack against his palm and then lit one with his Zippo. He sighed after a mo-ment. "You got the paper on this asshole?"

"Yeah," Roadkill said. "Seth was going to pick him up a few days ago, but his old lady got sick, so he asked if you and me could do it. I told him we would once you got back from your whirlwind tour of Bumfuck, Texas. He wondered what the fuck you were doing there too."

"Look, man," Heck said, "I know it sucks to have to keep so much of this shit on the DL, even from you, but you've got to believe me, it's for the good of the MC."

"Sure, but you can't tell me any more than that," Roadkill said, "and you shouldn't have even told me that much. Me, the guy who lied for you, took the hit and said *I* was the one who cut that supersonic, gross-as-shit fart in front of Kelly Burgess in eighth grade, because you were in luuuurvve with her . . . well with her boobs, anyway . . ."

"Jethro . . ." Heck said.

"Can't trust the guy who got you the last ticket in the fucking state to the Tom Petty show in Raleigh or bailed you out, how many fucking times?"

"I don't know . . ."

"Nineteen times," Roadkill said. "But, no. No-can-do. Big hush-hush top secret bullshit. Gotcha, chief."

"Shit, come on, man!" Heck said, shaking his head, cigarette smoke streaming from his mouth and nose, swirling around his head like a nicotine halo.

This was not a new conversation. It had become an ongoing sticking point between the two lifelong friends for the past couple of years, ever since Heck had learned the deepest secret of the Blue Jocks Motorcycle Club and had been thrust into a stranger world than he had imagined, which was saying a lot.

The Jocks were a Scottish-American motorcycle club started back in the late sixties by a group of Vietnam veterans, including Heck's grandfather, Gordon "Claymore" Sinclair and Roadkill's dad, Glen Hume. The Blue Jocks weren't just bikers; they hunted monsters—real monsters—unnatural things that seemed to thrive at the edges of civilization, that haunted the highways the Jocks rode upon, and that preyed upon the innocent, the isolated, and the vulnerable. Heck still didn't know the exact story of how Gordon, Glen, Ale, and the other "originals" of the MC had come to this path, but the Blue Jocks had been keeping the highways and back roads of North Carolina a little safer for fifty years, now.

It was this strange, almost-alternate universe Heck and Roadkill had grown up in: all-night parties, initiation of club prospects, getting hassled by the cops just for breathing. Wearing colors, gang wars, guns, drugs, and cash. Living outside the rules everyone else played by while having to adhere to a code to stay alive, to stay honest. Facing down monsters, mutants, and entities that defied any comprehension.

Heck's grandpa, Gordon, the first president of the MC, made it plain that the Blue Jocks would not get mixed up in running drugs or guns. He said they were dirty business and a quick road to nowhere. So the Jocks became bounty hunters to pay the bills, hunting normal, mortal criminals by day and supernatural abominations by night. Ale, Heck's stepfather, had been the Jocks' second president. Everyone figured that Heck would be the third, after Ale had gotten sick and passed away, but that hadn't happened, at least not yet.

The night they had scattered Ale's ashes, Hector's mother, Elizabeth, had told Heck a deeper truth, a secret that was part of the beating heart of the MC, and one that he had to swear to keep silent, even from his best friend. The Blue Jocks were a link in a far more complex and far-reaching chain, an ancient fellowship that protected the roads and those who traveled upon them from all threats, supernatural and all-too-real. These secret knights were known as the Brethren, and they hid in plain sight as truckers, bikers, cabdrivers, state troopers, RV gypsies, and others who lived or worked upon the highways and byways of America. Every leader of the Blue Jocks had been one of this secret society's number.

Heck became a squire to a knight of the Brethren—Jimmie Aussapile—at the urging of his mother. Jimmie was an old friend of the family. In the past year, Jimmie had fought side by side with Heck, teaching him so much about the secret world of the highways—the Road—and so much more about himself. Heck wanted to share all of it with Jethro, but he had sworn an oath of silence and had pushed that oath as far as he possibly could. Still, he knew it hurt Jethro, practically his brother, to feel left out, to feel a wall between them and not know its name or reason.

"To be continued," Heck said, dropping the butt of the cigarette and crushing it under his boot. "Where is this guy?" Roadkill drew a compact H&K 9mm from a shoulder holster under his hoodie and cut, snicked the slide back, and then clicked the safety on and returned it to its holster.

"About five minutes from here," Roadkill said. "His name is Julius Ovison. He's got nothing violent on his record. Just kiting checks and some identity theft charges. He rented a beach house off Virginia Dare Trail. I drove down after I got off work at Dad's garage and checked it out. His girlfriend's car is parked there, a few lights on. I doubled back a few times waiting on your lagging ass, and it hasn't moved."

"Okay," Heck said, "let's go get him and take him home. I'm going to sleep for a week."

"Should we call the cops and let them know we're serving paper?" Roadkill asked.

"Nah," Heck said. "I got my balls busted enough for one night from you, why double down?" Roadkill flipped him off and climbed back in the truck. Heck got in the passenger side. He sighed at the comfort of the old seat with its loose springs and torn upholstery and let his sore back rest heavily against it. "If I crash, wake me gently, luv," he said to Roadkill.

"I'm so glad you're here. My fucking hero," Roadkill said, starting up the old Ford. "I feel safer already."

The drive to the beach house was quick and uneventful. Heck did almost fall sleep all the same. This section of beach houses was designed to be rented out to tourists, and many of them were dark and obviously vacant. Heck could smell the salt off the sea and hear the crashing of the waves. It was soothing and hypnotic. He started to snore a little. A grease-stained hand caught him square in the chest, and he jumped forward, surprised and suddenly awake. "Wakey, wakey," Roadkill said. "That gentle enough for you?"

Heck rubbed his eyes and looked around. "Fuck," he grunted, "asshole."

They were in a small parking lot behind the house, facing the beach. There were two other cars in the lot. One of them belonged to Ovison's girlfriend from Cape Fear. There was also a squat, ugly green dumpster with heavy black plastic doors on top of it. A torn and stained sign on the dumpster said it was for use only by the tenants of the rentals. The rental house Ovison was in looked a lot like the ones to its left and right, worn, wooden shingles silvered and smoothed over time by sea salt and sand. The whole house was on stilts—wooden poles like you'd see supporting a pier with wide, wooden stairs taking you up from the beach sand to the railed porch that ran around the length of the house. Heck noted several neglected folding beach chairs on the porch overturned by an indifferent wind. Most of these houses were set up to handle two or even three tenants at the same time, but only one section, in the middle, had a light on in the window at present.

"Come on," Heck said. The two bounty hunters moved quietly across the stretch of beach between the parking lot and the house stairs and quietly ascended them with their guns drawn. Heck covered Roadkill as he ascended then moved up himself. Once they reached the door, they took up positions on either side. There was muffled music on the other side of the door, "Highway to Hell" by AC/DC. Heck began to position himself to kick open the door. Roadkill raised a hand to halt him. "What?" Heck whispered.

"I go in first," Roadkill whispered. "You come in behind me, remember?" Heck shook his head and rolled his eyes.

"Oh, come on," he said. "Okay, Dirty Harry, go for it."

Roadkill kicked the door beside the plate for the lock. The wood spider-webbed under his steel-toed boot and flew open. The slight biker pivoted into the open doorway and found himself looking down the barrel of an ugly double-barrel shotgun. Both barrels emptied into Roadkill's chest, and Jethro flew backward from the blast and tumbled over the rail of the deck to the sand below.

"Jethro!" Heck screamed and stepped into the doorway, ready to kill who-ever had just shot his best friend. The still smoking shotgun was mounted by vise clamps to a step ladder about ten feet from the door. The ladder itself had been weighed down and stabilized with plastic paint buckets full of beach sand. The piano wire assembly that ran from the door to the trigger was tight and vibrating now that the door had been kicked open. A trap, a very nasty one.

Heck swept the room from the doorway, covering the hard corners—the ones on the same wall as the door—first. Nothing. A boombox was playing music from a local radio station, WVOD, loudly on the floor, near the win-dow on the other side of the room. It was near a standing lamp that was on a timer plugged into the same outlet. "Jethro!" Heck shouted, still sweeping the room. "Hang on, buddy, I'm coming!"

As if in response, a section of the wooden rail behind Heck exploded, sending splinters everywhere. Heck spun toward the rail, taking a step to the side in case there was an attacker in the house and he was being set up in a kill box. Two men in dark hoodies, the hoods up to obscure their faces, were advancing from the shadows of the empty house next door across the sand toward Heck, firing their 9mm pistols as they advanced. Heck returned fire and ran down the porch toward the stairs, bullets ripping apart the wooden shingles and railing as he ran, staying low.

The two assassins lost sight of the target that hadn't been cut down by the shotgun trap as he darted into the tangled shadows of the stairs. The dark, cold ocean crashed and frothed beside them.

"That Heck?" one of them grunted, pausing in his advance to drop his empty magazine and reload with a fresh one.

"Should we call it up?" the other said, squinting, trying to pierce the darkness. "He said Heck would be trouble and to call it up if Heck was—"

"I don't trust the creepy-ass-motherfucker," the other interrupted, clicking the slide release and chambering a bullet. "I don't give a shit if it's on our side or not. We're normally hunting shit like tha—" A snarling thing launched itself from the sandy ground, driving yellowed needles of teeth into the face and throat of one of the gunmen. The man shrieked and popped off several rounds wildly as he stumbled backward and tried to pull the thrashing, clawing, biting thing from his tattered face. "Fuck, fuck, fuuuuck! Get it off me, get it the fuck off me!"

Before his companion could react, he was caught in the chest by three .45 caliber safety slugs that reduced his midsection to mangled hamburger meat. He was dead before his body fell among the bloody sand and sea grass. Heck lowered the pistol and walked toward the remaining struggling killer, who had fallen on the beach as well beside his dead ally. The thing sitting on the disfigured man's chest turned to Heck and hissed, showing bloody teeth and dead black eyes, flecked in red. It was a possum, a big one. Its ratlike tail smacked back and forth across the sputtering man's bleeding face. The possum hissed to Heck again, and the biker squatted down on his haunches only a few feet from the creature and its victim.

"Look," Heck said, "we've been over this since we were both nine. I don't speak fucking Possum, okay." The possum shook its narrow, pointed head and scampered back to the injured man's face. It gestured with one of its tiny pink hands. Heck shrugged. The possum put its little clawed hand to the side of its face and shook its head again. It then grabbed the injured assassin's tattered eyelids and pulled them up to let Heck look into the man's eyes. The possum gestured at the gunman's face, which Heck hadn't gotten a good look at yet. The man moaned and tried to bat the creature off his face, feebly. The possum gave the killer the finger.

"Holy shit," Heck said. "Spur, Tommy, that you, man? I didn't recognize you while you were busy shooting at me. What the fuck are you doing out here trying to kill us? I thought your stupid, scrub ass was in prison in West Virginia."

Tommy "Spur" Barnett groaned and attempted to sit up. Heck's boot pushed him back down and the .45 in his face suggested to him he should stay that way. The possum scampered off into the darkness, back toward the rental house. "Fuck you, Hector," Spur said through swelling, torn lips. "Fucking crazy-ass motherfucker. You don't got the sense or the balls to run the Jocks."

"You know, Spur, coming from a member, even a nomad, drug-dealing-junkie-piece-of-shit member like yourself, that hurts. Where are your and your buddy's cuts? Sell 'em to get well, 'cause your dealer wouldn't trade for blowjobs anymore? Or maybe Cherokee Mike told your stupid asses to ditch your colors in case you fucked up and didn't kill us. Which you did, by the way."

Spur's bloody eyes burned with rage and pain. He leaned up a little, despite Heck's boot on his chest. He held a small black sea shell to his lips and whispered into it. The nomad biker's blood and spit spattered against the shell. Heck felt something, something there wasn't a word for, a sense of something vast and unseen lurching to life, its attention turning toward him. He'd felt this sensation before, and each time it portended something bad. Heck kicked the shell from Spur's trembling hand and pointed his .45 at the nomad biker's shredded face.

"It was Mike, wasn't it? Set us up, put this whole thing together?"

Spur smiled.

"He's coming for you, Sinclair, he's coming for what's his. He's got your number, freak. Gave us something to deal with you. You're going to die, bitch."

Heck put a single .45 round into Spur's face.

"After you, Tommy," he said to the corpse.

The waves roared, and the wind off the sea picked up, a cold whistling whisper through the tall grass, carrying away the echo of the gunshot. Roadkill walked out of the inky shadows, zipping up his hoodie over his bare and unblemished chest. He held his singed and tattered System of a Down T-shirt in a rumpled ball in his hand. He grimaced when he looked at the remains of Spur's head.

"Ugh," he said. "Tommy, man, that shit ain't gonna heal if you keep picking at it." He glanced at Heck. "Well, no getting back up for him."

"You okay?" Heck asked.

"No, actually," Roadkill said, gesturing with his ruined shirt. "Fuckers ruined it! My favorite shirt! You know how long I've had that shirt?"

"Since 2003," Heck replied, patting his jacket, looking for his cigarettes and lighter. "Incidentally, the same year you last washed it."

"Har-fucking-har," Roadkill replied. "You're comedic gold. You should give up your full-time job as a raging dick to do stand-up. Oh, and 12-gauge slugs burn like a motherfucker, FYI, and . . ."

"Do not talk to me about 12-gauge slugs in the chest, motherfucker," Heck began as he popped a Lucky in his mouth, but Roadkill kept going.

". . . and, and I got sand *everywhere*! Fucking nooks and crannies, man! I don't even know what a fucking cranny is but I got fucking sand up in there!"

"But you'll live," Heck said.

"Yeah, shit, I'm all right," Roadkill said. "Werepossum, remember? Well, half-werepossum . . . on my mama's side. You can't kill me with no normal shit. Takes something special." Roadkill's face suddenly dropped, and panic began to fill his eyes. "Um, something like that, maybe?" He pointed toward the sound of the pounding waves, and Heck turned.

The creature's body was obviously a floater, a long-dead victim of drowning. Its skin was pale, mottled with blue and green, and bloated, splitting in places like ripped seams. Heck and Jethro could smell the gases leaking out of the putrid flesh from twenty yards away. It was a woman's dead body, with only a web of black, wet seaweed tangled around it like a gown. The head of the body was gone. In its place was a glistening glob that looked for all the world like a huge jellyfish. The soft, pulsating flesh glowed a yellowish green.

There were no eyes, no mouth, no features at all, only rows of slender, slime-covered tendrils near the neck. It looked as if some of the tendrils had actually insinuated themselves deep down into the stump of the corpse's neck, while others drifted from the gelatinous mass to silently wave three or four feet away from the body, as if they were floating in water. The sickly throbbing light carried from the central tumorlike mass all the way down to the tips of the tendrils.

The thing took another step and another toward Heck and Roadkill. The creature's human arms remained still at its sides as it advanced up the beach, away from the sea that had vomited it onto land.

"Yeah," Roadkill said, nodding as he drew his pistol. "I'm pretty sure something like that could kill me dead."

"Any fucking clue what that is?" Heck asked, spitting out his cigarette. "How we kill it? You got any goodies in the truck? Flamethrowers, grenades?"

"I got a clean pair of jeans to change into now that I just soiled these," Roadkill replied. "Sorry, man. I prepped for a guy that writes bad checks, not for jellyfish-zombie-mermaid-gal!"

"Your gun loaded with Safety Slugs?" Heck asked. The creature was getting closer now, lurching along. Roadkill nodded. "Give me it."

"What the fuck am I supposed to do?" Roadkill asked as he handed the 9mm over.

"I think Spur summoned this thing up. He had a little black seashell; he said something into it. I kicked it out of his hand and it went over there," Heck gestured in a vague direction. "Find the shell; I'll bet it's a focus for the summoning. I'll keep it busy while you get it."

"Great," Roadkill shouted as he stumbled toward that section of the sand-and-grass-covered lot, "find a black fucking seashell on a patch of beach at night! Fantastic plan!"

"Shut up and find it!" Heck raised the pistols, one in each hand, and opened fire.

Safety rounds had been invented initially for use by air marshals as a form of ammunition that it was safe to fire in a pressurized cabin. The bullets were designed to deliver all their kinetic energy to a single point as they hit. If the target was hard, like a wall, even a flimsy wall, it would flatten out and not go through the barrier. If the target was soft, like a beef carcass, a human being, or a weird jellyfish-zombie-mermaid-thing, then all the force would transmit through the tissue and cause massive damage. The Glaser rounds had a reputation for one-shot stops on most assailants. Heck and the other Blue Jocks often carried the rounds when on bail collection jobs because it limited the possibility of collateral damage, like an innocent person on the other side of a tenement wall being hit by a wild bullet, and even berserk, drug-fueled jumpers usually went down from a single round.

The first bullets out of the guns hit the creature square at center body mass and blew fist-sized holes straight through the thing's chest. It staggered and almost fell over. Heck never got a chance to put two more rounds into it. Two of the long, drifting tentacles sprang to life and shot out, extending in length as they did, and plucked the two pistols from Heck's hands. The tendrils retracted, tossing the guns back over the creature's shoulder and releasing them to fly away and disappear under the dark waves of the encroaching tide.

Several other tendrils launched out and whirred toward Heck. He tumbled backward, but he was tired and clumsy, and he forgot he was on sand. One of the thing's lashes struck his lower leg, and Heck screamed in brilliant, white-hot agony. It was like he had been hit by a lightning bolt of pure pain, searing his entire nervous system. He felt the tendril tighten around his leg and felt another one strike him under his arm and begin to wrap around his shoulder. Each touch was torment. It was getting hard to think, and Heck swore he heard some alien voice whispering to him behind the curtain of suffering. His fingers, of their own accord, found the cool butt of Spur's 9mm and managed to pull it up into his palm. He fired at the first tendril holding him and it popped in a splat of ooze. He took out the other one and staggered to his feet. The throbbing pain remained, but it was staring to diminish. Heck emptied the gun into the thing's pulsating head-sack. Chunks of its head splatted and sprayed glowing blood behind it. It still advanced, and now a writhing swarm of angry tendrils flailed around the monster, making an eerie whistling sound as they did. The gun was empty in Heck's hand.

"Got it!" Heck heard Roadkill's voice behind him. "Now what?"

"How the fuck do I know?" Heck shouted. "Crush it, crush the fucking thing!"

The monster took another step then paused as Heck heard the tiny *snap, snap, snap* of Roadkill crushing the shell. Its tendrils stilled and slowly retracted. It turned, lurching, and began to walk back toward the surf. Heck heard a squishing sound. He looked down and saw the two severed tendrils slithering like snakes after their parent. The monster disappeared out of view behind the dunes and the tendrils followed a moment later. Heck expelled a *whoosh* of air and put the empty gun in his jacket pocket. He traded it for a cigarette and his lighter. His leg and arms still throbbed but the pain was manageable. Jethro walked up beside him and opened his palm to reveal the remains of the crushed shell.

"This, this shit right here," Roadkill said, nodding in the direction of the dunes and the waves, "this is why I don't come to the fucking beach."

"It's all the same," Malyssa Dunning said, "local cops, state, FBI. Always the same." Malyssa was in her late forties. She had teased blond hair with warring roots of midnight black and steel gray. The hair was poofed up in front and long and straight in back, a style popular in the eighties during the reign of the hair metal gods. It was a safe bet that back then Malyssa had been a beauty, probably wedged against the stage on the front row at numerous Ratt, Poison, and Guns N' Roses concerts. She was still pretty, but the years and the mileage of life showed on her. She took a long drag on a Virginia Slim and exhaled through her nostrils. She wore a gray sweatshirt with the image of a teddy bear and some alphabet blocks on it. Above the pictures was an unfurling banner that read, "World's Greatest Grandma!" Below the image of toys was another banner that read "Spoil 'em Rotten!" The sleeves were pushed up to her elbows, and she had old, blurry, blue-ink tattoos on both forearms.

"They all say not to give up hope," Malyssa said. "That the investigations are still ongoing and that they are pursuing any and all leads. They say those exact same words, the same way." Malyssa stubbed out her Virginia Slim in an ashtray that declared it was from Pigeon Forge, Tennessee. Lovina noticed the corpses of a legion of dead cigarettes in the tray. "It's like a goddamned litany from church!"

"I understand how frustrating that can be," Lovina Marcou said, pausing to take a sip from the cold can of Miller Lite her host had offered her when Lovina had knocked on the door of her apartment here in Baton Rouge. "They're kind of required to say that just that way since your daughter's case is still open, and believe it or not, they are still investigating."

"Cold case," Malyssa said, sipping her own can of beer. She was still dressed in her powder blue, polyester waitress uniform. Lovina had caught her just getting off a shift at the restaurant this afternoon. "That's what you police call it, right, Ms. Marcou?" she pronounced Lovina's name with a northern accent as "Mar-Kaw." "Cold, dead. I watch *Investigation Discovery* as much as my nerves will let me. I know how it goes, and I do know they're trying, but I also know they got bigger fish to fry than a teenage girl gone missing over four years ago." Lovina knew this woman was no fool. This was not just a cold case; it was frozen. Those cops and feds were all telling her as nicely as they could that the odds were pretty much one hundred percent that her daughter, Raelyn, was dead. Lovina broke eye contact with Malyssa and opened the brown cardboard folder on her lap.

"So the last time you saw your daughter was at 11:20 p.m. on September 21, 2014? Is that correct, Mrs. Dunning?"

Malyssa lit another cigarette and leaned back on the couch, streams of smoke again coming from her nose. Someone had taught her that was the cool way for a woman to smoke a long, long time ago, Lovina decided. "Yeah," she said, "and please, call me 'Malyssa,' or 'Mal,' hon, everybody does. Rae was running late for her job at the factory. She was working third shift, started at midnight." Malyssa swallowed hard, and Lovina saw the whole slow-motion nightmare tumbling behind her rheumy eyes, the one you can never escape because you're awake. "She never made it there."

"That's the PPG plant over in Tyrone," Lovina said, flipping through the case file notes. Malyssa nodded.

"It was about a thirty-or forty-minute drive," Maylssa said. "Rae always tried to leave by eleven so she had time to stop at the gas station and get her smokes and some coffee."

"Why did she leave late that night?" Lovina asked, looking up from the file. Malyssa sighed and rubbed her eyes.

"We . . . we had a fight. Before you ask, it was about me watching my grandson, her boy, Beau."

Lovina was patient. It was part of the job, and she understood all too well how hard those last moments can be. The last time you see someone, the last time you talk. The things you said you wish you hadn't, the things you'd give a piece of your soul to get to say. It would seem like any other moment in the continuity of your life, but it isn't.

Malyssa took another long drag. "I yelled at her, told her if she was old enough to get drunk and spread her legs, old enough to end up a mama at eighteen, that she was old enough to figure out some way to take care of her baby without expecting me to do it every night. Me and Troy had just started seeing each other, you see and . . . I was tired of being her babysitter every night. She cried a little, told me she would see if maybe one of her girlfriends who lived near us could take him some nights. I argued with her over the cost of a pack of diapers. I was a bitch. We'd almost always tell each other 'I love you' before she heads off. We didn't that night, and I was so mad, even after she left." She looked up at Lovina with eyes that had cried too much, too often. "I wonder sometimes if it went through her head at . . . the end. I wonder if she knew how much I loved her, how proud I was of her."

Malyssa sniffled and wiped her eyes before repeating the ritual of crushing out the dying cigarette and replacing it with a fresh one. "But then your fellow cops all tell me not to give up hope. What they really mean is there's no body for them to be able to close the case for good, never mind ever catching the bastard who did this to her."

"They found her car up on I-80," Lovina said. "That's completely wrong for her to have been heading to Tyrone, isn't it? Malyssa, could she have been blowing off work to meet up with someone? Boyfriend, your grandson's father, maybe?"

"Raelyn was no slut," Malyssa said, a sharp edge of anger entering her weary voice. "She was wild in high school; a lot of kids are. She made a mistake a lot of girls make, and it changed her life, changed her. She was a good mother, Ms. Marcou, a good daughter. She was with Beau as much as she could be. She didn't party anymore. Her and her girlfriends would come over here and drink beer and watch movies and play on their phones and talk shit. There was no guy, especially not that piece of shit that was Beau's dad. No, whoever grabbed her left her car up there. The staties and the FBI, they both had those guys like on *CSI* go all over the car. Nothing, they said. She got it inspected over at Mike's Garage that morning, took it to get it washed and detailed. If there was anything in it from that night, it seems to me it should'a stuck out like a sore thumb. Nothing, they said."

"I'm not trying to piss you off, Malyssa," Lovina said. "I'm not trying to imply Raelyn was doing anything wrong, I'm just trying to find a place to start that maybe no one had thought of before."

"Why *are* you here?" Malyssa asked. "I mean, you're a Louisiana state cop. This all happened in Pennsylvania, in a poor-as-shit little borough, a long way from here. It happened to a person who only mattered to me and her boy. I'm thankful for your help, Ms. Marcou, but I really don't understand."

Truth be told, Lovina didn't fully know either. If she had told Malyssa the real reason she had driven from New Orleans to Baton Rouge to see her, the woman would think she was just as crazy as she felt. Instead she told her the official, rational reason. "It's just 'Lovina,' please," she said. "I used to be a cop in New Orleans, then I became an investigator for the Louisiana State Police. My job these days is to work as a liaison with other organizations, like the National Center for Missing and Exploited Children. Finding missing people is important to me. My . . . sister, she went missing during Katrina. She was . . . taken. I found her, but . . . it was too late."

"I'm so sorry, hon," Malyssa said, patting Lovina's knee. "So you . . . understand."

Lovina nodded. "Yes. I've worked a lot of missing person cases. I have to be honest—no cop-speak—most of them don't have happy endings, but at least it's an ending. It gives their loved ones some closure on what happened, and maybe even some justice, if we can find the perpetrator."

"You want to go looking for Raelyn," Malyssa said, wiping at her blinking eyes. The dregs of her tears had found her. Lovina opened the file again.

"I do," Lovina said. "When you moved to Louisiana, you sent a request to the state police here and in Pennsylvania to keep you informed on any developments in the case. I found that letter when I was reviewing the case files, and I decided I wanted to look into what happened to Raelyn."

It was a plausible enough lie. Malyssa nodded and accepted it, Lovina could tell. She wished it were true. What really led her to this woman's door was a lot more ominous.

Lovina had the first dream the night she arrived home from the mission with Jimmie and Heck in Texas. In it, she's driving home from Texas in the Charger along an empty highway at night. "Dark Horse" by Katy Perry is playing on the radio. She has the window down and it's cold, but it feels good as the night rushes by her. Her headlights catch the interstate sign, I-80, and then pass it, back to the void of the empty interstate.

Then the dream changes. Time becomes drunk and jerky, kind of like it did on the highway when she used what Max, the expert on all things weird, called viamancy, what Jimmie and Heck called road magic, to make the truck move backward in space and in time. Everything slows, takes on a quality as if you were watching what happens next from an old videotape, slightly out of sync. There's a car on the side of the road, a little burgundy Honda Civic with its blinkers on and driver-side door open. Lovina's headlights capture the moment of tumbling time as she drives toward it. A man outside the car, hunched over the open door, struggles with a young girl with blond hair in the driver's seat.

The man is tall and husky. He's in a camouflage thermal jumpsuit, like hunters often wear. Lovina's headlights catch a glint of something like glass in his hand, as he wrestles to put a cloth over the girl's mouth and nose with his other hand. She's fighting him, trying to get a hand up to claw at his face, the face Lovina can't see.

The look on the girl's face is one of defiant fear, of survival distilled down to its most pure state. Lovina had seen that face, with all the civility and all the soft emotions stripped away from it, many times in her life: on the battlefield, on the job, and in her brief time as a Brethren. The girl makes eye contact with Lovina for one horrible second, and there is pleading in those fear-frosted eyes, a tiny shiver of hope, of rescue. Then, Lovina's car is past them, the accusing headlights are a tunnel seeing only the road and the darkness again.

Lovina awoke, shaking and sweating, desperate to get back to the dream, to help the girl, but she couldn't. Until the following night when she had the dream again and the next night and the next and the next. She'd dreamed of the girl, of the faceless man, and the struggle on an unknown patch of I-80 for over two weeks, night after night.

Lovina took to keeping a yellow legal pad and pencil next to the bed. Each night, she gleaned more and more details from the slow-motion, tumbling nightmare. She got the license plate number of the car; a few letters and numbers at a time. It was a Pennsylvania plate. She gleaned more information on the car, it was most likely a 2008. There was a high school graduation tassel hanging from the rearview mirror, and she noted the color of it.

Lovina got as many specifics about the attacker and the victim as her nightly tour of the crime scene allowed. It was maddening to have the assault move past her so slowly and yet be over so quickly. She lost count of how many times in the dream she tried to jam on the brakes, or to swerve and hit the car door, to smash the attacker at seventy miles an hour. She never could, but she did discover some disturbing details about the faceless man. She pegged him at 325–350 pounds and about six foot eight in height. His head was shaved, and the color of his skin, his head, his hands, was a morbid, chalky white that almost glowed in her high beams.

As she gathered the information, bit by bit, Lovina decided to check and see if her dream was based on anything real. The license plate led her to Raelyn Dunning's disappearance in Coalport, Pennsylvania. That led her to her file, the letter from her mother, and finally to Malyssa's door.

"May I ask you something, Malyssa? Why did you leave Pennsylvania?"

Malyssa crushed out another cigarette, began to repeat her process and then stopped and put the pack and the lighter down.

"It was Troy's idea. He should be home pretty soon. I honestly don't know how I would have survived what happened to Rae if not for him. He loves me, even when I'm crazy. He looks at me like I'm some kind of goddess, even when I look like shit. You got anyone like that, Lovina?"

Lovina had someone she hadn't seen in close to a year appear unbidden in her mind, and then she pushed the ghost away. "Kinda, I guess . . . not really."

"Raelyn taught me not to wait," Malyssa said. "Say it, whatever it is, when you have the chance, because you never know when the last time out the door is the last time forever. Anyway, I was having bad dreams. I kept dreaming of her . . . of Raelyn. She was all cut up, in a lot of them, like in pieces. Her . . . head was . . . then sometimes she was cut in half, like one of those ladies in a magic trick would be. He . . . in the dream her mouth was split, cut wider. She was . . . littered across the courtyard of the trailer park." Malyssa's hands were shaking, and her eyes were becoming more unfocused. Lovina had noticed a row of brown plastic pill bottles on the counter in the kitchen, and she now had a pretty good idea why they were there. "I'd be walking in my nightgown; I swear I could feel the dew on my feet, cold and wet. I looked down at her head, and her eyes opened . . . she tried to talk to me with her torn-up mouth, but I think her tongue was . . . was . . ."

"It's okay," Lovina said. "Do you need me to get you some of your medicine? Maybe a glass of water?"

"There's some Jack Daniel's under the sink," Malyssa said. "Could you pour me a glass and get me two of my Xanax, please, hon?" Lovina thought to caution her on mixing pills and booze but decided to keep her peace. Malyssa Dunning had been surviving this for four years now and was still surviving, getting up and living. It wasn't her place to lecture her on how to manage her grief. Lovina looked at a photo resting on the counter next to the pill bottles. It was Malyssa and a younger version of her, both smiling widely, genuinely, at some kind of amusement park. The younger girl was holding an infant in her arms, the baby looked confused but happy. The girl in the picture with Malyssa was the girl in the Honda in Lovina's dream.

"This Raelyn?" Lovina asked, already knowing the answer as she opened a bottle and shook two pills out. Malyssa nodded.

"Yeah, it was the summer before she disappeared. We went to Hershey

Park. It was great. We couldn't fucking afford it, but I don't regret it one damn bit. They're the last good memories I have of my baby."

By the time Lovina returned with the pills and the glass of whiskey, Malyssa had lit another cigarette, and her hands were steadier. She popped the pills and drained half the tumbler before she began again.

"One time, in the dream, I touched her face and got her blood on my hand. The next morning, when I woke up, there was blood on my hand, and to this day I have no idea how it got there. Troy found me once, sleepwalking out in the courtyard. I was certain the place was haunted, that Raelyn's spirit was restless and reaching out to me." She rubbed her face and then drained the rest of the tumbler. "I know she's dead. I know it, I feel it. But there is something she is still trying to say, trying to get out. I started to obsess on her ghost, on the whole place being haunted."

"What place, exactly?"

"The trailer park," Malyssa said. "Where we lived when she went missing. I convinced myself it was full of ghosts and that Rae was trapped there. I had to see some doctors. They got me some pills and said I was suffering from nervous exhaustion, PTSD. I spent some time in grief counseling. But I kept having the dreams. I kept waking up in strange places in the park. Finally, Troy decided the place was making me sick, that there were too many unhealthy memories there. He had family here in Louisiana, in Baton Rouge, so we left, and we've been down here almost two and half years, now."

"Have the dreams stopped?" Lovina asked. She knew she shouldn't ask, but a morbid concern for her own sleep drove her to. Malyssa inhaled deeply and blew the smoke out her nose before she answered. She was looking past Lovina, past this box of a life.

"Some," she said wearily. "But she's still trying to tell us something real bad."

. . .

It was well after 10 p.m. before Lovina began to head home to New Orleans from Baton Rouge. She was making good time on I-10, and the Charger was purring like a big cat. "Exit" by U2 was playing on the alternative station, 91.5, KNSU. She was tired, and she knew she had an early morning meeting with Russell Lime to discuss the forensics of Raelyn's case. If she kept up this pace, she'd be home and in bed by midnight, maybe 12:30. She rubbed her eyes and wondered again why she was getting mixed up in this. Why had she been dreaming of it before she even knew it existed? How was that even possible? It was insane. Then again, her parameters for what was possible and impossible had been pushed pretty far in the last year since meeting Jimmie Aussapile and learning of the Brethren's existence.

In the Army, in Iraq, later, as a young cop on the beat around St. Bernard Street in the Big Easy, Lovina had brushed up against some things in this world that defied reason.

She had an inkling of it growing up. The Marcou clan had a long history connected to Voodoo and Hoodoo, but Pops would have none of it in his house. He kept Lovina and her brothers and sisters as far away from that world as possible. They attended a Catholic school that was closer to a boot camp. Pops worked three jobs for decades to pay the tuition, drove them there and back when Mama got sick, and never muttered a word of complaint. Thinking back, Lovina never recalled seeing her dad asleep or going to sleep. The most undressed she ever saw him was his socked feet propped up on the ottoman while he watched the *CBS Evening News* and read the newspaper or his Bible. They attended church as a family every Sunday.

She knew Pops had relatives that believed, still carried the gris-gris, still attended the rites, but it was the kind of conversation at family gatherings that always made Pops hustle the kids out to the car and had Mama making excuses for everyone leaving. Pops and his brother, her Uncle Lincoln, had a major argument about *"it"* out on the porch one Thanksgiving. They didn't talk again until Pops was in the hospital for the last time.

Now, years after Pops had passed, Lovina's sister, Delphine, had fallen prey to predators who existed in this hidden twilight world. Searching for her sister, Lovina had found herself in the world of fever-dream logic, secret cabals, witchcraft, and monsters.

Magic was real, secret worlds existed right beside the one we were so damned sure was solid. Even having met Jimmie Aussapile and Hector Sinclair, and become one of the Brotherhood, Lovina still knew so little of its secrets, and of the other two equally secret societies that worked hand in hand with them, the Builders and the Benefactors.

She thought of calling Max and telling her about her dreams, but Max was another mystery she had yet to fully comprehend, and in many ways Max frightened her more than anything else she had discovered so far. She wished Pops was around to talk to. She could tell him anything.

Lovina rubbed her face. There was a car coming up on the left shoulder of the highway, its blinkers flashing. She hadn't seen the lights a moment before. Lovina slowed, clicked on her high beams and felt herself falling, dizzy with fear. It was a burgundy Honda Civic with Pennsylvania tags, the driver's door open.

Her car slowed and she saw Raelyn struggling with the pasty giant, the faceless man, but this time her car *was* slowing and Lovina was filled with dread, with an unreason that had never gripped her before. An antediluvian alarm was shrieking inside of her, bypassing her logic, her wits, her training. Everything in her was screaming to jam the gas, to run, to live. Even though the car was obeying her desire to decelerate, her body, her mind, was paralyzed with inaction.

She had a gun under her coat and she was damn good with it. She couldn't will her hand to leave the wheel and draw it. She couldn't force the wheel to turn to crash into the hulking man, who was clamping a cloth over Raelyn's mouth and nose. Raelyn's face, her pleading eyes, were a ghostly green in the light of the instrument panel.

Her car crawled past the violent tableaux. There was a strange symbol in dripping, white spray paint on the driver's door that Lovina had never seen in any of her dreams. It was a rectangle with a single dot at its center. The pasty man turned to regard Lovina, even as Raelyn's struggle against him began to subside as the drugs on the cloth took her.

Lovina was less than five feet from the scene now, from him, as he turned. She got a good look at his face and immediately felt a sense of shock and fear run through her. It was a broad, fat face, wide, with a prominent wrinkled brow, bulbous nose, and heavy jowls. He was painted up like a circus clown. His countenance as chalk-white as the rest of his skin, the only color coming from gaudy, greasy makeup, the painted crimson triangles above and below his dead, Triassic eyes. A large black circle with two smaller ones off to one side of the larger covered his forehead. The black tip of his painted nose and flaring nostrils, and the wide, scarlet bow of a drawn-on counterfeit smile completed his false face.

His eyes tied her intestines in tight bands, filled her brain with screaming, burning adrenaline. She couldn't fight, couldn't run. With the hand he wasn't using to clutch Raelyn's face, he reached out to Lovina through the open window of her now motionless car. The pale hand encompassed her field of vision, her universe.

Lovina woke, jerking to a sitting position in her own bed in New Orleans, her pistol clutched in a trembling hand. She was still clothed, save her shoes. The sunlight filtering through her blinds told her it was after 8 a.m. She was panting, wet with perspiration. She lowered her gun as Wafflez, her only roommate, hopped on the bed and padded over to crawl into her lap. The tortoiseshell cat looked at her silently with wise, amber eyes.

"Yeah, I do feel like an asshole, thanks," Lovina said to the cat. "I'll get you some breakfast." Wafflez hopped off her lap and padded toward the kitchen and her food bowl. "I'm fine, by the way," Lovina called after the departed cat. She began to relax and feel the tension slipping out of her.

She wondered where her phone had gotten to, patting the pockets of her jacket. She began to rub her face and then froze. A smear of white greasepaint was on the back of her left hand.

Ryan dreamed of running through fields of chalk-white arms; the hands, like alien flowers with cracked, blackened nails, opened and grasped at him as he passed. He opened his eyes and felt his heart punching his chest. Instinctively, he patted the crotch of his jeans. They were dry, thank God. He was still in the car, headed to Granny's. Mom was driving, a cigarette dangling from her lips as she hummed along with the scratchy car radio, Elton John's "I'm Still Standing." Mom glanced back for a second and smiled. "Hey sleepyhead. How you doing, honey?"

Mom was pretty but she usually looked sad when she didn't think Ryan was looking. She had long black hair, usually tied up in a ponytail, and brown eyes. Mom was small, but strong. She was wearing cutoff jeans and an old WWE wrestling T-shirt with John Cena on it that had belonged to some guy, long, long gone.

"Choking," Ryan said, wiping his eyes and sitting up. He knocked a bunch of his comic books and his Game Boy to the floor doing so. He mock-coughed a few times. "Dying." Mom snorted and rolled down her window more and flicked her cigarette out onto the highway.

"Okay, okay!" she said. "It's gone. You're saved!"

"Thanks," Ryan said. He leaned forward so his head was next to hers. "We there yet?"

"Close," she said. "Maybe twenty, thirty minutes."

"Oh," Ryan said.

"Were you . . . having bad dreams, honey?" she asked, keeping her eyes on the traffic. "You were moaning a little and tossing and turning." Ryan slipped back to the dim recesses of the backseat.

"Nah," he said.

"Honey, Dr. Pangolos told us it was important to talk about what's going on in you, remember?" Ryan nodded sullenly. He recovered his Game Boy and switched it on. Mom tried again, not ready to admit defeat. "You know you can talk to me about anything, right, buddy?" Ryan nodded again, focusing on the screen.

"I know, Mom. I'm okay."

"I just want to make it better," she said. "That's part of the reason were starting over out here at Grandma's." Ryan almost said something about Mom having lost her job by missing too much work after . . . what happened, and that they couldn't pay the bills anymore was the real reason they were headed to Pennsylvania, but he knew she really meant it when she said she wanted to make it better. She was kind of a fuckup but she loved him more than anybody. "You want McDonald's?" she said as the Golden Arches came into sight on the side of the highway. Ryan smiled and leaned forward toward his mom once again.

· · ·

Crouched up in the bright yellow plastic hub of the McDonald's play area, suspended some ten feet in the air, Ryan was painfully aware that he was getting too big for the nest of tube-tunnels and pods. He had turned twelve in January and Mom remarked daily how tall he was getting, even if he was still skinny like a stick. He heard the echo of the children and grown-ups below and looked through a large round porthole to see the tables below. Mom was looking up at him, smiling, but he saw the shadow of worry behind her parent-smile. She had paid for the food with change from a Ziploc bag.

The little yellow room was like the hamburger Happy Meal Ryan had eaten, it was the same here as it had been back home. He liked the sameness, it had always made him feel safe, made it seem like the world was stitched together good and tight. Back in Baltimore, he had a clubhouse in his closet. He put his box of comics in there, his radio, a flashlight, and had used some old pillows and a blanket to make a bunker. Above him had been a sky of pants legs and plastic-shrouded jackets, lit by a 40-watt sun with a pull chain. The walls were tight and secure.

He had run to the closet, to his fort, to hide when mom had told him to. The blanket had been an impenetrable force field, it had stopped monsters and nightmares, but it couldn't stop him. Ryan had heard his boots thudding on the wooden stairs as he ascended, coming closer, seeing the doorknob to the closet begin to turn. He had wished the walls would fall away, that he'd discover some secret trapdoor, but he hadn't. Mom, her face busted up, bubbles of blood frothing from her lips, was screaming, begging him not to go up there, screaming.

There was a squeal that echoed through the play maze, then another, more high-pitched than the first. Ryan jumped at the screaming, blinking, not in the closet, not in that night. Here, now. It was okay. Two little boys, probably eight or nine, rushed into the yellow room from one of the tunnels, one child chasing the other. They paused when they saw Ryan. He smiled as best he could, just like Mom had done below. A mask to protect the innocent from the ugly truth that hid behind it.

"Ewww, you smell like pee," one of the little boys said, wrinkling his nose. Ryan looked down and touched his jeans. A warm, dark stain had spread across his crotch.

. . .

Ryan was quiet after they left the restaurant. His mother, Taylor, had hustled him to the bathroom and he now wore a clean and dry pair of sweats with his *Star Wars* BB-8 T-shirt. He had been mortified, of course, but Taylor— she insisted most folks call her "Tay"—understood. Since what they both danced around and called "the thing," Ryan had trouble sleeping, sudden, loud noises would put him into either a panic or an almost trance. When he did sleep he often wet himself, awaking from dreams soaked in sweat and his own urine. Dr. Pangolos had told her it was PTSD, and completely un-derstandable given what Ryan had been through that night. He suggested in-tense therapy, which Taylor couldn't afford, a few medications, that Taylor didn't want to burden her boy with, and that she really couldn't afford any-way, and a change of scenery, which they both were in need of.

"Ryan is a very intelligent young man," Dr. Pangolos had told her. "How-ever, this isn't about reason, it's about emotion, and his emotional state is badly damaged from the trauma he endured. With time, patience, love, and support, he can make it through this, Mrs. Badel. You will just need to be his constant, his lifeline to a sane, safe universe."

Taylor wanted another cigarette, but it bothered Ryan and she didn't want to do anything to make it worse for him right now. "Your ice cream's gonna melt if you don't eat it baby," she offered, her eyes searching the backseat of the car. Silence. "Baby, I know . . ."

"I'm not a baby!" Ryan said, almost a snarl.

"Of course you're not," Taylor said. "You're my guy. You've helped me through so much since your dad . . ."

"Stepdad," Ryan said, the anger still tight in his voice. "Kenny isn't my dad . . . wasn't."

"I know, I know," Taylor said, raising a hand from the wheel, palm up. "Shit, I'm just making this worse. I'm sorry."

They drove in silence for a long time. Taylor felt the burning, hollow ache, like an itch at the base of her brain. The urge to find a little shop on the side of the road and buy a pint, and sip it. How fucking good it would taste. How it would give her the strength to do this, to do it right. Not to get drunk, not to escape, but just handle it. She started looking for a place to pull over. One showed up on the left side of the highway, it advertised "Kool Kones" as well as live bait and "spirits." She started to slow, and then she sped up and kept going.

Fuck, like that's all Ryan would need. His only parent down a fucking bottle, and her mother . . . Jesus, that would be a nightmare. She kept going. She was leaving behind her meetings and her sponsor, Jamie. Hell, how was she going to do this? She glanced back into the backseat. Ryan was dozing again, curled up like a ball. He was beautiful, the only beautiful thing she had ever been a part of. She told the screaming thirst to shut the fuck up again. She placated it with a cigarette and kept on driving. They were almost there.

Coalport, Pennsylvania, had a brief moment of boom during the heyday of King Coal and the railroads. That ended a long time ago. Like a lot of small towns in America, Coalport had existed to accomplish one thing, cobbled together for a singular purpose. With that gone, it had dwindled, diminished into a shade, those who lived here did so mostly because they were born here and had no idea of where else to go, or means to do so even if they did. Fewer than five hundred souls lived in the town now and most of them drove quite a ways to make a living.

Taylor came up Route 53, which became Main Street. Old farmhouses, like faded matrons, stood beside colonial-style homes, and some mid-twentieth-century two-story houses that had seen far better days. There were more churches than businesses but she smiled when she saw the little blue farmhouse that was Josie's Restaurant. The few times she had come to visit Mom, they had eaten at Josie's and it had always been great. She passed a public housing apartment complex on her right and a funeral home on her left. The Minit Mart was most likely the only place to get gas around here from the number of cars clustered in its parking lot.

Taylor turned left onto State Route 3019 at a used car lot that was operating in the rusting husk of what had once been a gas station. She headed toward Irvona, now technically outside Coalport's limits. There was some movement and noise in the backseat and Ryan's face popped next to hers. He had cinnamon skin and light brown, curly hair that looked kinda golden in bright sunlight. For an instant Taylor recalled one of the few good memories she had of his real father, Tee. Ryan held a fist to his mouth and coughed, locking eyes with his mom in the rearview.

"Okay, okay!" Taylor ejected the cigarette from her window. Ryan smiled and kissed her cheek.

"We there?" he asked.

"Pretty much. You missed Coalport, but we're almost to Granny's."

"Hmm," Ryan looked around. "They got a comic book store?"

"I'm . . . sure they have one around here somewhere," she said.

"That's a no," Ryan said.

They drove over the concrete bridge that crossed Clearfield Creek and made a right onto North Hill Street. Ryan saw his new home coming up on his right.

"Well, here we are." Taylor tried to put as much excitement in her voice as she could muster. They turned right onto a short, paved private road with a large faded and rusted tin sign beside it announcing they were now entering the Valentine Trailer Park. The road intersected with two other paved roads that Taylor recalled from the last visit four years back; it was a circle. The main road also continued ahead, branching off left and right. They took the right branch and Taylor pulled into a bare patch of dirt in front of her mother's long trailer.

Ryan climbed out of the backseat. There were trailers on opposite sides of Granny's. One on the other side of the narrow road they had traveled down and another on the left side of Granny's trailer. An older-looking small camper, all worn silver and portholes, was across the yard from Granny's It reminded Ryan of a submarine or maybe a rocket ship from some old black-and-white movie. Duct-taped to the trailer's door was a weathered square of cardboard——it looked like the lid of an old pizza box flipped over—and on it "Trailer Park Manager" was written very neatly. Almost fancy, in black Sharpie. Below that was the times and hours the manager was in.

Ryan thought he caught a flash of something pink past the fifties rocket ship trailer, but before he could go over and check, the door flew open on Granny's trailer and she rushed down the small set of wooden stairs.

"There's my fella!" Granny shouted and wrapped her arms around Ryan, hugging him tight. Ryan laughed in spite of himself. He knew this was embarrassing as hell, but he loved Granny and he'd missed her.

Granny's name was Judy and she was about twenty years older than mom. She wore a tank top, shorts, and flip-flops. She was skinny with long legs, veined with blue, and she had faded tattoos, including one on her shoulder of a rose with thorns dripping blood. The Tasmanian Devil from the Bugs Bunny cartoons, his legs replaced with a spinning vortex of motion lines, the words "Bad Girl" below it was on her left biceps. A ring of strange black swirling flames she had told Ryan was called a "tribal" was on the other arm. Ryan wasn't allowed to see Granny's other tattoos. Granny kept her hair, which was the color of a carrot, but with black and gray roots, up in a bun thanks to a pair of wooden chopsticks. Granny's hairdo always reminded Ryan of a volcano erupting.

"Hey, Granny," he said.

"You had better not be giving my sugar away now," she said and kissed madly at his neck. Ryan giggled and squeezed his chin down to stop the tickling kisses. Granny looked up and saw Taylor stepping out the driver side of the car. The grin faded. "You've gained some weight and you've got dark circles under your eyes," Judy said. "You're not sleeping are you, or are you back on something?"

"Hi Mom," Taylor said. She walked over and hugged Judy. It was awkward for both of them and they didn't do it long. Ryan felt the badness between Granny and Mom, he always did, and he did what he normally did, he tried to ignore it and do something else. He plucked the keys from Mom's hand and unlocked the trunk with a click of the key fob.

"I expected you sooner," Judy said. "I hope you minded me, Taylor. It's a tiny little room, and you and Ryan will have to share with the cat. So, hopefully, you didn't bring too much junk."

"We don't have much to bring, Mom," Taylor said. "I appreciate you doing this until I get us a place of our own."

"Mhm," Judy said. "We'll see." Judy turned to look over at her grandson. Ryan was wrestling a red plastic storage bin out of the trunk of the car. It was covered with stickers, most of them comic book superheroes, or Vans skateboarding decals. "You need help with that, baby?"

"No Granny," Ryan said. "I got it."

Taylor wrestled her blue storage tub free of the backseat and followed her son up the wooden stairs and into the trailer. Granny's always smelled of stale tobacco and baby powder. The living room was narrow and decorated in dark paneling. The old, wide television was catty-corner and currently playing some Lifetime movie. Small shelves with tchotchkes and pictures were everywhere. Granny's old cloth recliner was in the corner next to the half-wall that separated the living room from the kitchen. Ryan knew the way to the back room. It was where he and Mom had always stayed when they visited. He went past Granny's bedroom and the bathroom to the room at the end of the hallway.

His and Mom's new room was half-full of cardboard boxes, a washer and dryer, and a litter box in the far corner. Granny had already blown up the air mattress and fitted it with a sheet, pillows, and a blanket. Ryan put down his box and turned to help Mom set hers down. Mom looked really sad as she stared at the two plastic tubs, the entirety of their possessions, and this tiny little room. Granny's cat, a Maine Coon named Reeses, yowled at them from her perch on a tower of boxes. Ryan gave his mom a hug. "Hey, Mom, it will be okay."

Taylor hugged her son tightly. "That's my line," she said. "It will, baby. It will. I promise."

. . .

Granny made dinner. It was blue box mac and cheese, chicken nuggets, and green beans, all Ryan's favorites. After dinner, Mom and Granny started arguing about Ryan and school. Granny wanted him to register as soon as he could, even though there was less than a month left in the school year. Mom wanted him to wait to enroll at the end of summer. Ryan dropped his paper plate and plastic cup in the trash and headed outside as they talked about him as if he wasn't there.

It was after seven and still light outside. Somewhere Ryan heard a lawnmower. He smelled grilling steaks and there was the hum of cicadas on the warm air. He looked to his right and saw a girl sitting on the wrought iron steps of a trailer with wooden lattice panels running along its base. She looked a few years older than him with hair dyed pink and turquoise the color of cotton candy. She wore a black Twenty One Pilots T-shirt and cutoff jeans shorts that showed off her tanned, toned legs. She looked up from her phone to catch Ryan looking at her. He smiled out of reflex and then looked down.

There was shouting and motion and whooping as a pack of boys, around Ryan's age, shot past him on bicycles and rounded Granny's trailer.

"'Vada!" one of the boys called out as he sped by. The girl on the stairs responded to the name. "We're going to the fort! Tell Mom!"

"Tell her yourself!" the girl shouted back, standing. Two more blurs shot by but another boy with jet black hair and a face covered with acne slid to a stop in front of the girl.

"Hey, you want a ride, bae?" he said smoothly. The girl barely batted an eye, as she picked her own bike up off the grass, climbed on, and started to pedal.

"Sam, what did I tell you I was going to do if you called me 'bae' again?" she asked.

"Punch me in the junk," Sam said, grinning, "But I know—"

The girl's fist shot out struck Sam square in the balls. The punch clogged Sam's retort in his throat. He grunted and nearly fell off his bike. Instead he pedaled sidesaddle for a moment and wobbled off to follow the other boys. He made a muffled coughing sound as he disappeared from sight. The girl glided past Ryan, then slowed and dropped her leg to balance hers. She paused a few feet from him.

"Hey," she said.

"Hey," Ryan replied. "That was a good punch."

The girl's whole face lit up for a second. "You new?"

Ryan nodded. "Yeah, me and my mom. We're staying with my Granny." The girl looked past him to Granny's trailer.

"Judy?" Ryan nodded. "She's real nice."

The shouts of the boys grew fainter. Sam called out, his voice echoing, "Naaaaaaavaaaaada, c'mon!" The girl rolled her eyes and shook her head.

"Nevada."

"Ryan."

"You got a bike? We're headed out to the fort."

"Skateboard," he said. "Sorry."

"It's peachy," she said, smiling. "I'll give you a ride, if you want."

Ryan climbed on the back of the bike. He almost wrapped his arms around her waist for a second, but then put his arms behind him and grabbed the handle behind the seat and pulled his legs up. Nevada smelled like soap and grape Bubble Yum. They took off onto the paved road and followed it past Granny's trailer to where it intersected with the circle road.

There were about a dozen more trailers behind Granny's, scattered about. Ryan saw a small green, plastic kiddie pool with a slide that was a smiling frog's tongue in the front yard of one of them. They sped between the trailers. Past them was a vast, empty grassy field and at the distant edge of that was thick, shady woods. The sun was fat and red, low in the sky to their right. The even ground gave way to a gently sloping hill and Nevada took them down that and into the field. Far up ahead Ryan could see the other boys riding their bikes into the forest, racing each other.

"Where'd you move from?" she asked.

"Baltimore," Ryan said. "We kinda had to."

"Yeah," Nevada said. "That's how me and my mother and brother ended up here too. It's not too bad. This place is a little weird, but it's pretty here and most of the people are nice. "

"Weird?" Ryan said, but before he could ask why they were out of the bright light of the field and under the thick, cool shade of the forest. Nevada drifted to a stop at the semicircle of the other boy's bicycles a few yards into the woods. The boys stopped an animated discussion of something and they all looked at Ryan.

"Hey," Ryan said, climbing off Nevada's bike.

"Who's this?" one boy asked, ignoring Ryan's greeting and looking at Nevada. It was the same boy that had shouted at Nevada to inform Mom he was headed to the fort, whatever that was. He had dark curly hair, a tightly held jaw and lips, and intense brown eyes. Now that Ryan looked closely he saw the resemblance to Nevada.

"This is Ryan, he's Judy's grandson from Baltimore," Nevada said. "They just moved in today. Ryan, this is my rude-as-hell brother Joe." Joe was maybe a little older than Ryan, but not much. He was about half an inch taller and he looked like he had some muscles under his old, faded U.S. Army T-shirt, probably a hand-me-down.

Joe nodded at Ryan, but said nothing. There was a little menace in his stare, but Ryan swallowed and shut up.

Two of the boys were sitting side by side on their bikes. They were Ryan's age. One raised a hand and waved. The other smiled a little too wide and revealed a few crooked teeth. It was obvious they were related; both had blond hair cut neat and short, blue eyes and the same basic features. The one that waved looked older. The smiling one with the snaggled teeth said, "Hey, I'm David. This is Patrick, he's my brother. Pleased to meet you." He had a little southern twang in his voice.

Patrick held out a hand. Ryan shook it. It was a strong grip, but Patrick wasn't trying to crush his hand or nothing. "Howdy," Patrick said, and meant it. He had the same southern accent in his voice that David had but not as pronounced.

"Pat's the smart one, David's the dumbass," Sam said. He was met by a chorus of "shut up's" from Patrick, David, and Nevada. Joe just glared.

Unhindered, Sam held out a fist for Ryan to bump. He looked Ryan over. "You half-brother or something, man?"

"Sam," Nevada growled, "you want me to punch you in the nuts again?"

"See," Sam said, looking to the other boys. "I told you she touched 'em!" Nevada began to climb off her bike menacingly. Sam cackled and rode off into the woods.

"Asshole," Nevada said. She turned to Ryan. "Sorry. He's not trying to be a douche, it's genetic."

"It's cool," Ryan said. "I got no problems. My dad *was* black."

"Mine's a redneck," Patrick said. "No, a real one. His neck . . . it's red. We're from Texas, and he used to do construction. Said he got baked for too long. Turned him pink to red." Patrick chuckled and Ryan smiled. Patrick gestured toward the narrow dirt path Sam had already ridden down. "We're headed for the fort if you want to come hang out?"

"Yeah," Ryan said.

"You ride with 'Vada?" he asked. Ryan nodded and climbed back on Nevada's bike and the group rode up the dirt path, single file. The trail was rough and a few times Ryan thought he was going to bounce right off the back of the bicycle, but he was too busy laughing to worry about it.

The bike trail branched off several times in different directions, looping about the forest, but finally the group stopped before a massive white oak tree that had been struck by lightning a very long time ago. The base of the tree still stood, about five feet high and a good five feet wide. The base had numerous names, dates, symbols, and some very gross swear-word-laden sentences carved into it. Sam was standing above them, up in the nest of the shattered tree's trunk, which with him standing there did look a lot like a small tower.

"Speak, 'friend,' and enter," Sam said in a booming voice. He was trying to do a British accent and kind of sucking at it. He held a stick as if it were Excalibur.

"Man, you have got to read another book besides *The Lord of the Rings*," Patrick said.

"I'm just shocked he can read," David chimed in. He walked behind the tree's base and began to walk up a long, dead tree branch, part of the upper part of the tree that had fallen long ago, but was still partly attached to the base by strips of thick bark. The branch was a wide as a two-by-four and David held his arms out from his side like a trapeze artist as he walked up the narrow ramp and joined Sam in the nest. Patrick followed and so did Nevada and Scott. Ryan walked up last.

"Screw all of ya," Sam said. "Best. Fucking. Book. Ev-ah."

"I liked *The Hobbit* better," Ryan said then folded in. Usually when he talked about stuff like this at school, he got looks like he had just sprouted a second head, or he got busted on, laughed at.

"Bull-fucking-shit!" Sam responded at once. "The Hobbit movies sucked!"

"But the book is really good," Patrick replied, "even if the movies did suck . . ."

"And they did," Ryan said, "hard."

"Yeah but *The Lord of the Rings* movies *and* books kick ass," Sam reiterated.

"They're really long," Nevada said. "And they are always stopping for food."

"I kinda liked those parts," David added.

Ryan felt a strange sense of peace settle over him. There were maybe two or three friends that he could talk to about stuff like this back home in Baltimore and he was resigned to never seeing them again. But now . . . Joe fished out a crumpled red and white pack of Marlboro cigarettes and a white Bic plastic lighter in a Ziploc bag from a crevice in the tree. He slipped one of the cigarettes into his mouth and offered one to Sam, who took it. He paused and offered one to Ryan. Ryan knew he probably looked like a scared little punk as he shook his head. Joe shrugged, seemingly to genuinely not give a shit, and lit his own smoke and then handed the lighter to Sam, who did the same. Nevada took out her phone and began to check her messages.

"What else you read?" Sam asked Ryan as he blew the smoke out the side of his mouth, trying to look cool. Ryan smiled and felt his whole body relax, down to his toes.

. . .

It turned out Joe, Patrick, David, Sam, and Nevada all read comics. They had a long debate on Marvel versus DC, Ryan threw in the wild card of Image Comics and said they were better than either of the others, and that seemed to make him the de facto authority on the subject, even though Sam told him he was full of shit, which seemed to be Sam's retort to most things.

They all played console games, Patrick and David had an Xbox One; Joe, Nevada, and Sam had PlayStation 4s.

"What you got," David asked Ryan as he absently stared at his smartphone's screen. The sun was almost gone now and the light in the forest was getting dimmer, becoming the color of ash.

"Uh, I had a PS," Ryan said. "It . . . got smashed up." No one seemed to notice the shift in Ryan's mood but Nevada. She held her tongue.

"That sucks man," Sam said. "You still got games?" Ryan nodded.

"We get together and team play a lot," Nevada said. "You still got your headset?"

"Yeah," Ryan said, brightening a bit.

"Okay you can come over and—"

There was a shout, echoing through the woods, then another, the sound of branches being pushed past, twigs snapping.

"Shit," Patrick said.

"Come on, let's go." Nevada started down the branch and back to the pile of bikes. "We'll take the switchback."

"Bullshit!" Joe said, crushing out his cigarette butt under his high-tops. "I'm sick and tired of this! Why the fuck run from that little chickenshit pissant Dickie! We got as much right to be up in here as they do." Nevada looked angry. She gestured for Ryan to come on, and he began to make his way down, with Sam in front of him and David behind. The shouting voices sounded closer, like they were coming up the bike trail.

"Joe, you know they'll kick your ass if they get ahold of you. Mom will freak! Come on!"

Patrick and Joe stood alone on top of the fort. "Come on, man," Patrick said. "Another day when 'Vada and Ryan aren't here, okay? We'll stomp 'em good." Joe sighed and made his way down the branch with Patrick following behind him. Joe muttered about it being bullshit. Nevada with Ryan on her bike waited, making sure her brother got on his too. She noticed Ryan's questioning look.

"Dickie Dennis," she said, "and some of his buddies. They're mostly seniors, some dropped out. Bunch of meth and potheads. They come up here to drink and get high. Sometimes they bring girls up at night and, y'know. They mess with us if they catch us in the forest."

"They fuck us up!" Sam said. "They put Danny Haas in the fucking hospital when they caught him up here alone."

"It's not even dang fair!" David said. "They got the cage, why do they care if we hang out at the fort."

"They figure they own all of it," Patrick said. "Jerks."

Joe shook his head but said nothing. They set off with him in the lead along the narrow bike trail. When they reached the first fork in the trail, Joe led them down the other branch than the one they had come in on. It was harder to see, night wasn't very far away. Branches *whooshed* and snapped close to their heads as they ducked, tilted, and pedaled wildly. Ryan's palms were sweating but he hung on to the passenger bar as tightly as he could. Suddenly there was shouting on either side of the trail. Shadowy figures jumped out from behind foliage and grabbed at the bikers.

"C'mere, you little shit-stains!" a gruff male voice snarled out of the darkness. Nevada screamed, so did Sam. Ryan thought he heard Joe shouting something, then a bright light strobed behind his eyes and his face went numb as he tumbled off Nevada's bike.

"Shit!" It was Nevada's voice, frantic. "Ryan, Ryan, get up, get up and run!"

"Grab that little cooz," another voice said. "We'll show her . . ." The voice was cut off and Ryan heard a roar that sounded like Joe, and wet smacking sounds.

"Get the fuck away from her!" Joe bellowed, and there were more crashing sounds. Ryan was back in his closet, back in his fort, the door splintering. No, no, he wasn't, goddamn it. Nevada was screaming. He was back. Ryan staggered to his feet and he saw some guy in a jeans jacket trying to wrestle Nevada to the ground. Patrick and Joe were fighting another guy, a lanky blond with long greasy hair, sideburns, and a patchy goatee.

"Hey!" Ryan practically screamed. He picked up a heavy stick and smashed it hard over the head of the guy in the jeans jacket. He went down hard and his scalp was bleeding. The guy struggling with Patrick and Joe paused, as they did, to gape at Ryan. Even Nevada froze. The guy Ryan hit rolled over, moaning and wincing. He looked to be eighteen, maybe nineteen. His eyes were glassy and his pupils tiny. He glared at Ryan.

"You little bastard!" he rumbled. "I'm fucking bleeding!"

"Your mama squealed last night," Ryan said and flipped off both the older boys. Two other older kids came crashing through the forest and saw what was happening. "Your mamas all told me you were a bunch of little punk-ass bitches!" Ryan began running and he heard the older boys chasing after him down the path. He heard Nevada shouting something about the wrong way, and the jungle, but he didn't understand. He heard panting close behind him and he sped up.

It was nearly dark and he had no idea where he was in the forest, where he was running to. He just knew that his lungs and blood were burning and he knew these guys would kill him if they caught him, when they caught him. He hoped Nevada was okay. He figured all four of the older boys were after him from the shouts and labored breathing behind him.

"I'm gonna break your fucking little chicken neck!" one of the voices panted. It was getting hard to see in the dusk. He heard the gurgling waters of a creek and slowed as he reached the bank.

"Drown the little fucker!" a voice too close to him gasped. Ryan jumped from one large rock on the bank of the creek to another on the far side. One of his legs slipped and splashed in the cold water, he scrambled up, hearing the splashing behind him and he kept running. There was no longer a bike path, just trees and bushes. He felt branches scratch at his still numb face and his eyes were tearing in pain and fear.

This had been stupid. Why the hell had he done this? He had almost died not too long ago and he'd sworn that he'd never be in that place again, and here he was. Why? He began to see the forest thinning up ahead, the dingy twilight beyond the maw of trees.

He cleared the forest and saw he was on the opposite side of it from the trailer park. The sound of cicadas was deafening, chanting their nocturnal songs. There was another sloping hill but this one was steeper and less inviting. Below was a small valley. In the dying daylight he saw the squat monoliths of old, dirty train cars scattered about like a child's discarded toys. High patches of grass jutted between the discarded cars. There were old carnival rides looking like the rusted skeletons of alien dinosaurs, looming. The shadow of a Ferris wheel was far off to the right past the sea of boxcars. Beyond the junkyard were old train tracks, choked with weeds, and past that Ryan heard the *whoosh* of a highway somewhere beyond sight.

His plan was to descend the ridge and try to hide. He never got the chance. Someone tackled him, spun him around, and pulled him off his feet. It was the kid with the sideburns and goatee. His face was red and blotchy and he was as furious as he was high.

"You little piece of dog shit," Sideburns growled.

"Fuck man! The little pussy done pissed himself!" the one in the jeans jacket said, looking at his palm covered in fresh scalp blood. "He stinks! Let me kick his fucking teeth in, Dickie."

Ryan had wet himself, he couldn't think. He looked into the face of his attacker and saw no mercy, saw nothing human, only anger and cruelty. He'd seen that face before, and he knew what to expect from it.

You think you can talk that way to us? I'm gonna fucking . . ." Dickie paused, looking past Ryan to something else. His eyes blinked and Ryan saw some of the cruelty and anger begin to slip away under a film of fear.

"Oh, shit . . ." Jeans Jacket said. "It's him, it's fucking him."

"Shut the fuck up," another boy's voice said. "That's just some old ghost story they tell to keep kids . . . from . . . coming back . . . here . . . Oh fuck . . . Dickie? What the fuck is that?"

Ryan looked over his shoulder. Below in the weed-choked boxcar grave-yard, a single figure was lumbering toward the collected boys on the ridge. The man was well over six feet and wore dirty old train engineer's overalls and unlaced work boots. He had no shirt to conceal his flaccid, hairless skin, his massive, loglike arms, and his swaying breasts. All of his skin—his chest, his arms, his face—was the color of greasy snow, flecked with dirt and blood. His skin almost glowed in the final, feeble scraps of daylight. The man's face became clearer as he walked slowly, purposefully toward them. He was painted. Around his eyes were black diamonds. His mouth was a black frown and his nose was painted a smudged blood-red. On his forehead was a black sun, radiating black waves. He was bald and he wore a pointed little hat tipped at a crooked angle. He began to ascend the ridge below the boys. He had a sledgehammer in his hands.

Dickie dropped Ryan and the boy fell. All the older boys ran back into the woods, screaming. Night was here. Ryan began to get to his feet, he turned and the clown's face was near his own. He screamed and the clown screamed back, almost parroting him. Ryan ran, he ran into the woods, a tangle of shad-ows, the echoing screams of the older boys and the gibbering laughter of the clown pursuing him.

He stumbled, fell, got to his feet. His arms and legs were rubber, he had no thought, he was light with fear. He splashed through the creek and up and out the other side. His wet clothes were so heavy. He heard the splashing of the clown crossing, coming, not stopping. The insane laughter. Ryan found himself headed downhill, back on the bike path, faster, a tiny flicker of hope for escape, for survival. He heard the thudding bulk of the pale giant thun-dering down the slope behind him. Ryan could see the sledgehammer in his screaming brain, ready to bash his skull in.

He saw the field ahead as he sprinted out of the woods. The forest was a slumbering beast, a huddled shadow. The sky above was purple and blazed with a million burning golden stars, scattered like sand on glass. He saw the older boys, back to the edges of the park now, bouncing silhouettes, then out of sight and then he saw Nevada and the others at the top of the hill, shouting to him. Ryan slowed and bent over, his side was stabbing him with pain. Over the gasping of his own breath he heard the swish-swish of the grass behind him, coming closer. He looked back and saw the clown lumbering, limping across the field toward him, raising the sledge. Ryan staggered forward, stumbled, ran, because he knew death was only a few yards behind him. He came up on the others, they were all shouting, screaming, pointing at the thing that continued toward them.

"You okay?" Nevada asked. Ryan managed a grunt.

"Everybody split up!" Joe shouted, grabbing Nevada's wrist. "Get home, lock the doors! It can't get all of us!"

They ran up the paved road, past the scattered trailers and then fragmented in different directions. Ryan sprang up the stairs of Granny's trailer, saw the warm light behind the windows. He expected the clown to spring into view at the edge of the trailer at any second. He swung the door open and slammed it behind him and locked it. He turned to find Granny in her chair half-asleep and Mom on the couch. They were watching some cop show on the old TV.

"You have fun, baby?" Mom asked, then saw his face and clothing. "Oh my God, what happened, Ryan, you're soaking wet and your face?"

"I was playing with some kids in the woods," Ryan lied. "We were just running around. I scratched my face on a tree branch. It's nothing, Mom."

How could he even begin to explain what had just happened to him? He wasn't even sure himself. Mom and Granny would think he had gone crazy. Given all the nightmares and the pants wetting since that night with Kenny in Baltimore, they might make him go to a hospital or something if he started talking about being chased by some nut in clown makeup with a sledgehammer. None of it seemed real. No, he needed to keep his mouth shut.

Tay sat up and examined Ryan's face. "God, maybe I should put some antiseptic ointment on that, honey."

"Oh, for God's sake!" Judy said. "Let kids be kids, Taylor! It's good for them to get out in the fresh air and run around. We're raising a whole generation of wusses! That's what Dr. Phil says."

"I'm okay, really," Ryan said. "I'm going to get ready for bed."

"Get yourself a shower and put on clean jammies," Mom said, and kissed his cheek.

He heard Mom and Granny arguing out in the living room. He walked back to the laundry room and stood in the dark room for a moment. He was shaking. Had that been real? Ryan sighed and rubbed his face. He walked over to the single window in the room and pushed the blinds aside an inch to peek outside. He hoped Nevada and Joe were home and okay.

The clown stood still, like a statue in the annex between Granny's trailer and the other three around her. The sledgehammer was slung over its shoulder, its black-diamond eyes glistened like oil in the reflection of a distant street light. Ryan felt his whole body tense, his stomach ate itself. The clown looked in his direction and waved with a wiggle of fingers before it lumbered out of view, vanishing behind Granny's trailer.

Ryan tried to sleep all night, but it hid from him. He listened to Mom's steady breathing, sometimes becoming a soft snoring, and it gave him comfort. Before dawn he peeked out the window again. There was no clown, only cigarette ash light growing in the east. He padded back to the air mattress and finally, thankfully buried himself in dreamless sleep.

SIX

Angelo Potts, better known to the streets and the Philadelphia PD as "Angie," pulled his stolen Ford Taurus POS into the Hamburg Wawa parking lot at four in the morning. The windows of the Ford were shuddering from the bass of "Dead Body Man" by the Insane Clown Posse. Angie wasn't thinking about the mutilated corpses in his trunk. He just wanted some smokes, a cheese steak, and some Red Bull. It had been a long fucking drive.

He climbed out of the car, leaving it running, his music thudding, droning on. "Hey!" an angry voice with a South Philly accent called out to his back, "Turn that fuckin' shit off, my family's tryin' to sleep in the car! I don't want them hearing that shit!"

Angie turned to the guy who was pumping gas into a minivan, his old lady asleep in the passenger seat. He saw two car seats with rug rats in them in the backseat. The gas pumper's expression changed from anger to shock when he saw Angie's face. Angie was about six feet tall, he shaved his slightly lumpy skull, and the scars from numerous childhood beefs made him look like he'd had multiple brain surgeries. His face and head was smeared unevenly in thick, oily clown-white and he had used a can of black spray paint to give himself a bar of a mask that looked like smeared, running bat wings. Another swipe of black paint over his lips and an uneven squirt of green paint on his nose made him look like a clown straight from hell. He smiled at the family man, but his eyes were full of barely contained violence. He lifted his huge, droopy, and stained ICP hockey jersey and showed the guy the 9mm stuffed in his waistband, squeezed up against his hairy, swollen stomach.

"You want, I can make sure they sleep forever, bitch," he said, his voice a little too lilting, too high-pitched for his hulking demeanor. The fucker better not say shit about his lisp either. The gas pumper said nothing and looked down at the hose and the side of his van. Angie chuckled and turned back toward the storefront, dropping his shirt. "What I thought. Punk."

Waiting for his food inside, Angie enjoyed the cushion of space everyone else waiting gave him. He caught the fearful, furtive looks and that just made him feel even stronger. At one point, this drunk-ass juffalo staggered up to Angie. This fake-wannabe motherfucker offered up his hand to fist-bump and gave the seminal Juggalo cry of "Whoop-whoop!" Angie stared down at the drunk long enough for the guy to rethink his decision.

"You into ICP, bro?" Angie asked almost like it was a challenge.

"Shit, yeah, man!" the drunk replied.

"Then you should man the fuck up and get with the squad, bro." The drunk looked confused. "The Lunatic Clown Squad, lame-ass," Angie said.

"I heard they were like fucking wannabes," the drunk said and immediately realized his mistake. "Uh, shit man. I don't know. They good, my ninja?"

"They're beyond, bro," Angie said and meant it. "LCS got it all over ICP. They got the real juice, little man. Evolve your ass."

The drunk scuttled away, promising he'd check Lunatic Clown Squad out. Angie snorted in amused contempt. Like you're gonna find LCS's music on iTunes or some shit. Please.

Resupplied, Angie shuffled back out to the jacked Ford. He headed out of the lot and toward the I-78 ramp. The Cooker was very clear that the body parts had to be placed near the interstate to complete the ritual. The Ford drifted up the on ramp and Angie slid into the sparse predawn traffic mostly made up of 18-wheelers, service trucks, and weary travelers with license plates from other states. The greenish glow of the instrument panel painted his ghostly face and the music droned a relentless beat into his brain. Now it was ICP's "Southwest Voodoo."

He knew he could just ditch the car and boost another and get on home to Philly, but he also knew what would happen if the Cooker found out he had done a half-ass job. Especially now that he was in the running to become a full-fledged Harlequin.

. . .

Angie grew up in North Philly, in the Badlands, that was the name the cops and the papers stuck on the neighborhoods, like Kensington where they lived. Lots of drugs, at one time, open-air markets for them. Lots of gangs, like the K&A that Angie hooked up with when he was thirteen. He joined the K&A, the street soldiers of the Irish mob, because he got tired of getting his ass kicked by the Puerto Rican gang assholes on his way home from ditching school.

When he started bringing home more money than his old man, he took his last beating from Pops. He pistol-whipped his father, stuffed a 9mm in his mouth, and told him if he ever touched him again he'd make his mother a widow. He left, moved in with some other guys in K&A, and never looked back.

Angie liked horrorcore rap and he first heard Insane Clown Posse when he was fourteen and fucking loved it. ICP was vulgar, crude, and so fucking real. They didn't give a fuck what they said or how they said it. They'd rap about shit Angie could feel, was living, and they never let anything hold them back, always forward, no apologies. He got his first ICP tattoo, the silhouette of the running Hatchetman, the same year. It was a jailhouse tattoo he got in a basement on Glenwood.

The Juggalo life embraced Angie full-on. He went to concerts, parties, and anytime he could he'd head out to the big Gathering of the Juggalos that was held annually for the family of fans. The Gathering was off the chain. There were carnival rides, food, drugs, booze, and naked people every-where. It was like a clown-face Woodstock minus the stinking hippies, or so Angie thought.

It was at the Gathering that he began to realize that he and his ninjas weren't like most of the pussy-assed motherfuckers that wore the paint. Most of them were about love and family and enjoying the music, and each other, and life. Lame-ass losers. There were fucking Christian Juggalos there for chrissakes, and fags, and cripples, and retards too. And these dopey moth-erfuckers would just welcome them on in. One big stupid, grinning family. It made Angie sick, and when he spoke up about it, it got him and his real-ass ninjas chased off site, almost got their asses kicked, but not before they set some fires and beat down some of the sub-juggs that didn't deserve to call themselves true Juggalos. That was when Angie was approached by some of the Harlequins, gliding through the Gathering like sharks in a sea of gup-pies. That was when he first heard about the Lunatic Clown Squad and he knew he had found his true home.

. . .

Angie took exit 49 at Fogelsville. He drove north on Route 100 and then took the left onto Old U.S. 22, then left onto Church Street. Angie chuckled at the name of the street. It was still dark but he could feel dawn coming and he knew this spot would have to do. He pulled over at the small wooded park and wiped the car down good, gathering up his trash and scattering it in the woods. He made three trips back to the car's trunk for the body parts, whistling an LCS tune as he did. The torsos and severed limbs were in clean garbage bags. The Cooker had cleaned the body parts and there was practically zero blood. Angie didn't fully understand what the Cooker did to the bodies, to the people they gathered up for him, but this was trash disposal. The Cooker got what he needed and he gave the Harlequins what they needed.

Angie placed the torsos and the hand-less, foot-less limbs in precise positions in the wooded lot. He referenced the map of how to place the parts that the Cooker had given him. The Cooker's diagram was written on very old, crinkly paper, like it was homemade and the style of his ink writing and drawing was intricate and complex like the way an old lady might write or draw, Angie thought. There were words in some weird-ass, Harry Potter language that he had to say as he placed each part, like he was putting a puzzle together. Angie struggled with the words but the Cooker had each word sounded out on the paper.

"*Masacre innocentium in sole et luna ut baptizentur,*" Angie mumbled as he placed the final arm, crooked at an angle four feet from the inverted female torso. Angie looked at his handiwork, nodded, and shuffled back to the car.

He gave the trunk one more good wipe-down and sprayed lighter fluid all over the trunk before he closed it with a gloved hand. He stuffed the garbage bags that had held the body parts into a park trash can that was overflowing with fast food wrappers, beer bottles, and cans. He took another can of lighter fluid and sprayed it all over the interior of the car and then tossed a lit match in and shut the door. He walked back down the road without a glance back as the burning car slowly began to brighten the dying night. Back on the Route 100, he used his cell to call Altair.

"Hey, yeah. It's done. I need a ride home. Ext. 49. There's a Steak 'n Shake over by the Goodwill. Pick me up there. Later." Angie hung up and slipped the cell phone back in his pocket.

Altair's real name was Dutch, and he was one damaged individual. He was a High Harlequin in service to the Cooker, and he was kind of like Angie's boss. Altair was his "Mystery Name" that the Cooker gave him when he first became a High Harlequin.

. . .

Altair had been with the other Harlequins that Angie had met years back at the Juggalo Gathering, along with another Harlequin, a guy who's name was

Agitprop. Agit's paint was whiteface with wide, crimson wings over his eyes and a black diamond formed around his cracked, red lips.

Angie had been in a circle with about a half-dozen guys and a girl, all wearing their clown faces, all drunk and high, the electricity of violence humming between them, an unspoken language they all understood, felt more than knew. Far away in the distance was the carnival, the rides, the laughter and the music from the stages, the lights of the Gathering. Angie had seen Agitprop around the Gathering the last few days and now he stood at the center of the circle. Altair, who was a big, scary motherfucker, stood mutely at Agit's side, staring off into the darkness, like he was seeing shit they weren't. His face was greasy and thick with clown paint and Angie figured him to be in his late thirties, maybe forties, it was hard to tell. Three dark blobs covered Altair's forehead. In time, Angie learned the dots represented the Star Altair and two other stars, Deneb and Vega.

"So you ninjas think this is all bullshit?" Agitprop said, his voice a tight hiss. "You don't think it's cute to see the little kid Juggalos and the Juggalos for Jesus? Think it's turned into some real PG-13, commercial shit? Right?" There was grumbling of agreement, a few curt nods of the head. Agit lifted a small glass pipe to his lips and fired up a handheld torch lighter. The meth crystals huddled in the pipe dissolved under the blue flame and the clown sucked in the thick white smoke. He exhaled and the smoke wreathed his pale, painted face, his bloodshot eyes rolled back into their sockets. Agit began to move around the circle, his cadence growing quicker and quicker as he spoke.

"Do you know where clowns come from, bitches? They come from Harlequins, like us." He slapped Altair on the chest and the giant didn't move, continuing to stare blankly. "The name Harlequin is a bastardization of the French *Hellequin*," Agitprop continued. "They were demons, straight from Hell, their faces painted as white skulls. The *Hellequins* roamed the countryside in packs, tormenting and slaying any unfortunate traveler who crossed their path. They were beasts, mockers of life and goodness." Agit gestured toward the distant noise and color of the Gathering. "Annnnd, now, now we have fucking Ronald the burger pimp, and a bunch of fucking old men driving around in little cars doing good deeds." He spat in the direction of the carnival. "Pathetic.

"Do you know what a clown really is? What it represents? Do you?" he screamed at the circle, his teeth and eyes the color of diseased phlegm from the meth, from his rotting soul. "Clowns are darkness hiding behind whitewashed light, blood lust peeking out behind a fake-ass smile.

"Goddamned Pogo the clown raping and strangling little boys in the night. Klutzo the clown—cop, Christian—such a good, godly man. He made children laugh and he made child porn, too. The faceless clown-gangs in France who stalked and beat people with crowbars and chased children with chainsaws in the night. Poisonous things in nature scream out warning behind bright, pretty colors."

"Hell, yeah," Angie had muttered. He felt himself getting hard just listening to this guy. He wanted to wild, to rage and burn.

"Clowns are the truth too ugly for us to face, the bad lie we tell ourselves about the universe, about ourselves," Agitprop said. "It's shoddy paint trying to cover the darkest of stains."

Angie nodded along, most of the others did too. "Fucking A," one of the guys to Angie's left said. Agit smiled a rotting, saffron smile.

"So," he said. "You ready to stop playing at darkness, playing at mocking the light like those fucking posers? You ready to sink deep under the black, sink so deep you know you may not make it back up, back out again? Are you?"

The circle erupted in snarling cheers. Agitprop refilled the meth pipe and passed it around the circle and everyone took a hit. Whatever was in the pipe wasn't regular meth, Angie thought. The rush of his heartbeat and breathing faded quicker and thescatter, the high, was . . . different. He felt like a fucking acid-blooded dragon god, like meth usually made you feel, but there was more clarity, less obsession. His thoughts didn't crash into one another like a thirty-car pile-up on the highway. Whatever this shit was, he liked it.

After everyone had a hit, Agit gave them their first trial, their first mission. "Every one of you," the Harlequin began, "is going to go find someone over there on the playground," he gestured toward the distant Gathering, "and pluck that pretty, foolish flower, convince them to come back here with you, and then you're going to kill them. Won't that be fun?"

One of the guys from the circle suddenly looked scared."Uh, you're fucking with us, right, man?"

Agit stepped toward the guy, inches from his face.

"You can't do it?" the Harlequin asked. The guy looked down, then shook his head.

"It . . . it all sounds so fucking cool, man," the shame-faced Juggalo said, "but there's a big difference between talking shit and doing it, y'know, ninja?"

"Oh I know," Agit said. "I get you . . . my ninja." Altair was a looming shadow behind the halfhearted clown now. Altair's massive fingers gripped the Juggalo's skull and squeezed. There was a thick, cracking sound, like wood splitting slowly. Blood gushed from the Juggalo's eyes and nose. One of his eyes popped out and dangled near his mouth by a glistening optic nerve. The dying clown made a nasal grunting sound for a moment and then went limp, falling to the weed-choked ground as Altair released his now misshapen skull.

"Dwamn!" the Juggalette shouted out. Her makeup was designed to make it look like her mouth was stitched shut. "That's some echoside shit right there, man!"

Angie grunted in agreement as did the other applicants in the circle.

"So, no more enlightened sense of morality bullshit," Agitprop said. "Go play." So they did, and that night Angie ground a broken beer bottle into the throat of a sixteen-year-old Juggalo boy and watched him bleed out at Agitprop's feet.

"Next level," Agit said. "Welcome to the Harlequins, Angie."

. . .

Angie was drinking his fifth Coke and finishing his third burger when he heard the car horn bleat in the restaurant's parking lot. He dropped a sweaty, crumpled wad of bills in the middle of his ketchup-soaked plate and gave his waitress the finger as he left. Altair was behind the wheel of a massive, black Dodge Ram pickup. The stone-faced clown grunted from behind the wheel as Angie climbed in the cab. The warbling strains of Roger Miller's "King of the Road" filled the extended cab. Angie didn't know the song, but he sure as hell knew better than to say anything to Altair about his taste in music. Angie noticed a sharp penknife and a few of the old Buffalo nickels the High Harlequin liked to carve on in a plastic bag next to the gear shift. Altair's carving was pretty much the only thing resembling a human habit Angie had ever seen in the clown.

The High Harlequin pulled out of the parking lot and headed for the highway ramp. In the distance, near the park, they could see a swarm of bright flashing lights, red and blue reflecting off the still dark foliage of the tall trees. "It . . . is . . . done?" Altair asked in his rumbling, halting tone. It always seemed to Angie that Altair fought for each word he spoke, struggling to form them. Angie nodded vigorously.

"Hell, yeah, Dutch!" he said, propping a muddy boot up on the dashboard of the truck. Altair looked over at him like he was dog shit he'd just found on his shoe. Angie put his foot down and lowered his eyes as he said, "Ye . . . yeah, Altair. It's done, just like the Cooker wanted." Altair looked back to the road and nodded slowly.

"Good," he said. The truck was on I-78 headed toward Allentown and I-476 and Philly.

"Something . . . for . . . you . . . from . . . the . . . Cooker . . . in . . . the . . . glovebox. A reward."

"Ballin' ass shit!" Angie exclaimed as he opened the glove compartment. He retrieved a freezer bag full of various drugs crafted by the Cooker himself, stolen credit cards, and a roll of cash. "How am I doing, man? Can you tell me? Give me a hint? Am I at least in the running?"

Altair was silent, passing headlights washing over his ghoulish, motionless face. Muddy Waters's "Champagne and Reefer" was playing on the radio now. Angie swallowed his anger at Altair's silence. He figured after all he had done lately for the Cooker, he deserved some idea of where he was in the competition to replace the dead High Harlequin called Luna.

· · ·

The first thing Angie learned after his initiation into the Harlequins was that they had their own music, a horrorcore rap group called the Lunatic Clown Squad or LCS. LCS was like Insane Clown Posse but under the radar more, and their music was full of codes, secret signs, and portents that all related back to the Harlequins and to their master, their founder, a man known to the Harlequins as the Cooker. A lot of Juggalos busted on LCS, calling them posers and saying they were trying to cash in on Insane Clown Posse. They didn't have a clue, and that was okay because you had to be strong and dedicated to become a Harlequin. Any bottom-feeder could be part of the Juggalo family.

It was almost impossible to find Lunatic Clown Squad music except at secret concerts and Harlequin gatherings. The music wasn't for the herd, only the anointed, just like the paint.

Angie's first Harlequin Hootenanny was held in a field somewhere out in Bumfuck, Pennsylvania. There were close to four hundred people there, getting into the concert and getting high, getting drunk, getting stoned, oh, and burning shit, shooting off guns, and setting off explosives. It was a lot more fun than that limp-ass Juggalo shit, more dangerous-feeling.

It was at the meet that Angie received his first jar of the paint and it changed everything.

"Here," Agit said handing him the small glass jar. "You pick up more when you get low at the gatherings like this. The Cooker has set up a network everywhere to distribute it. Don't get stupid and run out." It looked like clown-white makeup, but greasier and shiner, almost like the shit professional clowns used. Agit told Angie to smear it on his face and then use other paints to make his signature makeup which couldn't be the same as any other Harlequin's. If it was, the two Harlequins would have to fight to determine who got to keep the look. In that fight you either yielded your face or died.

"Over fucking makeup?" Angie had said, shaking his head. "Is it a pillow fight?" He realized immediately that was the wrong thing to say. Agit slapped him and held up the jar of paint.

"This is your face now," he said. "It's your colors, your cut, your country. You treat it with respect, and you fuck up anyone who doesn't. Understand, asshole?" Angie had nodded and taken the jar.

He didn't get why it was such a big deal, until he put the paint on and felt it working on him. The clown-white made Angie's skin burn and tingle at first but after a few days he began to feel better than he had ever felt in his whole life. It was like being high but with no fuzziness, no dimmed perception; if anything the paint made him feel like he was on coke or meth, only better. The stuff made him feel stronger and tougher and he discovered when he cut his hand on the window of a car he was breaking into, the paint healed the nasty jagged cut in hours. There was a downside, though.

The crash from the paint was bad, fucking-horror-show bad. Worse than speed, worse than H. Agit had told him to apply it to his face and body once a day, and after a maybe a month, there were a few days Angie forgot or just didn't want to do it. He woke up in the middle of the night shaking, drenched with cold sweat, his skull full of so much bright, jagged pain, he knew it was going to split. He puked and stumbled to the bathroom. He grabbed the jar with trembling hands and began to apply the clown-white to his forehead in hopes it would soothe his throbbing head. In minutes the headache was gone, all the sickness was gone. He never forgot to put his paint on again.

. . .

They were almost back to Philly. Angie was high and happy, even with Altair's shitty music. Now it was Woody Guthrie's "Hobo's Lullaby."

"Even if you won't say shit," Angie said, as they cut over onto I-76, "I know I got to be in the top five? Ten? Right?" Altair glanced at him but said nothing. "Yeah, I knew it. That's why he picked me for that other thing, right?"

Before he had dropped the body parts off at the park in Fogelsville alone, Angie had done a job with Altair earlier in the night for the Cooker. They'd dropped another cut-up body near Windber, among a bunch of old streetcars stacked up in the woods. They arranged the parts just as the Cooker had ordered, and Altair had dropped one of his hobo nickels near the body parts. That had not been part of the plan but Angie said nothing when he did it. The Cooker had stressed to them it was a very important job when he had personally delivered the butchered girl to the two Harlequins on the old abandoned stretch of highway near the Pennsylvania Turnpike.

The thirteen miles of abandoned turnpike was where the Cooker held all the High Harlequin rituals and meetings. Angie had heard about the meeting of the oldest and most loyal of the harlequins. Some High Harlequins came from distant towns and small boroughs across America, while others came from further away than that at the Cooker's summons.

The few High Harlequins Angie had briefly met besides Altair had some things in common with the giant. They were usually silent, words came to them slowly and with great effort, they tended to be scary strong and seemingly impervious to pain. The part that made Angie wonder if maybe the High Harlequins weren't entirely human was their eyes. The clown's eyes always seemed devoid of life, or empathy, or even awareness. They were the eyes of a corpse set in a chalky face of garish paint.

Angie had only met the Cooker twice. The first time was a few weeks ago when he and fifty other harlequins had been summoned to the abandoned highway. The Cooker was there, surrounded by a cadre of a half-dozen High Harlequins, including Altair and the equally hulking Helios. The Cooker himself was average height and gaunt, wearing jeans and off-brand sneakers. He wore a close-cropped gray beard, but the rest of his face was hidden by the hood of his black hoodie.

"Luna is dead," the Cooker had said. His voice reminded Angie of hot ashes and cold stone. "One of you will take his place as a High Harlequin and serve me." Angie and the others had cheered. The Cooker silenced them with a raised hand. "You will be given tests, trials to undertake in my name. From the strongest of you, from the most dedicated, shall I find Luna's successor."

The second time he met the Cooker was earlier tonight when he had given him and Altair the girl's body parts to ditch in the streetcar graveyard. The Cooker had stressed to him how important it was everything was carried out just as he instructed. "I have a very irritating thorn in my side," the Cooker said, "and you, Angelo, you are going to help me be rid of it. You alone are fit for this task."

"Yeah . . . yes sir," Angie had said. The Cooker had nodded to Altair and they had loaded the girl's corpse into the truck. He alone, fuck yeah. He had to be winning the contest to become a High Harlequin. He had met the man himself. Angie smiled and blew cigarette smoke out the truck's window and imagined what secrets and power waited for him on the other side. Moving up, baby, moving up.

. . .

For his part, behind the wheel, Altair kept his own counsel about the instructions he had been given by his master, the one these stupid, lazy children called by the disrespectful name of "the Cooker." They had no idea what they were dealing with.

Altair's given name was James Holt and he had gone by Dutch in his younger days. He had been born in 1901 in a little farming community near the Ohio River. He had served "the Cooker," the man he knew then only as Flamel since the twenties. He had donned the paint because he had been promised immortality if he did, only much later did he realize the cost that immortality required and by then it was too late.

Today, Altair existed as so many others did that Flamel had collected over the ages—alone, silent, wandering tiny towns and small communities across America—existing behind the pallid faces and the counterfeit smiles like leering ghosts, stalking those their master needed, and aiding in the disposal of the remains when he was done with them. James alone had kidnapped and murdered hundreds over his century of service to his master. Early in his service as a Harlequin he had reveled in his bloody tasks but thanks to the mind-deadening qualities of long use of the paint he seldom thought about what he had done or why anymore. Emotions were distant, shadowed memories.

He glanced over at the young fool in the truck beside him. Angie had no idea what lay ahead of him, of why he had been chosen for this task tonight. Some small crumb of James Holt that had not been devoured by over a hundred years of drug abuse, murder, and madness almost felt sorry for the boy and what lay ahead for him, but it was feeble ember of empathy and it was snuffed out almost instantly.

Philadelphia, glittering like a crown in the night's evaporating embrace grew up around them. James . . . Dutch . . . Altair—whatever name you chose to use—drove his foolish young charge into the heart of the city toward home, toward the next step in their master's plan. Angie smiled, happy to be close to his bed, unaware of what his role was to be. Altair remained silent, inside and out, still as stone.

Spring and summer had bickered over the last few weeks and, at least for this weekend, spring had won the argument in Lenoir, North Carolina. It was warm and mild, not sweltering like it would get very soon. Massive cloud castles drifted through a sky so painfully, brilliantly blue it made your heart ache.

There were more hot dogs than burgers on the grill in the Aussapile back-yard this Saturday afternoon. Hot dogs were cheaper. However, Jimmie's folks and his wife, Layla's, mom had brought plenty of burgers as well as some fresh ears of corn from Evelyn's—Layla's mom—garden. They were wrapped in blackening foil beside the sizzling burgers and swelling, charred-striped dogs.

Jimmie was wearing an apron that came to his knees. It was white and adorned with a cartoon-proportioned body of a woman in a pink bikini. The cartoon neck ended at Jimmie's baseball-hat-covered head. The cartoon fig-ure wore a banner, like a beauty pageant contestant, that said "All this and I can cook too." Heck had gotten it for him for Christmas last year and Jim-mie wore it proudly, even when Heck had nearly fallen off his motorcycle laughing when he arrived for the cookout.

Lovina had driven up from New Orleans for the cookout. The state police investigator had told Jimmie she had a case she wanted his take on, to see if it was Brotherhood-weird or not.

Jimmie's fifteen-year-old daughter, Peyton, had brought a bright red, pill-shaped, Bluetooth speaker and radio outside for music. After a few com-plaints by some of the "old farts" she and her friends had stopped playing their music and the radio was now tuned to a country radio station, 92.1 FM. "Body Like a Back Road" by Sam Hunt was playing, interspersed with the clang-clang of perhaps the most epic horseshoes battle in the history of the backyard, the Super Bowl of horseshoes. Don, Jimmie's dad, was facing off against the reigning champion, Layla. Heck, drinking his third Viking Fraoch beer, maintained a running commentary, using his beer bottle like a microphone, and both Don and Layla had told the mouthy biker to shut the hell up several times before tight pitches.

Jimmie liked watching his wife when she didn't see him doing it. Truth be told, he liked watching her when she knew it too. He thought Layla was actually more beautiful now than the day they first met, a damn hard undertaking, but Layla pulled it off.

Layla's legs were long and toned. She was wearing cutoffs, like she would for most of the summer, except for when she went to work at the Lenoir Walmart. Her tan came from hard work in her garden and her yard, from living life, not lying around in some UV bed baking like a potato. Her blond hair fell to her waist and was gently turning silver, her nose was narrow, one could say too pointy, her teeth, less than perfect. To Jimmie, those things just made her prettier.

Ella, Jimmie's mom, sat with Jimmie Junior—almost sixteen months old now—on her lap and cheered on the competitors. Jimmie Junior's chubby legs kicked excitedly as he watched his mom and granddad play. He made humming, burbling noises and would occasionally yelp whenever Grandma cheered for a throw.

Lovina, Evelyn, and Elizabeth—Heck's mother, and an old friend of the Aussapiles—were talking, sitting in folding chairs under the shade of the old water oak that had been one of the reasons Layla and Jimmie had decided to buy this house at the corner of Stonewall and Resaca. They paused their conversation to watch Layla take the throw that could end the game.

Layla was hunched, her eyes narrowed, as she took careful aim at the distant metal stake. She held the old metal horseshoe by its center, firmly, but not tightly; its two posts aimed away from her as she began to wind up for her pitch. Heck started to open his mouth to do a play-by-play, but Layla silenced him with a quick, withering "Mom's had enough" look. She wound up again, and let the horseshoe fly. There was a loud clank as Layla's horseshoe hit the post and looped before dropping, still touching the metal stake. Layla let out a loud whoop and did a little victory dance. The ringer gave her the points she needed to overcome Don's slow, methodical advance to victory. Jimmie let out a triumphant rebel yell for his bride. Peyton buried her red face in her friend Jennifer's shoulder in embarrassment at how her parents were behaving.

"Way to go, baby!" Jimmie shouted. Don glared at his son, and Jimmie, grinning ear to ear, held up his hand a small space between his thumb and index finger. "Close . . . so close," he mock-whispered to his old man. Don hugged his daughter-in-law and they both laughed.

"I almost had you, this time," Don said. "You wait till the Fourth of July, girl."

"Bring it," she said, almost giggling. She kissed him on the cheek.

"Truly," Heck said into his now fourth beer, doing his best Howard Cosell, which was difficult with a Scottish-southern accent, "a battle for the ages, but once again youth has overcome a fading gladiator in his twilight years." He held the bottle out to Don. "A few words on your stinging defeat, Don?"

"When Jimmie was my squire, he was never this mouthy . . . most of the time," Don said, walking around a grinning Heck on his way to the folding tables where the food was. "Hush up, boy, or this fading gladiator's gonna put his boot up your skinny bee-hind. See how much that stings."

"A terse 'No comment' from this once proud champion," Heck said into his bottle and then took a long pull off it.

"That's my boy," Elizabeth said to Lovina with a sigh. "I made him myself."

There was a post-game run on the food tables. A short line formed and Layla came over to help her mom up and lead her to the front of the line, so she could get her guidance on what food Layla should put on Evelyn's plate, leaving Lovina and Elizabeth beneath the tree.

"So tell me an embarrassing Lil' Heck story," Lovina asked Elizabeth. The older woman laughed and Lovina swore the sun got a little brighter. Elizabeth Sinclair, in her late forties, was a strikingly beautiful woman. Her hair fell to below her shoulders and was white, almost silver. Her eyes were a blazing green and as clear and bright as the spring sky, just like Heck's. She was slender, having managed to keep her figure, and her features were almost noble in their cast. Elizabeth wore an old white peasant blouse and faded jeans. When she shifted and moved, you could catch a flash of colorful ink near her neckline. Lovina felt like she was sitting next to royalty, and in a fashion, she was. Elizabeth's father, Gordon "Claymore" Sinclair, had been the founding president of the Blue Jocks Motorcycle Club. Elizabeth's lover, and Heck's stepfather, Ailbert "Ale" Mckee, had become the MC's second president when Gordon passed.

It had been almost two years since Ale died and the Jocks had been operating without a president all that time, the other officers of the club making the day-to-day decisions for the MC as best they could. Even though Elizabeth had been Ale's old lady, his counsel, and more than capable to lead, women were not allowed to act as officers in an MC. That being said, Elizabeth knew all of the other club officers since they had been children together, and her word was covert law.

Elizabeth looked across the Aussapile's yard to watch her handsome son talking and joking with Peyton and her young friends. Heck was oblivious to how many of the teenage girls were completely smitten with him as he told the story of his worst wipeout ever. Elizabeth sighed. Everyone was holding their breath, waiting, counting on Heck, and time was running out.

"A story about Heck when he was little?" Elizabeth replied to Lovina.

"Whoa," Heck suddenly called out from across the yard, "no, no, no!" The biker struggled through the chow line toward his mother and Lovina. "Hey! No fair, ganging up!"

"When Heck was eight, he wanted to be Batman."

"Who doesn't," Lovina replied, sipping her iced tea in a red Solo cup. Heck joined them, shaking his head.

"Stop right there, old lady," Heck said, "or no ride home for you."

"I'll drive her," Lovina said with a wide grin. "Go on, Elizabeth. Batman."

"Right," Elizabeth said, her eyes never leaving Heck's reddening face. "So, he decided to make 'web fluid,' I think it was . . ."

"Okay, if you're going to embarrass the Christ out of me, at least get the story right," Heck said, shaking his head. "It was *Spider-Man*. I liked his snappy patter. Batman was too fucking pompous." Elizabeth and Lovina laughed and Elizabeth snapped her finger and pointed at Heck as she took a sip of her Jack and Coke.

"Spider-Man, right!" she said. "Anyway, he got ahold of some Mason jars and some sinus spray and I think some gasoline from the can in the garage for the lawnmower, oh, and a roll of SweeTARTS . . ."

Jimmie walked over, a can of Budweiser in one hand, a cheddar brat on a bun in the other. "Oh, this sounds good," he said, around a mouthful of brat. Heck glared.

"Anyway, the garage was his 'Fortress of Solitude' . . ."

"That's Superman, another tit, like Batman." Heck sighed.

"Fine, then it was your 'web cave,' how's that?"

"Equally as wrong and humiliating," Heck replied, finishing off his beer.

"Don't mind him, Lizzie," Jimmie said. "What happened to Spider-Heck?"

"He nearly burned down the garage," Elizabeth said, trying not to laugh. Jimmie and Lovina didn't bother to try. As they laughed, Heck made silent, mock-laughing faces and then flipped off his fellow Brethren. "It was a miracle he came out without a burn or a scratch . . ."

Jimmie saw something pass over Heck's face, for just a second. He went somewhere else and it wasn't a pleasant trip. Then he was back. Jimmie glanced to Lovina, and noticed she had seen it too.

"Yeah I was fucking fine until Ale got ahold of me. He wore my ass out," Heck said cheerfully. "Thus ended my superhero career, my aspirations to be a chemist, and this embarrassing-as-fuck story I've had to endure about a million fucking times." Elizabeth grabbed the edge of his cut, his club vest, and pulled her son down to her. She kissed him on the cheek and ruffled his hair.

"You'll always be my superhero, baby boy."

"Mom! The hair!"

. . .

Several plates of food, drinks, and some of the worse backyard karaoke in the history of music later, Jimmie, Lovina, and Heck found themselves alone, sitting together at a patio table under the shade of a huge umbrella. Peyton and her friends had fled inside, saying that old, drunk people trying to sing Rihanna was just wrong.

The others—Jimmie's and Heck's parents as well as Layla and Evelyn— were sitting in a loose semicircle of lawn chairs under the oak tree, catching up on family gossip and who was in the hospital now and for what. Layla had laid the exhausted and increasingly fussy Jimmie Junior down for a nap in a portable playpen in the shade of the ancient tree. The radio was playing "Ain't Too Proud to Beg" by the Temptations under the conversations.

"A jellyfish-zombie-mermaid?" Lovina said. Heck drained another beer as he nodded. "Did it have a plucky crab sidekick and sing Disney tunes?"

"I fucking swear it's goddamned Cherokee Mike," Heck said.

"Language," Jimmie said. "That's my mom over there, and yours."

"Fucking sorry, Jimmie," Heck replied. "Shit, I mean, fuck . . . sorry."

"Just tone down the GD," Jimmie said, shaking his head. "I don't expect miracles. You said the guys who jumped you and Roadkill were Jocks."

"Yeah," Heck said, glancing over to Elizabeth for a second. "Mom told me Cherokee Mike's been traveling to other chapters outside Cape Fear, stirring up shit and recruiting. If the Blue Jocks had a fucking proper president, Jimmie, Mike's sketchy ass would be deader than that thing that came up out of the ocean and tried to kill us."

"Heck, you know the deal," Jimmie said. "Your granddad Gordon wasn't just the first president of the Jocks, he was a member of the Brethren, and he made it plain that every president after him had to be one of the Brethren too. Ale was, and you will be too, in time."

"'In time' . . . great. And until then I just sit on my thumbs and watch Mike fuck over the MC? Fuck over my friends and family?" Heck asked.

"How could this guy get something like SpongeBob there to work for him anyway?" Lovina asked, trying to change the subject. "He got magical juice?"

"Hell, no," Jimmie said. "I remember Mike Locklear from my old days riding with Ale and Roadkill's dad, Glen, a few of the other original Jocks too. Mike's no magician, he's a hustler. He's got a gift for slick-talking to be sure but no mojo."

"Jimmie," Heck said, "I'm ready."

"Heck . . ." Jimmie said.

"The president of the MC has always been a member of the Brethren," Heck said. "It's to make sure whoever is in charge is not going to drag the club down into the dirt. Jimmie, I've been shadowing you for over a year now, man. You know I can work without a net. I'm ready."

Heck had been sent off by his mother to seek out Jimmie Aussapile and become his squire a few months after Heck's stepdad's death. Heck had been with Jimmie since then, learning the secret history of the highways, and of the ways of the Brethren knight and squire had fought side by side many times over the year.

"Are you?" Jimmie said. "What do you think? Be honest with yourself and with me."

Heck paused for moment and looked into the face of his friend and mentor. "I'm not, am I?"

"When you're ready, you won't need to ask me or yourself that question," Jimmie replied. "I'm proud of you, Heck. Ale would have been proud of you too. Be patient."

"I don't do patient," Heck said, "but I'll keep trying. This thing brewing with Mike, I need to see to it."

Jimmie nodded. "If I can help, you holler."

"Same," Lovina said.

"Thanks," Heck said.

Lovina slipped a thick sheath of brown cardboard folders out of her beach bag and set them on the table before Heck and Jimmie. "In the meantime, I want both your takes on this," she said.

"This is the thing you're looking into?" Jimmie asked. "The thing you think the Brethren should take a look at?"

Lovina nodded.

"It starts with a cold case: Raelyn Dunning. She went missing back in 2014. Pennsylvania troopers and local PD found her car on Interstate 80, about thirty miles in the wrong direction from where she was supposed to be at, her job in Tyrone. Nothing from forensics on the car or the scene. No body ever found. Nothing."

"It's sad as hell, Lovina," Jimmie said. "But how does it—"

"I dreamed about her, Jimmie," Lovina interrupted the trucker. "I dreamed about her before I'd ever seen her case file."

Jimmie and Heck looked at each other. Lovina sipped her iced tea and nodded. "Yeah, I know just how crazy that sounds, trust me. But the dream led me straight to this cold case and from what I saw in my dream . . . I think it might be our kind of job."

"Why's that?" Heck said. Jimmie nodded.

"You'll laugh at me," she said.

"Hey, I owe you for that Spider-Man shit with my mom," Heck said.

Lovina sighed and paused for a moment. "In my dream, she was abducted . . . by a clown."

"A . . . clown," Heck said. Lovina nodded. "You mean, 'honk-honk, do-you-have-these-shoes-in a-size-80, tons of them packed into a smart car,' clown." Lovina nodded again. Heck burst out in laughter. "Aw, fuck, are you yanking me?" the biker said. "Was it fucking Krusty or Ronald? You had me going there for a second, Army. You aren't seri—"

"What kind of clown?" Jimmie asked, stone-faced. Heck snapped his head around to stare at his knight. "Can you describe it?"

"What?" Lovina and Heck said in unison, looking at Jimmie with equally surprised expressions.

"Jimmie, are you fucking kidding me, man?" Heck asked.

Jimmie took a sip of his sweating can of beer before he replied.

"For as long as anyone can remember," Jimmie began, "there have been stories about people . . . sometimes things . . . dressed up like clowns and associated with the Road."

"The Road" was a mystery unto itself. Something about highways and back roads attracted disturbed personalities—serial killers, maniacal hitchhikers, rage drivers, human traffickers, and worse—but it also drew unnatural predators from dark and alien places, entities—things—that couldn't possibly exist, but did in the shadow of the Road.

The Brethren and their allies, like Heck's club, the Blue Jocks, patrolled the Road, vigilant for the appearance of monsters, supernatural and all too mundane. Sadly though, there were far too many miles of highway, and far too few Brethren left anymore.

"You ever seen one?" Heck asked, semi-joking.

"Nope," Jimmie said, "but Brethren I know and respect have. A fella I know ran into one of them on Highway 74 in California. Plenty of stories of them trying to lure kids to abduct them. Heard that from Brothers in Tennessee, North Carolina, South Carolina, and Georgia. Lovina, you run any of this past Max?"

"No," Lovina said flatly and maybe a little too quickly. "She's busy with her own things."

Mackenzie Leher, Max to her friends, had aided Jimmie, Heck, and Lovina on their first joint mission together. The bookish Builder had proved invaluable in the field, a place most of the scholars of the Builder order would rather not venture. Max had headed home to Georgetown when the dust had settled, but she and Lovina had kept in touch.

"Max's a crypto-zoologist, among other things for chrissake," Heck said. "I figure she'd love a chance to lay eyes on some evil Bozo and see how it ticks."

Lovina's eyes dropped from her friends to look at the case files in front of her. "I . . . I didn't want her to think maybe I was going crazy," she said.

"The road witch stuff?" Heck said. Lovina nodded, still not meeting his gaze.

"Yeah," she said.

"Lovina," Jimmie said, "are you feeling like it's starting to affect you, darlin'?"

What Jimmie and most other Brethren called "road magic" was called viamancy by pointy-headed scholars like Max. Pure and simple, it was the power of the Road itself, the power of motion and velocity, time and space. Lovina had learned when she, Jimmie, and Heck first met that she had the gift, or curse, of being a road witch. Viamancers were powerful, able to trap you on the same endless loop of featureless highway, or make a gallon of gas last for a trip of a hundred miles, but it was an old trucker story that all road witches eventually went mad, and then just disappeared. Jimmie knew where the mad witches went and the thought of that being Lovina's fate tightened his throat.

Lovina looked up. "I honestly don't know, Jimmie. I do the exercises, the meditations Max showed me. They do help me focus and I've been able to do some pretty amazing things with it . . . but sometimes it feels like I'm seeing things at the edges of my vision. Other times it feels for a second like I'm traveling at a million miles an hour without moving an inch, like I'm everywhere at once. I think it's directing my dreams too. It feels sometimes like it's driving me, more than I'm driving it. Does that make any kind of sense?"

"Yeah," Heck said grimly, "it does. Just try to remember who's in charge. Don't let it give you any shit."

Lovina smiled.

"Thanks," she said. The three were quiet for a moment. The sounds of birds singing, a droning lawnmower off in the distance, the soft conversation of the others over the radio playing Smokey Robinson's "Tears of a Clown," filled the silence, and made Lovina's fear diminish. She pushed the file folders across the table toward Jimmie.

"Cecil Dann helped me do a nationwide VICAP search for any other disappearances or murders with a similar pattern," Lovina said.

"And what did Cecil and the FBI come back with?" Jimmie asked.

" A long string of disappearances along I-80 that stretch back over thirty years," Lovina said, beginning to open the folders on the table, "across multiple states—a large concentration in Utah, Northern Nevada, and northern California—thousands of miles of highway, and with no discernible connection as far as victimology."

"So a serial killer," Heck said. "Some sick fucker riding the interstate, making totally random kills."

"That's Cecil's and the federal boys' take on it," Lovina said, hesitating a little.

"But . . ." Jimmie said.

"But there is a pattern, Jimmie. It's scattered throughout the cases and the decades, but it shows up in some of the crime scenes again and again. Enough times to make me think it's connected to Raelyn's disappearance. Here, check it out."

She opened a folder and pointed to a faded color Polaroid stapled to the inside cover's paperwork. The photo was of a woman in her seventies with curly gray hair and kind, brown eyes.

"Her name's Natalie Dyer. Sweet lady by all accounts. A grandmother of five. She was traveling from Rock Springs to Rawlins, Wyoming, along I-80 September 22, 1978. She never made it to her destination. Hunters found her car driven over a ravine a few years later. There was no body and she's never been found."

Jimmie looked up from the case file and glanced over toward the others. Layla was watching him and Lovina and Heck. She had a worried, sad look on her face. She noticed Jimmie looking at her, smiled and went back to her conversation with Ella, Evelyn, and Elizabeth.

"I don't see the connection to your girl, yet, Lovina," Heck said.

Lovina had opened another folder. This one contained a photo of an older gentleman, fit with a fringe of white hair on his bald head, glasses, and wearing a navy polo shirt. The man's arms were crossed and his faithful dog, a German shepherd, sat next to his owner at the edge of the photo. "This is Paul Carney, eighty-six years old. He was driving from Nevada back to his home in Ohio in 2011. They found his car abandoned on I-80. They never found him." She slid another folder forward.

"Two thousand one, Judith Block, sixty-two. They found her Mazda off an exit of I-80 in Indiana. Two thousand fifteen, Holly Newman, twenty-three, no body, no trace evidence. They found her car on the side of I-80. Nineteen ninety-two, Joshua Winterbrook, forty-one, they found his sedan at a rest stop off I-80 in Pennsylvania but no body, no trace. There are more, Jimmie, a lot more. Unidentified skeletal remains in several states, most of the bones indicating severe mutilation of the bodies, abandoned cars, and people who vanish without a trace, all up and down I-80, all across America."

"And you think Pennywise is what's behind all this?" Heck asked.

"I don't know," Lovina said, "but it sure sounds like the kind of thing the Brethren should be looking into." She looked to Jimmie.

"Yeah," Jimmie said. "It sure is. I'll put a call in to the Builders, see if we can determine if this is Zodiac Lodge business, or some freelance serial killer, or killers. What you planning to do next, Lovina?"

"Backtrack my cold case," she said, gathering the folders together and putting them away. "I figure that dream of mine means something, so I'm sticking with Raelyn. I got Russell Lime with the Louisiana state crime lab to make a formal request of the Pennsylvania authorities to review their forensics and see if we can shake anything new loose. I'm headed to where Raelyn lived at the time of her disappearance, a little town in Pennsylvania called Coalport. See what I can see."

"You need backup, Dogface?" Heck asked.

"If I need you, I'll let you know, Jarhead. Thank you."

Heck hefted a fresh beer and tipped it to Lovina. "Oorah," he said and drank.

"How about me?" Jimmie asked. Lovina looked over Jimmie's shoulder and frowned. Jimmie followed her stare and saw Layla, looking almost grim, walking away from the others, headed for the side of the house. Don caught his son's glance and mouthed "go get her" to Jimmie silently.

"On second thought . . ." Jimmie began.

- - -

Layla stood beside Jimmie's rig, parked next to the carport, her arms crossed, holding herself tightly. Jimmie came up behind her and enveloped her in an all-encompassing hug. He held her tight and felt her begin to relax.

"My old man talking shit about you cheating at horseshoes again?" Jimmie asked, kissing her ear.

"Those are bullet holes, Jimmie," Layla said, nodding to the side of the cab. "You never came home with bullet holes before."

"I'm sorry, honey. I wanted to get it all spruced up but the Brother who got it street legal for me couldn't afford to do all that bodywork for the money I could give him. Me and Dad are going to fix it right . . ."

"I'm afraid you're going to die out there," Layla said. "I hate myself for being so selfish. This is like being a cop's wife or a soldier's. I know how much good you do out there, how many lives you save . . . but, baby, I'm so much more afraid of losing you since the baby came along. I don't want him growing up without a daddy."

"I know, baby," Jimmie said, keeping her close. "I know it doesn't help, but I keep myself safe out there, as safe as I can possible be."

"I know, sweetheart," Lalya said. "I also know that against an army of criminals with machine guns, or some weird, unnatural . . . thing, or even gods—gods, Jimmie—or demons . . . lord. When you're just flesh and blood, standing against that, 'being as careful and safe as you can' doesn't mean very much.

"Every time I see you and Heck and Lovina start talking business I get so frightened now. I love them like you do, like family, and I know they both need you, but we need you too, Jimmie."

"I'm not going," Jimmie said, turning Layla around, so he could see her beautiful, damp eyes. "Dad's got some engine rebuilds at the garage. He could use some help since Edger's tending to his wife, Pauline, after her surgery. Plus, he knows we need the money. Heck's taking care of MC business and Lovina's chasing down her own case. If either of them need me, I'll go. I swore an oath, baby. I'm sorry it conflicts sometimes with the one I swore to you. But if it comes down to the Brotherhood, or our family, you win that, every time."

"It won't come down to that, Jimmie," she said, and touched his stubbly cheek as gently as the rain leaves kisses. "You were straight with me from the beginning. I knew what I was signing up for and I will never, ever, regret that. I love you, Jimmie. You're the best man I've ever known."

"Well, it's a good thing you kinda like me," Jimmie said, smiling, "'cause you're stuck with me."

Lalya choked back a sob of relief and he pulled her to him, lifting her off the ground.

"You and the kids," Jimmie said softly. "You're the reason I go out there, the only reason I fight. You're my world, darlin'." They kissed, losing themselves in it, forgetting everything that existed except the softness of each other's lips, the warm, steady anthem of each other's hearts. The baby was crying in the backyard. They broke the kiss and both sighed.

"Five-second date," she whispered. "To be continued tonight, mister."

"Oh, yeah," Jimmie growled. "I say we chase them off now." He lowered her back to the ground but didn't let her go.

"Son," Don's voice called out. "Layla! Diaper! Grandpa and Grandma don't do diapers no more!"

"You do poop, I do pee?" Jimmie said, taking Layla's hand. Layla stopped walking and looked at Jimmie. "Right, I do poop, you do pee." She kissed him gently on the lips and squeezed his hand tighter. They began to walk together again toward the backyard.

Layla only glanced back at the bullet holes once.

Valley Hills Mall was pretty much every mall in America. The massive two-story building had a sky made of tinted glass and echoed with the sounds of the hundreds of people wandering the vast open spaces between the store-fronts, a river of murmurs above the air-conditioning, punctuated with the squeals of children, booming laughter, and the occasional shout. A Muzak version of Disturbed's "Down with the Sickness" wafted softly on the pro-cessed air. Valley Hills was the regional mall for the foothills of North Caro-lina and people drove from pretty far away to buy sneakers, eat frozen yogurt or bad mall Chinese food, and shop at national retail chains too big to ever consider setting up shop in their small towns.

Heck moved through the crowds without hesitation or pause. His biker cut ensured he was given a wide berth as shoppers, elderly mall walkers, and sullen teenage kids steered clear of him. He looked dangerous and he was. He couldn't help notice that there were more vacant storefronts now than there had been the last time he had made it over here to Hickory from Cape Fear. At one point sixty percent of the furniture made in America was pro-duced within two hundred miles of Hickory. Today, it was much less.

When the mall had opened in the late seventies, there were massive foun-tains set up inside. The time of the fountains had passed, however, and now where one of them had once been there was a food court with a central hub of tables and chairs. Heck walked past a Dippin' Dots kiosk and spotted Cher-okee Mike sitting alone at a table near the center of the food court. Heck walked toward him and Mike waved.

Cherokee Mike Locklear was a big guy. A few inches over six feet, mus-cular, and maybe a little puffy in the face, which could come from too much boxing, booze, or steroids. He was in his early forties and clearly got his nick-name from his evident heritage. Mike had long, thick, raven-black hair that fell to his shoulders. Some silver had crept into his hair since Heck had last seen him, but only a little. Mike's eyes were so brown as to seem black and a little too close to the crooked bridge of his prominent nose, which looked like it had been broken a time or two.

Heck had heard a lot of stories of Mike's romantic conquests over the decades. He was handsome but he was the kind of handsome that required some charm to seal the deal. In fact, Cherokee Mike gave off an air of oily menace that he had obviously learned to overcome by talking a good game. Mike smiled a friendly but crooked smile, and stood as Heck approached, offering his hand. Heck had a sudden flash of recognition about Mike's looks—Gene Simmons, or maybe that shitty actor guy from that movie *The Room*.

"Heck! Great to see you, man! You're looking good." Heck ignored the offered hand and sat opposite Mike at the table. Mike was dressed much like Heck, a T-shirt, jeans, and boots with his MC cut—a black leather vest with his club patches on it—over his leather riding jacket. One difference in the patches was that Mike had a rectangular patch on the right breast of his cut with the word "Nomad" on it.

"Yeah, no thanks to the late Spur Barnett or Sal Hopper, or you for that matter," Heck said.

"Oh, yeah," Mike said, snapping his fingers, "I heard about that. They got whacked on some bail bond bullshit down at Nags Head. Dangerous work, bounty hunting."

"They got whacked because you sent them down there to hit me and Road-kill," Heck said. "You set us up. The same way you had AJ Nye, and Keith Creasy, and Billie Ould all killed."

"Me?" Mike said, looking genuinely shocked. "Why the hell would I have a bunch of brothers killed, Heck? Shit, it sounds like all these years of bounty hunting to pay the bills is finally catching up with the club."

Heck's hand slid under his jacket to the .45 in his shoulder holster. "How about some of this shit catches up to you, now?"

Mike shook his head.

"Hector, come on man. Think. Don't let that famous bat-shit-crazy streak of yours make you do something stupid . . . or irreversible." Mike waved to someone over Heck's shoulder. Heck glanced back and saw a Blue Jock he didn't recognize against the rail on the second floor of the mall, looking down into the food court. The man's shoulder holster was hanging out from under his jacket as he leaned over the rail and he clutched the butt of his holstered pistol, ready to draw it. A group of excited children ran past the table and clambered onto a small merry-go-round ride a few feet away from the bik-ers' table. One of the kids eagerly fed quarters into the ride and jumped on with the others, jostling for space. Some off-tune carnival music began to play as the children hung on for dear life and cheered happily as the ride spun them around gently. Heck turned back and narrowed his gaze at Mike's smil-ing face. "You pull on me, I pull on you. My man, Will, up there, shoots you in the back. Maybe a few stray bullets hit a few innocent bystanders. A mess, right?"

Heck set his jaw. His green eyes burned. "More than you know, Mike." A green dot appeared on Heck's chest. It was from a laser sight. It slowly crawled along his shirt and then disappeared as the beam intersected with Mike. "My, man, Dave, who the fuck knows where his sneaky ass is, will blow the back of your head clean off if you start some shit. I guarantee you the only person he's going to hit is not fucking innocent."

Mike's eyes got a bit darker and his smile slipped away. "You going to kill me, Heck? I told you I don't know shit about what happened in Nags Head, or those other guys who got killed on bail jobs. You gonna whack a brother without a shred of proof? That won't sit well with a lot of the Jocks."

"I know it's you," Heck said, sliding his hand away from his gun. "I know what you're trying to do to the club, and I'm going to shut your ass down. This is your warning. You get one. Quit the Jocks and ride away."

Mike laughed and leaned back in his chair, stretching. "Heck, listen to yourself, man. You sound tweaked. You on something?"

"Just high on Jesus," Heck replied, his predatory gaze never shifting.

"It occur to you that someone else on the outside was doing this?" Mike said, leaning forward. He was so fucking earnest that for a second Heck doubted himself. Mike caught that momentary doubt and ran with it. "The Jocks have plenty of enemies. We've put a lot of pissed-off guys away. A lot of them have squads. Then there's the other clubs, the Aesir Mauls, those crazy viking motherfuckers, and the Bitches of Selene, they fucking hate the Jocks for all of their members we've taken down. Any of them, all of them, and a whole lot more, could be setting up these ambushes for our people, Hector."

Heck searched Mike's eyes, his face for some telltale hint of a lie. He couldn't find anything. Mike nodded. The warbling carnival music contin-ued from the merry-go-round as the children laughed and played.

"I know Ale and me had issues," Mike said, "but that doesn't mean you and I have to. It's my club too and I want to help if someone is trying to fuck with it."

"What you got in mind? " Heck asked.

"How about I get my people on this, see what they can dig up. Whoever is doing it, they are convincing our own crews to turn on us. You find the dickhead who was supposed to be serving that paper at the beach?"

"Seth Dodds?" Heck asked. "No. He's gone, his old lady and kid too. We're reaching out, trying to find him. The cops at the beach found the check kiter we had the paper on. He was locked in the trunk of his girlfriend's car, a dozen bullets in him. I can't believe Seth set us up. Me and Roadkill have known him since we were all teenagers. His old man was an original. Died of a stroke about five years ago."

"Let me see if I can find him for you," Mike said. Heck held Locklear's gaze for a long moment, then he nodded. The music from the merry-go-round ended abruptly as the time ran out on the quarters.

"Okay," Heck said. "Find him, just find him. No collecting him, no questioning him, no nothing. Find him and call me or Roadkill."

"Will do," Mike said, the smile returning to his face. "I think you're going to find we make a very good team, Heck. I'm going to help you shut down the cornhole fuckers doing this to our club. You have my word on that."

Mike stood and offered his hand to Heck again. Heck took it and shook it, never taking his eyes off Mike's face. "You screw me, you screw with the MC, I'll kill you," Heck said. He let go of Mike's hand. "You have my word on that." Mike walked away without another word or a backward glance. Heck waited until he and his guardian angel, Will, on the second floor were gone. Then he stood, gave the Archangel Dave the all-clear sign and headed out of the mall to the parking lot and his bike.

. . .

The trip back to Cape Fear took about four hours and Heck used the time to tumble a few things over in his mind. He didn't trust Mike. He knew at his core that Mike was behind all this shit. He'd been scheming since he got out of Central to take over the MC, and run it into the ground. But goddamn if he wasn't as smooth-talking a bullshit artist as everyone said. Heck had walked in there half-ready to kill him, and walked out unsure if Cherokee Mike was his culprit.

The traffic along I-40 was steady but not bad. The sky was clear and it was hot today, a summer day muscling its way into the end of spring. Heck felt the lukewarm air slip up his jacket sleeves and cool him a little, but not much. The dry heat made him think of Afghanistan and the desert. That heat always stirred a very old memory in him, like he had been in the desert long, long ago, when he was just a child. The memory was slippery, like trying to catch a fish with your bare hands. Most of Heck's memories of Afghanistan always led him to the same place, to the desert, to the laughing fire.

. . .

Heck's nature didn't lend itself to too many friends, but over time he had become tight with the other guys in his fire team. It was kind of hard not to. When you lived together, fought together, watched each other at your lowest points, laughed about stupid shit no one else would get, and—most important of all—didn't just trust, *knew* the people beside you had your six, they became more than friends, they were your family. For Heck, family in Afghanistan was Javon, Abe, and Rich.

Javon Little was from Allendale, South Carolina. He joined the Marines straight out of high school, buying all the bullshit the recruiter fed him. Abe Toth was from Chicago, a really smart guy. He had joined up after college— he had a degree from the University of Chicago's Department of Economics— but he wanted to serve, wanted to do his time in the shit before he took a six-figure job. Maybe he wasn't that smart after all, given what happened to him, but his heart was in the right place and he never made anyone feel stupid or small. Then there was good old Rich, the best damn NCO a solider could ask for. Sergeant Richard Pham's family had been shrimpers in Galveston, Texas, for a few generations now, since they came over in the late seventies from Vietnam. Rich had been over there for three deployments. Even though he was only twenty-six, he was the oldest, their pappy, or, as he used to say, their "Cha."

Winter was coming on and the days were bright and sharp with cold. Snow constantly spun about in the air. They were on the knife's edge, the barren, rocky hill country at the terminator of the Azra district and the flat river lands of the Logar Province to the east. Their team had been tracking a Haqqani squad roaming from village to village, "recruiting" the men, young and old, to the cause and killing anyone who refused or got in their way.

The word from the politicians, the brass, all the OGAs and the POGs was that they were drawing down even more, and everyone would soon be home. However, in the meantime, until the mutual dick-sucking and champagne commenced, they were humping through a cold-as-hell, rocky desert, hunting Haji.

They were supposed to meet up with two other teams in their squad in a village the next day and receive any new FRAGOs, updates on operation orders. It was getting colder as the crimson, swollen sun fell to the teeth of the mountains, bleeding out across the horizon. That was when they had spotted the jagged, crumbling walls of the ruin.

There were ruins all over Afghanistan. The fucking Taliban had been blowing up a bunch of the more ancient Buddhist ones—some almost two thousand years old—in the country since 2001. This one looked like it had once been a temple. None of them knew a temple to what, exactly, but as the frigid night came on, none of them cared.

There were sections of remaining thick outer walls made of piled flat stones that skirted the edges of the temple. A single, arched entrance remained to the partially collapsed interior. Inside, it was little more than a cave with empty alcoves along the walls, piles of smashed pottery and thick gray ash in the corners. They didn't find any trash, like cigarette butts, ration wrappers, dried scat, or crumpled cans, indicating any recent occupants, NATO or otherwise, which was kind of weird, but Rich figured they were the first to discover this one.

"We're probably the first folk in here in a few thousand years," he said in his Texas twang, shining his flashlight around the thick walls stamped with crude ancient markings. The simple, stick and feathered, fletchlike symbols scratched into the walls when the clay was still wet didn't resemble any language Heck had ever seen in his time over there. It looked older, primal. He saw a large symbol, prominently repeated again and again all over the temple. It was a curve that rose up into jagged, uneven edges, and even across the eons, Heck knew it represented fire. Looking at it in the harsh halogen beam and the looping shadows of the flashlight lens made something squirm in Heck's mind and in his guts.

"I don't like this shit," Javon muttered around the cigarette at the corner of his mouth. "Feels like someone stepping on my grave in here, Rich."

"Well," Rich said, turning to face all of them, "we can crash here, or up against the walls outside, maybe in the frankenstein." The slang term referred to their piecemeal, spot-wielded armored truck. "But I guarantee we're going to freeze our nips off out there. We've done that before. I'm feeling nothing. It's a hole. The walls are thick and it's cold as a sumbitch outside."

"Last time we camped in the Humvee, Heck fucking nerve gassed us all night," Abe said. "I say screw camping out in the frankenstein, man."

"Then let's get shit secured," Rich said, and that was that.

Heck was the SAW component of the team, short for squad automatic weapon. He carried the M249 light machine gun for when the serious party got started. His shiny new M27 machine gun was lying next to him, wrapped up like an unwanted Christmas present from a distant aunt. A year ago the word had come down that the M249 was being replaced by the M27. The older gun was too heavy and gunners couldn't keep up with riflemen, especially in house-to-house city fights. Heck had never had that problem being strong and fast enough to wield the heavy weapon like a rifle. Heck carried the damn M27, but he had never used it in a scrap. He qualified with it, but he relied on the M249. Heck knew it was a violation of regs, but Rich had seen the skinny redhead in action with the older, bigger gun and he looked the other way. The old machine gun may have been replaced but it had gotten the team out of some serious shit and Heck trusted it a damn sight more than some gun approved by some fobbit who never stuck his lily-white ass past the wires.

Heck mounted the big gun on its bipod near the door along with most of his fifty pounds of battle rattle. Under his IBA, he wore a tattered, bullet-riddled Ghost Rider T-shirt. He'd caught shit about it more times than he could remember, but it was worth getting written up. Rich let him get away with it when they were out on patrols. Ale had bought the shirt for him the week before they had their big throw-down, the last time they talked. It was his good-luck charm.

They ran a cold camp, but the wind off the mountains moaned loudly enough that Rich was cool with a little music, playing low, so Javon set up his little wireless speaker and played music off a small radio. They sat around and ate their MREs, fucked around on their phones, and listened to AFN radio. "Gotta Get Away" by the Black Keys was playing.

"Rich, what the fuck are we still doing out here?" Abe finally asked. "Everyone else is packing up shop, and we're still out there playing cowboys and Indians with Haji?"

Rich sighed and set down his Meal Everyone Refuses. "I'm pretty sure this is our last ride," he said. "I think tomorrow when we hook up with the other teams and the OIC they are telling us we're bugging out. We're finally handing all this shit over to the ITGA, the new Afghani government."

"'Bout fuckin' time," Heck said.

"So we're finally going home?" Javon said, a wide smile breaking across his face like the dawn. "Hot damn." He retrieved a rolled-up plastic baggie from the liner of his helmet and unrolled it. He opened it and removed one of the sorriest-looking joints Heck had ever seen. "I say we celebrate! Rich?"

The sergeant looked from one face to another and sighed. "Yeah, okay.

What the hell, right? Besides, that rangy-looking spliff couldn't get my granny high." Everyone laughed. Javon shook his head, dismissing the taunts.

"Ye of little motherfucking faith," he said. "This, gentlemen, is the last of that dank fucking shit that TCN trucker from Nepal gave me. It will knock you on your disbelieving asses. Buy local, smoke local."

"Hey," Abe said. "You told me we smoked the last of that shit back in Kandahar! You lying hillbilly motherfucker!" Javon laughed as he lit the joint with a white plastic Bic lighter and took a long drag. He held the smoke and passed the smoldering cigarette to the left, to Heck. Finally when he exhaled he nodded to Abe.

"A country boy always prepares for the worst," Javon said. "This is the last one and hopefully the last smoke I'll be blowing in this shithole."

"Amen," Rich said, the pungent smoke spilling from his lips. "I'm going to fucking sleep for a goddamned month and shoot any motherfucker that tries to wake my ass up."

"I," Abe said, "am a little more ambitious. I'm planning to fuck my wife for a month . . . then sleep for a month."

The guys laughed and kept passing the joint. On the radio, the DJ was taking requests over the radio and from cell phones from excited soldiers all over the country. Every one of them was talking about heading home soon, about the draw-down. "Unsteady" by the X Ambassadors began to play softly in the ancient, heavy air.

"How about you, Braveheart?" Javon asked, passing the joint to Heck again. "What you going to do when you get back?"

Heck held the smoke deep in his lungs. All the hard, jagged edges of this place, all the sharp places inside him, were softer now, and he smiled and let the smoke roll out of his nostrils and mouth. Just breathing was a pleasure. This *was* good shit. "What? You my fucking travel agent, now?" Heck asked.

"Just wondering," Javon said. "I know you said a while back your mom emailed you that your dad—"

"*Step* dad," Heck interrupted. Javon continued.

"Whatever, man, at least you got one. If he's not doing too good, you going to see him?"

Heck snatched the joint out of Abe's hand, breaking the circle.

"Rude!" Abe said. Heck took a long drag and then passed it back to Abe.

"I'm going to get pished," Heck said, "and throw 'bows with a bunch of right cunts . . . wash, rinse, repeat. Fuck my old man. Bitter old bastard didn't even come to see me off. Fuck him."

"Heck, man," Abe said across the circle, "I didn't talk to my old man for years, fucking years. I'm glad we got that shit sorted out before I came over here . . ."

"Shit," Heck rumbled, dragging the word out a bit, his southern accent coming to the fore. His buzz was evaporating quicker than the joint. "Good for you, Doctor-fucking-Phil . . ."

"Look, you're right," Abe said. "I don't know your old man, but I know you pretty well, so I figure you're kind of alike. Whatever shit went down between you, you might want to make your peace with him, for your sake, Heck. You don't want to choke on that regret the rest of your life. I don't want that for you, bro."

Heck was silent. Finally he said, "Thanks. I appreciate it, man. It's just . . . you don't know him. It's like trying to fucking talk to . . . you don't know Ale."

"Fair enough," Abe said, snatching the dwindling joint from Heck's fingers and tipping it in salute to Heck. "To not knowing Ale!"

"Fucking numpty bastard," Heck said, shaking his head, and then laughing.

They passed the joint a few more times until it was a sad-looking roach. Javon put it in a clip and they passed it again. Eventually they laid it to rest. Rich and Abe broke out a worn deck of cards and began to play some gin rummy. Javon went out into the brutal cold and took a piss. He came back and settled in with his Gameboy. Heck volunteered to take the first watch.

By 0100, everyone else was asleep except Heck. He sat, smoking the $40 pack of shitty Marlboros he'd bought off a dirt sailor, a Navy Seabee, who was shipping back to the world before they had gone out on patrol. Beyond the open archway was deep space, impenetrable darkness, icy cold, and merciless wind. Heck sat in the archway and tried to scry out what he would do when he got home. The darkness was empty, no answers. There was the MC, the Jocks, of course, but since Ale had bucked up against the Big C, he had felt the pressure from his mom and the other officers in the club to step up, to become president. The fight he'd had with Ale was mostly Ale screaming at him about how he was fucking up his life and letting everyone down. The memory stung and a hot anger welled up inside him again. He pushed away those feelings and tried to make his insides as empty and cold as the void outside the arch, but his anger was a brilliant jewel at the heart of him.

Something stirred in the darkness inside Heck. It twisted in the silence. He turned, instinctively toward the corner with the shattered pottery. Something was swirling there, above the floor. It was ancient dust and shadow, moving, spinning like a tiny tornado. Heck stood and pulled the machine gun to him as he did. He leveled the M249 at the growing whirlwind. It was starting to glow and smolder.

"We got a situation!" Heck shouted, his voice almost muffled by the thick clay walls. The others rolled from sleep to weapons at the ready. Rich snapped on his flashlight and ran the beam over the growing thing. Heck smelled smoke coming off the thing.

"What the fuck is that!" Abe shouted, as he slid back the bolt on his M16A4 rifle. Rick was in a crouch, his own rifle sighted on the spinning funnel of fire.

"Be cool," Rich said evenly. "Heck, it moves, light it up."

Light it up, a growling, alien voice whispered in Heck's mind. It chuckled and it sounded like two dried femur bones being rubbed together. *Very well.* The cyclone of shimmering dust erupted into flames, dispelling the chill and the shadows of the temple, making it like an oven in a second.

"Shit" Javon shouted and began to fire on the twisting, growing pyre. The deep, bass, inhuman laughter Heck had heard in his mind continued but now it also echoed throughout the chamber as well as in his skull. Heck stood transfixed, it was like trying to recall an old memory, on the tip of your awareness, but unreachable. The bodiless voice murmured inside him, almost a chant. He didn't know the language but part of him felt like he understood it.

"Heck!" Rich shouted, firing too at the thing now. Heck blinked and shook off the fog, but the thing was already moving quickly. A hissing, living thing, it reached Javon, and the tendrils of brilliant flame grabbed him as if they had mass, as if they were flesh. Javon screamed as his flesh crackled and sizzled. Heck fired the big machine gun jumping and sputtering in his arms. The chug-chug-chug of the rounds belching through the muzzle, the clatter and smell of hot brass as the bullet casings tumbled to the floor. It did nothing. The thing laughed louder as it devoured his friend. Javon's body was crumbling to ash. *You called to me, my little barādar, my brother,* the voice in his head said. It spoke in the old, alien tongue, a thick-crowded language, but Heck now understood every word. *You and I are of the same tribe, the same charm. You called to me in my sacred place, out in the darkness, and by the pact of our blood, I answered.*

Even as Javon's screams bounced and echoed in the temple, the thing began to spin and turn toward Abe. Heck knew it had names, *Jinn? Ifrit?* Heck tried to clear his head, he was still firing on the laughing pyre but he might as well have not been. "Out the door, out the fucking door!" Heck shouted over the thudding drumbeat of the machine gun. The thing caught Abe as he was turning to flee. It swallowed him whole. His throat had only seconds to let slip a scream at the horrible, freezing pain as his nerve endings were scorched to nothing. Then all he was, all he had ever been was reduced to a cloud of charred ash and greasy smoke.

"You fucking bastard!" Heck bellowed. The room was a furnace now. The heat rippled in the air. The stench of burned pork was everywhere. The *Ifrit* only laughed louder and made its way toward Rich, who had reached the door. Heck howled and charged the thing, trying to block its path to the last of his team, his friends, his family. The flames enveloped his body and mind. He saw, felt, the totality of the *Jinn*.

Why do you struggle so? It asked even as it passed through him, and he was unscathed. The flame was nothing, it felt like cold water to his skin. *They are nothing, insects that live a moment, nothing more. We are born of the dust, the flame, the void, my clansman. They exist to amuse us, to covet us. We exist to challenge their faith, to make it shiver like an old woman in the desert.*

Rich was in the archway and he was screaming. The thing was eating him, smoke streamed from his eyes, like Hell's tears. He looked into Heck's own eyes, pleading, terrified, then they sizzled and popped like hardboiled eggs left too long in a microwave. Rich's face was wreathed in brilliant flame, the skin curled up and crisped away, like blackening paper, leaving a gasping, grinning skull, the bone sputtering and popping with cooking fat. His scream was his legacy, it lasted an instant longer than him. Another step and he would have made it into the darkness and the blissfully freezing cold.

"Fuck you!" Heck felt the smoke clawing at his throat, he wanted to cry but there was no place for the mercy of water here. The dried salt caked at the edges of his eyes, wide with rage and fear. The fire wrapped itself about him as he fell to his knees, holding him as a mother might hold a weeping child. Its laughter was the universe inside him and out. It whispered to him all the rest of the night, sang to him stories of the unforgiving, otherworldly deserts that never encroached upon this world. It told him secrets. At some point Heck tried to put his rifle barrel in his mouth, but the hot metal sloughed off in his hands like dough. There was no escape.

At dawn, he returned to awareness. He was unmarked and naked, alone on the cold stones surrounded by the ashes of his brothers. Every scrap of the presence of his comrades and of him was gone. Only new piles of dust remained in the corners. His mind was empty, lost to him. He remembered a single word, *qareen*. Heck stumbled out of the ruins, oblivious to the sting-ing cold and the steam rising off his untouched skin. He found clothes in the Humvee and he dressed and then drove to the village in the harsh morning light. In the days and months to follow, he was put under suspicion of hav-ing killed his team. Eventually he was cleared and the incident was marked as classified. For the record, the Haqqani squad had caught wind of them tracking them and had doubled back with a flamethrower. The doctors called his blackouts PTSD. Heck wasn't sure himself for a long time if maybe he hadn't just snapped and killed his team, his friends, buried the bodies, the gear, maybe burned it all. In some ways that fucked-up scenario was more comforting to him than the shards of memory that would flash through his mind nightly as he courted sleep.

. . .

Heck physically shook the memory off like a chill. For a terrifying second he felt completely disoriented. How long had he been driving on autopilot? He was off I-40 and riding along Route 421, turning now onto State Route 902. Why? This wasn't a way home, and he had a MC meeting he had to get to.

A green road sign on a steel post caught his eye and he knew exactly where he was. The sign marked a side road and said "DEVIL'S TRAMPING GRD RD." Heck turned onto the yellow-line-divided road and slowed as his bike glided through the deep forests on either side of the one-lane. It was late after-noon and the sun flashed in dappled patches through the thick canopy of dark green leaves. He passed a house with a work truck, a pickup, and a child's swing set in the well-tended yard. He passed a few small churches, their gravel lots already filling up with folks coming for the Sunday night service. Cica-das hummed and birds sang in the thick, warm air.

He hadn't been here since he was . . . thirteen? He'd been with Roadkill and a few older teenage members of the Jocks then. They came here to smoke weed and drink stolen beer, and of course, see if the stories were true. He didn't recall much of the trip. Actually, now that he tumbled it over in his head, there were holes in Heck's recollection of the trip. Probably just age, and weed, but the absences seemed familiar in some way language and defi-nition could not lay claim to.

Heck saw the yawning gap in the foliage on the right side of the road, near a couple of power poles and the large white cross someone had spray-painted on the left side of the asphalt, opposite the gap. It looked like one of a million access roads used by farmers or utility workers to reach property not connected by an official roadway. He pulled over onto the grassy shoulder, kicked down his stand, and shut the bike off. He removed his steel demon mask and helmet and set them on the handlebars. He unzipped his leather jacket and ran a hand through his tousled red hair. He walked down the worn, rutted dirt road that led into the woods. The path was littered with flattened PBR cans, cigarette butts, and Snicker wrappers faded from rain and time. Old, dead leaves were decaying on either side of the dirt road, being slowly devoured. Seemed the Devil didn't keep a tidy residence.

Heck entered the clearing. There were no sounds of birds crooning, no cicadas humming a song here, no signs of any life. There were logs and more trash scattered about. The blackened corpses of old logs huddled, evidence of campfires. There was an uneven circle of powdery gray soil that stood out from the rest of the ground. They called this place the Devil's Tramping Ground.

Heck slowly walked around the edge of the circle, counterclockwise. He remembered Roadkill whispering, as if he raised his voice too much it might summon the Beast himself. "They say nothing's grown in that circle for hundreds of years," Jethro said breathlessly. "They say the Devil paces this circle. He dances in these woods at night."

"Bullshit," thirteen-year-old Heck had said to his friend. "Bullshit," Heck echoed across the gulf of time. "Well, if you're fucking around in these woods, come on, then. I got a few questions for your tail-y ass."

The woods were silent. The wind picked up a bit but there was no sound of the leaves on the trees rustling. Heck saw in the distance a pickup on huge, knobby tires zoom down the road, but he didn't hear the growl of its engine. Heck spit and stepped into the circle. Nothing.

"Well?" Heck said, looking about. "Got nothing to say?"

"*Soon,*" a voice that was one part honey to two parts rotgut whispered. Heck turned, thinking someone was right behind him, but no one was there. He smelled the greasy stench of burnt pork, burnt flesh; it seemed to cling to him like a drunken lover. From the road, which was now at his back, he heard the throaty bellow of a motorcycle engine. For a second he thought someone was stealing his bike, and sprinted toward the highway, but then he stopped as he realized the engine sounded wrong, different.

He saw a blur heading down the road in the opposite direction he was heading. All he could make out was that the rider's bike had the long, stretched-out forks of a classic '76 Harley chopper, that the rider wore a black leather MC cut and no helmet, and that a mane of bright red hair streamed behind him like a banner of fire. By the time Heck reached the road, the biker was gone.

. . .

Heck was late. He was really, really fucking late to church, to the meeting at the clubhouse. He had to make a case to the MC's officers that they needed to step up and call for a meeting of all the chapters to resolve this Cherokee Mike thing once and for all. He may not be the president of the Jocks, but his name carried a lot of weight. It was his grandfather's name, his mother's name. He had to make them see what they needed to do.

The Blue Jocks conducted their business and their pleasure in Cape Fear in a large two-story building and garage that set back a ways from Jethro's dad, Glen Hume's, towing, salvage, and garage business just off Carolina Beach Road, a little ways past Martin Self-Storage. The sun was low and smeared across the edges of the clouds as Heck sped down 421, and turned off at the large chain link gates to Glen's empire of junk. The gates were open.

Wilmington police cars were clustered around the entrance, their blue lights pulsing. A young cop with a haircut as fresh from the academy as he was held up a palm and blocked Heck's way. Heck saw more cops now, and ambulances. There were over a dozen Jocks milling around outside the clubhouse, all of them penned in by cops. It didn't look like a raid or a bust. Heck slowed and dropped a leg to regard the young cop behind his demon face.

"You missed the party your asshole friends threw," the cop said. "Pull over there and park with the rest of your skel butt-buddies. An investigator will be over to—"

"What the fuck happened?" Heck said, pulling his mask and helmet off. "I want to talk to Detective Elkins."

"He'll get to you," the cop said, obviously annoyed that Heck wasn't quaking in fear. "Now move your ass over there like I told you, boy."

Heck saw the large dark truck from the Coroner and Medical Examiner's Office, and a high-pitched scream, like a tea kettle bleeding steam, began in his mind, through his nerves. Someone was dead. He punched the rookie cop in the face with his helmet and was speeding through the gate before the kid had hit the ground.

He pulled up next to the truck, oblivious to the shouts of cops. He let the bike hit the ground and ran toward the technicians rolling stretchers out the clubhouse doors. Four bodies in dark green zippered bags were rolled toward the truck. Jethro was wheeled out on a stretcher too, surrounded by

EMTs working on him, trauma bandages covering his pale skinny chest, an oxygen mask over his nose and mouth, and several of the paramedics calling out his vitals. The bandages were saturated with blood, his blood.

"How . . . how the hell did he," Heck stammered. He couldn't think, couldn't breathe. "What the fuck happened?"

"Get the fuck out of the way!" a paramedic shouted and pushed Heck back.

"Your buddy's shot twice in the chest," another medic said, sparing Heck a quick look. "Some kind of clubhouse beef. Two of your guys started shooting up everyone in your meeting. It's a fucking slaughterhouse in there! Now get back! If you want him to live we have to get him to the hospital!"

"Shot, Jethro? That's . . . that's fucking impossible! I'm goin' with him," Heck said, his jaw tightening. That was when the cops fell on him. He was sleepwalking, but hitting the cops gave him something to do with his fists, with his body, which felt like it wanted to fly apart, explode like a grenade. He hit them, he kicked them, and they returned the favor. He thought he heard some of the Jocks calling out his name but by then he was burning with numbing fire as the stun guns hit him. He punched a few more cops, and staggered toward Roadkill's ambulance before the pavement rushed toward him and the darkness claimed him. He fought it all the way down, especially when he heard the laughter in the fire once again.

NINE **"10-43"**

The Pennsylvania State Police headquarters and forensics lab in Greensburg was a complex of squat, brick, two-story buildings with numerous windows. The complex sat back off of Westmoreland Avenue, bordered by well-manicured green lawns and gently rolling hills. As Lovina turned off of Westmoreland and up the asphalt drive to the parking lot full of marked and unmarked police cruisers, she thought the buildings looked like they may have once been utilized by the public school system.

Greensburg was about an hour and a half from Coalport, where Raelyn and her mom had lived at the Valentine Trailer Park. Lovina parked her Charger and walked toward the cement stairs that led to the lobby. There was a tall man standing by the reception counter talking to the uniformed trooper behind it. He turned when Lovina entered and nodded to her.

He looked like he might have played football in high school about three decades ago. He was bald with a border of thick, dark, russet hair circling his skull and a bushy mustache to match. He had dark brown eyes and a nose like a big slightly lumpy potato. He wore a shirt, tie, and jacket from the clearance rack of the local Walmart. Lovina was pretty sure they had a "broke-ass-cop" section just for uniform guys that made their way up to plainclothes duty. He had a small American flag pin on his lapel.

"Investigator Marcou," he said, offering his hand, "I'm Dave Wojick. Good to know yunz. I hope the trip up was h'okay."

Lovina shook Wojick's hand and accepted the visitor pass attached to a lanyard he offered her. "It was fine. Some beautiful country you got. Thank you for your help on this."

"Your boss must have some juice," Dave said. "He made this happen pretty snappy."

There was an electronic click as Wojick led her through a security door behind the reception counter, which the trooper on duty opened with the press of a button. The corridors of whitewashed cinder block were a maze of cramped offices, interview rooms, and alcoves filled with file cabinets.

"I got to let yunz know, I'm kind of puzzled," Wojick said as they navigated the corridors. "A Louisiana statie coming up, bringing her own forensic guy to kick around a five-year-old missing persons case? Yunz guys got a connection to an ongoing down there or what? Should I expect the feds to be knocking at my door too?"

"I've got a complainant, the vic's mom," Lovina said. "She moved to our state and she's still concerned about the case, obviously. I work cold cases in cooperation with the Center for Missing and Exploited Children, so I came across the mother's letter and after interviewing her I decided to give it another look. It's got nothing to do with the feds."

Dave stopped and turned to look at her. Lovina knew exactly what he was doing, he was smelling bullshit. Wojick gave her the bland cop-stare for a moment to see if she'd give him anything more. Lovina was silent.

"Hokey-doke," Wojick said, turned, and kept walking. A few more turns and Dave opened a door and led them across an open-air breezeway to a second brick building with a sign next to the door saying it was the state lab. They entered the lab and made their way to a corridor with elevator doors on either side. Wojick pushed the up button and they waited. The Pennsylvania cop crossed his thick arms across his wide chest and regarded Lovina.

"Look, Investigator Marcou . . ."

"Lovina."

"H'okay, Lovina. Lovina, don't piss on my leg and tell me it's raining, h'okay? This is all pretty hinky, right? Why is a senior director of your state lab rooting around in our cold case? You thinking the guys who caught this case fucked up or what?"

"Dave," Lovina said, "I'm not here to jam you and yours up. I have a . . . personal interest in this case, especially after talking to the mom. I'm just here to backtrack, okay? I need your help, I'm not looking to jerk anyone off. Russ Lime is here because he's the best lab man I've ever seen. Not looking to throw dirt on anyone or start a war. I swear."

There was a feeble ding and the elevator door opened. Wojick kept looking at her, then, finally, he uncrossed his arms and gestured for her to enter the elevator first. "Umhmm," he muttered, stroking his mustache. "I guess we'll see what your swear is worth, huh?" he said as the doors closed.

The conference room's window A/C unit was on the fritz, sputtering and blowing out stale, warm air. There were three cardboard file boxes on the long conference table, each box was affixed with an evidence sticker next to the Staples logo printed into the cardboard. Russell Lime, the senior technical director of the Louisiana State Crime Labs, was sitting at the table, his skinny legs crossed, leafing through a file folder from one of the boxes, an evidence bag full of loose coins sitting on the table before him.

Russ was a short, rawboned man in his seventies. He had a full, thick head of snow-white hair that he kept swept straight back from his face in his own take on a pompadour. His bulbous nose and cheeks were florid, like he just had a stiff drink or heard a good dirty joke. He always reminded Lovina of a cross between one of Santa's elves and an elderly Tom Waits.

Russ looked over his glasses and saw Lovina enter the room with Wojick. Russ stood. The younger man next to him in a lab coat glanced up but didn't stand, continuing to type on his phone. Russ spared him a momentary glance to look at him like he was a virus, then the charming smile returned as he looked at Lovina again.

"Why Inspector Lo-vina Marcou, as I live and breathe," Russ began. "You look scintillating, as always, *chère*." Lovina gave Russ a hug and noticed he was a bit thinner than usual. He looked like he wasn't getting a lot of sleep. Lovina had a pretty good idea why and it made her very sad.

"Hello, Russ." She stepped back and took a seat at the conference table beside Wojick, across from Russell.

Russ gestured to the twenty-something in the lab coat. "This is Assistant Lab Director Chapel. He has been so gracious to spare a little of his time for an old man."

Lovina and Dave both chuckled, but Chapel didn't as he looked up from his phone and addressed Wojick. "Look, I got a class of twenty rookies to teach in twenty and then back-to-back meetings with the superintendent and the fucking AG. Let's do this." He looked back to his phone and commenced to type again.

"De-lightful?" Russ said, the smile never leaving his lips or voice. He matched glances with Lovina and wiggled his bushy eyebrows. Lovina tried not to laugh. "Let's get this show on the road then, shall we, investigators?"

It took less than twenty minutes to lay out the case, the last story Raelyn Dunning would star in as the main character. The local police and the staties had all done their jobs and done them well. The girl had simply vanished and left no apparent clues to where she had gone or why. Lovina noticed Russ was pensive as Chapel droned on about the evidence collected, including photographs and a cast made of the set of size 19 boot prints found near Raelyn's driver-side door. Chapel forgot or mispronounced Raelyn's name about four times during his lifeless recitation of the forensic files. Russ made a few notes and pushed the evidence bag of loose change found on the floorboard of the abandoned car around the conference table.

"We good?" Chapel asked Wojick, standing and gathering his folders and a laptop. The investigator nodded.

"Yep," Dave said and nodded to the lab director as he hustled out without so much as a good-bye. Wojick waited a moment and then looked from Russ's face to Lovina. "Yeah, sorry about that. He's kinda a dick. But he's a dick that knows his job, and he laid it out straight for younz."

"Dave," Lovina asked, "did the investigating officers reach out to the feds to check on any serial offender patterns in Pennsylvania and the surrounding states?"

Wojick nodded.

"Yeah," he said, "after every other lead dried up. We sent the information into VICAP. Nothing useful. The information we got back was so broad it really didn't help us. Lots of girls go missing on the highways. Nothing jumped out to give us a direction."

Lovina frowned. "That's odd," she said. "I did a little digging myself and found a lot of disappearances running all along I-80. Several with similar crime scenes to Raelyn's. Hard to believed that the feds missed it."

"We asked about Pennsylvania and the neighboring states," Dave replied. "We don't have the personnel or the resources to go fishing for national serial killers unless they are working or dumping in our backyard."

"I understand," Lovina said. "No offense intended."

"None taken," Dave said, cracking his first smile since Lovina had met him. His teeth were yellow, probably from smoking, and he had a chipped front tooth. "Hell, I wish we had the money to send folks all over to dig and follow up, but we don't. Hell, they're closing state police barracks all over PA, as it is. We gotta do more with less."

"I get you," Lovina said. "My boss is paying for a couple of nights at a hotel and my gas. Otherwise, this is out of my pocket. Did the lead investigator get any kind of a feel for this? Anything?"

"Sorry to say, but nope," Wojick said, shaking his head. He looked down at the open file folder in front of him. Raelyn's senior high school picture looked up at him. "A goddamned shame." He closed the file and returned it to one of the boxes. "Yunz got access to these files for as long as yunz need 'em. Anything I can do to help you out, I'm your guy." He stood and shook both Lovina's and Russ's hands, then shuffled out to deal with his next problem.

"Well, that was productive," Lovina sighed. She leaned back and stretched in the chair. 'They did everything we would have done. There's just . . . nothing."

"Not quite, Love-ly Lovina," Russ said with a smile. He put the evidence bag with the loose change back in a box and stood up. Lovina heard his joints pop and crack. "Buy me lunch on that grand expense voucher Leo Roselle sent you up here with. I got a story to tell you."

"Hell," Lovina said, standing, "if we're lucky I can afford to buy you a hot dog at Wawa."

They went to a place to eat down the street from the state police head-quarters. A good rule of thumb was that any eating establishment that was near where cops worked and stayed in business probably had decent food for cheap. They decided on Bubba's, a local place the trooper at the front desk recommended.

Lovina snagged a booth in the back corner and they ordered. Russell had the homemade Golabki, cabbage rolls stuffed with ground beef, onions, and rice, then smothered in tomato sauce. He got it, on the waitress's recommendation, with a side of mashed potatoes. Lovina decided to try the deep-fried Pierogies with a side of sauerkraut. They both drank cold Yuengling draft beers.

"Okay, *chère*," Russ said, dabbing his lips with a napkin, after a sip of his beer, "'fess up. Why you so interested in this particular little girl gone miss-ing? I know you take them all personal, but this seems more like that mess with those Black-Eyed Kids a while back."

"God, I hope not," Lovina said, adding a dollop of sour cream to a Pierogie. "Well, this will sound crazy, but . . ." She told him about her dream with the clown-thing, and how it had led her to Raelyn's case. Russ listened, nodded, and ate and drank. Occasionally he'd stop her to ask a question or clarify a detail. There was no mockery in his tone or demeanor. When Lovina was finished, she took a long draw off her beer.

"I've heard stranger," Russ said. "About twenty years back I did an autopsy on a wino who got himself killed down by the 17th Street canal. He had bites in him from what the cops swore up and down was an alligator man. I saw the bites. They were consistent with a 'gator damned sight bigger than any I ever seen 'fore or since. There were muddy footprints too that no human made."

Lovina chuckled. "Never heard that one," she said. "So you think a killer clown abducted Raelyn Dunning off the side of I-80?" Russ shrugged. Near the front of the restaurant someone dropped some quarters into the old Rock-Ola jukebox and it began to play Bobby Darin's "Long Line Rider."

"These clown sightings have been all over the internet the last few years," he said, "but they go back almost forty years, at least here in the States."

"First of all, how do you suddenly know all things evil clown?" Lovina asked. "And secondly, you're serious about this stuff?"

"I had a good friend of mine, we came up together in NOPD back before you were a twinkle in your daddy's eye. He moved to Chicago eventually and ended up working the Gacy case in Illinois," Russ said. "He told me things about that man, about what he did to those boys. My friend didn't hold much stock in God or the Devil, or anything else really . . . until he went into John Wayne Gacy's house. Gacy was fascinated by clowns, did you know that? What would make that kind of mind respond to that archetype? Why? So I have to admit a certain morbid fascination with clowns, myself."

"As a kid," Lovina said, "when we'd go to the circus or carnival, they'd scare the hell out of me, even if they were nice old Shriners."

"Coulrophobia," Russ said around a mouthful of cabbage roll. "A fear of clowns. A very common phobia, *chère*. About forty-two percent of people say they have it to some degree. It's fascinating. They think it's a phenomenon called the Uncanny Valley Effect. Some very old, deep, dark parts of our brain respond to things that replicate human beings but aren't. We respond to human-seeming things—robots designed to mimic human appearance and speech, the concept of the zombie, ventriloquist dummies . . ."

"Don't get me started on those creepy little bastards."

". . . and clowns—with a sense of primal unease and revulsion," Russ concluded.

The waitress came by and inquired about the meal and replaced their empty beer glasses with full ones. Once she was off to another table, Russell raised his full beer in a toast, "To the human mind: what the hell *is* going on in there?" Lovina smiled and raised her own glass. They clinked them and took a long drinks of the Yuengling.

"I've never understood why clowns became a thing in the first place," Lovina said, wiping her lips with the side of her hand.

"Chaos," Russ said, earnestly. "The earliest celebrations were ritual, sanctified rites designed to bend nature to our little monkey wills, or placate it so it didn't kill us, at the very least. In other words, magic. Even in those primordial occult ceremonies, we humans insisted on introducing chaos to the natural order, thumbing our nose at the gods and spirits whose favor we were currying.

"The Hopi have a ritual dance that is interrupted by the arrival of a band of fools who mock the ritual, their faces painted with mud and animal fur. The earliest Greek theater had the Doric Mimes, comical figures in absurd grinning masks mocking the plight of the heroes and the gods. Almost every culture, almost every time period has them: ritualized disorder, chaos, madness peeking out from behind a mask. That was when Gacy's fetish began to make sense to me."

"So today we have Homie the Clown wandering beside the highway, or in some vacant lot, with a machete, scaring the shit out of people and blowing up the internet," Lovina said. Russ shrugged.

"Today our rituals are through celebrity, our gods: the internet, social media. It makes sense the oldest human archetypes would find their way there, *chère*. So, as to your clown dream, I think there may be something to it, especially in light of the evidence I found."

Lovina arched an eyebrow while Russ smiled and shoveled in a mouthful of food.

"Why Russell Lavon Lime, you have been holding out on me. You gave those staties the impression you hadn't found anything."

"It may be nothing. Tell me, *chère*, do you know what a hobo nickel is?"

"I think I'm about to find out," she said.

"It is a rather unique form of folk art practiced primarily by the nomads traveling the rails across America in the early to mid-twentieth century. Buffalo nickels were their preferred medium because they were larger coins and bit more malleable. Some of them are really quite exquisite, especially in the amount of detail and creativity in altering the profile on one side and the buffalo on the other."

Russ reached into his shirt pocket and removed a small plastic baggie containing a single coin. He handed it to Lovina.

"I found this in the evidence baggie of loose change they found on the floorboard of your girl's car. It was logged in as '$1.37 of assorted change,' that's it. Some technician didn't give that beauty a second glance."

Lovina held the evidence baggie close to her face. In it was a coin roughly the size and heft of a nickel. However, there was a profile of a face on one side that had been engraved in bas relief to resemble a grinning human skull with a cadaverous neck, the vertebrae, like bone plumage, fanning out. Very tiny and ornate script work curled around the circumference of the coin. Lovina didn't recognize it as a language she was familiar with. The only part she did comprehend was the date, 1913, which was in the left lower section of the coin.

"Russ, you stole evidence!"

"Nonsense. I replaced it with a perfectly good nickel, so even their math is still correct. I could have stolen that jackass Chapel's wallet out of his pants for all he would have known or cared. Smartphones are a pickpocket's best friend. Besides if they want to lock me up for it, they are more than welcome to."

Lovina set down the baggie with the coin and reached across the table to take Russ's hands in hers. They were soft, and dry, and a little cool. She searched her old friend and mentor's face and found the pain pooling behind his kind eyes.

"How is Treasure?" she said, asking about Russ's dear wife.

"That last bout of the cancer a year or so back," he said. "It didn't go back into remission like it should've this time. It's eating her up, Lovina."

"Oh, Russ, I'm so sorry." She squeezed his hand, he squeezed back.

"It's eating her a little piece at a time," he said. He suddenly looked very, very old. "The pain is so bad, the drugs don't ease it. They just make it bearable. The pain, the medicine, they're stealing her mind away too. She's my best friend, y'know, always was . . . my partner in crime." Russ's voice cracked a little. The human frame can only hold so much. He began to sob silently, his whole body shaking. He held on to Lovina's strong hands tight and she didn't let go.

Lovina remembered Russ and Treasure all those years at Thanksgiving, Christmas, birthdays. She remembered Treasure hugging her tight at Delphine's funeral. She recalled Treasure in her little turquoise slacks and matching flowered blouse that had been out of style since the seventies, those big, black cat-eyed glasses that she wore, reading to Pop as he lay in the hospital bed too close to his end to respond to her. Her lilting drawl as she sat watch and made sure Pop knew he wasn't alone.

In a world full of the things Lovina had seen: immortal murderers, highway magic, secret saints, and truck stop miracles, it seemed supremely wrong that such a decent person should pass this way. She felt a hot tear run down her face. It felt strangely cool on her skin. Her stomach was tight. She felt helpless and she hated that feeling. Russ plucked a folded handkerchief from his pocket and offered it to Lovina. She smiled as she sniffled, a little in awe at the simple gesture, and took it.

Russ wiped his own eyes with his napkin and then then cleared his throat before he spoke. "Well, me and my girl, we had a good run. Didn't we, *chère*?"

"She's not gone yet, Russ, and neither are you. You hang on, *béb*, you hear. She's a strong lady."

"That she is." Russ nodded and sipped his beer. "That she is." Russ looked down at the coin in the baggie. He slid it back across the table to Lovina. "Now flip that doodad over and see what you make of the other side." Lovina went along with the conversational detour and picked up the bag. The waitress, who had been giving them a few minutes, brought by a few napkins and asked if they wanted dessert.

"Yes, please," Lovina said. They both ordered the homemade bread pudding with a side of caramel sauce and two glasses of milk.

"My gut's gonna have a mad-on for you, girl," Russ said as the waitress departed. "But what the heck, right? What you think of that?"

The other side of the coin had also been altered. It had a strange symbol on it, a sideways teardrop with a small cross to the right of the teardrop's tail. Lovina looked up and shook her head.

"What is it?" she asked.

"Beats me," Russ said. "I tried a quick internet search on the way over, but nothing popped up."

"So what are you thinking? My dream clown dropped a hobo nickel while abducting Raelyn?"

"Perhaps," Russell said. "Perhaps it's a calling card. Some serial killers leave them. In any event, it is the only abnormality we have in the crime scene and so I intend to pursue it and see what shakes out. I managed to get it out of their evidence bag and into mine without much handling so hopefully we'll be able to get some trace and fingerprint evidence off it."

"Nimble fingers," Lovina said, raising her glass of milk in salute.

"You should ask my girlfriends," Russ said with a wink and a grin, but Lovina still saw the pain, dull behind his bright eyes. Russ often joked about how much of a ladies' man he was. If that had ever been true—and given his considerable charm, it might very well be—all that ended the day he met Treasure. Russ was in agony, but he was too much of gentleman to let it slow him down, especially as far as his work. "I will, of course, get all the results to you as quick as I can, *chère*. I'm headed back now. I need to get home."

"Thank you, Russ. I'm so sorry about Treasure." Lovina took a small Zip-loc bag out of her purse and handed it to Russ. In it was a crumpled tissue. "Here. Give this a good going over too, please."

"What is it?" he asked.

"When the clown grabbed me in my dream . . . it left makeup on my hand. I had the presence of mind to collect it, to make sure I'm not losing it." Lovina saw the curiosity flash across Russ's face. He was intrigued and excited to see what he might find.

"Well, *cho! co!*" Russ exclaimed with a grin and wagging eyebrows. He took the baggie and slid it into his pocket along with the hobo nickel.

Outside, in the parking lot Lovina hugged Russ tight one last time.

"You be careful," she said. "There are crazy people on the roads."

"About to be one more," Russ said and kissed Lovina's cheek.

"Give Treasure my love."

He climbed into his car, an old '67 Corvair ragtop that was in need of new paint and a roof. "Thank you, *chère,* for everything," he said, the hurt leaking out a little again. He was trying so hard.

"That's my line," she smiled. "Don't commit any more felonies if you can help it."

"No promises. Don't get in no scraps with any circus folk," he said. "You be careful Love-ly Lovina. I'll call as soon as I got something."

He drove away and Lovina watched him go. She wished she could fix it for Russell, fix Treasure, fix how unfair it was to be a decent person your whole life and still get screwed in the last act. Pops used to say, if you couldn't fix it, you had to bear it. It was true, but it still sucked. Russ's car was long gone and Lovina realized she had been staring off at the road and the humming flow of traffic for a while, lost in almost a trance, as if the traffic was whispering to her in some shifting language of motion, telling her a secret of the world just for her. Finally, the spell broken, she headed to the Charger, slipping into the flow of traffic and beginning the long drive to Coalport and the Valentine Trailer Park.

Ryan ended up going to the new school after all. It was only for a little over a week and with everyone so excited to be getting the hell out for the summer his appearance hardly made a ripple in the social swamp that was seventh grade. Hopefully, by the fall he'd be headed back with friends by his side and not have to deal with being the kid no one knows twice.

The whole thing that happened with the clown wasn't even discussed by any of the other guys the next day. Joe gave him a slap on the back and joked that he should go out for track. The others seemed glad he was okay and admonished him for running the wrong way.

"Always toward the trailers," David said earnestly, like he was repeating something he had been taught by rote in school, "never toward the trains."

"Guys, what the hell was that?" Ryan asked. The guys looked at each other, then back to him.

"Don't worry about it," Joe had said. "Come on, let's get to the bus stop."

And that had been it for the last few weeks, nothing more. No one wanted to hang out at the fort, nobody wanted to go anywhere near the woods. Instead they took turns hanging out at each other's homes, playing video games and watching TV.

One afternoon, they were all together, even Nevada, sitting in Granny's living room, reading Ryan's comics from the big plastic tub he had brought with him from Baltimore.

"Hey," Sam said, holding up a dog-eared copy of *Invincible,* "Where's the next one, man?" Ryan remembered what had happened to it and his face dropped a little.

"It, uh, it got, messed up. Sorry," he said.

"That sucks," Sam said, digging through the tub. "Ah, okay, here's the one after." Sam went back to reading.

Ryan noticed Nevada looking at him. He glanced at her and they both looked away quickly.

"This *Saga* thing is pretty cool," Nevada said. "You're right, about Image."

"If Dad knew we were reading zombie comics," David said, "he'd drop a load. We're not allowed to watch the TV show."

"*You're* not," Patrick said. "They give him nightmares."

"Shut, up, Pud," David said to his brother.

"How can anything scare you guys?" Ryan said. "You live with a killer clown in your backyard." Joe chuckled and looked up from the copy of *Black Panther* he was reading.

"Clowns," he said. "There's at least three of them back there."

"Holy crap," Ryan said. "Why hasn't someone called the cops on them?"

"They have," Nevada said, putting down her comic. "After Virginia Burkes went missing, her mom and the park manager, Bob, called them. Her boyfriend, Eric, told the cops about the clowns. They tore up the railroad graveyard. They didn't find nothing. For a while they figured Eric had killed her and hid her somewhere, but they never found her and they never saw a clown."

"Missing?" Ryan said. "Shit! Are you guys for real or is this some kind of scary story?"

"Both," Sam said. "Since my folks have lived here, I guess two or three people have gone missing because of the clowns."

"I think . . ." David began.

"Shut up, Dave," Joe said. "Yeah, new kid, welcome to Weirdville. Some of the old-timers, been living here since the seventies, they say it's always been like this, the clowns prowling around the railroad graveyard, people going missing, all the deaths . . ."

"Deaths?" Ryan said, a little louder then he intended to. "What deaths?"

"Lots of people who live in the park, they just up and die all of a sudden," Patrick said. "No rhyme or reason. 'Natural causes,' they call it. Like Joe said, it's weird."

"Well, my theory is . . ." David tried to interject.

"Shut up, Dave," Nevada said. "The police looked into all of it a bunch of times over the years. They never found anything. Eventually they started calling it an old wives' tale, the bums over at the trailer park drinking too many beers and smoking too much meth. But they know it's real, the townies too. It scares the pee out of them because they can't explain it, so they pretend it ain't real. But you ask anyone who's lived here a while, and they'll tell you their stories."

"I think the clowns are ghosts," David said, obviously very happy to finally get a word in, "left over from the carnival. They're mad they're stuck here."

"Get out of here, dumbass," Joe said, tossing a cushion off Granny's couch at Dave. It hit him square in the face and dropped into his lap. "The clowns and the ghosts are two totally different things, okay?"

"Hold it," Ryan said, raising his hands as if he were being attacked. "Ghosts? There are ghosts too? It's a killer-clown-infested, *haunted* trailer park. You guys are messing with me."

"No, it's true," Sam said. "My mom says it's because of all those people dying here. They kinda, y'know, stuck around. There's an old lady ghost that stands out by Mrs. Joblanski's clothes line after dark. She just stands there and cries some nights, covering her face with her hands."

"Then there's the body parts," Joe said. "Heads, and arms and chests, all cut up and bleeding . . . just . . . laying there in the grass. One minute they're there, the next . . . nothing."

"There's the ghosts of the dogs," David added, "all howling and bleeding. They chased me to the public road once."

"The old bum, carrying his head and the head's got no eyes," Patrick said. "He stumbles around. He almost touched Howie Newcomb once while he was fumbling around. Remember Howie? His folks moved out a little after that happened."

"The worse is the scar lady," Nevada said softly. The others all nodded in agreement.

"Yeah," Joe said, nodding.

"She's scary," David said.

"Yeah," Sam agreed. "I hate seeing her."

"Scar lady?" Ryan asked.

"She's really pretty, but like old-time pretty, fancy, y'know? She's got black hair and she's . . . naked." Nevada blushed a little. "But she's been all cut up, like her boobs and . . ." The girl trailed off for a second and gave a little unconscious shiver. "Her . . . her mouth's been cut on both sides, like she's grinning. She's bleeding and screaming and trying to run away from something you can't see and then she falls over in the grass and she's gone. I saw her one night over by Karl and Tony's place."

They all fell silent for a moment, there was only the hum of Grandma's A/C unit, surrounded by wadded-up Walmart bags and peeling duct tape filling in the gaps where it didn't fit right in the window. Ryan looked at his new friends. He recalled how he felt after his first night with the clown. He wondered how he'd do after seeing a few of the trailer park's dead residents. His chest felt tight at just the prospect of it, but then something unexpected pushed aside the fear, the realization that being chased by the clown, that seeing ghosts, weren't the worst things he'd ever been through in his young life. That thought gave him a little comfort and strength. It also made him a little sad.

"Hey, Dave," Ryan said, pointing to his friend. "You said something about a carnival? Is that what all that old junk is back by the railroad tracks? It looked like old rides and stuff."

"Yeah," Patrick said. "There was like this old-timey carnival a long time ago. It went all over the country on a train and it finally went broke and shut down and this is where they stopped at."

"It was called the Valentine Carnival," Nevada added. "I looked it up on Google once. It was like a real circus, it had acts and animals and a freak show . . . and clowns too."

"Those old railroad tracks don't go nowhere anymore either," Patrick said, nodding. "They're broke down. Dad says the railroad that used to run through here closed up after the coal boom went bust. The carnival just ran out of money and they stopped here, broke it all down. 'End of the line,' he said."

"A bunch of the carnival folks were too poor to move or go anywhere, so they kind of set up a little community here," Nevada said. "At some point it turned into the trailer park."

"You guys believe all this stuff?" Ryan asked, looking from face to face, "for real, not just trying to get me."

"Yeah," Joe said, "it's real. You'll see you live here long enough, you stay alive long enough. My oldest brother, Jack, he's stationed in Germany now, he and his buddies they used to hang out in the woods when they were our age. They saw all of it too. He told me, he told me the same thing. He lost a few friends to whatever those clowns are, just disappeared. He told me to remember this, and I'm telling you, Baltimore. Stay away from the woods at night. Stay out of the railroad graveyard and stick together, travel in pairs. Those are the club rules."

"Joe!" Sam said, sitting up. "That's a secret, man! We ain't voted yet!"

"I say he's in," Joe said. "Anyone who can get away from Dickie Dennis and his douchebags and one of those things is tough enough . . . he's in." Joe looked to Patrick.

"He's in," Patrick said, nodding to Ryan.

"I say yeah," David said.

"In," Nevada said. She smiled at Ryan and he smiled back.

"Yeah, okay, I guess," Sam said.

"Welcome to the club," Joe said. "You don't say nothing to nobody about it, okay. You gotta swear."

"You talk about it to anyone, even your mom or Judy, and we can cut your nuts off," Sam said.

"I put that part in," David said, beaming.

"Okay," Ryan said. "I won't say nothing, swear."

"This club goes back a long time," Patrick said. "To kids who have already grown up and are old folks now. We're the latest ones. We look out for each other and for anyone else who wanders around here and don't know about the clowns and the ghosts and the other dangerous things in the park."

"Like Calvin," David blurted out. Ryan had no idea what a Calvin was, and at this point he didn't want to know.

"We try to warn them and keep them from getting hurt," Patrick continued.

"But mostly we take care of each other," Joe added. "I ain't sticking my neck out for some dumbshit who goes looking for trouble."

"How come all this stuff happens here?" Ryan asked. "I mean if kids have been knowing about it for all these years, one of them must have kept looking into it when they got older and grew up, right? Somebody must know how it all got started."

"Who cares," Sam asked.

"Because," Ryan said, "if we figure out how it started, then we might be able to figure out how to stop it."

. . .

It was hot enough that weekend—Memorial Day Weekend—for the tub to "officially" open. Sam, Patrick, and David collected Ryan and told Judy where they were taking her grandson. Mom was off working her new job as the cashier at the Minit Mart.

"The tub?" Ryan asked as he grabbed his Orioles baseball cap.

"Yeah," David said nodding and grinning. "It's cool!"

"You make sure you tell Dickie Dennis I will tell his mother on him if he gives you kids any shit," Judy said, wagging a finger as if Dickie was right there. She was in her faux-leather recliner, a jelly jar full of white wine from the box in the fridge in her other hand.

"Yes, ma'am," Patrick said. "We'll look out for Ryan, ma'am." With that, the boys spilled out the door to the trailer and jumped off the porch to the ground below and began to run, whooping and hollering as they went.

The sun was high, brilliant, and merciless in the sharp blue sky. The air was still and humid. It carried the scent of fresh mowed grass, meat charring on a grill, and suntan lotion. Several different radios competed for the ears of anyone in the park. As the boys passed by the "four o'clock" alleys of trailers in the big circular road that was the hub of the park they heard Kendrick Lamar's "Humble" blasting. As they cut through to the cluster of trailers at the center of the hub, the rap began to be drowned out by "Hurricane" by Luke Combs. Ryan paused for a moment as they cleared a corner and a sea of pink plastic filled his field of vision.

"Wow," was all Ryan could get out. The large grassy courtyard between four of the trailers was home to a large shade tree, an old sugar maple. A few wooden benches, maybe old church pews, circled the wide trunk of the tree, facing outward. They were weathered from years in the sun, the rain, the snow, carved up from obvious generations of pocketknife poets, and splattered with white bird shit in a few places. A few old people sat on the benches, talking softly to each other, or just staring. A little blue-haired lady waved to the boys as they turned the corner. The rest of the courtyard was populated with plastic pink flamingos, hundreds of them of all different types and styles.

"Hi, Mrs. Harris!" Sam called out to the old lady, who waved back. He lowered his voice then and spoke to Ryan as they all began walking again through the maze of plastic birds. "Mrs. Harris kinda likes flamingos, if you hadn't figured that out. They're all hers. She cleans them and replaces the old ones when they get too faded, or start dry rotting."

"Weird," Ryan muttered as he sheepishly waved to Mrs. Harris.

"Yeah," Patrick said. "She's been doing that since her husband died. Dad says there seem to be more of them every year." They cleared the flamingo gauntlet and passed between two more trailers to another clearing. Ryan heard laughter, splashing water, and music, "Loud and Heavy" by Cody Jinks, before they rounded the corner.

"Welcome to the tub," Sam said with a grin. Ryan guessed there were about fifty people in the clearing. There were beach towels, folding chairs, and blankets scattered everywhere. Some people were sitting on blankets drinking a cold beer or soda, others were tossing Frisbees, or flirting, talking with their neighbors, or dancing to the music. There were coolers scattered everywhere and jambox radios and Bluetooth speakers were playing everything from hip-hop to country and everything in between. "Highway Tune" by Greta Van Fleet was dominating his ears at this moment.

There were the wheel-less skeletons of three old pickup trucks squatting in the center of the activity, side by side. The long truck beds of each had been sealed with heavy plastic tarps and filled with water. About fifteen or twenty people were splashing, chilling and enjoying the three impromptu pools. Fresh, but cold, water for the tubs came from hoses that were still pumping into all three pools as the water sloshed out from the occupants' excited activities. One truck bed was exclusively for younger kids, the other two were for teens and adults.

"The tub's what us poor-ass folk got instead of a swimming pool," Sam said. "Cops used to try to shut it down, back when they gave a shit about what happened out here. Now they just let us alone as long as nothing gets out of hand." A very large, almost obscenely muscled man with long platinum blond hair, wraparound sunglasses, a whistle around his neck, and a clipboard circled the pools and seemed to be policing behavior and regulating who got in and came out of the water.

"That's No-Balls Trey," David said pointing to the muscleman. "He's kind of like a lifeguard . . . if the lifeguard didn't have balls no more."

"Hey, Trey!" Patrick called. The blond lumbered over, a perfect bleached-tooth smile on his square-jawed face.

"Hey, Pat," Trey said, his voice higher pitched than Ryan had anticipated, like he had been breathing helium from a balloon.

"This is Ryan Badel," Patrick said. "He and his mom just moved in. He's Judy's grandson."

"Oh, yeah," Trey said, nodding and shaking Ryan's hand. "Betty told me you guys had come from Baltimore. Good to meet you, Ryan."

"Which Betty?" Patrick asked. "Regular Betty, or one-leg-shorter-than-the-other Betty?"

"Regular Betty," Trey said. "You guys going to take a dip?"

"Yeah," David said, "please. It's hotter than the Devil's jockstrap." Trey scribbled their names down on the clipboard's list and then examined a stop-watch he clutched in his massive tanned fist. He clicked the watch to stop and blew the whistle around his neck.

"Nice to meet you, Ryan," Trey said and then bellowed in the direction of the truck beds, sounding for all the world like a belligerent Mickey Mouse, "Okay, José, Doug, Debbie, and Stu, outta the water! Phil, Chuck, Tim, and Shellie, you're in!" Trey headed back to his charges.

"Um, his voice?" Ryan asked.

"He was a professional lifter," Sam said. "Too much juice. His nuts turned into raisins."

"Juice, nuts, raisins," David said. "You're making me hungry! How much you got on you?"

Between the four of them scrounging change, the boys were able to buy two hot dogs, a can of Coke, and a small bag of chips to split between them. A couple of the park's residents, Marion and Boyd Wuxler, set up a grill when the tub opened and sold food and drinks. David told Ryan how George Bosque tried a few summers back to compete with the Wuxlers and how that summer the prices for the food and drinks plummeted. Dave recounted the event as a golden age of cheap junk food. It sadly only lasted a season, since George moved out of the park very quickly with his family after a nasty encounter with the mysterious aforementioned Calvin.

The boys had polished off their food and were in a spirited debate over whether Holly Mueller or Christen McCoy, two park girls a few grades older than the boys, looked better in their swimsuits, when Trey's whistle chirped and he called out their names to take their turn in the tub. As they ran over to the teen pool, one of the dripping kids getting out, a skinny black youth with his hair shaved down to shadow, slapped Sam on the back hard.

"I just peed in there," he mock-whispered in Sam's ear. "Enjoy the warm water," and laughed as he ran off, waving to Patrick and David as he sprinted to join his wet friends crossing the courtyard.

Sam winced at the slap and shouted after him, "Screw you, Gino!"

"Hey!" Trey shouted, brandishing the whistle like a weapon. "Sam, language!" Sam held up a hand in apology. The boys climbed up a set of slick, wet stairs nailed together from two-by-four remnants and jumped into the cold water, sending gallons of it flying as they did. Ryan gasped for a second at the cold and then submerged up to his chin. In a moment the cold faded and he sat on on the hump of one of the wheel hubs. David submerged completely for a moment and came up, his wet hair plastered to his narrow face.

"Dude," Sam said, "Gino just peed in that."

David grinned. "Me too."

"Ugh!" Patrick groaned.

"Gross," Sam said.

"Hey, it's really cold," Dave said with a shrug. The boys settled down and enjoyed the water's reprieve from the muggy, oppressive heat. "What do you think, Ryan?" David asked after a few moments. "You like it?"

Ryan looked around at all the people, laughing, drinking, dancing, eating, playing. "Yeah," he said. "I do. It reminds me of when we'd go to the pools in the city, back in Baltimore. Kids squealing, music, everybody having a good time and trying to stay cool. This is not what I expected at all."

"From a bunch of Pennsylvanian trailer trash?" Sam said. "Yeah, don't think it's always all sweet like this. It's opening day, by middle of July we'll have drunks fighting over someone jumping Trey's line for the tubs. It can get ugly."

"Hey," Patrick said, "don't listen to Sam's crap, Ryan. Dad says not to judge people. There are a lot of really good folks who live here, like your grandma, Judy. They're down on their luck, but that don't mean they're bad."

"Just stay out of the southeast part of the park as much as you can," Sam said. "That's where the cookers and dealers live, mostly. Bob tries to keep most of the folks who he thinks are going to be trouble over there."

"Bob?" Ryan asked.

"Mr. Valenti," David said. "He's the park manager. He's cool, I think he's an old hippie. He lives right across the way from your granny's trailer, that little, old silver one that looks like something from an old space-man movie."

"Oh, yeah," Ryan said. "Um . . . is this Calvin guy you all keep mentioning a drug dealer?"

"He's worse," Sam said. "He's killer-clown, screaming-cut-up-ghost worse. Don't let him paint anything on you either!"

"Shut up, Sam," Patrick said. "It ain't that bad, Ryan, honest. There are some crazy folk, but they keep mostly to themselves. I think there are like only two or three guys who do all the drug stuff now. The cops rounded up a bunch of them back at Thanksgiving . . . and Calvin, well, he never comes out in the daytime, so just steer clear of his trailer at night and you'll be okay."

"It's okay," Ryan said. "I . . . like it here. I thought this was going to suck, but meeting you guys . . . well . . . y'know." The boys were silent for a little bit. Sam cupped his hands together near the water and squeezed, squirting Ryan square in the face. Ryan choked and coughed, then laughed as he swept an arm and splashed Sam back. The war was on. The boys cackled in between sputtering and wiping water out of their eyes and noses and then beginning the next volley of attacks. It ended with the shrill toot of Trey's whistle and an order for the boys to jump out. They did laughing and blowing water out of their noses.

They found a dry, old, wooden picnic bench, its wood warm to the touch. It had only been abandoned a few minutes earlier and they climbed up on it.

David and Sam lay on the table, drying off in the sun, Dave on his belly, Sam on his back, while Patrick and Ryan sat on the bench.

Ryan saw a dark blue four-door with several antenna mounted along its trunk slowly drift by on the circular road that looped the central hub of the trailer park. The driver was a big white cop, bald with a bushy mustache. The woman cop in the passenger seat was black and pretty, with long straight hair. They both wore cop-style sunglasses.

"Police," Patrick said, seeing the car too. "Don't look like the Sheriff's Department either. I wonder what's up?"

"Hey, Ryan," David said, sitting up on his elbows, "you said you wanted to know how all the weird stuff got started, you should ask him!" David pointed to an old guy making his way in a big hurry down a set of stairs from a trailer. He was in pretty good shape for his age, with forearms thick, strong, and hairy poking out of his rolled-up shirt sleeves. He wore a light blue button-down shirt tucked into somewhat baggy seersucker trousers. He wore old tennis shoes and he stuffed a battered straw porkpie hat with a maroon and black hatband on his head as he strode away from the trailer.

"Who's he?" Ryan asked.

"That's Karl," David said. "He and his roommate put out the *Arrow*. He knows a lot about the park. They've lived here for a long time, since they retired from some newspaper."

"The *Arrow*?"

"The *Valentine Arrow*," Patrick said. "It's the park's newspaper."

"It's a crappy photocopied newsletter," Sam said. "They still type it on a typewriter. It comes out every few months. And I don't think Tony is his roommate. They fight like an old married couple."

The door to the trailer banged open and a portly older man with prominent jowls and snow-white hair swept backstepped out onto the stair's landing. He wore tan khakis and a bowling shirt with a print as loud as his voice. There was a scowl that seemed almost carved into his wrinkled face. "Karl!" the man bellowed. Ryan got the feeling the old man yelled that a lot. Karl paused in mid-stride and winced as if he had been physically hit by Tony's voice.

"See?" Sam said.

"They worked for a newspaper?" Ryan asked. Patrick nodded.

"I bet they could tell you all about the park," David said. Karl walked back toward the trailer and he and Tony were engaged in an animated discussion, voices raised and arms flailing wildly.

"Why haven't you guys ever asked?" Ryan said. Sam held out a hand toward the two old men bickering as if he were presenting evidence.

"They're really nice," Patrick said. "And I think they really like each other . . ." he paused and looked to Sam, ". . . but not that kind of like. They just shout a lot at each other, but not really at anyone else. They're really smart. I heard they both worked on a lot of big stories before they retired. Go on, Ryan, ask 'em." Ryan stood up. His legs were shaking a little. He walked across the courtyard toward the two men as they continued to argue, seeming oblivious to everything else.

"Karl, how are you going to grocery shop without the grocery list?"

"I don't need a list, Tony, you get the same things every single time I go. I have a memory, a good one too. I don't need a list. I'm insulted you think I do!"

"Is that a racing slip in your back pocket, Karl? You planning on sneaking over to Philly and betting the ponies again? Like the last time you lost our grocery money?"

Karl raised a finger as if to defend a point. "I . . . I . . . I don't *lose* it, Tony! Not at first. Beside I have an informer at the track and I need to talk to him about this Liberty Bell phantom . . ."

"Oh for heaven's sake, Karl!" Tony interrupted. "Not another word about this ridiculous ghost story of yours . . ."

"Ridiculous!" Karl said, indignantly. "You wouldn't know a good story if it mailed itself to you, first class!

"If you mailed it, it would be postage due," Tony replied, jabbing his cigar at Karl.

"Um, excuse me," Ryan said his voice trembling a little. Both men immediately stopped in mid-argument and turned to regard the boy.

"Yes, young man?" Tony said, his tone completely different now.

"Um, my name is Ryan, Ryan Badel, and . . . um, I heard you were newspaper reporters?"

"I was, kid," Karl said, giving a sideways glance to Tony. "He was an editor." He said the word "editor" like he was diagnosing a disease. Tony bristled, but remained calm.

"That's right," Tony said. "I *was* a reporter, but I was so good at my job they promoted me to editor." Karl let loose a quick, squawking outburst of a mocking laugh, but held his tongue. Tony narrowed his eyes at Karl but then continued. "What can we do for you, Ryan?"

"Um, well, Me and my mom just moved here . . ."

"You're Judy's grandson," Karl said, nodding. Tony looked at the old re-porter quizzically. "It's called knowing your beat," Karl said, gesturing to Ryan. "Something editors don't know squat about. Go on, kid."

"Well my friends said you would be the people to ask about the history of the park . . . all that old carnival stuff behind the woods?"

"Have you seen the ghosts yet?" Karl blurted out.

"Karl!" Tony's voice sounded like Zeus throwing thunderbolts.

"The undead cultist in the painted trailer, have you run into him yet," Karl continued, "because if you haven't kid, don't! How about the evil clowns? The thing that moves between cell phones? The demonically possessed Shih Tzu . . ."

"Karl!"

"The propane elemental? The monster in the water tower? Drink bottled, kid, drink bottled!"

"Karl! That's enough, you're going to scare the child!"

"Scare? Scare? Shows all you know! I'm trying to warn him," Karl said.

"I, uh, I have seen the clown," Ryan said sheepishly.

Tony rolled his eyes and sighed a world-weary sigh. "He's one of yours," he said to Karl, like admitting defeat. Karl grinned and groaned a little as he went down on one knee to look Ryan square in the eye. He put his hand on Ryan's shoulder.

"That's great, kid, great. Tell me all about it. Tony, could you go get my tape recorder?"

"Karl, the groceries," Tony shook the list in his hand, "now. Campfire nonsense later."

"Okay, Tony, okay!" Karl struggled back to his feet. Ryan helped the old man up. "Listen kid, I have some business with a source of mine . . ."

"You have business with a shopping cart," Tony interjected. Karl contin-ued, unabated.

"Come on by anytime. We'll swap information. Deal?" Karl thrust out his hand. Ryan shook it.

"Deal," Ryan said. "Thanks!"

Karl snatched the list out of Tony's hand and resumed his purposefully stride away from the trailer, Ryan, and his former editor.

"Oh, and kid?" Karl paused and looked back.

"Yeah?" Ryan said.

"Come before dark."

"Hand me that 14mm, son," Don Aussapile said, bent over the open hood of the weathered '94 Toyota Camry. "I can tell you what, this through bolt is gonna be a bear." Jimmie handed his dad the socket wrench and went back to working on the air conditioning in the Ford Focus Steve Hall had brought in yesterday. The bays of Don's Wreck and Repair, Don's gas station, echoed with tinny music from the old grimy duct-tape-covered jambox that was on top of the file cabinet in the room that doubled as the customer counter and Don's "office." It was playing O. B McClinton's "Don't Let the Green Grass Fool You" off the country oldies station Don kept the radio on most of the time.

"Todd told me he'd have the rebuilt over here by this afternoon or tomorrow morning at the latest," Jimmie said. He and his dad were back to back, but he knew Don just smiled a little.

"Gotcha," Don said. "So we'll see it here day after tomorrow."

Jimmie chuckled and nodded. "Yep, that'd be about right for Todd."

"It's nice having somebody to take care of managing stuff like that," Don said. He grunted, struggling with the stubborn through bolt.

"What are you talking about?" Jimmie said, looking over his shoulder, "Edger's been doing all that for you since I was crawling around here."

"Edger's getting old," Don said. He strained as he tried to loosen the bolt, the thick muscles in his forearms tensing with the effort. The faded USMC anchor tattoo on his forearm rippled like a flag. Jimmie had the same tattoo on his forearm. Don stopped the struggle and took a break, turning to face his son. He sighed. "We both are."

Jimmie wiped the grease off his hands with a rag and turned as well. "Happens to the best of us, dad. Edger still breaks his back for you."

"Oh, I know. He's a good man. I'm lucky to have him. Remember that kid, what was his name, worked for me a few months last summer?"

"Justin?" Jimmie offered. Don snapped his fingers and nodded.

"Justin. Twenty years old, pants down to his butt-crack. Spent more time playing on his phone than working. I'm lucky to have Edger, but he's talking about retiring pretty soon. Don't blame him. He wants to spend all the time he can with Pauline. They both know what's coming."

"Y'know, Dad, there are a lot good kids out there," Jimmie said. "You can find one to help you out when Edger does retire."

"I already have," Don said, smiling. Jimmie looked genuinely surprised. Don chuckled. "What, you never considered working with your old man full-time? You used to, remember? Back before you and Layla got married, when you first got back from the Gulf."

"Yeah, Dad, but I was such an angry fuckup back then," Jimmie said.

"Language," Don interjected.

"Yes, sir. You and I fought all the time, Dad. I figured you were glad to get rid of me."

"You did irritate the blazes out of me," Don said, nodding. "But I understood it. You came back from being deployed. You had to get your head right. I get that, I had to do the same thing when I got back from Vietnam. God bless your mother. Another woman would have kicked my sorry ass out and be right to do it too."

They were both quiet for a moment, neither sure what to say, neither wanting to discuss that experience they shared. The only sound was the traffic *whooshing* by on Jennings Street. The radio was playing "El Paso," by Marty Robbins. Dad never spoke much about the war. When Jimmie was a kid that always seemed strange to him, but Mom told him to leave his dad be about it. After Jimmie came back from Iraq in 1991, he understood why Dad had been silent. Finally, Jimmie spoke.

"Well, if you need the help, Dad, you got me. I just don't want to make anything bad between us, like it was then."

"You're a different man, now, son," Don said, walking over to a large red-metal tool chest. He began searching through a drawer. "I know it would mean less time on the road, but with Jimmie Junior here that's not such a bad thing, is it?"

"Truth be told," Jimmie said, going back to work under the F's hood, "I've been thinking about that anyway. Layla would love it, at least until I got on her nerves, and, well, I'm not sure there's much future in driving anymore, Dad."

"What you mean?" Don asked, retrieving a long extension rod and fitting it to the socket wrench. "You've always loved driving."

"I still do. It's just . . . well, you hear all the news talking about these new 'robot trucks' they're going to have out on the road to replace us in a few years. A lot of gear-jammers are worried they ain't gonna have a job before too long. Me too." Don chuckled and shook his head.

"I wouldn't lose any sleep over that, son," he said, looking at Jimmie. "They said barbed wire would be the death of the cowboy, they're still kicking."

"A damn sight fewer of them kicking than there used to be, Dad," Jimmie added. Don slipped back under the hood of the Camry. He applied a little oil to the back side of the stuck bolt and then fitted the socket in place again.

"Well, sometimes things look worse 'fore they look better," he said. "Take a look at that thing over there." He nodded toward a computer console and monitor with numerous wires and cable draped over it. The console was on a wheeled base and Don had it setting in a corner of the bay, like a bad child being punished. Jimmie had seen it numerous times and he had a pretty good idea what it was, but he couldn't recall ever seeing his dad use it. "That thing there talks to the computers in the engines of the newer cars, asks them what's wrong, gives you a code that you look up in a manual that looks like the New York phone book. I hardly ever use the damn thing. I can know more about what's ailing an engine by listening to it, feeling it, taking the thing out for a drive. It's a handy tool, I don't begrudge it. Tools help." Don grunted and gave all his effort on the stuck through bolt, talking between grunts. "But people made the tools, and people fix them when they break. People can think outside of sense, react, and make a choice when there's no good one to be made. They can remember the pain of mistakes and why, sometimes, you have to make them over and over again anyway. The barbed wire doesn't know or care if there's a calf caught in it, but the cowboy does, that's why they're still around."

Don continued using the longer lever of the extension to try to turn the socket through gritted teeth. "I see more and more folks come through here who don't understand *how* a thing works, or even *why* most of the time. They're willing to just blindly accept how things are. As long as the engine turns over, as long as the call goes through on the cell phone, as long as the bank card pays for their seven-dollar coffee, they don't want to know. They don't realize how much control over their lives they're giving up to strangers. I'm pretty sure that's the point."

There was a groan of frozen metal, and a crack and the bolt gave and began to loosen and turn. Don grinned, the tension slipping out of his body. "Lost Highway" by Hank Williams Sr. was playing on the old radio now. "A machine can't predict on instinct how the jackass in the F-150 is going to swerve right up under your grille at eighty miles an hour in complete defiance of all logic, reason, and common sense," Don said. "Or how to drive with english, like you're playing pool, going down the icy side of a mountain, trying to not slide into that school bus. They can't tell the difference between the drunk driver and the SUV full of kids, between when you can make it another couple of miles on the fumes of that tank to shave some time off that damn log book, or when you can't. And if they ever can do all that, son, well, I'm pretty damned sure they'll start asking for better pay than nothing and get themselves a good union to boot." Jimmie laughed.

"Who knows," Jimmie said, "Maybe by then they'll be members of the Brotherhood."

"Maybe, and we'll welcome them in. You always remember, son," Don said, "and you make sure those grandchildren of mine remember, it ain't the wheel that's important, it's the brotherhood part that matters."

. . .

It was mid-afternoon by the time they paused to eat. Don drove them in the wrecker to the Hardee's over on Morganton Boulevard. They picked up food and took it back to the garage and ate it in the front office. The jambox was playing Loretta Lynn's "Don't Come Home A Drinkin' with Lovin' on Your Mind." They sat and ate without talking for a while, watching the traffic rush by.

"You said you think that's the idea," Jimmie said. Don looked up, confused. "All that you were saying about people not knowing how things work, about them giving up control to strangers, you really think that's on purpose, part of somebody's plan?"

"Yep." Don popped a French fry into his mouth. "There are a lot of folks in this world whose only business and sport is power. They want as much control over people as they can get, which is funny because they are also usually the ones who care the least about those same people."

Jimmie was quiet for a moment, then, "Dad, how much do you trust the other orders? The Builders, the Benefactors?"

When the Templars had dissolved and re-formed in secret, they had created three orders, three "spokes" on a wheel. The Brethren, who Jimmie, Don, and Don's father were all members of, was one spoke. The Brethren had taken up the burden of protecting "the ways between"—the highways, the skies, the waterways, the rails, even the "information superhighway" of the internet.

A society was only as healthy as its roads, an old saying proclaimed, and the Brethren helped hold society together by protecting those roads and those who traveled upon them.

The other orders, the other "spokes," were made up of the Builders, like Jimmie's friend, Max Leher, who operated to gather and protect all knowledge, be it mundane or supernatural in nature. They operated through schools, universities, libraries, hospitals, and laboratories, as well as occult and religious organizations.

The final spoke of the wheel was the Benefactors, the masters of financial and political power. They operated through governments and trade markets, media, and military. All three spokes were independent but offered aid and resources to each other, with the implicit understanding that without any of the three spokes, the wheel itself would collapse.

"Trust the other orders?" Don echoed. "Well enough, I guess. I haven't mixed company with too many Builders, even fewer Benefactors. We don't exactly rub elbows in the same social circles." Don grinned. "Oh, wait, I think I saw one in Hardee's getting a sweet tea."

"Come on Dad, I'm serious," Jimmie said, leaning forward in his chair. "That business a while back with that Vanishing Hitchhiker, the little girl, and the Black-Eyed Kids?"

"Yeah." Don nodded and took another bite of his burger. "I remember."

"We had a Builder out in the field with us, a real nice lady, a professor from D.C. Her name was Max Leher."

"A girl named Max?" Don asked.

"Short for Mackenzie," Jimmie said. "Anyway, Max had this crazy theory about the highways, about why the Road is the way it is."

"The Road" was the name the Brethren used to describe the supernatural nature of the American highways. The Road drew things to itself, evil things, and they preyed on travelers and those who lived near the highways. Why the highways attracted such supernatural and mundane predators had long been a mystery to the Brethren.

"Max's notion was that the highways were built along very specific lines of magical energy, ley lines," Jimmie said. "She thought the route numbers of the roads and their sequences were hidden magic formulas, part sacred geometry, part numerology, and a bunch of 'ologies' I didn't understand. She said it was only a theory, but everything I've experienced out there and all she did seems to support it, Dad. I was just wondering if maybe someone built the Road to do what it does."

Don whistled, and leaned back in his old rolling chair. "That's a hell of an undertaking," Don said. "Just the money part alone . . . all those jurisdictions, the politics involved in highway money between the states and the feds . . . I don't see how anyone could pull that off without the Benefactors knowing about it and only the Builders would have the occult know-how to make that happen, so if they didn't know about it . . ." Don stopped, an odd look came across his weathered face. Jimmie nodded slowly.

"Exactly," Jimmie said.

"You think the other two orders teamed up to create the Road?" Don said. "Why in God's green earth, son?"

"That's what I've been trying to figure out," Jimmie said. "But I don't know of any other outfit with the know-how and connections to do it, do you?"

"No," Don said. "Not even close. But why would they? The Road causes so much trouble. You remember that stretch of I-444 in Oklahoma that was taking people straight into that other universe last year? What was it called?"

"Irkalla," Jimmie said. "It's got something to do with the Babylonians, I think."

"Right, right, Ikea," Don said. "Texas Pete and his crew had to go in there and deal with 'The King of Sunset,' that Nergal-god-thing. It was a mess."

"Made for a great story when Pete told me about it at the Pilot Flying J in Augusta," Jimmie added.

"My point is," Don said, "the Benefactors have to use their press connections all the time to keep a lid on some weird thing or another that happens out on the Road. What's the benefit to them, and why the hell wouldn't they tell us about it? We Brethren bleed out there. We're on the front lines."

"Maybe that's why they don't tell us," Jimmie said. "We're the ones who do the fighting and the dying. How well do you think it would go over if we found out our fellow Templars were the ones who created the meat grinder they dropped us into?

"What you were saying earlier, Dad, what if it is all some kind of plan to control people's lives, to control the Brethren? Max seemed to think the Road was built to act as a way of damming up all the magical power of the world, to aim it, like changing the course of a river. You could do an awful lot with that kind of power on tap. What if they're just using us to police their little experiment?"

Don sighed and took a long sip on his tea. "I can't believe that, son. We're all in this fight together. The other orders, they just contribute other things besides a strong arm is all. You know I've had my differences with the home office, but I can't imagine they'd do us that dirty. I think your friend is wrong. I sure hope she is."

"Yeah," Jimmie said, "me too." His cell phone began playing the Eric Clapton song and Layla's face popped up on the screen. Jimmie reached over, picked up the phone, and answered it. "Hey, baby, what's up?" He listened intently and Don saw a shadow pass over his son's face. "Okay . . . okay. Damn. Do we need to get Peyton? Okay, hang on a sec, and I'll ask." Jimmie lowered the phone. "Dad, can Peyton and Jimmie Junior stay with you and Mom for a spell?"

"Sure," Don said. "What's going on, son?"

"Something's happened with Heck and the Jocks . . ."

. . .

Jimmie rushed off in his pickup headed for home. Don sat in his office chair for a few moments thinking about what Jimmie had told him. He sifted and tumbled decades of life through his mind. Every once in a while the replay would pause on an event, an odd occurrence, a strange phrase someone had said.

He recalled his old buddy and fellow Brethren, Clifford Swanson. Cliff had been one of the best mechanics he'd ever met. He was a churchgoing man, always made his wife and his mama feel like a queen. He raised decent kids, and he always dressed smart for any special occasion. Cliff could play the jessie out of a guitar, and Don's memory lingered on several New Year's Eves at the VFW where he had watched Clifford and his band play bluegrass while couples clogged, whooped, and spun around the dance floor.

He missed Cliff. The older you got, the more holes appeared in your life where people used to be. Then Don thought back to that January night in 1974, to Nebraska, to I-680 and Clifford bleeding out on the ice-cracked asphalt of the highway, nearly cut in two by the rending claws of that . . . thing, that thing with breath like the stench of a slaughterhouse and the tittering laughter of a little girl.

"We got it . . . we got it, didn't we Donnie?" Cliff had muttered through a bubbling fountain of his own blood. The thing was still and burning on the side of the road. The Willie Pete grenades had done their job, but they had done it far too slowly to save Cliff. Clifford looked up with his strong, kind eyes and took his friend's hand and squeezed it tight.

"You got it, Cliff," Don had said. "You got it, man. You did good. Hang tough now."

"Worth it . . ." he said. "The wheel turns," He squeezed Don's hand for all it was worth. Don watched Cliff's blood seep into the fissures in the Road.

"Hang on now, Cliff. You wait for the medics, y'hear."

Cliff couldn't. The kindness and awareness bled out of his eyes and drained into the Road just like his blood. As a grown man, Don Aussapile had only cried a few times. He wept like a baby, cradling his best friend's body on the side of that empty Nebraska highway as the winter wind keened.

Something colder than the memory of that night unwound in Don's stomach. He reached for the phone on his desk, punched in a code he knew by heart, but hadn't used in almost twenty years. It answered on the first ring with a single electric beep.

"The wheel turns," Don said. There was a pause, then a woman's voice, or as close an approximation as a computer could produce, responded.

"Confirmed, Stovebolt," the voice said. "How may we assist you?"

"Patch me through to Moonshiner," Don said. "Authentication, Whiskey Epsilon Howard 313, break." Again there was silence then the normal tone of a phone ringing. After half a dozen rings the receiver was picked up.

"Hello?"

"Billy, it's Don, Don Aussapile. I hope I'm not calling at a bad time."

"Don! Hell no. How are you? How's Ella and little Jimmie?

"Ella still puts up with me for some reason and Little Jimmie has a little Jimmie of his own now," Don said with a chuckle. Billy laughed on the other end of the line. It was good to hear that old, familiar laugh. It helped ease a little of the old hollow pain that came with Cliff's memory.

"How's Rose?" Don asked.

"Better'n I deserve," Billy replied. "My youngest, Carrie's, a beautician now if you can believe that."

"That's great, Bill," Don said. "Congratulations!"

"What can I do you for, Don?" Billy asked. "Ain't like you to call out of the blue on a secure line just to jaw."

"Billy, how many friends have you and I lost to the damn Road over the years? Good people, the best." The line was silent for a moment.

"Too damn many," Bill finally replied with a sigh. "Too many. Donnie, you okay? What's wrong, pardner?"

"Bill, you ain't gonna believe this . . . it sounds crazy," Don began, "but I've heard tell of this . . . theory about the Road . . . and I think as Grandmaster of the Order of the Brethren you should hear it out. The Brotherhood may have a problem, a big problem."

TWELVE "10-14"

Dusty Acosta's shoulder throbbed as he hung on to the handrail by the door of the slowly moving boxcar. The train swayed and each movement tugged at his pulled shoulder as he waited for the right moment to swing off and drop to the gravel and grass alongside the tracks. He had pulled the muscle when he had to catch the train in New York on the fly. He had tried not to sleep on it funny in the car, but he had. Dusty counted silently to himself and then tumbled as the boxcar reached a particular soft-looking patch of grass. There was the dizzy uncertain thrill of free fall and then the tuck and the roll on the carpet of green. Two rotations of tumble and Dusty ended up on his knees, crouched, watching the freight train drift into the depot. He noted with some pride, and a little regret, that the fall hadn't been anywhere near as scary as it used to be when he was a greenhorn. As B. B. King had put it, "the thrill is gone."

Dusty stood, brushed the grass off the legs and chest of his old, stained jean bib overalls. He was in his early twenties with dark hair and eyes. He did a quick check that he hadn't lost any of his kit in the tumble. His pack was solid, no harm done. He used the skank tied around his neck to wipe away the dust and grime of the train trip. The black and white paisley hand-kerchief was pretty much a required bit of gear for any serious train hopper. You got dirty traveling this way and a skank was a kind of code to other hobos and nomads that you were of their tribe.

"And welcome back to Philly, Dusty," he said, wiping his mouth and looking around the rail yard. "I love what you've done with the place." The longer Dusty was on the road, the more he had discovered the value of talking to himself.

Stacks of red, yellow, and blue cargo containers the size of 18-wheeler trailers were piled four-high in rows all along the edges of the yard like a child's city of giant Lego bricks. It was after sunup and Dusty figured he had better get out of the yard before the railroad bulls spotted him. He slid his old multi-frequency crank-powered radio out of his pack and snapped it on. The radio was held together mostly with generations of many-colored duct tape and some Disney stickers. It had an old camera strap affixed to it so Dusty could keep it hanging around his neck. He had it tuned to the frequency used by the railroad dispatchers and rail yard security here in Philly. The blog post from wanderlost.com he had read on his phone gave the frequency to spy on the rail authorities and rail cops. It also said that this particular stretch of the Philly yard was easy to get off at since it was sparsely patrolled and parts of it were a security camera dead zone. Hopefully the blogger wasn't a green-horn, or worse, a hawk, setting folks up to fail for their own troll-ish amusement.

It was already getting muggy and the sun hadn't been awake that long. It was going to be a hot one. He slipped the shoulder straps on his overalls off and let the bib drop to his waist like a loincloth. He pulled off his sweat-and-dirt-stained ICP T-shirt, wrung it out, and stuffed it in his pack.

Dusty moved between the numerous lines of rails, looking for his way out, when he felt an invisible tug at his stomach and his balls as he crossed a deep-sunk pair of tracks. It was the same feeling you might get if you were suddenly afraid or caught. Instinctively, he knelt low to the rails and ran his hands along the steel tracks, still warm from a train's passing. He could smell the brasslike scent of the metal, the earthy musk of the hot gravel. Dusty closed his eyes and read the rails, letting the faint vibrations and resonance tell him the story it had been trying to tell.

Someone on that train got off here a little while ago, the Rail said to Dusty, *her name was Alice,* and he could almost make out her face, the faint scent of sweat and soap on her skin, though he had never met her. *Something . . . b . . . a . . . d . . .* a strobe of red light, a smear of greasy white . . . the Rail grew silent. He stood up, that was all of the story the vibration had held. Something bad happened to this Alice. Well, that sucked. He'd help her out, if he knew any more but that was it. The Rail had gone silent. "Sorry, Alice," he said.

Dusty headed toward the high chain link fence with the coiled barbed wire at the top and was gratified to see the torn flap in the fence right where the blogger, Sunshine Sister, had said it would be. Her hoboglyph was there on the steel pole beside the flap, drawn in pink and silver Sharpie. It would look to most like some random graffiti, perhaps a tagger's signature, but to those who knew the secret language it said this was a good road to follow.

A lot of nomads didn't use the hobo symbols anymore, depending on online message boards, texts, websites, and emails to pass along information, but Dusty and a few others respected the old ways, and the Code of the Road that all real hobos followed. "Should never have doubted you, *hermosa*," he said to his long absent fellow nomad. *"Gracias."*

He lifted the loose bit of steel link fence and slipped under and onto the public street. His arm reminded him it was unhappy, but, all in all, his trip back east was going pretty well. He had already applied through his phone to a couple of tech temp agencies that needed experienced coders and he had a crash space lined up with his friend Moxie Dolittle until his first paycheck arrived. He still had walking-around money in his pockets, and he thought about finding a nice air-conditioned movie theater today, eating popcorn, chilling and seeing if he could find a good flick until he met up with Dolittle tonight at the bar.

A patrol car with flashing yellow lights and a CSX railroad corporation logo on the door sped around the corner and pulled up beside Dusty. A bull-necked white guy with a crew cut and wearing a security guard uniform, complete with name tag that said "Marty" on it, climbed out the car.

"What the fuck you think you're doing, amigo?" Marty asked, the challenge implicit in his voice.

"Just walking down the street, man," Dusty said. "You?"

"That's 'officer,' not 'man,' sport," Marty said. "You freight-hopping? You jump off that train that just came through?"

Dusty shook his head and laughed.

"No, man," he said. "Just passing through, but great interrogation technique. Keep that up."

Officer Marty was now nursing a full-on mad. "Let me see some ID, shithead. You legal?"

"Ask your mom," Dusty said and wished he hadn't. Marty started to grab him, but Dusty took off a second quicker than the musclebound rail bull. He sprinted toward the freeway underpass down the street, hooking his bib back up to keep the cloth from slapping against his legs. That had been stupid, but it felt good. Marty shouted and took off after him, shouting into the radio mic mounted on his shoulder.

"Dispatch, I got a trespasser near lot 11," Marty rasped, already getting winded. "Hispanic male, early twenties. I caught him on the lot. He got abusive and violent. Send backup and notify Philly PD, he's headed north on South Delaware. I think he's high."

"Fuck you, *hijo de puta!*" Dusty shouted over his shoulder. He was catching his stride and starting to pull out and away from the cop. He heard the squeal of tires and another CSX security car came into view headed straight toward him.

This was going sideways fast. There wasn't a whole lot of anything to hide behind out here. Vast wooded, undeveloped vacant lots lay between the warehouses and the rail yards. He cut left sharp and headed for a field and treeline he saw in the distance. If he made it a big enough pain in the ass to catch him the bulls would most likely give up. Dusty slid down a low gravel ravine and crossed two more sets of train tracks. He heard Marty shouting to the cop in the car back on the road, then he heard him begin panting again and the screech of the car peeling out.

Dusty reached the edges of the wooded lot. It looked to be a few acres of undeveloped grassy field with small stands of trees dotting the land. He heard a rapid chirp of static-y conversation over his radio between bulls and the rail yard dispatcher. The real cops were on their way now too. Swell.

"Yeah, welcome to fucking Philly, Dusty," he muttered as he hit the first patch of trees and dove into the cover. He turned the radio off and peeked back after he was about fifteen yards into the trees, no Marty. He paused for a minute and tried to assess his options. He could come out and try to show the real cops he wasn't high and deny the rail bull's charges. But that was risky. A lot would depend on the Philly cops that showed up and how closely they worked with the rail bulls. Fuck.

He wondered for a moment if he had the time to try to work a little Juggalo Juju. He had his Joker Cards and maybe a swallow or two of Faygo soda in a plastic bottle in his pack to try to wake the Great Milenko of the Dark Carnival, weave an illusion to hide him, or distract the bulls. Probably not. Most of his magic didn't work well in broad daylight and it was doubtful the cops would be nice enough to wait for dark.

Dusty decided to skirt the edges of the trees and stay low in the grass, try to work his way back to a factory and warehouse complex further back on the other side of the empty lots. He heard Marty nearby, gulping down air like it was Mountain Dew. He heard the rail cop thrashing around in the tall grass, searching for his quarry. Dusty was still, silent. He waited until the sound grew fainter and then he moved low and slowly, making sure he wouldn't give away his position.

It was times like this he wondered if maybe his folks had been right in trying to talk him out of taking up the pack and joining the Brotherhood of the Freight Train Riders, as some nomads—modern-day hobos—called themselves. His dad had been a civil rights organizer for his fellow produce pickers in Pullman, Michigan, where he had grown up. His mom was a nurse and volunteered weekends at a needle-swap clinic in Detroit. They were both very civic-minded people and they tried to instill that in all their kids.

Dad had did what he always did when he was pissed and disappointed with one of his kids when Dusty had told them at dinner shortly after his eighteenth birthday that he was going nomad. Dad looked down at his plate, his knuckles white as he clenched his fork. Dusty knew dad was counting to ten just like *Abuelo* had taught him to do as a kid. Dusty still heard his father's words today, three years later, right now, hiding from the bulls in the tall grass. *"So, you've decided you're going to be a bum? You've been listening to all those bullshit stories from Uncle Tomás, huh?"*

And he had. Uncle Tomás, Dad's brother, drove a long-haul produce truck and he had done a stint in the Army and then went nomad for almost a decade when he got home from the Gulf. His stories were amazing, the things he'd seen out on the Rail, on the Road. The people he'd met, the adventures he'd had. Hell, yeah, Dusty had been listening to his uncle and he was going to go out there and experience it for himself. And it had turned out to be about 50-50 as to how much bullshit and how much truth was in Uncle Tomás.

Bullshit or not, none of his uncle's words of wisdom were going to help him out of this. He risked a peek up through the tall grass. The CSX security car and a Philadelphia police car were parked on the side of the road at the edge of the field. The city cops and the bulls were talking and scanning the field. Dusty shrunk back down, keeping his eyes on his pursuers, and reached out with his hand to move along the grassy floor toward his only hope of escape. His fingers touched something wide and cool. It felt like smooth leather, then his fingers touched something wet and sticky. Dusty gasped and his head shot around. He was touching the severed torso of a woman.

There was no head, no arms, only bloody stumps. His fingers were wet from touching the pooled blood of the skinned patches where her breasts had been cut off. She had been severed below her rib cage and her nearly bloodless entrails spilled out, but some part of Dusty's screaming brain registered that the grass was unstained with blood. He stood without even realizing what he was doing. In a distant part of his awareness he heard the cops shouting at the edge of the field, but he had forgotten about them, about escaping. He was looking at the dead woman's severed torso lying in the grass, and the other torsos, like pale mottled islands, scattered across this part of the field. There were a half-dozen victims, or part of victims.

A strange familiarity overtook Dusty's perceptions as he looked at his fingers stained with blood, a certainty that had no logical inference. *This blood.* "Oh, Alice," he whispered. There was something else about this grotesque scene too, something familiar and old . . . something about a hobo jungle and murders . . . it was on the tip of his brain, struggling against his fear and Alice's silent screams.

They tackled him hard, his face was in the scratchy grass. He saw an ant climbing Alice's sickly flesh. "Don't you fucking resist," the cop with a knee in his back and his voice in his ear said. "You understand? *Me tienes?*"

"Yeah, yeah," Dusty shouted. The pain had shaken him out of his horror and chased his memory away. "I'm not resisting, officer, fuck!"

"Watch your goddamn mouth, kid," the cop snarled.

"Sweet Jesus." It was Marty's voice. "Look . . . what is . . . is this real?"

"Awww shit," said another voice, another cop. "We need to call somebody . . . everybody. Fuck me."

They pulled Dusty to his feet, and he saw the sick horror on the bulls' faces as they looked across the archipelago of bloody meat. Dusty figured he should at least try to see if any of these guys were members. It was worth a shot. He looked from face to face. "The wheel turns," he said.

Marty narrowed his little spit-colored eyes at him, "What the fuck you talking about, asshole?"

Dusty sighed. "Nothing." He looked at the madness laid out before him in the field. "Nothing at all."

Heck sat on the hard plastic bench in the waiting room of the Cape Fear Valley Medical Center ER, his face a mottled patchwork of bruises and cuts. Televisions bolted in brackets near the ceiling droned on. One was on ESPN, another CNN, a third, the Weather Channel. Heck had no idea what any of them were saying. He stared at the six inches of scuffed floor in front of him and occasionally over to his mother, Elizabeth, who had finally fallen asleep on the bench next to him, Heck's riding jacket draped over her as a blanket.

It had been thirty-six hours since they had brought Roadkill and the other survivors of the clubhouse shooting here. It had been twenty-four hours since Elizabeth had bailed him out of the Harnett County Jail and they had come straight here and began the wait. Most of the local club members and their family were here, though hospital security had tried to chase them off. Elizabeth finally told the bulk of them to head over to her house and she and Heck would keep them posted if anything changed. A few had remained, loitering outside the ER, to act as security for Heck and Elizabeth, just in case. Occasionally, a member would show up with coffee and food. Heck declined the kind offers, despite Elizabeth's urging.

Jim Gilraine, the MC's road captain, was out of surgery and in the ICU. His wife, Wendy, had been allowed to be back there with him. Wendy was a head nurse at the VA and knew a lot of the staff at Cape Fear Valley, so they let her sit with her husband.

When Heck had first walked in to the ER, Wendy had strode over to him and slapped him hard across the face. "God damn you, Heck!" Wendy had said, hot ribbons of tears running down her cheeks. "Everything's gone to shit since Ale died and you came back!" By the time the doctor came out and told her how Jim was doing, Wendy had apologized. Heck hugged her and told her it was okay. Thing was, he agreed with her.

Time passed. Heck knew that by the face of the clock on the ER wall and the fact he was out of cigarettes. The surgeon, a tired, pissed-off looking man in his early thirties with blond, receding hair, dressed in green surgical scrubs, walked out and approached Heck.

"You the Humes family?" he said. His voice had a tight angry edge to it. He looked with disgust at Heck's MC cut draped over Elizabeth as she began to blink and awaken, sitting up.

"Yeah," Heck said standing. "How are they?"

"Jeffery," the doctor began.

"Jethro," Heck interrupted.

"I don't care what his bullshit biker name is," the doctor said. He was tired and the anger slipped out. Unfortunately, Heck was tired too. He began to reach for the surgeon, rage flashing in his eyes.

"Watch your goddamn mouth . . ."

"Hector!" Elizabeth said. Heck stopped and took a step back. "Please, doctor," she continued. "How's Jeffery?"

"We got the bullets out," the doctor said, keeping his eye on Heck as if he were watching a venomous snake ready to strike, "but the bullets seemed to be made of a soft metal and they fragmented. There was a lot of damage to his lungs and his intestines, but we managed to get all the fragments out. His vital signs are looking strong, especially considering the damage and that's optimistic. He's stable now, but still not out of the woods."

"And Glen?" Heck asked.

"Mr. Hume . . . didn't make it, I'm sorry," the doctor said. Heck slumped back on the bench next to his mother. "There was just too much damage, too much trauma." He looked to Elizabeth. "Is there a Mrs. Hume? Any other relatives we should notify?"

"Glen's wife is deceased," Elizabeth said, her voice catching. "We're all the family Jethro has left."

The doctor nodded, and rubbed his face. He sighed. "I hate to say this, but your family needs to be more damn careful how they play with guns. The nurses will be bringing you some paperwork we need to have filled out in regards to Mr. Hume's body, and the homicide investigators will want to interview you as well. I am sorry for your loss." He walked away.

Elizabeth hugged Heck tightly and he hugged her back. A lifetime of small moments created a mosaic, glittering flashes of a life of compassion, integrity, and most of all love. When you have no real father, men come into your life to fill those shoes. If you're lucky they are good men. Glen Hume had been one of the best men Heck had ever known. Glen had treated Heck like his own, especially when Heck and Ale fought, which was often. Jethro was his brother in all the ways that mattered.

Crushing sadness and stinging anger struggled through the fog of exhaustion for control of Heck's soul. His mom sobbed a little but she composed herself quickly; she knew she had to. Heck suddenly felt sad for her, she didn't get the luxury of opening herself up to grief, letting it run and drain away. She was a Sinclair, and now, even if she could never wear a cut, never hold a leadership role, she was still an original in the Jocks, and they needed her.

"Go home," Heck said. "I'll deal with the cops."

"The way you almost dealt with the doctor there?" she said, rubbing her eyes. "No."

"I'm good," Heck said. "That's shit, I'm not good, but I can handle the cops. I know one of the detectives and I'm pretty sure he'll be running the show."

"Who?" Elizabeth asked. "Royal?" Heck nodded. "He and Ale always got along pretty good."

"We can talk," Heck said. "I swear we'll be cool." Elizabeth hugged him again, tighter.

"If you had been there," she said in his ear, her voice and heart both cracking, "I don't know what I'd . . ."

"It's okay Mom," Heck said. "It's okay."

"I love you, son."

"I love you too."

. . .

A hand held out a fresh pack of Lucky Strikes a few inches from Heck's face. He couldn't say how much time had passed since Mom had departed with a Blue Jock security escort back to her house. He glanced past the smokes to the ever-vigilant wall clock. It had been forty-five minutes. Heck took the pack of cigarettes and looked up into the clean-shaven face of Detective Royal Elkins with the Harnett County Sheriff's Office. Royal was black. He wore his hair in a short fade haircut. He was a good half a foot taller than Heck and was wearing a rumpled Persian blue sports coat, a button-down cream broadcloth shirt, black slacks, and a pale blue tie loose around his neck. Royal looked like he hadn't slept in a spell and mostly likely the last time he did it was in these clothes.

"You still smoke these nasty things?" Royal asked

"That I do," Heck muttered, taking the cigarettes. "Thanks."

Royal sat down next to the biker. "What happened, Hector?" he asked. "I need to know."

"Me first," Heck replied, tapping the box of cigarettes against his palm. "I need to know what the fuck happened in church. I was late to the meeting." He nodded toward the ER doors and got up. "You show me yours and I'll show you mine." Royal followed him outside and waited for him to light up and take his first drag of a Lucky.

"Okay," Royal said. "Just don't jerk me around, Heck." Heck nodded and remained silent. Royal retrieved a slender notebook from his jacket pocket and flipped it open. "Okay, the shooters are a Jordan Arwood . . ."

"Lance," Heck said with a sigh. "Our secretary."

". . . and Kenneth Roxler," Royal concluded.

"Ghoul," Heck said. "Our treasurer. You're fucking kidding me. Two of our officers, both of them members of the MC for over fifteen years."

"Apparently, they just opened up in the executive meeting," Elkins said. "They shot and killed Brandon Coons, Jason George . . ."

"Fisheye and Torque," Heck said. "Shit."

". . . and wounded the Humes. I'm sorry Glen didn't make it. The docs told me it looks like Jeff will. Your road captain, Jim Gilraine, shot Arwood and Roxler dead, but he was hit prior to returning fire. I just tried to talk to him a while ago."

"What did he say?" Heck asked.

"He told me to talk to his lawyer," Royal said with a chuckle, "and a few other colorful things. Most are physically and ethically impossible for me to do."

"Jim's got a concealed carry permit. He's got a wife and kids. He's legit."

"Yeah, I know, and it sounds like it was a good shoot. I understand why he lawyered up, I'm the Po. I'm not after him. I'm just trying to figure out what the hell is going down with the Blue Jocks, Heck. I've got reports over the past six months of half a dozen Jocks from different chapters all over the state getting busted for transporting heavy weight and distributing. Ale Mckee would never have stood for that, or let those kind of scumbags wear Jock colors. I suddenly got Jocks showing up dead on what should be routine bail jump apprehensions, and now two of your club officers suddenly decide to shoot up the rest of the Jocks' leadership? It's sounding to me like a civil war is brewing in the MC. Now, your turn. What's going on?"

Heck blew smoke out of his nostrils and regarded the cop. "I can't tell you shit about club business or club members," he finally said. "I also can't refute a single thing you just said." Royal nodded.

"Who's doing this to Ale's club, Heck?" Royal said. "I've heard you and Ale had a rough finish, but I also know how proud he was of you. The Jocks were very important to him, to your grandfather. Now someone is turning them into something ugly and wrong. You going to let that happen?"

"No," Heck said, dropping his dying cigarette and crushing it under his boot. "No, I'm not."

"Let me help you, then," Royal said. "Give me a name."

"I'm not a hundred percent on who it is yet, Royal." Heck looked across the crowded hospital parking lot. The sun was spilling umber fire, bleeding ribbons of pink, orange, and violet across the darkening blue horizon. The gasping light was reflected across the windows and roofs of the parked cars. Night was still a ways off but it was coming, inevitable. "When I'm certain, you'll know. You'll know."

"Don't do anything stupid, Heck," the investigator cautioned. "Whoever it is, they ain't worth spending the rest of your life in a box." Royal slipped a business card out of his shirt pocket and handed it to Heck. "I'll let you know if I turn up anything on my end. You be sure to do me the same courtesy. I got to go take a few more statements and collect the bullet evidence. Get some sleep."

Royal walked away. Heck watched the sky for a while. His gut told him Cherokee Mike was behind all this, but what if it wasn't? Mike had made a good argument that the Jocks had a long list of people who wanted to do them harm. It could be any of them. A suspicion twisted in his mind like a fat worm on hot concrete. He pulled his phone out of his jacket pocket and called a number from his contact list.

"Big Papa," Heck said when the call went through to a certain club member. "It's me. Yeah, I'm still at the hospital. Jim and Roadkill's out of surgery. They think they're going to be okay. Listen, man, I need you to grab a few of the boys and get down here. I have a bit of misdirectional fuckery I need your help with . . ."

A half-hour later, a dozen loud, cussing, angry Blue Jock bikers streamed through the sliding doors of the ER like a raging leather-and-denim-clad tsunami. They began to demand information about the condition of their fallen comrades, dead, and still breathing. They berated, threatened, bellowed, and snarled. Leading this full-frontal assault was Mason "Big Papa" Shupe, a roaring redheaded and bearded giant who looked like he might have just stepped off a Viking longboat. Mason had been a member of the Jocks for almost ten years and he had more than little bit of Loki in him.

The bikers badgered the staff behind the admissions counter with belligerent questions and growing threats and soon had the staff from the triage bays and even the ER security guards all engaged in the growing ruckus. That was when the bikers began to argue, push, and scuffle with each other. Things rapidly began to spiral into a full-fledged riot. Under that cover Heck slipped back into the ER through the ambulance entrance, unnoticed in the chaos.

Heck turned a corner and found himself face-to-face with the doctor who had come out to waiting room after Jethro's surgery. The doctor's eyes widened in recognition, and then fear, as his weary mind suddenly caught up with his senses. Heck cold-cocked him in the nose and pulled him into a room that was labeled as storage, tossing him to the floor and locking the door behind him. The doc was clutching his bleeding and swollen nose as he glared up at Heck.

"You little bastard," the doctor snarled through his cupped hand. "I'm going do have you and your mouth-breathing friends arrest—" Heck pulled the 9mm pistol Mason had brought him from the back of his jeans waistband. He aimed it at the doctor's face.

"Shut up," Heck said. The doctor shut up. "Now, where do I find Jethro and those bullets you pulled out of him?"

"I'm not going to help you." The doctor gingerly poked his obviously broken nose.

"Yeah, you are," Heck said. "I've had about a pitcherful of a day in a fucking shot glass, doc. I'm done even trying to be nice. Tell me or I'll pistol whip you until you have to breathe thorough a straw, motherfucker, and we'll see if your goddamn insurance company covers the straw."

Heck rapped the side of the barrel of the gun across the doctor's nose and the man on the floor gasped in pain and jumped in fear. "Mr. Hume is in ICU recovery bay 23, straight down this hall. The bullets are still in the surgical theater. It's around the corner to the left, second door. It's labeled, if you can fucking read, you redneck moron."

"Wallet," Heck said, still pointing the gun. The doctor fumbled and handed a slender leather Burberry wallet to the biker.

"You robbing me now too?" the doctor said sullenly. A light flared behind Heck's green eyes and he cocked the pistol and ground the barrel into the bridge of the doctor's nose. The doctor looked to the floor and visibly shuddered.

"One more fucking word, one syllable . . . one cross look and I'll spray your fucking brains all over this room. I lost friends today, family, and I don't really give a shit what you think about any of it." Heck pulled the driver's license out of the expensive wallet. He tucked it into a pocket of his leather jacket and dropped the wallet into a sharps container with the bio-hazard symbol bolted to the wall. "Now we know where you live, where your family fucking lives. You whisper a word about any of this to a cop, to your fucking priest, to your goddamned barista at Starbucks, and we'll pay you a visit. We clear? Are we?"

"Yes," the doctor said, nodding. "Yes!"

"Got another smartass comment to share, asshole?" The doctor shook his head. "Good. Now sit there and you wait at least twenty minutes before you walk out of here and remember, we'll all be watching you."

Heck exited the room. He slid the gun back into the waistband of his pants and pulled the driver's license out. He paused for a second and noticed the blood on his hand from breaking the doctor's nose. He dropped the license into a trash can in the hallway and headed toward Jethro's room.

"Heck!" The voice came from behind him. He spun and began to go for the gun but stopped when he saw it was Jimmie Aussapile.

"Jimmie? What are you doing here?"

"We heard what happened," Jimmie said, walking toward his squire. Jimmie was dressed in work jeans and steel-toed boots. He wore a jeans jacket with a Harley patch over the left breast and a black T-shirt. The ever-present *Squidbillies* baseball cap remained planted on his head. Jimmie looked half-worried and maybe a little pissed. "Me and Layla rode up to see if we could help. She's at your mom's place. What the hell is going on out in the lobby and what are you doing back here?"

"Getting to the fucking bottom of this," Heck said, and began walking again.

"Why you got blood on your hands?" Jimmie asked, hurrying to follow him.

"'Cause I've been dicking around for too goddamn long," Heck replied. "People have paid for it."

Heck and Jimmie entered Jethro's room like they were entering a church, slow and silent. There were machines huddled around Roadkill's bed, breathing for him, easing his pain and listening to the shaky song of his heart. Heck had never seen Jethro so still, so helpless. His throat tightened and the breath froze in his lungs.

"I'm sorry, son." Jimmie's voice behind his right shoulder. "Jethro's a tough knot, he'll pull through."

"I'm going to kill them all, Jimmie," Heck said in that even, cold voice that never seemed to be entirely his own. "Every son of a bitch that did this, that made this happen. They're all six feet under."

Jimmie started to try to calm Heck down, but he understood exactly what he was feeling right now and he knew he'd be a liar if he said he hadn't been here himself many times over the years and the battlefields. He stayed silent and placed a hand on his friend's shoulder.

"I got your six," Jimmie said softly. Heck stepped beside the bed and clutched the cold steel rail, looking down at Jethro.

"You keep napping, you lazy sod," Heck said with a knife cut of a smile. "I got this one, man. You rest." He stood beside Jethro's bed for a few moments and then turned and headed for the door.

"Now?" Jimmie asked, following him.

"Bullet," Heck said.

"Bullet?"

The surgical theater smelled of industrial cleaner trying to smother out the fresh smells of bowel and blood. Heck looked around the room and then found two slightly deformed bullets in a small, stainless steel, kidney-shaped tray. A tagged police evidence bag was on the table next to them but they had not yet been bagged. Heck picked up one of the bullets and held it up in the bright lights of the theater.

"Fucking silver," he nearly spit. "They don't flatten out as much as lead rounds do."

"So the shooters were gunning for Roadkill," Jimmie said. "They knew he was werefolk."

"That ain't public fucking knowledge, Jimmie, outside the Jocks," Heck said, slipping the bullet in his jeans pocket. "They wanted them all dead, they just knew they'd need something special to take Jethro out. You don't just pick up silver bullets over at Dave's Gun O' Rama."

"You figure the bullets will lead you to who put the shooters up to it," Jimmie said. Heck nodded.

"It already fucking has." Heck held up the bullet he left in the tray for Royal to bag and tag. "This mark right there, that's not rifling, it's a maker's mark." Jimmie squinted at the round and saw a tiny mark, like a "c"—a crescent. He looked back to Heck, who had dropped the bullet back into the tray and was already headed for the door. "Goddamned Bitches of

Selene," he said. "Only folks around here that routinely deal in silver ammunition."

"Wait, Heck!" Jimmie called out. He quickly wiped any prints off the silver round and hurried to follow his squire through the door into the hall. "The Jocks carry silver rounds too!"

"I know, but not with that fucking mark, Jimmie," Heck said, heading for the ambulance entrance he had initially come in through. "The Bitches have hated us for years, since the beginning of the MC back in the seventies. My granddad and Ale had to scrap with them."

"Yeah I remember," Jimmie said, "I was along on a few of those runs, but—"

"Looks like they've decided to get some payback," Heck said, interrupting.

"Wait a second," Jimmie called out, following Heck into the parking lot. "The Jocks and the Bitches have had a truce, a peace that's held for over twenty years. I was around for that too. Why would they suddenly decide to piss all that peace and quiet away to start a war?"

"Ale's dead," Heck said. He'd reached his T5 Blackie and was putting on his helmet. "The MC's in limbo. Cherokee Mike is sniffing around smelling blood. The Bitches are predators, top of the ladder, maybe they figured it was time to make their move."

Heck climbed onto the bike and it snarled to life.

"Where you going?" Jimmie asked.

"To get some straight goddamn answers," Heck said. He slid the steel demon mask over his face.

"Wait, wait!" Jimmie said stepping toward his squire. "Heck, you go off half-cocked and everything is going get worse!"

If Heck had a response it was lost to the bike's revving engine and muffled behind his mask as he sped out of the parking lot and vanished from sight.

"Damn it, Heck!" Jimmie said. He ran around the corner of the building toward the parking lot that faced the ER's main entrance. There were police cars at the curb, their blue lights strobing. Jimmie saw several grinning Blue Jocks being led away in cuffs and a crowd of ER staff and patients watching the show.

Jimmie reached his own bike, a 1980 Harley-Davidson Shovelhead FXE 1200. The tank on the 1200 was black with the silver, three-spoked symbol of the Brotherhood of the Wheel on either side. His handle, Paladin, was inscribed in the same cursive script as on his rig under the symbol. The bike had wide and high ape handlebars. Jimmie had managed to find one of the bikes with the engine package used by biker cops back in the day. The extra power of the cop engine let the bike travel much faster, but the trade-off was that it was a bear to handle. Jimmie had bought it when he was still in high school and he and his dad had tinkered with it for years.

He and Layla had ridden the bike up. It was like waking up a part of him that had been hibernating for a long, long time. The weather had been good and given what was going on, Jimmie figured he might be riding with the Jocks again until things got resolved. That was the excuse he gave himself anyway. The sensation of having the love of your life's arms tight around your waist while the road, the world, rocketed by, smears of kinetic color, the burning morning sky spread out before you like a painting wrought just for you, was like feeling the music of the world, the song of life in the rush of wind and the pulse of the motor.

Jimmie took off his baseball cap and stowed it in his saddlebag. He slipped his half-face helmet and sunglasses on and keyed the Bluetooth CB mic that was built into his brain bucket. "Break 2-3, Break 2-3 . . . Heck you there? Come back." He thumbed the electronic ignition and the Harley grumbled to life, like a slumbering dragon who didn't care to be disturbed. There was no answer to Jimmie's hail. "Well," the trucker said to no one in particular, "shit." He sped away from the parking lot and out onto Village Drive. Jimmie knew where Heck was headed and he knew he had damn well hurry.

Jimmie caught a red light at Roxie Avenue. Another bike, a 1976 Harley chopper with stretched-out forks and ape bars like Jimmie's own ride pulled up alongside him. Jimmie glanced over at the other rider. His heart jerked and spasmed in his chest.

The rider wore no helmet. He was a giant of a man, close to six foot five, with a toned, muscled body. His hair was an inferno of red and fell to his broad shoulders. He had wide muttonchops and a handlebar mustache the same color. His eyes were hidden behind Ray-Ban aviator sunglasses. He smiled at Jimmie with perfect white, even teeth.

"Jimmie Aussapile!" the rider said. "Long time, no see. You got fat, brother. I'm surprised you can still keep it up on that hog." The rider laughed, it sounded like a rain of gravel. Even though Jimmie was wearing a helmet and both bikes were idling loudly, he could hear every word the rider said perfectly, as if he were speaking into Jimmie's ear.

"Why'd they let you out?" Jimmie asked. "And what the hell are you doing here?"

If you had to guess the rider's age, he was probably in his late thirties to early forties. Intricate and colorful tattoo work of various snakes crawled up both his muscular arms, the colorful scale patterns almost seemed to slither of their own accord. He wore a black leather cut over an immaculate white T-shirt. The cut had a circular patch with a red 13 over the right breast. Jimmie was struck by and horrified by the association of resemblance that shot through his mind.

"I got time served for . . . community service, I guess you could call it," the rider replied. "Plus I owe the warden a few favors now, but I intend to make good on them for him."

"You stay the hell away from them," Jimmie said, "from him. We kicked your sorry ass once, Viper, we'll do it again."

"You sure did," Viper said. You, and old Ale Mckee, and Glen Hume . . . the others. Life takers and ball breakers that you were. You did what no one had ever done before." Viper's smile grew larger and his eyes dark. "You should be proud of that, Jimmie. Are you? Are you proud?"

"I try not to think about it, about you—what you did—any more than I have to," Jimmie said. "We did what we had to, and we'll do it again if you don't git."

"We?" Viper said. "Most of them are dead now, Jimmie. You can only cheat that big old black dog for so long, good buddy. Take the hint."

Viper blipped the throttle on the bike for emphasis. Jimmie glanced at the light to see if it had changed. When he looked back at Viper he saw the giant of a biker merged with his bike—Viper's chest melted, flowing into the body of the chopper, joined in a mass of black blood, oil, guts, and cables, a bizarre centaur of meat and machine. "Stay the fuck out of my way this time, old man," Viper rumbled, his voice vibrating with the power of the bike's engine.

Jimmie blinked and Viper was normal again, just a big man sitting on his chopper. Viper shot through the intersection while the light was still red. Cars honked and swerved to avoid the chopper. Jimmie watched him vanish from sight and finally let the fear trickle through him like ice water. He sighed and when the light turned green he sped off to find Heck and stop a war.

The closest hotel Lovina found to Coalport was a Hampton Inn thirty miles away in DuBois, Pennsylvania. She checked into the cookie-cutter room and settled in. The latter process took about five minutes. It consisted of hanging up a few clothes and dropping her toiletries bag next to the sink located outside the closet of a bathroom. Everything else was in an Adidas gym bag she tossed on one of the two beds, the one closer to the door.

She called her boss, Lieutenant Leo Roselle, and updated him on her progress and assured him that she would pay for the room if she was here for more than a few days. They talked briefly about Russell and his wife and they both mourned a little for their mutual friend and colleague and for Treasure. Leo paid her the courtesy of not telling her to be careful. He ended the call by reminding her to collect receipts. She called Russ briefly to make sure he got home okay. He was at the hospital with Treasure and he sounded tired and sad, although he tried not to.

Next was a call to Jimmie where she learned of the horrible news about Heck's MC brothers. Jimmie said he and Layla would be in Cape Fear for at least a few days but to "holler" if she needed any help. Lovina ended the call and held her cell for a moment looking at it, then looked around the empty, silent room.

She cycled through her contacts list and found Max's number. The picture that came up under Max's name was one of her caught in mid-laugh, taken on their road trip to drop Max back off in D.C. It was rare for the shy professor to bust out in laughter but Lovina had caught it when they had stopped at a Shoney's in Virginia to eat. They had been talking about Heck's weird southern-Scottish brogue and both of them had tried to imitate it. The results, plus many hours on the road and not a lot of sleep, resulted in twenty minutes of giggles and the rare photo.

Max was beautiful, Lovina thought for the millionth time. In her photo, Max had a mane of curly black hair that fell below her shoulders and dusky skin, hinting of a Middle Eastern ancestry. Her dark brown eyes were behind glasses and they gave her an owlish look. She wore no makeup and Lovina didn't think she needed any. Her smile, her laugh, were rare but they were like the sun.

Lovina lay back on the still made bed and regarded Max's picture. The big green "call" button just below her laughing, frozen face. She'd done this so many times in the past year, wrestled with feelings inside her that she had no words, no frame of reference, for.

Lovina had had relationships, boyfriends, lovers, since she was seventeen, from high school, to her time in the Army, and then after with NOPD. She had dated, committed, and even had a scant few casual hook-ups and friends-with-benefits arrangements during her life. Some of her unions had been brief, others had lasted years. None of them had ever touched her as deeply as the way Dr. Mackenzie "Max" Leher had from the moment Lovina laid eyes on her in a Memphis juke joint.

In most cases Lovina was the one to walk away from her relationships. When she was young she always figured it was because she had so much she wanted to see, to do. She saw too many of her schoolmates, her cousins, get pregnant, get married, and never get out in to the world after that. She knew she didn't want that. Later, she thought it was because of her career, her desire to rise in very competitive and traditionally male professions like solider and cop. Then it had felt like it was the loss of her sister, her drive for justice, for the other forgotten victims, that seemed to make all her attempts at getting together with someone feel muted and distant. All that changed with Max. It terrified Lovina, more than any battle, any perp, any monster ever had. Max unlocked feelings in her that she had pretty much decided weren't in her. Until Max.

Lovina sat up and cleared the screen on her phone and plugged it up to her charger next to the bed. Until she knew and could define what she was feeling toward the Builder scholar, she needed to keep it to herself. It would be selfish and unfair to do otherwise.

She read an Octavia Butler novel she had downloaded to her tablet until she realized she was hungry, ordered a pizza and ate half of it while watching a *Law & Order* rerun. She fell asleep by 10:30.

The nightmare woke her at 4:30 in the morning. Lovina was sheened in sweat as she sat bolt-upright in bed. She had her .40 Glock in her hand aimed at nothing. She lowered the gun and rubbed her face. It had been the recurring dream of passing Raelyn on the side of the road again, only this time Raelyn is being led from the car, away from the hulking, advancing clown, by a boy probably no older than eleven or twelve.

The kid was a very light-skinned black kid and had a wild tangle of curly reddish brown hair. He was wearing a faded Baltimore Ravens jersey, jeans, and Walmart sneakers. He was frantic to get the girl away from the steadily approaching, gaily painted monstrosity. She could hear the clown's deep bass giggling this time as it closed in. Lovina tried to stomp on the brakes, tried to stop the car, but she couldn't. She wanted to grab her gun and shoot the lumbering thing that was passing her window intent on its prey.

She began to feel her dream fingers fumbling with the butt of her pistol. She looked down and some part of her realized she was altering the dream. The car jerked to a complete stop and Lovina snapped her head to the window. The ghastly, bloated face of the clown eclipsed her view. His teeth were yellow and his breath reeked of decay and blood. The pale paint only hid his pockmarked face at a distance. It reminded Lovina of the craters on some demonic moon. His eyes were not human, they were dirty windows peering into a void where a soul should be. His massive, viselike hand gripped her throat and began to squeeze. Panic swallowed her like frigid wildfire in her brain and guts.

"Keep driving . . . Loooo-veeeee-naaaaaa."

That was when she woke, her throat aching, clutching her gun. She staggered to the sink, gun still in her hand, and clicked on the harsh light above the large mirror. There was more grease paint smeared on her neck but this time she didn't save it. She scrubbed it off furiously, water splashing everywhere. She felt the fear eating her up, the fear of what was happening to her, to what she was becoming, and to how it was granting a window into her for some inhuman intellect to climb through. She almost cried, she was sobbing, her breath and the fear catching in her lungs, her diaphragm, choking her like the clown had tried to.

"Get it together," she croaked to her reflection, like a DI to a shavetail in Basic. "Get . . . it . . . together. You are no good to anyone like this."

Pops and Delphine came to her then and threw blankets on the fire eating her reason, stomped it out. Jimmie Aussapile was there too, surprisingly, a comforting presence, fighting the fire beside her dad and sister. Slowly, slowly, her breathing eased and her heart slowed. Her eyes stayed dry and that she counted as a victory. She took a long, hot shower until she was convinced there was no taint on her from the clown, then she slid into the bed and slept dreamlessly for another few hours.

Dave Wojick was waiting for her in the parking lot in an idling, dark blue Ford unmarked patrol car. The old police cruiser had whip antennas mounted all over the trunk. He offered Lovina coffee in a green paper cup as she got in the passenger-side seat.

"Didn't know how you took it," he said. "There's some cream and sugar in the bag."

"Thanks," she said. He pulled away from the hotel. For several moments there was only the sound of the struggling air conditioner and the squawking chatter of the police radio. "I appreciate you doing all this, Dave, but you really don't have to, especially on a Saturday."

"I kinda feel like I do," Wojick said, keeping his eyes on the road, "since it's an old friend of mine's case you're mucking around in, you get my meaning?"

"I see," Lovina said. "I already told you, I'm not here to make anyone look like an asshole. I'm just trying to find out what happened to this girl. I think her mom deserves that."

"Yeah, I know," Wojick said nodding. They were heading south on 219 now. "See, the thing is Jim Lubke caught this case and he was my old training officer. Jim was a good guy, a real good guy. He passed away a while back, right? Heart attack over in Philly. I feel kind of like I need to make sure, y'know, that you . . ."

"Don't fuck his case up?" Lovina said, nodding. Wojick chuckled. She sipped the coffee black. "I get that. I can respect it. I just don't usually work with partners and the ones I got are . . . well . . . unconventional."

"Speaking of unconventional," Wojick said. "I hear tell this trailer park is pretty weird. The guys in the Clearfield barracks, they usually respond to stuff in Coalport. That's the way it is in a lot of these little boroughs, they don't even have a sheriff, so we're the closest law."

"Same way with a lot of tucked-away parishes in Louisiana," Lovina said. "I get it."

"So anyways," Wojick said, nodding, "I've heard some pretty whack-a-doodle stuff about the Valentine Park."

"What kind of stuff?" Lovina asked.

"Believe it or not, clowns," Wojick said with a snort.

"Clowns," Lovina said flatly. She unconsciously glanced out the window to the side of the road but there was only the blur of passing trees.

"I know, right? I don't know what the freakin' world's coming to. Like we don't got enough real crap to deal with, people gotta make up crazy stuff to boot." Wojick looked over to Lovina. "You okay? You looking kinda . . . I don' know."

"I'm good," Lovina said, as much to herself as to Dave. "So, there've been clown sightings in Coalport? In the trailer park?"

"Yeah for like, I don' know, years." Wojick said. "The old guys who were on the road in the sixties and the seventies, most of them are retired, they got stories too. It kicked up a bunch in the last few years since everybody, all over, is going cuckoo for clowns all a' sudden. We still get about a half-dozen calls a year, people in Coalport reporting seeing stuff. Most of them come from the park. Me, personally, I think they're drinking too much cough syrup." He laughed, then looked over to Lovina, and stopped laughing. "But you don't do you?"

"I don't know," Lovina said. "Honestly, I've seen some strange things. I just don't know anymore. I try to keep an open mind best I can."

"Un-huh," Wojick said and went back to watching the road. "Keep an open mind . . . about evil clowns." He sighed and kept his eyes on the road. "Okey-doke."

. . .

It was midday by the time they reached the Valentine Trailer Park, coming in on Route 53. The summer sun was merciless, beating down on the grassy lots carved out of the thick, surrounding woods. The gravel road to the park was just off of State Route 3019 and shifted to a well-paved, unmarked black flattop once they passed the sign at the entrance. Wojick took a left into what appeared to be a circular road around the hub of the park. A small sign indicated this was the way to the manager's office. They drove slowly past a courtyard where a large crowd of the park's community was enjoying the summer weekend. For a second, Lovina thought they had several above-ground pools for the residents, then she realized they were the hulls of old pickup trucks converted into makeshift pools. For a second, she recalled her and her brothers and sisters playing in the spray of an opened hydrant down in the heart of the Tremé on a painfully hot August day when she was nine. The memory and the sound of the shrieks and laughter of the children made her smile. The circle continued south and at around roughly the six o'clock position there was a sign with an arrow indicating the way to the manager's office. Dave pulled the cruiser off to the side of the blacktop, parking in the grass. The two investigators climbed out of the cool car into the stale, hot air.

Lovina noted that past the circle and another row of trailers was a rolling hill that meandered into a vast, grassy field easily the length and width of several football fields. At the edge of that was deep, dark, shaded woods. Wojick shucked off his sports coat and tossed it in the car. His service sidearm, badge, ammo pouches, and cuffs were all clipped to his belt and visible. He was wearing a gray polo shirt and slacks. He kept his aviator sunglasses on and wiped his forehead with a hankie.

"Jeez, summer, right?" he sighed, heading toward the smaller courtyard the sign pointed to. Lovina had worn a white T-shirt and jeans. Her gun and police gear were also visible around her waist. She wore her police credentials on a lanyard around her neck and round, wire-rimmed sunglasses.

It was only a few yards to the front door of the small, classic Airstream trailer with the cardboard sign on the front door. Wojick's shirt was already darkening with sweat. He rapped on the door and after a moment there was a muffled "Yeah, yeah, coming!" and then the door creaked open. "Whatcha need?" the old man asked as he stepped out of the shadows and into the bright daylight. He was an inch or two under six feet and gaunt. His hair was thin and gray and pulled back tight away from his prominent widow's peak. He had a close-cropped gray beard and warm, but slightly unfocused, brown eyes. He was dressed in a rumpled Hawaiian shirt, blue with pineapples and gold apples all over it, and baggy cargo shorts. He had on black knee socks and leather sandals. He smiled like a child or someone high as a kite.

"Mr. Valenti?" Dave asked. "I'm Investigator Wojick with the state police. This is Investigator Marcou. I called you yesterday about the Dunning girl."

"Yeah," Valenti nodded, suddenly remembering. "Yeah, right, right. How you doing?" He nodded to Lovina. "How you doing?"

"Thanks for your time," she said.

"Hey, always want to cooperate with the fuzz, man." Valenti said. "Call me Bob." Lovina made a face, stifled a grin, and glanced over to Wojick, who didn't look quite as amused.

"Well, on behalf of the fuzz," Lovina said, "we appreciate it, Bob."

Valenti invited them inside the tiny trailer for coffee or pop, but the two investigators refused. Lovina noted that while the Airstream had every kind of imaginable antenna mounted on its roof, only adding to its overall UFO-like appearance, it didn't look like it had any air-conditioning and she imagined being inside the shiny metal trailer on a day like today would be like how a baked potato felt wrapped in foil. Valenti shrugged, gave them the goofy stoned grin again, and shut the door to the trailer. He flipped over a laminated magnetic sign on the door to indicate he was out, and ambled back in the direction of the parked police cruiser.

"Not a lot to tell you," Valenti said. "Malyssa and Raelyn were good tenants. Paid their rent, not late too often and never any complaints. It was a shame what happened to that little girl. Mom's moved away now, been years. Mississippi, I think."

"Bob, did you know of anyone in the park with a grudge against Mrs. Dunning or her daughter?" Lovina asked. "Boyfriends? Wannabe boyfriends? Anyone close to them who might have a grudge, or an obsession with Raelyn?"

"You get any prowler or Peeping Tom complaints from the Dunnings?" Wojick added as they passed his car and headed to the other side of the circle, into a crowded tangle of corridors between trailers of all shapes, sizes, and ages.

"Anything like that, we pass along to you staties," Bob said, weaving through the maze. You could hear babies crying, lovers and parents shouting, TVs blaring. You could smell bacon cooking, and catch the pungent odor of weed, failing septic tanks, and even the weird chemical stench of someone cooking something illegal, moving between the tiny pocket worlds of different residents' lives.

"Well, I looked and we didn't get zip," Dave said. "Hardly any calls except for some emergency services, a few domestic brawls, and that big narc bust with the DEA last winter." He sniffed the air. "From the smell of things, we need to get the feds back out here again."

Valenti stopped and turned to face Wojick. "Yeah, well look, man, a lot of the stuff that happens here, you cops didn't believe it, didn't do nothing about, right?" The trailer manager stepped back a few steps from the big trooper. "Look, no offense, right, but after a while people just, y'know, stop calling for help, when nobody believes them, okay?"

"You tellin' me this has to do with the clown crime wave, Bobbie?" Wojick said, giving Lovina an eye roll as he said it.

"No!" Valenti said. "Look man, I think all that clown stuff is just because this park kinda got started from some old circus or something a long time ago, like back in the thirties or forties. There's all this rusted crap left over from whatever it was parked out by the old railroad tracks." He gestured in the general direction of the field and the woods. "The property owners never hauled any of it away. The park kids they tell stories, y'know like ghost stories, but the ghosts are clowns. I heard a few of the old-timers even talk about the stories they heard when they were kids, about the ghosts of hobos killed on the tracks before the railroad shut down. They've been doing it since before I got here and that was"—Bob seemed to struggle with chemically shrouded memory—"the seventies? The eighties? I don't know. Forever. People build stories, like houses, it's just what people do. All I'm trying to say is the cops stopped believing the people and the people just stopped trying to call out, y'understand, man?"

"An obvious failure for community-based policing," Wojick said dryly. "How about you, Bobby, you ever seen any scary clowns?"

"I . . . I don't know nothing," Valenti said. "You asked about police calls and I told you."

"Bob, what do the people say?" Lovina asked, stepping between the park manager and Dave, making eye contact. "The tenants? What do they tell you they don't say to the cops?"

"I don't think you'd believe it," Bob said. "This is a real strange place, officer."

"Lovina," she said. "I've been to a few strange places . . ."

"I'll bet," Wojick snorted, and crossed his arms. Lovina ignored him.

"Try me," she said to Valenti.

"Well, Raelyn asked me once, about a month or two before she went missing, if I had seen a particular car around the park, or if anyone here had a car like that. I told her no, no one I knew did."

"What car?" Wojick asked.

"She said it was like an old Ford," Bob said, struggling to recall. "It followed her to work a few times and then home. It scared the hell out of her because one night not too long before she vanished, the guy was waiting just out on the access road by the entrance to the trailer park. He followed her halfway to Tyrone that night. The next morning she came banging on my door, asking if that was a tenant's car. I said I didn't think so. I'm pretty sure I'd recall a car like that if I'd seen it. She was really scared and upset. That's how come I remember it so good."

"What kind of car was it?" Lovina asked.

"From how she described the grille maybe a Fairlane? It sounded like maybe it was a '66 from the way she described it, baby blue. Man, oh, man, I have some great memories of those days . . . at least I used to."

Lovina held eye contact with Valenti, trying to keep him focused. "Bob, did she get a tag, or anything off it, that might help us track it?"

"She said once he come up beside her and she saw him for a second before he passed. It was night but she said she could see him by the instrument lights."

"Did he have a big red nose and orange hair?" Wojick asked with a smirk. Lovina glared at him.

"Stocky," Bob said, fighting to pull the memory out of the swamp. "White guy with a crew cut, like military. He had a CCP parking sticker on his back window. She saw it when he passed her."

"CCP?" Lovina looked to Dave.

"Community College of Philadelphia," Wojick said, nodding as he made notes in a small notebook he had pulled out of his back pocket. "So Bobby, why the fuck didn't you tell any of this to the troopers who initially investigated after the girl disappeared?"

"I thought I did," Valenti said, looking like a deer in the headlight between the two investigators. "Didn't I?"

Wojick sighed and put the notebook away. He whispered, "Okey-doke" under his breath.

"You did good, Bob," Lovina said to the old hippie, but she was disappointed too. How many years were lost? Had this cost Raelyn her life? Most likely. Valenti sheepishly led them a few more yards around a few more corners to a lot that was currently occupied by a trailer with white vinyl shingles and a small enclosed porch shrouded in mosquito netting.

"This was their spot," Valenti said. He pointed to a small asphalt side road a few dozen feet away that trailed off from the main circular drive. "They used to park right over there. Like I said, not a lot to tell."

"What," Wojick said, "in the name of Sister Mary Elizabeth is that?" He nodded to a trailer on the other side of the road. It was an older model, a long, aluminum, 1950s Spartan, and it was painted completely jet black, even the windows. The surface of the trailer was covered with a strange pattern, a kind of squiggly bright yellow triskelion that looked like a union of stylized question marks and meat hooks. The whole pattern had an almost hypnotic effect that Lovina felt just looking at it. It was like the symbols were bright yellow worms twisting and undulating on the hot metal surface. It made Lovina's eyes itch and ache.

"Oh, that's just Calvin's place," Valenti said. "He kinda fancies himself an artist, I guess."

"You guess," Wojick said. "So, what's his story?" He live here when the Dunnings did?"

"Calvin? He's lived here since before I moved in, man. Yeah, he was one of their neighbors," Valenti said.

"Groovy," Wojick said and walked across the road toward the strangely painted trailer. Lovina followed as did Bob, but the manager stopped at the road and went no further. Wojick banged on the door, unclipping his badge from his belt. Lovina's hand dropped to rest on her holstered sidearm as she took up a position behind and to the left of the Pennsylvania trooper. There was no response to the knocking.

"Uh, Calvin, he, like, works nights, I think," Bob offered from back by the road. Wojick banged on the trailer door harder.

"State police," he said loudly. "Open up." After another long wait, the trailer door opened into cool darkness. A woman, curvy and pale with silver, purple, and blue hair that fell to her breasts opened the door. She wore a tight black T-shirt with the squirming yellow triskelion symbol prominently displayed on the chest. She had wire-rimmed glasses and her eyes were the color of pale blue glass behind them.

"Praise be to Hastur," the woman said in a soft, melodic voice. "Have you come to commune with madness and oblivion?"

"Uh . . . I'm . . . um, I'm Investigator Wojick," Dave said, holding up his badge. "Who are you?"

"The high priestess," the woman said. Another woman appeared out of the darkness, equally as pale with blond and pink hair, shaved close to her skull save for a long lock that fell across half her face. Her eyes were a darker blue and she had a tattoo of the strange squirming yellow symbol on her wrist. She wore a black tank top and cutoff jeans shorts. The new woman took up a position on the other side of the doorway.

"I am the acolyte," the other woman said. "How may we serve you," she nodded toward Dave's badge he was still holding, as if he had forgotten it, "and the false gods you grovel to?" Wojick seemed frightened and entranced by the two women, and Lovina stepped between the trooper and the doorway, her hand still on her gun.

"Calvin," Lovina said. "We got a few questions for him. Get him."

"The high priest, Hastur's beloved vessel, slumbers," the high priestess said.

"The sanctimonious light offends him," the acolyte said.

"Go get him," Lovina said, "or the sun won't be the only thing offending him. Now."

Lovina noticed now that the increasingly frigid darkness emanating from inside the painted trailer wasn't just shadow or an absence of light, it was like some kind of void that seemed to devour the sunlight that leaked in through the open door. There were no details of wall, furniture, anything past the doorway. Lovina's instincts tugged at her gut, her brain shouted for her to step back away from the door, from these people, if they were people.

"What the fuck you want, Jane Law?" a gravelly male voice said from the darkness. The accent was southern. It reminded Lovina of Pentecostal preachers and used car salesmen. A shade of a man appeared at the termination of the invading light. He was tall and gaunt, with pale skin covered in tattoos and a fringe of a blond beard. He had long, thinning blond hair that swept down from a prominent widow's peak and came to rest past his shoulders. He wore a ratty bright yellow terrycloth bathrobe that fell open to reveal his bare, wiry-muscled chest, and loose-fitting black pajama pants. Both women took up places on either side of the man, who seemed to glide silently to the very edge of the doorway and brace himself, with both arms raised, against it. He leaned into Lovina and she could smell alcohol, stale cigarette smoke, and perhaps a hint of charred meat. "You got my ass up now, what you and that stammering dickhole back there want?"

Wojick, seemingly free of the spell now, thanks to the insults, took a step closer to Lovina's back. "I'm sorry, scum-bucket, I didn't quite catch that," the statie said. The gaunt man laughed and shrugged. Tight, slender muscles rippled along his chest with the motion, like darting fish in a shallow pool.

"Just fucking with you, orificer." His eyes flicked to Lovina and he licked his lips. "So how can I help *you* today, lovely?"

"Calvin, I take it?" Lovina said.

"If you say so," Calvin replied.

"We're looking in the disappearance of Raelyn Dunning," Lovina said. "You were her neighbor. What can you tell us about that?"

Calvin's gaze became slightly hooded and he looked past the cops to Valenti, standing back on the narrow access road. "Nice. Thanks a hell of a lot, Bob!"

"Sorry, man!" Valenti called back. "They just kinda wanted to talk to you. I told them you work nights!"

"Hey, shit-for-brains," Wojick said, "talk to us, not to him!" Calvin's gaze snapped back to the cops, like a switchblade popping from its handle. "What do you and the Manson girls know about Raelyn?"

"She got herself lost," Calvin said. "Happens a lot around here, not that you fuckers give half a shit what happens to a bunch of trailer trash." He paused and focused on Lovina, as if he was only now seeing her for the first time. "Scratch that. You," he said to the Louisiana cop, "you do actually give a damn." He sniffed her and nodded, a wide smile coming to his skull-like face. "You've suffered loss, at our hands, well, the hands of my sibling, anyway. That's why you care. We walk numb in this life until we taste real pain. It's the greatest gift you can ever receive."

"What?" Lovina said. She had a strange sense of déjà vu, as if she had met this man, somewhere before. Calvin seemed satisfied with her response.

"Someone you loved was sacrificed to one of my family," Calvin said, "to him. I can smell it on you like a dollar whore in the summer sun."

"Hey, jackoff," Wojick growled, pulling the distracted Lovina away from the door and getting up in Calvin's face, "Shut the fuck up, or how about we toss your little shithole of a trailer and see if we find some magic mushrooms or somethin'."

"Or something," Calvin said. "Might not care for what you find neither. You got a warrant, pig-pumper?"

"I don't need a fucking warrant, asshole," Wojick snarled. "You're the poster boy for fucking probable cause."

"Really? 'Cause I got an ass-ton of witnesses right here that I'm sure will be glad to testify about how you violated my civil rights by illegally searching my residence after you got pissed off at me exercising my constitutional rights to free speech by calling you a jackass."

Lovina put a hand on Wojick's shoulder. "Dave, it's okay, it's okay. We need to do this right." Wojick turned and looked at her. "Cross every 'T,' dot every 'I.'" Wojick let Lovina lead him away from the door. She looked back at Calvin and his women. "We'll be back," she said. "I got some more questions for you."

"Ph'nglui mglw'nafh Cthulhu R'lyeh wgah'nagl fhtagn," Calvin said, looking at Lovina. "You come on back, sweetheart. Come on back! I'll tell you what's what." The door to the trailer banged shut, seemingly on its own. It took a moment for Lovina to reorient herself to sunlight, the hum of cicadas, the distant music from some radio, the sensations of life and sanity.

"You good?" Wojick asked. Lovina nodded.

"Yeah," she said. "I'm okay."

The drive back to her hotel was quiet except for the chatter on the police radio. Bob Valenti had offered to give them a copy of Calvin's lot application but when he returned with a tattered old file folder all it contained were few pieces of yellowed paper. The paper was a handwritten contract dating back to the early fifties that said the lot was rented for $20 a month in perpetuity to one "Calvin Luthor of Staunton, Virginia." No Social Security number, no previous address, no job references, nothing. It had been signed by Calvin and the owner of the property at that time and Bob told them that owner was long dead.

"Well, you were right to come down here," Dave said after a while. "We got some solid leads out of all this crap today, right? I'm going to run this guy's name and description and check with the cops in Virginia and maybe we'll get lucky and he used to own a Ford Fairlane." He glanced over to Lovina. She was looking out the window at the blur of forest passing by. "You, ah, you okay? What was that shit about sacrifice he was going on about? And all that weird shit he said there at the end, sounded like he was gargling a chain-saw covered in lube. You acted like it meant something to you, not just crazy falling out of that asshole's mouth. If you don't mind me asking. Not trying to neb into your business."

Lovina smiled a little at the courtesy tagged on at the end. She nodded, but kept looking out the window. "During Katrina, my sister was abducted by a bunch of sick sons of bitches, cultists to some weird ancient religion. They worship this . . . giant octopus-thing with bat wings. They ritually raped and murdered her and then left her in the ruins of a house that got hit hard by the hurricane, so no one would ever think her death was anything but an act of God. I guess in a sick way, it was, just not one of the gods everyone prays to. They didn't count on her sister being a cop with the NOPD. I think our buddy Calvin has got himself a similar cult running with his girlfriends."

"Shit, I'm sorry," Wojick said, and Lovina could tell the big cop meant it. "You think this asshole had something to do with your sister's death?"

"No," Lovina said. "All the members of that cult in New Orleans were murdered," she said. "Cases are still open." Wojick gave her a hard look for a moment.

"You seem awfully sure that none of them got away," he said. Lovina locked eyes with the trooper.

"I am," she said. "Awfully sure."

They drove the remainder of the trip in silence. It was late afternoon by the time the cruiser pulled back into the hotel lot. Wojick left the car idling so the A/C would remain on. Lovina gathered up her things.

"Thanks for the ride and the company, Dave," she said. "Keep me in the loop if anything comes of your digging?"

"Yeah, sure, you bet," Wojick said as she opened the passenger door and climbed out. "You know, you don't seem to like our boy Calvin for Raelyn's disappearance."

"I don't," Lovina said, "but I couldn't tell you why."

"Is it because he ain't dressed up like Bozo?" Lovina smiled and shook her head.

"Be safe, Dave." She shut the door and headed toward the motel. The cruiser drove away and was gone by the time she had entered her room. Lovina sat on the edge of her bed and enjoyed the air-conditioning for a moment, then she stood and began to gather up some of her stuff and pack it into the gym bag. She plugged her phone in to charge and kicked off her shoes and socks and lay down on the bed and closed her eyes. Eventually she slept.

When she woke it was cooler and the sun was lower in the sky. She gassed up the Charger at a local Wawa and bought a Coke and Snickers bar for her late lunch and forgotten breakfast. Soon she was on the road, headed back to Coalport.

When Lovina arrived in town she drove around to see the sights. That took about ten minutes. She was surprised to discover that Coalport had a museum dedicated to coal's importance to the town's creation. It kind of made sense, Lovina thought, given the name. She was even more surprised to discover a place on what passed for a main drag in the town called the Central Hotel. It looked more like a neighborhood bar to her than a hotel, but she went in just as the sun was ducking behind the treeline and got herself a small but comfortable room for the night. By the time she had finished a couple of brown, fat bottles of Old German beer and some excellent pizza, she figured it was time to go back to the Valentine Trailer Park.

The drive took a few minutes, and she parked the Charger just off North Hill Street in sight of the weathered sign and the one road into or out of the park and waited for the night to swallow the town whole. She fiddled with her radio, looking for something, anything. She found a few Christian music stations and some religious sermons on a few channels. Finally she managed to get a Top 40 station out of Altoona, playing a remix of "Despacito," by Luis Fonsi, Daddy Yankee, and Justin Bieber. She saw a few cars drive into and out of the park and a guy on a scooter with an orange plastic milk crate bungee-corded to the back to hold his gear. None of them were the mysterious classic Fairlane Bob had said had been following Raelyn.

The night was cooling off after an unbearable day. Lovina had the usual craving for a cigarette she would get on a surveillance, but she had quit over ten years ago and if ink-eyed monsters and homicidal shadows hadn't made her start back up, a little boredom sitting in a car wouldn't.

At nine, a Pennsylvanian State Police cruiser drifted down the gravel access road and stopped directly in front of Lovina's car. It kicked on its blue lights and she found a halogen spotlight stabbing into her eyes. She reached next to her for her ID.

The trooper, a tall, muscular white man, approached her with his Maglite trained on her eyes and hand on his gun.

"Evening," Lovina said through her open window.

"You lost, homegirl?" the trooper asked. "This ain't Philly, or even Dauphin, y'know? What you doing out here? Waiting for somebody to drop something off from over there at the park?"

Lovina felt all the irritation, all the frustration of having to deal with this idiot start to come out of her mouth. Then Pops was there. She remembered what he told her when she was a teenager, told her again when she had come home from her time in the Army. *"I don't care what your rank was or what you did for this country over there in the war; I don't care if you do become a police, you listen to me and you listen good, girl. When that flashlight's on you and that cop has his hand on his gun, all he's seeing is black. All it takes is one fool with a badge to destroy your life, maybe end it. You be polite, and you move slow, and you tell that cop every single thing you going to do before you do it. You hear me?"*

She sighed, flipped open her ID case and held it out for the cop to see. "I'm a cop," she said, "working a surveillance." The trooper took the case and looked at it, then back to Lovina. The irritation was beginning to well up into anger, but Lovina held it in check. She stayed cold and looked straight ahead, her hand on the steering wheel.

"This says Louisiana," the trooper said. "You're in Pennsylvania. Let me see your driver's license and registration."

"Yes," she said and tried to keep her voice even and neutral. "I am reaching over and getting them out of my purse now." If she had been Leo Roselle, or any other white cop, this wouldn't be an issue. "I'm working a case that occurred in your jurisdiction and was reported in mine." She handed the cop the identification. "I'm working with Investigator Dave Wojick out of the Greensburg barracks." The trooper was silent for a moment. Lovina knew he was making her wait for no reason other than he could. He was debating getting her out of the car and searching. She had to stay cool, even though the fact that she had to display such extraordinary discipline just made her more angry.

"Let me check it out," the cop said. "Keep your hands on the steering wheel." He used his belt radio to call it into the dispatch. Lovina waited. Several cars pulled into the park off the access road and more departed. They all got a good look at her and the trooper. Finally after about ten minutes, the dispatcher responded and gave the trooper the all-clear. The cop handed everything back to Lovina. "Okay, you check out," the cop said, handing the IDs back to Lovina, not even a hint of apology in his voice. "What *are* you doing out here in the middle of Bumfuck, Egypt?"

Lovina let some of the anger burn through her eyes. "My job." The cop waited to see if he'd get more. He didn't. He nodded and ambled back to his cruiser, driving off, and killing the light. "Fuck you," Lovina said to the cruiser's disappearing taillights as they bounced down the gravel road back toward Route 3019. Her cell phone buzzed, it was Wojick's number. She turned the phone off and stuffed it in her pocket. "And fuck you too, Dave," she said.

She decided to walk into the park, leaving the car out on the access road. She slammed the car door. Instead of following the circular road she and Wojick had driven in on, Lovina walked down the main road that led into the cluttered heart of the park that the circular road surrounded. In a few minutes she had let most of the anger go. Anger made you sloppy, could get you killed. At the point the road branched, Lovina kept walking straight, off the road and into the grass lanes between the trailers. It was well after nine now, but it was a summer night. She heard TV programs and music and human sounds of life in the trailers she passed. She walked past a double-wide where a group of people were sitting out in folding lawn chairs, talking and drinking beers. They got quiet as Lovina came into view.

"Evening," Lovina said, and flashed her badge. Several of the partiers, especially the younger-looking ones, tried to hide their beer cans and red Solo cups. Lovina gave them a dismissive wave. "You're cool. I'm looking into the disappearance of a girl, not checking IDs."

"Which one?" a young, pretty brunette in a pink bikini top and cutoffs asked.

"Which what?" Lovina said.

"Missing girl," the girl said. A boy, probably twenty at the oldest, nodded. He was wearing nothing but ripped-up faded jeans and lots of tattoos. He was smoking a cigarette.

"People go missing here all the time," the boy said. His eyes were glazed, probably weed. "If they send anybody it's a statie after everything done gone down. Nobody gives a shit."

"I do," Lovina said and almost immediately wished she hadn't. How many times had a cop said that to her growing up and she knew it was bullshit. They wanted something, and it wasn't to help. The kids got quiet. Childish Gambino's "Crawl" was playing thorough the screen door to the double-wide. "Her name's Raelyn Dunning and her mom's worried sick about her."

"I remember her," the little brunette said. "She had a baby. She lived here with her mom, right?"

"Yes," Lovina said. "Can anybody tell me if you heard anything about what happened to her? Anything could help."

"I heard Emmett got her," another girl said. Several of the kids nodded. A few chuckled.

"Emmett?" Lovina asked.

"She'll think younz all high," the cigarette boy said, pointing his smoke at Lovina.

"I don't give a fuck about the weed, or the beer, or the nine your friend over there's got stuffed halfway down his ass-crack, as long as he's not high enough to point it at me," Lovina said to the boy. "Who's Emmett, and what did you hear about Raelyn?"

"Emmett's a ghost," the brunette said. "He haunts the park, him and a bunch of other ghosts. He's a circus clown. He, like, died, when the train carrying the circus to another town derailed and crashed back there in the woods by the old tracks."

"I heard he was hobo," a boy who had remained silent until then added. "Got his throat cut by some psycho who escaped from Torrance and dressed himself up like a clown. He killed a farmer and his family and then he killed Emmett and some other hobos back there in the woods. When they found their bodies their faces had been so drained of blood they all looked like clowns too!"

"Gross!" a kid uttered. Several kids laughed nervously.

"Ewww," another kid said, looking up from her phone.

Lovina remembered her and her friends telling stories to each other about the Devil Man of Algiers. It could have been the same conversation transported through time. Each kid had a version of the myth, each added something in the telling and the hearing. If it weren't for the dreams, the white makeup, she would dismiss it all, but she had seen too many things and fought too many things to dismiss "Emmett" outright as an urban legend, at least not just yet.

"What about this Calvin guy?" Lovina asked. "What's his story?"

"I heard he's like a cult leader, y'know like that Jim Jones guy," one kid offered.

"Yeah, he's killed people," another kid said, "buries the bodies out in the woods. The ghosts are from his victims. That's what Roy's sister's friend Trish told me. She saw him and his crazy bitches dragging a body away."

"He's a vampire," the brunette said earnestly. "He sold his soul to Satan, or the Elder Gods or something. You stay out of the southeast part of the park. That's where all the drug dealers and Calvin live."

"I see," Lovina said. "Raelyn and her mom's trailer were in the southeast part. Is that where most of the kids go missing from?" She received an assortment of noncommittal shrugs that told her nothing. Lovina sighed and tried again. "As far as you know, Calvin never had anything to do with Raelyn?" All the kids shook their heads or muttered "no." Lovina thanked the kids and headed deeper into the park, toward the south. The park got quieter and darker. No residents out, no signs of life or activity. She checked her phone, it said it was 9:30. The phone's bars for service were empty too. She kept walking.

Lovina reached a large courtyard swarming in mute, still, plastic flamingos of every shape, size, and style. Lovina smiled a little and shook her head. She began to weave through the maze of fake birds. Maybe she'd find a little convention of garden gnomes around here too. She was halfway through the courtyard when she stopped. There was something at her feet.

It was a bloody human torso. It had been a man, his genitals had been hacked off, his neck, arms, and legs were raw stumps of tattered meat and snapped bone. Scattered between the flamingos, she saw islands of pale, bloodless flesh jutting up out of the grass, arms, hands, feet, and even more torsos, more bodies. She turned and saw a man's head, his face scratched, his eyes closed, his black hair cut short and neat, slick with blood. The head's eyes opened and Lovina jumped, feeling thin, plastic bird bodies bump against her. She felt a hot sting along her back, like razor blades and an odd sound behind her, like something whirring, thudding against something else rapidly. She turned, reaching for her gun. The path she had followed through the flamingos to that point was no longer there, filled now with more of their number.

The strange, echoing, shuffling sound again, this time to her right. Lovina spun and was face-to-face with the dead black plastic eyes of one of the larger birds, which hadn't been there a moment ago. A trickle of black blood ran down its hooked beak, dripping quietly into the grass below. Lovina looked back to the scattered body parts and they were all gone, as was her path, still blocked by birds. The sound again directly behind her, and she knew it this time, her mind had filled in the blanks. It was the sound of hollow plastic wings flapping, fluttering, moving.

She whirled, feeling the sharp sting on her arm as she turned; her incredulous brain told her where the pain came from but it was simply not possible. Her pistol was leveled at more flamingos and a dead woman now lay in the grass about five feet away from her.

The girl was nude and young, probably in her twenties. She had been beautiful in life, with black, curly hair, but now her face was carved in a wide, grotesque knife-grin that made Lovina think of the clown's leering face, his painted smile. Her pale blue eyes were vacuous in death. The girl's arms had posed above her head and her nipples had been cut off. She had been savagely severed below the rib cage. The girl's pale abdomen and legs, splayed open, were a foot away from the torso. Strangely, her entrails were neatly tucked under her buttocks. There was a remarkable absence of blood from the gaping wounds.

"He . . . harvested . . . us," the dead girl said to Lovina. "Drained, took . . . our precious light into himself. The light . . . in our skull."

Lovina lowered the gun. The girl's dead eyes followed her movement. "Who?" Lovina said. "Who did this to you?"

"Stop . . ." the girl's split mouth whispered, "stop . . . So many of us . . . so many. Please." Something sharp tore at Lovina's hand and the pistol fell to the grass. Lovina winced at the pain, rubbed her bleeding hand and squatted to retrieve the gun. When she came back up, the girl's corpse had vanished and the path through the flamingos was where it should be again. Lovina hurried through the gauntlet to the other side of the courtyard.

"It ain't me," a familiar gravelly male voice said. Calvin, in an olive drab military trench coat wrapped tight around his cadaverous frame, stepped out of the shadows between two trailers. His face and hands were painted bright yellow, the strange black triskelion symbol was painted carefully all over his yellow face, hands, and arms. Lovina brought the gun up and aimed it square at his chest. Calvin didn't even seem to notice. "I know you're thinking you got your man, Jane Law, but you don't. Hell, I ain't even a man no more. I evolved, praise be to Hastur . . . technically, to me."

"Why should I believe you?" Lovina said.

"'Cause, darlin', I *know* things," Calvin said. "Like I knew about what happened to your . . . sister, right? It was your sister, wasn't it? Got fed to one of the big boys, one of my kin. Finger . . . lickin' . . . good."

"Shut your goddamned mouth," Lovina said, her finger slipping to, tightening on, the trigger of the Glock.

"You got that part right, toots," Calvin said. "That little girl you're looking for, those human chop-shops you jist seen, not my work, not my style. I'm a big-picture kinda guy—universal heat-death, asteroids smacking into the planet, a good-old fashioned viral serial killer strangling millions—now that, that gives me the jollies, officer. Fella you're looking for is a lightweight . . . at least as far as me and the big boys are concerned."

"Then tell me his name, Calvin," Lovina said.

"Where's the fuckin' fun in that?" Calvin said. "Way I figure it, there's going to be a hell of a lot of people dyin', a bunch of running around, and fussin', and hollerin' 'fore you're done, original recipe. And chaos, well, chaos is always good for business."

"What if I think you're full of shit," Lovina said. "A pissant lunatic with delusions of godhood who likes to hunt and disappear innocent people."

"Nobody is innocent, Lovina," Calvin said. "You know that better than most, don't you, Officer Marcou. You had a hell of time hunting down that cult that killed your sweet baby sis, didn't you? What if I told you every single one of those deaths you caused were sacrifices to the same things your baby sis got fed to? You just made the hole a little bit deeper, darlin', think about that."

Calvin shrugged at the shocked look on Lovina's face. "How do I know about that? How do I know you don't think I'm your bad guy because I'm not dressed up like fucking Puddles Pity Party, right? The same way I know about the screaming city, about how at your weakest, at your most isolated, and vulnerable, and desperate, it calls out to you from across the wasteland of dream. I am a killer, but I ain't your killer, Officer Marcou. But I'm going to enjoy the hell out of seeing if you can bag 'em."

Calvin chuckled and began to walk away.

"Maybe one day, I'll be coming for you and the boys," Lovina said.

He paused and looked back. "Maybe. We'll talk again, Lovina . . . a long talk, when you finally come to the screaming city." The dry chuckle again, then shadow and silence.

Lovina skirted the edge of the flamingo courtyard, doubling back to her car. She sat there for a time trying to calm her racing mind and thudding heart. Her temples throbbed and she closed her eyes tightly against the pain of the headache. White light flashed behind her eyelids and when she opened her eyes, she could she the vast alien silhouette of the city from her dreams squatting along the starry horizon. She shut her eyes again breathing, deeply. "Not there . . . not there. It's not really there." She opened her eyes and the city was gone but the headache remained.

Calvin's words were like gnawing insects chewing on her brain. She reached for her phone, pulled up the contact, and hit the dial button. It rang several times and then a sleepy, melodic voice answered.

"Lovina?" the woman's voice, "are you okay?"

"Max," Lovina said, "I'm sorry. I really need your help."

FIFTEEN

The Bitches of Selene's original MC chapter hung out at a little dive bar over in Cape Fear called the First Bite. The Bite was on K Avenue near the intersection of Atlantic Avenue and spitting distance to the Kure Beach Pier. It was owned by a member of the MC and it was rare not to see at least a half-dozen motorcycles lined up in front of its uninviting dark-tinted glass doors.

Heck pulled up on the sidewalk and dropped his bike's stand right by the front door. He pushed the tinted door open and strode into the Bite. Music was blaring from the speakers around the bar, Lordi's "The Riff." The TVs mounted high in the corners behind the bar were mute and showing the NASCAR race at Talladega. There were about two dozen patch-wearing members of the Bitches in the bar and another dozen or so civilians, mostly boy- and girlfriends of club members, the staff and a few wannabes hoping to become patched prospects. Some of the MC club membership were playing pool, others clustered at the bar or sat at pitted old wood tables and booths. As Heck walked in, several Bitches and Bastards stood to confront him.

The Bitches of Selene, or BoS, was a rarity in outlaw clubs, almost unheard of. They had male and female membership and women were allowed not just to ride and wear colors but to vote and hold office. In most one-percenter clubs, women were treated as second-class citizens at best. They were usually relegated to being "party-favors" at MC functions: "sweet butts," "sheep," or "Mamas." The pinnacle a woman could hope to achieve in most MCs was becoming a member's "Old Lady," his steady girlfriend or wife.

The times had been a'changin' slowly, though, with the Motor Maids, an all-woman MC forming up in the forties, right alongside the earliest male-only clubs. While there were female-only MCs and one-percenter clubs, the Bitches, or Bastards, of Selene, whichever the member chose to go by, was one of the only outlaw MCs that allowed full membership to women, men, and LGBTQ bikers. The question of how the BoS managed to survive, thrive, and navigate in the violent, machismo-soaked world of the outlaw could be answered only by those few who knew the club's deepest secret. All of the BoS membership were of shapechanging blood, the werefolk, and those related to werefolk.

You got a hell of a lot more tolerant of diversity when regular bullets and knives didn't kill the biker you just tried to shoot and they grew claws and fangs and proceeded to rip you several new assholes. A lot of traditional MCs didn't like the BoS, but they knew enough not to fuck with them.

Heck knew all that too. He had been raised around all kinds of weird-ness in the Blue Jocks: monsters, magic, spirits, and shades. His best friend, lying half-dead in a hospital bed, was werefolk. Right now, however, he didn't give a shit how dangerous the Bitches could be. He was too fucking mad.

"So which one of you assholes is the Bitch-in-Charge?" Heck asked to the tightening circle around him.

"That," a woman leaning against the bar said, turning to face Heck, "would be me." Her voice was even, she didn't need to raise it. It carried no fear, no anger, and no welcome. She had long reddish brown hair. Her eyes were blue stars and her skin was pale. A well-rendered and colored crescent moon tat-too was visible on the back of both her hands, waxing on her left, waning on her right. She was slender and beautiful with a tight, wiry strength in her. She bore herself like a queen ready to throw down bare-knuckle if she had to. The jukebox had switched over to the Fumes' "Jazz" now.

Heck felt his anger gutter for a moment, replaced by something else pri-mal. He swallowed hard and narrowed his eyes, pushing the other emotion aside, remembering the bodies, Roadkill's unmoving form. "You know who I am?" he asked.

"You're one dumb bastard to come in here and interrupt our wake," the leader said, "especially wearing enemy colors."

"Enemy." Heck nodded, a cruel smile played at the edges of his mouth. "That we fucking are, Scooby. So the truce is fuck-gone then, right?"

A flicker of blue, angry fire jumped in the woman's eyes. "After what just went down, what do you think?"

"I think, this," Heck said and drove a fist into the face of the closest of the bikers surrounding him. The Bastard flew back, stumbling and crashing into a table, overturning it as he hit the floor. Three other bikers launched at Heck, two grabbing him by the arms. Heck pulled his arms forward, expecting the two grapplers to fly across the room like normal. They didn't. They jerked forward, one losing balance, but it was clear they were as strong as Heck. Heck felt a sharp pain in the back of his head and bright light flashed behind his eyes as the third attacker broke a pool cue over his skull. Heck stumbled forward, feeling dizzy and nauseous from the hit, and bent his shoulder low to send the off-balanced BoS member clutching his arm crashing into another table of MC members who had been rising to join the fray.

Heck used his now free arm to grab the shoulder of the BoS still holding his other arm with a slight crunch. Heck threw her, using his hips for torque. The biker flew high and crashed into one of the bar's TVs in an explosion of glass and plastic. She tumbled to the ground with the rain of debris. Heck felt another blow to the back of his skull from the joker with the broken cue. Heck wanted to puke in pain. He felt jagged shards of agony in his skull. Instead he drove a fist into the pool enthusiast, who tried expertly to parry the shot with the pool stick. The thick wooden cue shattered into splinters from the force of Heck's fist, and landed squarely in his upper chest, sending him hurtling backward into more of his charging biker brothers and sisters.

A pale fist bearing a waxing moon snapped Heck's jaw around and his head followed. The leader's punch nearly took him off his feet. If he hadn't had his legs planted to throw the grappler, it would have. Heck's face was numb and he tasted his own blood. He looked the leader in her now bright yellow eyes and licked the blood from his lips with a smile. She smiled back, fangs barred.

Heck jabbed at her face, but the leader blocked it with a forearm and counterpunched with another hit to Heck's ringing head. He grabbed her wrist as she snapped her fist back, however, and pulled her forward, driving her own jaw into his extended elbow. They both staggered back after the exchange of blows, shuffling a few steps, then circling each other. The rest of the MC in the bar backed off, and let the alpha claim her kill. Calls of "Get him, Ana Mae!" and "Kick the fucker's ass!" came from all around Heck.

"That was pretty good," the leader, apparently Ana Mae, said, searching for an opening. "You don't punch like the rest of those fly-weight Jock-offs do. You got a little of the blood in you?"

"I don't think so," Heck said, keeping his guard up. "I haven't had the urge to chew on my own asshole, or needed a flea and tick dip lately." A fist flashed out and caught Heck in the stomach. He lowered his guard a second too late to stop it but just in time for Ana Mae's follow-up with her other fist to break his nose with a wet popping sound. Heck took a wild swing as he stumbled backward, but Ana Mae danced away from it.

"You're too funny for your own good," Ana Mae said. "You drop your guard just a little when you think you said something funny. You want to see the reaction to your words."

"Yeah," Heck said, addressing the middle of the three blurry biker goddesses he currently saw. "I'm a card." He felt the furnace of anger that always licked at his belly roar. This time he didn't try to hold it down. Heck bellowed and came all-in on Ana Mae, driving wild, rapid punches one after another at the MC president. Ana Mae blocked several of his clumsy roundhouses and jabs and took advantage of Heck's practically nonexistent defenses to chop hard on the battered biker. Heck kept coming, taking the blows, snarling and punching, hitting again and again and again. Ana Mae found herself against the bar, Heck right on top of her, his punches relentless, nothing aware behind his eyes but dark rage. She snarled and her now-yellow eyes flashed as she grabbed the berserk biker by his throat with all her superhuman strength, pushing his head back, baring his throat. Her ears grew longer and pointed, her teeth bigger and sharper. Her other hand, raised high, now bore sharp, knife-like claws replacing human nails. Ana Mae howled and Heck matched her in ferocity.

A blast of gunfire took down one of the bar's ceiling fans. Debris spilled everywhere, crashing to the barroom floor. Everyone in the bar was frozen in stunned silence, including Heck and Ana Mae. Jimmie Aussapile, his sawed-off shotgun pistol still smoking, stood just inside the doors to the Last Bite. Jimmie scanned the hooded hunter's eyes of the assembled pack, searching for any sign of weakness. "Enough of this bullshit, right now," Jimmie said around a lump of tobacco in his cheek. He chambered a fresh round into the shotgun and spit brown tobacco juice beside his booted foot. "Heck, Heck! Get over here, now. We're going."

"You and the Jock aren't going anywhere, shit-kicker," one of the BoS prospects said. "I ain't afraid of you or your little spud-gun. I'm of the blood." He lunged toward Jimmie, who lowered the shotgun and fired. The kid screamed as his knee and lower leg exploded. The prospect fell back thrashing in pain from the wounds, clutching his leg and knee. Several other members of the MC started to move on Jimmie but when they saw the prospect's wounds they took a step back.

"That sure does look like your blood, kid," Jimmie said. "That was silver nitrate and rock salt. This," he said, jacking another round into the shotgun's pipe, "is silver birdshot."

"Dumbass," another BoS member said, kneeling by the whimpering prospect. "That ain't no ordinary redneck. He's a Templar. See that cross on his gun's grip?"

"So," Ana Mae said, releasing Heck's throat and lowering her claws, "you're Jimmie Aussapile aren't you?"

"Yep." Jimmie kept the shotgun trained on as many of the bikers as he could. "Heck, c'mon now."

"I've heard of you," Ana Mae said. "Always heard you were good people. Tell me straight, is the Brethren declaring war on us, using your old proxies, the Blue Jocks, to do your dirty work?"

"What the hell are you talking about?" Jimmie asked. "Nobody's declared war on nobody."

"Tell that to the three members we lost yesterday," Ana Mae said, talking more to Heck now than Jimmie. "Tell it to their families. Your goddamned Blue Jock monster-hunting parties have been hitting us for months, whittling us down."

"Don't you fucking even try to play the injured party," Heck said, his voice rising. "You turned our own, gave them the fucking silver bullets they used to kill our people, to almost kill Jethro! How'd you do it? Kidnap their families?"

"Are you out of your mind?" Ana Mae said. "You're the ones who broke the truce. We caught one of your boys too late to stop him from killing Jodie, Finn, and Sara." She turned to one of the Bitches to her left. "Show them." The MC member, a twenty-something girl with dyed gray hair streaked with blue, reached into a backpack and pulled out a torn, bloody jeans vest. She turned the cut around to show off the patch on the back: a circle of Celtic knotwork with a sword intersecting the circle horizontally. The slogan *Braithreachas* emblazoned on the sword's blade. Above the circle a crescent patch, a rocker curving downward, said "Blue Jocks," and below the circle another rocker, curving upward, said "North Carolina." When she turned it back around, Heck noticed that the patch over the left breast said "Dollar."

"It's one of ours," Heck said. "But I have no fucking clue who the hell 'Dollar' is."

"Right," the gray-haired girl said with a sneer. She put the cut back in the backpack.

"Okay," Heck said, stuffing his bloody hand into his jeans pocket. He held up his other damaged hand to Ana Mae to assure her it wasn't an attack. He placed the silver bullet on the bar beside her. "Explain that. They dug that out of my best friend." Ana Mae picked up the bullet and examined it. "There are ones just like it in three dead Jocks, put there by two more dead fucking Jocks at your say-so. That was fucking two days ago."

"It's one of our bullets," Ana Mae said to her people. "Got our mark." She turned to Heck. "We didn't do this. I swear."

"It sounds like someone is trying to get you both riled up and turned about," Jimmie said. The shotgun didn't waver. "I suggest you hold the truce in effect until you can both talk to all your people and see what's going on here."

"Yeah, sure," one of the Bastards that Heck had laid out on the floor said, rubbing his tender jaw. "Give them time to hit us again? I call bullshit on that!"

Several other members of the MC nodded or grunted their agreement with that assessment.

"What kind of assurance can we have," Ana Mae said. "Whose word can we count on to hold the peace. The Jocks have no president, no leader . . ."

"They do now," Heck said. He glanced over to Jimmie and then back to Ana Mae. "Me."

"Who the fuck are you?" another Bastard asked.

"Hector Sinclair," Heck said. The grumbling in the room stilled. "You have my word, my father's word, my grandfather's word, that the peace will hold until I get to the truth."

"So you're Ale's son," Ana Mae said.

"That I am," Heck said. "I'll need that cut."

"I'll need that bullet," Ana Mae said.

"Done," Heck said and held out his bloody hand.

"Done," Ana Mae said. She took his torn hand in her own bloody, now human hand. They held the grip, flesh to flesh, blood to blood, and their eyes held each other's as well. Finally, they stepped away. Heck limped across the room to Jimmie.

"We'll be in touch with what we find," Jimmie said. He nodded to Heck, who began to make his way to the doors of the bar while Jimmie covered him. They stepped out into the hot summer sun. "Can you ride?" Jimmie asked his battered squire. Jimmie's Harley was parked on the sidewalk next to Heck's

"Hell, yeah," Heck said, groaning as he got on the T5.

"Follow me out of here," Jimmie said, starting up his own bike and holstering the shotgun in a leather rifle sheath. "And try not to do anything else stupid for at least ten minutes!"

. . .

"What the hell got into you!" Jimmie said, his shouting beating out the waves roaring past them. They rode a bit down Atlantic and parked at a pier just off Avenue M. Jimmie had waited until they were out on the pier and alone before be began to dress down his squire. "You think because you're crazy enough and lucky enough to take on a bunch of banditos in Texas, or a greasy spoon full of batshit crazy serial killers, you can just wander on in and piss off a bar full of *werewolves*?"

"Hey," Heck said, leaning his throbbing head on the wooden rail of the pier. It sounded like the gulls were laughing at him. "To be fair and balanced, not all of them are werewolves, and I was the one who saved your ass from those Zodiac Lodge assholes in the diner, remember?"

"Yeah, and I just saved your ass," Jimmie said.

"So we're even," Heck said. "Can we stop and pick up some beer and ice cream?" Jimmie made a sound like his internal plumbing was backing up. He threw up his arms to the beautiful sky and then made a gesture like he was choking someone.

"You would have died in there, you get that, right?" Jimmie said. "You're just lucky they went along with that crap you fed them about being the Jocks' new president."

"That wasn't BS, Jimmie," Heck said quietly. "I'm doing it. I'm stepping up and taking Ale's place."

"Heck, you can't," Jimmie said. "You're not a full member of the Brethern yet, and that shit you just pulled back there is a perfect example of why you aren't ready. The tradition is—"

"Fuck the tradition," Heck snarled. "And fuck the Brotherhood too. People are dying, Jimmie. People I know, people I love. My friends, my brothers, my family. I'm done sitting on my goddamn hands here. This isn't some fucking fairy tale, this is my life! It's the only life I've ever known."

Jimmie was silent. The water lapped against the posts of the pier. Finally, the trucker spoke. "You do this, Heck, you're going to end up destroying what you're trying to save. You'll end up being the people you're fighting. That's why Gordon and then Ale made it a secret requirement for the president of the MC to be a Brethren. To be sure that power was always tempered with wisdom and with mercy. Knights in leather, riding steel. Protecting the weak with strength and honor from the evil and the unjust." Not Jimmie's words,

Heck could see him recalling them from a shining memory of another time. "That was their dream, Heck."

Heck looked out into the restless ocean. One of his eyes was nearly swollen shut. His head stabbed with sharp pain. Everything that had been kicked, or punched, or jostled was stiffening up. A line of dark clouds had formed, stirring far out at sea, lightning dancing between the sky and the water. He closed his eye and he saw blood on white hospital sheets, Jethro's pale face.

A moment later the rumble of thunder rolled into shore with the waves. Heck stopped leaning on the pier rail, he stood. He turned and looked at Jimmie with his one open eye. There was nothing but exhaustion and anger in his voice.

"Then fuck them, and fuck their dream too," he said. He bumped into Jimmie as he pushed past him, headed back for the bikes. "I got a club to mind and a war to win. You go save the fucking world, Jimmie."

Dr. Max Leher tried to think of some quiet, polite way to dislodge the drunken gentleman snoring in the bus seat next to her from her shoulder. The gentleman was originally from Haiti and he had told her he was on his way to Philadelphia to see his children, who lived with his ex-wife there. He also told her the only way to endure a long bus trip was to get good and ripped, which he had done in the D.C. Greyhound bus terminal prior to getting on this bus. He offered Max a few of the small sample bottles, like they gave out on airplanes, out of his stash in his gym bag at his feet. She heard the bottles clink as he sorted through his sizable collection. His breath reeked of gin and the smell wafted across Max's face with each window-shaking snore.

"Um . . . sir?" Max said, almost whispering. The gentleman had not offered his name when he had embarked along with Max. "Sir? Could you, maybe, um . . ." She struggled to gently push him to the other side of his chair, but Max was short, only a hair over five feet, and her toes barely touched the edge of the bus floor, so she didn't have much leverage as she presently sat. Max had a mane of thick, curly black hair that fell well below her shoulders. She wore glasses and her eyes were large, dark, and intelligent. The glasses made her look almost owlish. Her skin was olive like she was of Middle Eastern or Mediterranean ancestry. Her best friend in high school, Julie Silverman, had tried to teach her the esoteric craft of makeup but she had never got the hang of it and seldom wore it. She was dressed in a pair of her most comfortable jeans and a Georgetown University T-shirt, a dark blue hoodie, and her old Chuck Taylor sneakers. Her ever-present leather messenger bag was at her feet.

The bus was dark and about half the seats were full. It had been packed when they had departed Washington, but several stops later, having passed through Maryland, they had lost more passengers than gained new ones.

It was around three in the morning and most of the people riding were asleep, trying to sleep, or listening to something on their phones with ear buds in. Max wondered again if maybe this hadn't been the best way to reach Lovina after her call for help last night.

The morning after Lovina's call, Max had contacted her friend and mentor in the order of the Builders, Dr. Norman Pillar, to inform him she would be leaving town.

"You want to run off into the field again," Norman had said, sipping his tea from a white mug with a quote from Thomas Aquinas on it. Dr. Pillar had always reminded Max as a child of a malnourished Santa Claus. He had a luxurious white beard and had managed to retain a full head of snow-white hair. Norman frowned and shook his head. "Mackenzie, are you sure? Think about this."

"You only call me Mackenzie when you disapprove," Max said. "Lovina— Officer Marcou—needs my help! Norman, the case sounds fascinating. There's been so little research done in cryptozoology and Urban Mythology on the clown phenomenon. Think of the feather that will be in our cap!"

"More like a big orange wig," Pillar said, shaking his head, "or perhaps a red rubber nose. This is ridiculous. Chasing after phantom clowns is a waste of your talent and your time. I'm your proctor in the order, or at least I used to be. I think you'd better serve the order, and yourself, by staying put and continuing your lecturing schedule, your real research."

Max had grown up around the magic, the myths, and the secrets of the Builder order. Both her parents were career academics and members in the order, following in the tradition of her paternal grandfather, whose name was also Max. Growing up, her grandfather had been Max's everything. They were virtually inseparable. He was "Big Max" and she became "Little Max."

She recalled Grandfather buying her first telescope, letting her stay up past bedtime and stand on tippy-toes in the back of his old Toyota pickup, Big Max showing her how to peek in and say hello to the universe. He had taught her Latin at seven, Aramaic at nine, differential calculus at eleven. He taught her how to play canasta, and what a pun was, and how listen to jazz. She owed her passion, her hunger for knowledge, to him.

Norman was an old friend of the family and had been Grandfather's best friend and, for a time, his lover. The two of them had been recruited into the

Builders together right out of university. When Max had joined the order, Norman had taken her grandfather's place, after his death, as her "proctor," her mentor, advocate, and instructor. It was a process similar to the knight-squire relationship the Brethren developed with their new recruits.

"That can all wait," Max had said as she hurried about her Georgetown office, grabbing small items off of shelves and packing them in her leather satchel. She paused to flip through a slender book, searching to see if it was the one she needed to take, while guzzling down about half a can of energy drink. While most of the Builder archives were now available online, Max had learned to not always trust that everything you needed would be there. She nodded and slipped the thin book into her satchel.

"This isn't about getting back out in the field to test your theories, is it?" Max blushed a little. It was one of the reasons she wanted to go.

Max had developed a theory as to why the roadways of America attracted so many supernatural horrors, so many disturbed personalities. She believed that the highway system had been intentionally built over or near the invisible lines of energy the ancients had called dragon lines, and modern occultists called ley lines. Ley lines stretched and branched across the earth's skin like arteries and veins, conducting raw magical energy. Max believed that the highway system had been created to channel all that massive supernatural power and tap it through a complex system of hermetic magic involving numbers, like those found on highway signs. The bleeding of raw, magical power attracted creatures and madmen like a lantern in the night drew moths. The question of who created the system and why were still mysteries, but Max was convinced her theory was sound. Her colleagues in the Builder order were less convinced and had not yet even given her thesis on the subject a hearing. Academics, either mundane or occult, were always plagued with politics.

She was going out to gather more data, and that was the excuse she gave herself when her heart had jumped at seeing Lovina's name on her phone's screen. The true reason, the most important reason fell from her lips as easily as breath. "Lovina needs my help, and I'm going to go help her."

"She's a *Brethren*," Pillar stressed. "They have their own haphazard way of doing things. She should know that to request your help requires more than a panicked phone call in the wee hours. I mean, really! We have protocols for this! There was no formal request put through channels. This could cause you and her a great deal of trouble, you know. You don't want another reprimand do you? It would not look good on your record, dear, especially since you still want to present your research to the Imperceptible Perceptory. Such rash behavior on your part could jeopardize that."

Max paused in her whirlwind of packing and turned to look at her old friend and colleague. "It could? Really?"

"We're not the Brethren," Norman said. "We're seekers of truth, beauty, and knowledge. Flying off the handle, guns blazing, into some ridiculous adventure is not our way of doing things. You know that, Max."

. . .

Max's order, the Builders, was dedicated to the discovery, accumulation, and dissemination of all knowledge, occult, religious, and secular in nature. They worked through scientists, artists, and priests, research facilities, museums, and mystic lodges, deep space probes and oracles.

The underpinning of all civilization was the safety and reliability of their roads. A Brethren, Jimmie Aussapile, had told Max that shortly after they had first met on a mission Jimmie had requested Builder assistance about a year ago. The mission became much more than just that and Jimmie, his squire, Heck Sinclair, and Lovina Marcou had all become Max's good friends, especially Lovina. Max couldn't quite pin down how to quantify the way the beautiful Louisiana investigator made her feel, but she had missed Lovina terribly and knowing she was out in the field and in need of her help seemed much more important than politics of her orders.

"You're right, Norman," Max said. "I am acting emotionally, not rationally. And I'm still going."

Pillar shook his head. "I know that look. It's the same one you had when your parents and I tried to talk you out of going on that infernal carnival ride after you ate all that deep-fried garbage and cotton candy. You were nine, I believe, and you vomited everywhere."

"And Grandfather said he'd go on the ride with me," Max said, a smile coming to her lips from the memory. "He cleaned me up and we both laughed the whole time. He said, sometimes for life to be fun it had to get messy."

Norman made a "hrumph" sound. "You threw up on him too, dear. Sometimes, Mackenzie, life is no fun at all, and it can still be damn messy." He sighed. "Go. I'll cover your classes for you."

Max squeaked and threw her arms around his neck, her legs kicking off the ground. "Oh, thank you, Norman!"

"Don't thank me, dear child. You have no idea how awful it can be out there on 'the Road,' as I believe the 'gear-jammers,' 'grease monkeys,' and transients call it. I never cared much for Kerouac, myself. He was a Brethren, you know?"

"Not to worry," Max said with a grin and more than a little pride. "I've been out there and made it back. No problem!"

"Well, then Alexandria Quatermain," Norman said, smirking, "tell me, how do you plan to get to the middle of God's Green Earth, Pennsylvania, when you can't even drive a car?"

"Oh," Max had said.

A quick search of the internet had not made the prospect any cheerier. The quickest and closest way to reach the tiny borough of Coalport was going to be to take a bus to nearby Altoona. Which brought Max back to her present predicament with her inebriated friend snoozing on her shoulder.

Max had a flash of inspiration. She began to lightly tickle the rather prominent thicket of nostril hairs growing out of the man's nose. The man snorted a few times, like a cold car trying to turn over, scrunched up his nose, and then grunted and rolled over to the other side of his seat to resume his snoring.

Max, pleased with herself for solving the problem, reached down to celebrate with the last can of energy drink from her satchel. The bus shifted abruptly and the can slipped away from her fingers and rolled forward under the next row of seats. She heard its metallic "tink" as it stopped a few rows up. Max sighed and then slipped past the snoozing man, out into the aisle, and made her way quietly past the few sparsely populated rows of passengers. She paused to lean over, balancing herself on the back of the aisle seat and caught a quick glance at her wayward can. She slipped into the empty outer seat of the row where it had come to rest.

"Excuse me," Max said softly to the passenger, a young man, who was in the window seat. "Um, my drink rolled under you, um, your seat. I was wondering if I could . . . Uh, sir?"

The young man, in his twenties, was not moving. His head was lolled against the window, his longish brown hair fell into his eyes. Max leaned close to him and could hear music seeping out of his ear buds, a cover of Katy Perry's "Dark Horse" by Our Last Night.

"Poor boy's been sleeping the whole trip, dear," the powder-haired old lady in the seat across the aisle said softly. Max nodded to the elderly woman absently and gave a faint smile. She leaned down awkwardly around the boy's lap and splayed legs and retrieved her can of life-giving caffeine. It was as she was coming back up that she saw the blood on the left side of his shirt.

Max quickly checked the boy's throat for the jump of a pulse. There was none and the skin had grown cold.

"Is everything all right, dear?" the old lady was asking, starting to sound concerned.

"Um, just a sec," Max said as she lifted the boy's shirt where she had seen the blood. The shirt and the dead boy's side under it had identical puncture wounds through them. There were four circular wounds, side by side, in a row. Each wound approximately an inch wide, about a quarter of an inch apart. The edges of each puncture were ragged but there was surprisingly little blood. This was familiar to Max, from somewhere, some when . . . she knew this. *Think, Max, think . . . push back the panic . . . think.*

"Are you all right?" the old lady asked, concern written all over her face. "You look like you've seen a ghost. Is he okay?"

"Yes, ma'am," Max said, pulling the boy's shirt back down over the wounds. She stood. "Everything's okay. Excuse me." She started down the aisle toward the driver. She had to convince him to stop the bus, to get everyone off of it. She couldn't recall the exact memory, but she knew they were all in terrible danger. Her heart was thudding. A horrible recollection fell on her, and it was followed by another one almost immediately. The woman at the window seat next to the old lady had also been slumped as if sleeping and Max now recalled seeing a dark stain on her side too in the instant they had passed a lighted billboard on the highway. Max knew what it was that had killed those two people.

A powerful vise gripped her shoulder and Max felt awful pain and a burning cold even through her hoodie and her T-shirt. "Have a seat, dear," the old lady said, her liver-spotted hand on Max's shoulder, as she practically wrenched Max into a vacant window seat, and then joined her in the empty seat beside her, blocking the Builder in. "You need a rest. You look ill."

The old lady made a face like she had just tasted rancid milk. She rubbed the palm of her hand furiously. It was the same hand she had used to grab Max's shoulder.

"You killed those people!" Max said before the old lady's hand shot out and covered the younger woman's mouth. The skin was so cold it felt like she was getting frostbite. Max started to struggle and try to scream.

"Hey, yo! Shut the fuck up!" A groggy man's voice said from the darkness a few rows away. "Trying to sleep on this bitch!"

The old lady's eyes were watery and brown, rimmed in bloodshot sockets. "Listen to the man, dear," she whispered. "Keep quiet or I'll kill you and everyone else on this bus. I can do it too." Max nodded slowly and stopped struggling. The old woman released her face and smiled the same, fake placid smile she had when Max had first seen her. "Much better, dear," she said. "Isn't it? Quiet keeps everyone alive. Especially you."

They sat silently in the seat for a few minutes while Max caught her breath. It was hot in the bus. The air conditioner wasn't working very well, pushing around lukewarm air. The old lady was wearing a pink vinyl raincoat tightly about her. She wasn't sweating at all and Max leaned in closer to examine her face.

"Can I help you?" the old woman said, a little irritation creeping into the sweet granny cadence of her voice.

"Y . . . You're a Carriage Ghoul, aren't you?" Max asked. The old woman smiled.

"Now how do you know about such things, you darling girl?"

"I know there was a recorded incident of such a creature in California in April of 1867," Max said. "It murdered all the passengers on a Wells Fargo stagecoach and then simply vanished. All the victims were drained of blood, silently and within a few feet of each other in a cramped compartment. No one raised an alarm. No one heard anything."

"Silence is an ally to the predator," the old woman said, "dear."

"A . . . all had four cir . . . circular puncture wounds on their side," Max continued. The implications were dawning on her. This creature had already silently murdered at least two people on this bus. For all she knew, she and her snoring Haitian friend, the angry man who shouted, and the driver might be the only living human beings left on board.

"You are a very clever girl," the Carriage Ghoul said, still sounding like a jovial granny. "I've lived my whole life and never run into anyone who actually knew of our kind. We've worked very hard to remain anonymous. We fed on you in the olden days in coaches. Today, it's subways, airplanes, trains, and of course, buses. We're very good at what we do."

"Why?" Max asked. "Why do you do it? Why kill people?"

"My sweet girl," the ghoul said, "you're not people, you're food, nothing more. I do what I was created to do. I feed until I'm full enough with blood to slumber. I awake hungry and I hunt again. When I have reached the proper age, I create a child. I insert it into one of my prey without their notice and then I die, my reason for existence complete. My egg grows in one of you and eats away all the soft, human parts for substance. Then when it's matured it begins to hunt as its instincts direct it, using this shell of human meat as camouflage."

The ghoul had turned to face Max as she had talked, and now she leaned in toward Max. The raincoat slipped open, peeled back from within by brown, squiggling, bony, fingerlike projections that reminded Max of wriggling crab's legs. Each of the brown, segmented "fingers" ended in a hollow nail-like point. Whatever else lay hidden behind the coat, Max was thankful it was obscured.

"You all fret too much about the why's and the how's, darling," the Carriage Ghoul said. Max thought she saw tiny toothless mouths puckering, opening and closing—like a baby trying to suckle—just below the dark-stained nails. Max felt dizzy and dumb with fear. The old lady's face was close to her now and she seemed to have no breath, no odor at all about her, and that made the oldest animal parts of Max's highly advanced brain shriek a primal alarm. "It's simple, love. We eat you, we use you to breed, and we die. That's all there is to existence, to mine and to yours."

The ghoul stopped and sniffed Max. She made the grossed-out face again and gagged a little. Max saw the tiny finger-mouths that had crawled out from under her coat gag too. She sniffed Max's shoulder and then moved back in her seat, the things in her chest retreating back under the raincoat. The old lady pulled the coat closed and looked around. Then she leaned back into Max, but not as close.

"Here's what I'm willing to do for you, sweet, bright girl," the ghoul said. "I will let you live. You will sound no alarm, you will forget our meeting. You will allow me to feed in peace until I reach Philadelphia, where I will be leaving your sweet presence. If you honor our agreement, I will let you live and I will only eat a few more passengers before the night is done." The old lady's face smiled. "There is no weapon on this vehicle that can harm me, no person capable of stopping me. If you try, I'll kill everyone but you and then I'll lay my egg in your pretty little body and gobble up your soul."

Max blinked. Her fear was bright and it made everything seem unreal, like some dream movie in which she had no volition, only a part to play out.

"Good, dear," it said. "I'm so happy you understand." The Carriage Ghoul stood and backed out into the aisle. She sniffed her hand again, distastefully. "Now, be a good girl and go back to your seat." The old woman moved further back in the bus and disappeared into the shadowed recesses of an empty seat, next to some unsuspecting passenger.

Max sat there for a few moments and tried to not cry. She was shaking and she wished she was back in her bed in Georgetown and had never left, never found out that this particular bit of obscure monster lore was true. She folded her hands together into a fist and rested them against her forehead. What could she do, what should she do? She could get people killed by trying to stop the creature, but people would surely die if she did nothing.

There were a few sounds of coughs and sniffs. The stale warm air of the compartment stank of the chemical toilet in the rear of the bus. It was all so human, so normal. The words of the ghoul echoed in Max's mind. The notion that mankind was on this earth to act as food, as incubators was obscene. She refused to believe it. Humans had minds, minds that had let them escape the trees, had let them fell animals that should have easily devoured them into extinction. There was a weapon on this bus that could stop that thing, and she needed to get it back under control. As the fear retreated a bit her mind began to tumble it over like an equation missing some elements. *Search for variation in pattern, find for X. X was the way to destroy that thing.* Max cracked open her can of energy drink and sipped it, trying to recall any facts, any myths, any data, about the Carriage Ghouls that might be the key to a weakness. There was so little information about the creatures, however. Nothing, there was nothing that would help.

Observation of the organism. Its form and functions. Max looked out the window into the hurtling darkness. They might as well be on a spaceship between worlds. The desolation of the highway offered no answers. She suddenly envied her friend, the Haitian, for being drunk and passed out through all this.

Drunk.

The ghoul had grabbed her by the shoulder, and then acted like something it had touched had irritated and sickened it. *An aberration in behavior.* It had gone in for the kill with her. It made much more sense to ensure her silence by killing her than threatening her. It was ready to kill her, it wasn't motivated by anything but the cold logic of evolutionary response. *Another aberration in behavior . . . or an override of predatory instinct for . . . survival?*

It had sniffed her, sniffed her shoulder. Sniffed the same shoulder she had grabbed her by and acted repulsed. Max sniffed the left shoulder of her hoodie. It smelled faintly of gin, of the breath of the drunk man who had rested on her shoulder, on *that* shoulder.

Drunk . . . Alcohol.

It was a wild theory with absolutely no way to empirically verify, no way to present in a controlled environment, no way to prove without getting a lot of people killed. Maybe she just didn't taste very good to Carriage Ghouls, maybe it was just a coincidence? Maybe they hunted by blood type like some vampire breeds did? Maybe she was vanilla and the ghoul like chocolate? Maybe . . . maybe. Max saw Lovina in her mind's eye, Jimmie and Heck beside her. And Grandfather stood with them too. *"Life is messy, Max . . . No easy answers, that doesn't mean you don't try."*

No more time to think anymore, no time to second-guess and doubt. This wasn't a lab or a classroom, it wasn't some academic lounge where you could bat around theorems all day. People had died. More were going to die if she didn't at least try.

Max drained her energy drink and stood, she began to walk even though her legs wobbled in fear, even though she thought she might stumble and fall. She didn't. She paused at her row and knelt down by her still snoring companion and scooped up a handful of his small sample bottles. By the time she reached the row the ghoul had settled into, she had twisted the lid off one.

The old lady was sitting, smiling, looking straight ahead. Her coat was partially opened but the nightmarish fingers had not yet crawled out. The woman sitting next to her was black and dressed in military BDUs. She was sleeping quietly, her chest rising and falling. Max wasn't too late.

"What is it now, dear?" the Carriage Ghoul asked, sounding irritated at the interruption, like she was scolding a child. She looked up at Max. "Yes?" Max grabbed the thing by the old woman's jaw and poured the contents of the small sample bottle of vodka into its open mouth. She tried to think of something witty to say, like Lovina or Heck might, but it took all she could to not run screaming down the aisle.

The ghoul's eyes rolled back in its head and it struggled feebly against Max's hand. Its strength seemed to have fled quickly, and the alcohol might be having a paralytic effect on it. It made no noise a human being could hear. Max poured a second bottle into its now slack mouth and noticed that the watery, blood-rimmed eyes were melting into indistinct pools, like chemicals separating, draining back down into the upturned skull.

Max closed the old woman's eyelids and left the empty bottles in the old woman's lap. She splashed a few drops on the vinyl raincoat for good measure. The lady soldier began to sniff from beneath her pulled down lid and Max hurried back to her seat, where she returned the rest of the bottles to the Haitian's backpack, save one. She settled in, pulling her legs up into the seat, so they weren't dangling in the darkness below, and wrapped her arms tight around them.

She listened to each sound on the bus, carefully, holding tightly to the tiny bottle of booze. She listened to the coughs, the sniffles and sneezes, the flatulence, and the grumbles, all the human sounds. Her companion snored louder, and it was the most beautiful sound Max had ever heard. She didn't sleep until the sky outside her window was on fire with the colors of dawn.

. . .

Lovina Marcou sat on a plastic bench and checked the arrival times for the buses on a wavering old TV monitor in the Greyhound terminal on 11th Street in Altoona. A PA system announced the arrival of a bus but it was too distorted to make out any specifics. Lovina stood and waited and waited. In about fifteen minutes bleary-eyed passengers began to shuffle in through a tinted glass door.

One of them was Max.

The slight Builder waved shyly and smiled. Lovina walked up to her and Max wrapped her arms around the detective tightly. Lovina was a little startled, but then was even more surprised when she hugged Max back deeply, holding her and neither seemingly wanting to let go.

"Thank you for coming, Max," Lovina said. "The trip okay?"

"Uh, well, you know . . . buses," Max said into her shoulder. She pulled away a little from Lovina for an instant. "You, uh, you think you can give me a lift home when we're done?"

"Sure," Lovina said. "Come on, let's get your bags and get on the road. I'll tell you everything on the way."

Ryan knew he was being stupid, dangerously stupid. He walked through the tall grass toward the dense, dark woods behind the park. The June sun was high in the crystalline sky and the heat and humidity beat down on him like a hammer. He could turn back, make up a lie to tell Nevada that he had tried to get her stolen property back, maybe even embellish it a little to make him sound extra heroic in her eyes. No, lies were an awful way to treat people you cared about, and he obviously . . . cared about Nevada.

Nevada had let Cody, one of the teenagers that hung with Dickie Dennis, borrow her grandpa's harmonica. He had promised he'd bring it back as he kissed her forehead and headed off into the woods with the other guys. Cody told her that night that he had lost it in the woods, but she knew he was lying.

"I was so stupid to trust him," Nevada had said. She and Ryan had been sitting on a bench near the courtyard of flamingos. "He was being so nice, and he told me he was in a band and they were going to do some blues stuff and he wanted to learn how to play it for that. I told him about Grandpa giving it to me. I'm an idiot!"

Ryan had felt a hot flush of jealousy. She thought that asshole was cute, and she had fallen for his bullshit. The angry part of him felt like saying, *"Yeah you were an idiot, and now it's gone!"*

Nevada began to cry. She had been trying to be cool, but she had lost the battle at the summoning of her grandfather's memory. "He . . . he acted like he really understood how it was the only thing I had left of him since we lost everything in the stupid hurricane and had to come here. I thought he was being nice." The tears became sobbing, as her shoulders heaved and Ryan was ashamed for what he had been thinking.

Now, heading into the the woods, Ryan remembered the look on Nevada's face, a look of soul-deep sadness and betrayal by someone you truly wanted to believe in. Mom had that same look on her face the night Kenny beat her, the night "the thing" happened, the night they had both nearly died. Ryan would have given anything to take that look off his mom's face, to take that cataract of pain from the light of Mom's eyes.

He had hugged Nevada and told her it was going to be okay. He held his friend. That was the moment, Nevada's wet hot face on his shoulder, her long tanned arms around his neck, that he decided he was going to get Nevada's harmonica back.

He liked Nevada, really liked her. The feeling ballooned inside him whenever she was around. It was too big for him to find words for. And at twelve Ryan knew, he *knew,* he'd never feel this way about another girl again. He wanted her to be happy and he wanted her to notice him. He really liked her. Why else would he be doing something he knew was idiotic, especially after all the stories Karl had been telling him. Karl apparently had been a really great reporter. He had worked at major newspapers all over the country. Tony had been his editor at many of his jobs. Karl's problem, the ex-reporter told Ryan, was that he was too dedicated to getting the truth out and he ended up being fired and blacklisted for his trouble.

"Tell him *why,* Karl," Tony had said from the kitchen of their trailer. Karl and Ryan sat at the small kitchen table, Tony was cooking.

"I just did, Tony!" Karl said, going from calm to agitated in an instant. Ryan had noticed that while the two men seemed to be as close as family, the only way they seemed to know how to talk to each other was by yelling.

"Tell him about the vampires, or the zombie, or maybe that swamp monster," Tony said, almost sneering as he put a pinch more paprika in his sainted grandmother's spaghetti sauce. "That one was rich."

"I was getting to that!" Karl said.

It turned out Karl had an awful habit of running into monsters of all kinds. Every time he tried to report what he saw, his stories got canned and he soon followed. He'd even written a novel about his misadventures in the occult, but no publisher would take him seriously, which led to a rant about the secret occult conspiracy hidden at the heart of the publishing industry. He'd usually be the only one to believe what he saw and it usually fell to him to hunt down and destroy the creatures before they harmed more innocent people.

"Why?" Ryan asked. "Why you?"

"Because, kid," Karl said, "if you see something wrong happening and you don't try to do something about it, you're as guilty as the ones who did it."

The words made him flash back to Baltimore, to his closet fortress, and to that terrible night. Mom screaming, Kenny's rage as he smashed at the gates to Ryan's closet fortress.

Ryan had been coming back often to meet with the old newspapermen. They always fed him until he was stuffed. Ryan ended up helping them to put out and deliver the *Valentine Arrow,* the photocopied newsletter of happenings at the trailer park and the doings of its citizens. Tony and Karl put the *Arrow* out with a printer and a copy machine in the living room of their trailer, which resembled a newsroom more than a living space.

Karl still used an electric typewriter that had PROPERTY OF THE NY TIMES written on the side of it in permanent marker. Tony would argue over the content of the stories Karl wrote, saying it was too long, too sensational, not on point. Karl would decry that Tony was a blind buffoon for not seeing the vision of his work. "Pearls before swine, Tony! Pearls before swine!" Ryan would deliver the copies of the *Arrow* for the two old men, stuffing a copy inside the screen door or the jamb of each trailer's door.

Karl had made copies of all his notes and research on the Valentine Trailer Park and gave them to Ryan in a folder. "Here you go, kid," Karl had said. "This should keep you busy. I'm going to be out of town for a while. I'm meeting up with this guy in D.C. I met him in an online chat room. He claims to be with the FBI and have some strong leads on UFOs. He seems a little spooky to me, kind of obsessed, but you go . . ."

". . . Where the story leads you," Ryan finished. Karl smiled at him, a warm, genuine smile and ruffled Ryan's hair.

"Atta boy," the reporter said, grabbing his battered straw hat from a peg near the door and stepping outside. "We'll make a muckraker out of you yet, kid. Stay out of trouble. I'll see you when I get back. Remind Tony to pick up his foot cream at the pharmacy."

Ryan had pored over the file every night before bed. Karl's notes were close to impossible to read, and a lot of them didn't make sense, but Ryan got the gist of it. There were reports of hauntings of all kinds going back to the sixties and seventies, especially of chopped-up bodies and a beautiful but savaged woman cut in two, her face sliced into a bizarre smile.

Karl had interviewed dozens of residents, past and present, who reported the things they had seen. There were notes mentioning other strangeness besides clowns, including the mysterious Calvin everyone was so afraid of and about the plastic flamingos in the courtyard coming to life and attacking people, and an alarming list of all the residents of the park who had died of seemingly natural causes or simply gone missing in the last few decades.

There had been more in the file, lots more, but most of it didn't make much sense to Ryan and read like a history book from school, with big chunks of the text missing. There were photographs in the file that Karl had taken over the years of weird symbols drawn in chalk all over the trailer park and apparently all over Coalport too.

...

He showed the pictures to the guys, and Nevada, and they all agreed they had seen the symbols around as long as they could recall.

"I heard they were death marks Emmett the clown puts on his victims' trailers to claim them," Patrick said. "I know they've shown up on the homes of a lot of the folks who died here over the years."

The six of them were walking down Main Street into Coalport to visit Ryan's mom at the Minit Mart, where she worked now. It was insanely hot and bright out. Taylor, Ryan's mom, would treat them to Slush Puppies as long as the manager wasn't around.

"Emmett, the ghost clown?" Ryan clarified.

"Or ghost hobo killed by a psycho clown," David added. "I like that version better."

"That's all bullshit," Joe added. "My old man told me they're bum signs. Homeless guys use them like a code to tell each other stuff when they're passing through. They mean stuff like 'the people at this trailer will give you food' or 'don't go to this house, they'll kick your ass for buggin' them.' Shit like that. One thing you can always count on in the warm months is bums wandering through."

Nevada shook her head and looked over at her little brother, "Joe, that's mean. They're not bums, they're just people who are down on their luck. Some of them have mental problems but can't afford to get help."

"Cut the bull crap, 'Vada," Joe said. "Dad says they're lazy bums, who won't get a job. Stop being a hippie."

"Like Dad's an expert on having a job," Nevada said. "He's drunk half the time he comes to see us."

"Shut up, 'Vada." Joe said.

"Yeah, lots of homeless folks walk through on the old railway trails back at the edge of the woods in the spring and the summer," Patrick offered to

Ryan, trying to disarm the fight that was brewing between Nevada and Joe. "Sometimes a bunch of them camp out in the jungle."

"The jungle?" Ryan asked.

"The boxcar jungle," Sam said, pausing to kick a discarded plastic Dr Pepper bottle on the side of the road that looked like it was half-full of pee. "You know, that junkyard at the bottom of the hill back behind the woods. It's where all the old carnival rides and trailers ended up, along with a bunch of old train cars, when the carnival went bust. They all ended up back there. Whoever owns the land just let it all sit out there and rust."

"Bad place to go," David said. "Some homeless guy killed a little kid back there in like the eighties, I think?"

"I heard the nineties," Nevada said. "It's pretty creepy, Ryan, between the clowns—whatever they are—and the dead bodies that are supposed to be buried back there, and the homeless people. Everybody stays away from there, even Dickie Dennis and the older kids, even the cops are scared of that place."

. . .

Ryan stepped into the cool darkness of the treeline and headed up the bike trail, looking about, waiting for the maniac clown with the sledgehammer to step out from behind every tree. His heart was thudding in his chest, as fast and as hard as it had during "the thing," during that horrible night in Baltimore with his mom and . . .

He pushed the memory out of his head, pushed away the hulking silhouette ripping open the door to the closet, the bulb swaying, that horrible near-human sound of rage, the rain of blood. He checked to see if his pants were dry. They were.

Lit, he thought. He hadn't had an accident since he'd been threatened by a band of snarling, teenage boys and by a psycho clown. It was a slender hope but maybe he was getting better, stronger. Ryan decided to cling to that hope. He reached the branch in the bike trail where he knew if he veered to the right, he'd reach the fort. He headed to the left, toward the switchback where he had encountered Dickie and the older boys that first time in the woods.

. . .

Taylor Badel had been happy to see her son and his new friends come through the doors of the Minit Mart. She was true to her word and let all of them get small Slush Puppies from the machine. She always slipped a few dollars into the till to cover them at the end of her shift. It probably wasn't the exact amount but it made her feel like she wasn't taking advantage of the store's owner and manager, Charlie.

"Inn keeper!" Sam bellowed as they burst through the doors of the convenience store. "Slushies for me and my men!" Ryan and Nevada both gave him a frog punch, a quick, tight jab in the arm designed to make your arm twitch like a jumping frog. Sam groaned even as he laughed.

"I'm not a man!"

"Shut up, Sam! Don't talk like that to my mom!"

Tay laughed. "You all look cooked," she said. "Go ahead." The kids ran to be first in line at the machine. Patrick paused.

"Thanks, Mrs. Badel!" he said.

They were good kids, and Tay couldn't help but notice that Ryan let the little girl, Nevada, cut in front of him in line. The girl smiled at her son and Ryan lit up like a Christmas tree. In the two months since they had arrived Tay had seen the change in her son, and it made her think she had made the right decision to come to Coalport.

"Thanks, Mom!" Ryan said heading out the door with his friends.

"See you back at home tonight," Tay said. "Be careful!"

The kids sat on the steps of the church next to the store and drank their Slushies. Nevada slipped a harmonica out of one of the pockets of her overalls and began to play "You Are My Sunshine."

"That was really good," Ryan said. Nevada stopped.

"Thanks." She held up the harmonica. "It was our grandpa's," she said. "He used to play it for us when we were little. He taught me how to play a little. Grandma gave it to me when he passed away."

"I got one of his pocketknives," Joe said, slipping the knife out of his jeans pocket.

"Cool," Ryan said, examining the knife and handing it back to Joe.

"Yeah he was a pretty cool old guy," Joe said. Nevada went back to playing her harmonica.

"So you going to keep checking out all this stuff Karl told you about?" Patrick asked Ryan.

"I don't know," he said, shrugging. "It's all really cool, but I don't see how I could find out anything Karl and other people over the years haven't."

"Well that old man and those other guys didn't have the dream team here to help 'em out," Sam said, not even looking up from his phone. "If we find some real ghosts we could end up on TV, maybe get our own reality show.

Kid Ghost Hunters." Sam did a pretty good Eric Cartman impersonation. "Kick ass."

"I'd watch that," David said. "It's got legs as a midseason replacement, I'd say," nodding. He took a big slip from his straw. He gasped, groaned, and clutched his head. "Ahh, brain freeze!" Sam smacked the suffering boy's forehead. David fell back on the stairs.

"It's a miracle there's a brain in there to freeze," Joe said.

. . .

Ryan paused for moment in his advance along the bike trail. The sheer enormity of what he was undertaking hit him. He was looking for a place in the woods he'd never been to and that place was the den of the teenage assholes who beat the shit out of people. This was amazingly dumb, to try, and for what? To impress Nevada? It was her own stupid fault for falling for Cody's crap in the first place.

Now, deep in the woods Ryan remembered the look on Nevada's face. *If you see something wrong happening and you don't try to do something about it, you're as guilty as the ones who did it.* Karl's words found him. He was sick of letting fear own him, drive him. Sick of the ammonia smell of fear. In that moment, alone in the woods, he decided some things were a lot worse than getting your ass kicked. Ryan straightened his shoulders and kept going.

It took a while and a little backtracking, but Ryan found the small, worn, dirt footpath off from the bike trail that the guys had told him about. It was a little ways past the creek. He headed down the path, his legs trembling. If any of the older boys were there, he'd have to run, or try to hide. The foliage on either side of the path narrowed and thickened. Ryan kept thinking that at any moment an angry, pimpled face or a chalk-white hand would spring out at him. He flashed to the dream he'd had during the trip from Baltimore to Coalport, a field of white hands grabbing at him. The realization came to him that the field in his nightmare was the field behind the trailer park, the field that led to these woods. He felt numb with the sense that something much larger than this forest was swallowing him up. He felt like running, but where do you run from something that can sneak inside your head? He kept going, trying to focus on the physical elements of the woods, and ignore his thrashing mind.

At the end of the path was a small clearing, surrounded on all sides by thick brush, bushes and trees. The clearing floor was littered with flattened, faded Milwaukee's Best beer cans, old condoms, and cigarette butts. Half-devoured by the foliage was a rusted, old tear-drop-shaped cage that had long ago been part of some larger carnival ride.

Ryan moved closer to the cage. He froze when he heard a rustling sound in the bushes. After a moment he heard the fluttering of a bird's wings and then silence. He stepped up to the cage's door and lifted the latch. The steel mesh door opened with a loud creak that seemed to echo through the forest. Ryan stood still again, paralyzed, waiting for one of the attackers in his mind to manifest, but again there was only silence. He looked inside the cage.

The back, top, and sides of the cage were covered in plant growth that acted as an effective seal and shelter. Some of the bushes' limbs and fronds had grown through the mesh walls and poked out here and there. The whole inside of the cage smelled of stale marijuana and cigarette smoke. There were two long, smooth metal benches built into either side of the cage. The benches could probably accommodate three carnival patrons to a side if you jammed them in. One bench had been made into a makeshift bed, covered by a stained tattered old cargo blanket, like the ones found in the back of U-Haul trucks.

The other bench was bare, covered with symbols scratched into the metal with a knife. Some of the stuff etched on the bench looked like the weird signs Karl had photographed all over the trailer park. Others were crude depictions of penises and vaginas, or naked people doing it. There was also words, things like "Anne and Steve 4-ever," or "2 good 2 b 4 gotten." Ryan was surprised at how many girls' names and phone numbers were scratched in and shocked at the claims of what these girls would do.

Prominent among the scratched messages on the bench were drawings of clown faces. Two faces, to be exact: one clown's makeup was like a bird with spread wings fanning out over both of his eyes, the other's face looked was like he had stitches holding his face together. The two faces were accompanied by the letters "LCS" or the words "Lunatic Clown Squad." Ryan had heard of the rap band through YouTube. They were kind of a rip-off of ICP, and Ryan's mom didn't like him listening to that kind of music because of the language and the violence. Of course, Ryan had checked them out anyway, and decided they weren't the kind of music he liked.

There were two small Igloo coolers in the cage, under the bed-bench. Ryan slid them out and opened them. The red one held a few cans of warm beer, a baggie with a few weed stems, a small glass rainbow-colored hash pipe that looked a little like a mushroom, and a white Bic lighter. The blue one had a half-empty box of Trojans, some small empty plastic vials Ryan was pretty sure had held crack, a Swiss Army knife, and Nevada's harmonica.

Ryan scooped the harmonica up and stuffed it in his pocket. He closed the coolers and slid them back under the bench. That was when he heard the voices further down the path. He recognized one of the voices as Dickie.

"Shit," Ryan said under his breath. He got out of the cage and shut the door. He looked around the clearing, searching for any way out. His mind was like a panicked animal and he began to imagine what Dickie and the others would do to him, then he was back in his closet fort in Baltimore, back to the night of the awful thing that had nearly devoured both him and mom.

No. He shut that movie down, and was surprised with himself when he did. The voices were closer. Ryan began to climb the door of the cage, slipping his fingers in between the gaps in the steel mesh. His Chucks' rubber soles gripped the smooth metal of the cage and in a moment he was on top of it, brushes and branches poking him. From his new vantage point he could see the boys coming down the footpath to the clearing. Their voices were distinct now. He had less than a minute before they'd see him.

"So did you fuck her?"

"Yeah, did you?"

"What the fuck yunz homos think I did!" The voice was Cody's, the asshole who had stolen Nevada's harmonica. "I fucked the shit out of that little bitch. She loved it."

Ryan felt anger fill him. He preferred it infinitely to the old, familiar fear.

"Shit." Dickie's voice now. "What is she? Twelve? Thirteen?"

"'Vada's almost fourteen," Cody said. "She was fucking sweet too, man. I was her first."

"Look out, man," Dickie said mockingly. "Her pissant little brother will get you!"

The teens all laughed. Ryan wished he had a machine gun or a flamethrower. He didn't, though, and he wasn't in a video game. He had seconds before they would see him. He looked up, there was a thick tree branch stretching out above the clearing. He reached out on tippy-toes, grabbed it, and pulled himself up. He crawled along the branch back toward the trunk of the tree that was behind the clearing. The tree rustled with his moving weight.

"What was that?" one of the teens asked. It might have been the guy in the jeans jacket that Ryan had hit with a stick on his first trip into the forest. Ryan was clear of their sight now and hugged the trunk of the tree tightly. He still had to get down.

"Yo," Dickie called out. "Paul, that you, man? You up there?"

"Maybe one of those bums camping out?" Cody asked. "Or one of those little shitheads."

"It could be one of, y'know, *them*," another teen's voice said, tense with dread.

"Shut the fuck up," Dickie said. "We made a truce with them. If it's some old alkie or a little snot-nosed piece of shit, we'll send their asses straight to the hospital, or the morgue."

"If it's that little half-nigger bastard that hit me, I'll cut off his fucking head!" That was definitely Jeans Jacket.

Though he couldn't see them anymore because of the wall of foliage, Ryan could tell they were in the clearing now, at the cage.

"Nobody," Dickie said. "Probably a fucking squirrel. We still got any beers left?"

Ryan hugged the rough bark of the trunk and tried to twist around it to reach a lower branch on the other side. He heard the teens opening beers and rummaging through the coolers.

"Hey," Cody said. "One of you assholes take that harmonica?"

"Why the fuck would we . . ." Dickie began. Ryan lost his grip on the trunk as he reached his leg out for the lower branch. There was a dizzy eternity of free fall, then he was tearing, falling through thick bushes and sharp branches, then impact. He gasped and tried to breathe but he felt like the wind was knocked out of him. He wheezed and scrambled to his feet. Walking in a panicked circle, trying to catch a breath.

"What the fuck was that?" one of the teens said. Ryan heard movement on the other side of the wall of foliage. The older boys were on the move, heading down the footpath to double around to him. His skin burned everywhere from the cuts and scratches the foliage had given him on his way down. He felt his breath return and he gasped, drinking in the sweet air. He looked around and saw the bright light of the edges of the forest a few yards behind him. He couldn't head back toward the creek, they were coming that way. Ryan ran toward the edge of the forest and the jungle.

Clear of the woods he heard Dickie and his crew shouting as they made their way toward him. There was a deep drop, close to five or six feet, along most of the rim of the jungle, but there was a gentler slope near where he came out of the woods this time. And he sprinted for it. In less than a minute, he was among the tall yellowed grass of the floor of the boxcar jungle. There were dozens of old boxcars scattered about with no discernible pattern. Some were on their sides, but most still stood upright on corroded wheels. Ran sprinted for all he had in him toward the closest car. He slipped behind the corner of it just as Dickie and his boys cleared the woods.

"Where you hiding, you little shit?" Dickie called out. Ryan tried to stay quiet, as his chest heaved and he fought to gulp in air as quietly as his burning lungs would permit. "You better get back up here! What's down there will have you begging for us to come save you!"

"Screw this, man," Cody said. "Let's go on down there and find that little bitch."

"Fuck, yeah," Jeans Jacket added.

"Be my fucking guest," Dickie said. "You heard what they told us, stay the hell out of the jungle until they call for us."

"Dickie, come on, man. They ain't fucking ghosts, they're just weirdos, gangbangers. Come on."

"You two badasses go right on down there," Dickie said. "I'll tell your mamas, and fuck your sisters when you're both dead."

The gang was silent for a time. Ryan crouched near the side of the boxcar, and tried to be as still as stone. The sun was bright and hot, the cicadas hummed and a dry wind tousled the grasses.

"Well?" Dickie asked the two-would be rebels. If the other boys said anything, Ryan couldn't hear it. "That's what I thought," Dickie finally said. "Let's go." Ryan could hear them retreating back to the shadowed womb of the woods. "Hey, Helios, Phobos, he's all yours!" Dickie called out in a booming voice that echoed across the jungle and between the old rides and train cars, rusting gravestones of another age. "Enjoy the little punk." Then the teenagers were gone, lost to the woods again. Ryan couldn't shake the sick feeling that maybe he would have been better off if Dickie and the boys had caught him.

Heck stood at the maw of the tunnel on the Road to Nowhere, the bloody sun struggling at the treeline as it was strangled by the night. Before him, over a hundred Blue Jocks, their bikes idling, growling like chained junkyard dogs, stood, most of them armed, ready to ride and eager to throw down. The call had gone out to the club's entire membership all across the Southeast. A rough head count told Heck about ninety or so members were absent. That meant almost half the MC had been assassinated, were in jail, gone rogue, or were sitting this one out. None of those options were pretty. He wished Jimmie had come tonight, or Mom, but they had both made it clear to him what he was doing was a mistake. He was on his own on this one.

The Road to Nowhere was a monument of sorts to a whispered history of America. During the Second World War, the Tennessee Valley Authority, backed by the federal government, seized 68,000 acres of land for a dam project here in Bryson City, North Carolina, just a few miles into the Great Smoky Mountains. The project ended up displacing 1,300 families and flooding ancestral homesteads and family graveyards. Only six miles of road, a bridge, and a tunnel that ended nowhere were ever built of the road the feds promised the families so they could visit the graves of their loved ones and kin that hadn't been destroyed in the flooding for the dam. The Road to Nowhere was a monument to lies by the powerful to the powerless and it was holy ground to the Blue Jocks. On the other end of the tunnel that was at Heck's back the club had been born.

Roadkill stood beside Heck. The MC's sergeant-at-arms's wounds completely healed by his supernatural constitution once the silver had been removed from his body. Heck knew nothing could heal the pain that twisted inside Jethro at the loss of his dad, though. A massive sword, longer than Jethro, was scabbarded at an angle on his back. Jethro looked grimmer than

Heck had ever seen him in his life. Roadkill stepped forward, put his fingers to his lips, and whistled loudly. "Yo!" Roadkill called out to the suddenly silent bikers. "Listen up! You know me, and you all know Heck Sinclair, here. You know his family, know what they've done for the club, and you know he's pretty much my brother. Heck's fought and bled for our country and for the Jocks, and he deserves your attention, so pipe down and listen good!" Road-kill stepped back as the bikers cheered their approval with their voices and their throttles. Heck stepped forward and raised an arm. The crowd grew still and waited.

"We all know what happened to our leadership back in Lenoir," Heck be-gan. "We've lost some damn good men." There was a murmur of agreement and a surly undercurrent of anger. "Someone is trying to fuck with us, to take us down." More anger from the crowd and Heck felt his own smoldering em-bers of rage stoked as he thought of Glen, Jethro's dad, of all the other friends lost in this madness.

"I know a lot of you are like me," Heck continued. "You grew up in this club. Your dads, your uncles, your grandfathers, they wore the colors and they rode with honor and pride. They fought the same battle we fight every night. To keep the things in the darkness from chewing up the innocent, the weak. The Jocks isn't just our club, that word on a cut isn't just some old bullshit saying that means nothing. It's our code, our word, our honor. *Bráithreachas.* We are *Bráithreachas,* a brotherhood born of blood and fire, flesh and iron! Each and every one of you is my brother, my kin. Now, some sorry piece of shit is trying to destroy us, brothers!"

The crowd was a single organism, growling in anger and protest. Loud catcalls and boos punctuated the pause Heck took. "We've lost family to these bastards, we've lost our elders." He looked to Jethro, who wore a face Heck had never seen before. "We've lost our dearest blood! The question I've got for you, brothers, for all of you here, and I expect a goddamned answer," Heck called out, his own anger taut like rope inside him, "is what are we going to do about that?"

There was a roar from the assembled Jocks. Fists, bottles, rifles, and shot-guns were held aloft. Heck snarled like an angry wolf and Jethro screamed in anger, in vengeance, tears streaming down his rage-filled face. Heck grabbed, Jethro hugged him, and raised his fist with his brother to the dark-ening indigo sky.

A chant went up among the bikers "Sinclair, Sinclair!" Others chanted "Heck, Heck, Heck!" The motorcycles revved and roared but their masters were louder still. Roadkill joined it and slapped Heck hard on the back. The chant lifted and echoed through the forest that surrounded the assembly. Heck shouted out and beat his fist against his chest. The thing in him shouted too. His anger gave him power and made him burn with brilliant pure light.

Finally, Roadkill screamed out over the chanting and the bellowing of the bikes, "I say there is only one man to lead us in this fight, brothers! One man to hold this club together and lead us to victory and payback! As the only surviving officer of the Blue Jocks present, I nominate Heck Sinclair as president!" A cheer went up from the assembled Jocks. "Do I have a motherfuckin' second?" Jethro called out. A storm of "ayes" responded. Jethro looked over to his oldest friend and smiled. "The ayes have it. Heck Sinclair is the president of the Blue Jocks!"

A thunderous roar came from the assembled, louder than any before. Throats and engines screamed for their new leader, for Heck. Jethro slipped the massive sword off his back. It was a Claymore, over six feet long. It had been in the Sinclair clan for centuries. It had been Gordon's, Heck's grandfather, when he became the first president, and he'd passed it to Ale when it was his time to lead. Now Heck took the massive blade and cradled it in his arms. He unsheathed it and held it over his head with both hands. "Bráithreachas!" he called out to his leather-clad fellows.

"Bráithreachas!" the assembled responded as one booming voice, raising their own weapons skyward.

Heck opened his mouth to say more but at that moment the chanting was silenced by a chorus of howls coming from all around the bikers in the darkening woods. Eyes of green fire appeared everywhere in the shadows of the forest.

"It's the goddamned Bitches of Selene!" a gruff voice called out from the crowd of Jocks. "Let's light those fuckers up!"

The wolves burst from the cover of the treeline. They were the size of bulls. Their thick, shaggy fur was a deep emerald green that shifted to an almost luminescent white as they cleared the foliage and began to attack. Their tails were long and plaited. To their credit the Jocks were only surprised for an instant, but it was enough time for men to die, ripped and shaken to pieces in the slathering maws of the giant wolves.

Years of hunting and killing the terrors that bled out of the night gave these bikers an edge most wouldn't have. The automatic weapons fired and the shotguns went off a second later and the massive beasts howled in pain.

Some fell to silver shot and bullets, but the wolves hit with conventional rounds shrugged the wounds off and kept fighting, kept killing.

"No, wait!" Heck said but his voice was lost in the opening clash of the two forces. "Shit!" These weren't the Bitches of Selene, but in the gathering darkness they sure looked like them. Heck drew the Claymore from its sheath and moved into the fray, swinging the massive sword in a continuous figure-eight pattern before him, building momentum with the ten-pound blade. One of the monstrous wolves loped toward Heck and launched itself at him. Heck swung with all his considerable strength and what remained of his anger. The creature's whine was cut short as it was hacked in twain by the blow of the ancient highland sword.

Heck turned, spun his body even as he rebuilt the momentum of his twirling blade. Around him he heard gunfire, the *whoosh* of a flamethrower, the screams of dying men. He heard the beasts dying too, mostly from silver rounds and flame, but a few succumbing to prolonged weapons fire from regular bullets. These were no werewolves, but someone wanted the Jocks to think they were.

Motorcycle engines rumbled as several of the Jocks sped around the road and the surrounding treeline. They cut in between the trees, turning sharply and firing pistols and machine guns at the monstrous canines as they deftly maneuvered, catching some of the wolves in a deadly crossfire. The beasts could keep up with the speeding bikes, however, and a few more Jocks died as they were torn from their seat, ripped apart on the forest floor.

Heck saw Scotty Mcgraff and the Fortune brothers forming up a circle around a group of the injured Jocks off to his left. The injured men who were not in shock from bleeding out kept firing, or reloaded guns and handed them off to the men on the front line. That was all Heck had time to see before two more of the wolf-things lunged at him. One wolf fell to his sword, but the other was quick enough to slip in while Heck was killing its companion. The Claymore was a powerful weapon but slow, even in the hands of someone as strong and quick as Heck. The wolf's fangs were close to Heck's face when the back of its skull exploded. He looked to his back where the shot had some from and saw Jethro behind the scope of a .30-30 hunting rifle, cocking the lever forward to clear the breech and then locking it back to chamber another silver round. He nodded to his grim-faced friend. Roadkill's target had fallen on Heck and he took a second to toss the creature's massive corpse off to his right where it hit a tree and slid to the ground. He pulled the sword free from the other dead wolf-thing and advanced with Roadkill as his rear guard.

Part of the forest was on fire from the flamethrower. The remaining creatures, outgunned and outnumbered, fought on till the last. That made no sense to Heck either. Why didn't they run? It was their instinct, but something was overriding that instinct.

Within ten minutes, the woods was quiet again, save for the idling engines of bikes, the soft moans of the wounded, and the snap and pop of the fire as it devoured the forest. The bodies of dead beasts and dead men littered the road to the tunnel and the surrounding treeline. The trembling light from the flames gave glimpses of the bloody spectacle between the deep shadows of the night.

For a second, Heck thought he was back in Afghanistan, then he looked down at the bloody blade in his hands and he was grounded once more in the present.

"Jesus," Roadkill said, standing at his side. "What a goddamned mess." Jethro looked at Heck, who was staring down at the ripped and savaged body of James, the younger of the two Fortune brothers. James's empty eyes stared back at Heck. "Heck, we gotta go man. This is fucking bad." Heck nodded and ran a bloody hand through his mane of hair.

"Yeah," Heck said. He looked to Jethro and raised his voice so the ragged clumps of survivors of the battle could hear as well. "We take our dead, every single one. No one gets left here. No one."

"What about their bikes?" one of the Jocks asked.

"Leave them," Heck said. I want everyone out of here in five minutes."

"But Heck, the VINs on the bikes? The cops?"

"I'll deal with it," Heck snapped. "Get our wounded and our dead out of here. Ride for the armory we have at that self-storage place over in Bryson City. We'll meet up there." The bikers obeyed their leader. Several bikes started up and headlights winked on as the MC prepared to bug out.

Heck turned to Roadkill. "Call 911. Get some fire and park personnel up here. Then I want you call that street doc that Muskrat and his chapter use. Tell him we got wounded on the way and God help him if any of them die. Use two separate burners to make the calls." Roadkill nodded and began to step away to use the untraceable cell phone. He paused and looked back at Heck.

"You okay, man?"

"Far the fuck from it," Heck said, the fire from the woods flickering in his eyes, "but I'll get myself there." Roadkill nodded and went about making the calls. Heck walked to his bike and removed the handheld CB unit and the Bluetooth headset. More bikes were departing and smoke was beginning to drift along the road. Heck turned the CB to channel 23.

"Break 23, Break 2-3. This is . . . this is a Brother. I'm in need of some serious help ASAP . . ."

. . .

"What the hell were you thinking?" Jimmie roared. "You used Brethren to help you tidy up a crime scene? Have you lost your mind?"

They were in Elizabeth's living room, at her home in Cape Fear. The house looked a little like an armed camp. MC members were camped out everywhere, guarding their new president's mother. The sun was up, barely, and Heck had just got in the door when Jimmie had jumped his shit for getting help with the dead and injured Jocks' bikes. Elizabeth had been sleeping on the couch while Jimmie stood watch in Ale's old leather recliner. Now both of them were awake and his knight was up in Heck's face.

"Hector," Elizabeth said, "some of the guys got back here about three hours ago. They said you were attacked? That it was werewolves?" Heck held up his hands for both of them to back the fuck off.

"Yeah, I did," Heck said to Jimmie, "and no, Mom, they weren't fucking werewolves. I've seen plenty of weird shit over the years, hunting with the MC, and I don't fuck-all have a clue as to what those things were but I know someone is going to a lot of trouble to get us and the Bitches of Selene to go to war."

"Well, there's a shocking revelation," Jimmie said. "I told you that when you were ready to take on their whole club because you were angry! But you were too pissed off to listen, until they almost killed you."

"You're fuck right I'm pissed," Heck shouted. "I got friends dying in this, man! Where the fuck were you, partner, when my people were getting torn up by those things? Back here being smug and practicing telling me 'I told you so'!"

"Heck," Jimmie said, backing off and trying to clamp his own temper down, "you aren't a Brother yet," he said. "You can't call other members in like that, not now, not yet."

"Oh, but once I get a fucking pat on the head from you, and a my gold star, then it's okay, right?"

"No," Jimmie said, his anger resurfacing, "that's not how we do it, and if you'd stop letting Cherokee Mike jerk you around, maybe you could think clear enough to realize that."

"How could that fucking bastard be doing all this?" Heck said, pacing the room. "He had those things attack us, had them fight till the last one dropped. It was like he was controlling them or something, but he doesn't have any mystical juice."

"Maybe he's an old dog that learned a new trick," Elizabeth said. "Perhaps he has help."

"Help? Who?" Heck asked. Jimmie and Elizabeth traded looks and then Jimmie spoke. "I ran into an old . . . acquaintance of your mom's and mine. He might be helping Mike out with all this supernatural backup."

"Who?" Heck looked back and forth between his mom and Jimmie. He could tell they weren't giving him the whole story. "Tell me who this guy is, Mom. I need to know if I'm going to fight him." Elizabeth sighed and rubbed her face.

"He goes by Viper," she said. "That's the only name I ever knew him by. Jimmie said he ran into him a few days ago and I think he may very well be Cherokee Mike's silent partner."

"He got some mojo?"

Jimmie nodded. "He's pretty deep into black magic," the trucker said.

"He a former Jock?" Heck asked.

"No," Elizabeth said, some sadness in her voice. "He rides with . . . another club. My father, Gordon, didn't trust him enough to ever let him join. But he had power, terrible power."

"I've never heard anything about this guy," Heck said. "When did all this shit go down?" The look again between Jimmie and his mom.

"Just before you were born," Elizabeth said.

Heck slipped the Claymore scabbard off his back and leaned it by the fireplace. He sat back on the sofa and his mother sat beside him. Jimmie hadn't noticed until Heck slumped back on the couch just how worn down his wayward squire was looking. He had dried blood on his hands, hair, and clothes, and he seemed so goddamned young, and so lost. Jimmie sat back down on the edge of Ale's old recliner.

"The last time I got my shit jumped like this I was thirteen," Heck said. "I came home at 7:30 in the morning on Sunday, coming down from being drunk and stoned. Ale read me the fucking riot act." He looked to Elizabeth. "Told me how worried you had been about me, and then the son of a bitch dragged my ass straight into church feeling like warmed-over shit."

"Ale?" Jimmie said, "In church? An actual church?" All three of them laughed. Heck nodded.

"Yeah," Heck said. "He just drove us around, yelling at me, until he found one that looked good and pious. Sat us right in the front row. Scared the hell out of the preacher. I think Ale was more hungover than I was."

They laughed again, then it got quiet. Heck rubbed his bloody face and sighed. "I know you both love me. I know you both care about me and the MC, and I know you both think I'm doing this ass-backwards. I've tried to think how Ale would have dealt with it. It's hard to second-guess a fucking ghost. I'm president now. This is all on me." He looked over to Jimmie. "Sorry I overstepped. I knew I was when I did it. I knew I was when I brought your name into it. But I was trying to save my people and I was going to use anything I could to keep them safe and out of jail."

Jimmie nodded. He reached over and placed his hand on Heck's shoulder. "If it makes you feel any better, Ale would have done the same damn, stupid thing, and I'm pretty sure he wouldn't have apologized."

"Describe the beasts that attacked you to me, Hector," Elizabeth said. Heck did, mentioning their massive size, the changing color of their pelts, the braided tails, and how they fell to sustained fire from nonsilver ammo. Elizabeth nodded.

"Cu Sith," she said. "They were Cu Sith. Very rare beasties. They come from the Fae realms."

"Sith?" Heck said, "like *Star Wars*?"

"I believe Mr. Lucas borrowed the term," Elizabeth said.

They heard the guarded kitchen door open, and Roadkill and two other Jocks, armed with AR-15 assault rifles, entered the living room a moment later.

"How are our people, Jethro?" Elizabeth asked. Roadkill looked exhausted and far too young too. Jimmie recalled all the faces of the children he'd gone to war with in Desert Storm. War grew you up fast and it left the debris of your childhood in its wake.

"Fifteen dead at the scene," Jethro began. "Of the eight injured, it looks like three of them aren't going to make it. We dropped them off at a hospital in Asheville, in hope they might be able to do something the street doc couldn't."

"Shit," Heck said, leaning back on the couch. "It's like we were in a fucking meat grinder. How about our missing members?"

"The hits keep on rocking," Roadkill said. "Most of our no-shows are backing Cherokee Mike. He's claiming the presidency of the whole MC now. Says you're soft on the Bitches of Selene and all the other monsters we've hunted over the years. Claims you're working with some of the critters to eliminate your rivals in the club."

"Ballsy motherfucker," Heck said. Jethro nodded.

"The other Jocks not with him are either dead or missing. Some of our guys from the firefight last night are making noise like they're going over to Mike. A lot of them think those things were members of the BoS or allied with them. He's running rings around us in propaganda, Heck."

"Numbers?" Heck asked.

"We've got maybe sixty solid with you after the casualties last night. That's the Cape Fear, Asheville, Raleigh-Durham chapters, a few strays here and there. He's got close to seventy-five, eighty-five loyal, mostly from this home turf in the western part of the state. Maybe a few more, maybe a few less. Too close to mention."

"You got a civil war on your hands, son," Jimmie said. Heck looked to his mother. Elizabeth looked pale and close to tears. He knew what she was feeling. Her family was tearing apart. This was the nightmare she had hoped to avoid when she had sent him off to squire with Jimmie.

"Mike's holed up somewhere in Swain County," Jethro continued. "He's back to cooking meth and he has his Jocks retailing it. He's been cutting into MS-13's, the Outlaws', and the White Knights' business in the western counties for months now, all on the DL. He's pissing off the Dixie Mafia boys too."

"I knew he was ambitious," Elizabeth said, "but I had no idea the scope of what he was capable of. He will drag the Jocks down, Hector, if we . . . if you, don't stop him."

"I know," Heck said. "The cops are already looking at us sideways. Royal Elkins tried to tell me that when he showed up at the hospital after the shooting at Glen's. Mike's fucking it all up. He's going to piss away decades of goodwill Gordon and Ale tried to build up for the MC. He's turning us into just another bunch of scooter trash drug dealers."

"He's telling his people that drugs are better, safer money than monster or bounty hunting," Roadkill said. "He's not wrong, Heck. There was grumbling about that long before Mike ever slithered his way into the club. Ale was strong and straight-edge enough to crush it down, but he's gone now."

It was quiet and everyone in the room looked at Heck. Heck glanced to Jimmie for wisdom, but the trucker kept his own counsel.

"Ale is gone," Elizabeth said. "What do you plan to do, Hector?" Heck groaned a little as he got to his feet, and slung the heavy Claymore on his back again.

"Get our members' families together," he said, "loyal and even the ones who are on the fence. Get their kin here to Mom's and make sure we keep enough men on site to defend the place proper."

"Even the ones turning their backs on you?" Roadkill asked. Heck looked to Jimmie and Elizabeth and then nodded.

"Yeah. Families have falling-outs, don't make them any less family. Make it voluntary. They don't want to come, we leave them be. We're not collecting hostages like fucking Mike is."

"Done," Roadkill said.

"You get the word out to every one of our people. Those things last night were not Ana Mae's crew, they were not the Bitches of Selene. You tell them the truce holds and if they got a problem with that, come see me." Roadkill nodded.

"Won't go over well, but okay, boss. Anything else?" Jethro said.

"Get some solid intel on Mike's meth labs," Heck said. "I want locations, defenses, whatever you can confirm and keep it quiet. Is Bobby-Ray still with us?"

"Shit," Jethro said. "He and his crew are ready to eat nails and shit bullets."

"Good," Heck said, smiling. "Tell him to get a raiding party together. Time we put a crimp in Mike's cash flow. See how he likes being on the defensive."

"Hot damn," Jethro said with a grin. It was the first one to cross his face in a while. "Now you're talking, Mr. President."

"What you planning on doing?" Jimmie asked Heck.

"Recruitment drive," Heck said, "using a little diplomacy."

"You?" Jimmie said. "Diplomacy?"

"I'll have you know I can be one charming motherfucker when I want to be," Heck said.

Ryan sat against the side of the old railroad boxcar, his knees close to his chest, and waited. He was scared to move and scared not to. Finally when he began to feel the cool sweat trickling down his back from the baking afternoon heat, he stood and wiped his brow. He was thirsty and tired and all he wanted right now was a cold glass of Granny's grape Kool-Aid in one of the yellow plastic glasses she had in her cupboard. But he was a million miles from Granny, or Mom, or the guys, or Nevada right now.

He looked around the jungle and started walking back toward the abandoned train tracks. He could follow those tracks down about half a mile and come out in Coalport and then walk up the street to the park's main entrance, swing by Nevada's to give her her harmonica back, and then home to Granny— keeper of the Kool-Aid—by dark. It was safer than backtracking through the woods where Dickie and his goons could be hiding or even waiting in the field for Ryan to come back. The grass was almost as tall as he was in places and yellowed from the unforgiving summer sun. He walked between the old boxcars, like corridors. The cars were mostly open, their side doors probably too rusty and corroded to be pulled shut now. They bore ghostly painted images of elephants and balloons, clowns and big-top tents from the days they had been used to ship the carnival from one town to the next. Painted over those images on many of the cars was the looping scrawl of modern graffiti and more of the strange symbols that were seen all over the trailer park and, apparently, the jungle too. Two symbols, side by side, seemed to be everywhere, on the sides of boxcars, some of the symbols were made with dripping spray paint, others were put on with white chalk. The first one was five vertical lines, angled right, with two parallel horizontal lines intersecting the tilted vertical lines, like a crosshatch. The other mark was a four-sided diamond with a vertical line projecting from the apex of the diamond.

A third symbol, which Ryan had seen marking trailers, benches, and light poles all over the park, was everywhere here too. The symbol was a strange teardrop-shaped marking with a small T or cross at the tail end of the teardrop. He had no clue what the symbols meant and wondered if Joe had been right about them being "bum marks." Ryan kept walking. The only sound was his own labored breathing, the thud of his heart and the hot, dry wind caressing the tall grass.

He approached the looming, rusting hulk of the old Ferris wheel near the right side of the jungle and almost to the tracks. Several of the wheel's passenger cars had crashed to ground over the decades and lay half-buried in the dirt and weeds at its base, like rotting fruit dropped from a rusting iron tree. There was the sound of metal bolts and joints creaking and Ryan stopped, his head snapping in the direction of the sound. Another of the old rides, the flying scooters, where the rider controlled the ride by use of two paddlelike fins, now squatted, half-decayed behind him and to his left. One of the lower-hanging passenger compartments was swaying back and forth, its rusted chains softly clattering against each other, the metal joints holding the compartment and its chains up groaning at the movement. The wind wasn't strong enough to have moved it.

Ryan forced his legs to action and he headed for the tracks. He felt like he was going to pee himself and he didn't want that, not after all he had endured today. *No,* he told himself, *don't do it.*

He heard the tall grass rustling behind him and he spun around. The clown stood there, a garish nightmare that had congealed into this world. It was the one with the black sun painted on his forehead, the one with the sledgehammer, still gripped in his pale, giant hands. The clown smiled with yellow, rotting teeth, and desolate eyes.

Ryan ran for the tracks. He could hear the clown's labored breath behind him as it loped after him. There was a new sound off to his left, the swoosh of more grass moving, and a pale blur at the corner of his eye. He glanced over and his heart punched his chest like a fist.

A second clown had appeared from behind an old ride. This one was thin, fast. Its skin was the same sickly, greasy white as the other clown's and its face was a gaunt, garish mask with red diamonds around his eyes, trimmed in black, a wide ruby mouth, traced in yellow, and a yellow nose. The clown had a black crescent moon on its forehead. Whereas the lumbering giant wore filthy coveralls, this one wore the dirty tatters of a gentleman's fine suit from maybe the twenties or thirties. A bandolier made of stitched-together old, red cummerbunds was strapped across the clown's chest, sheathing a half-dozen ice picks, one of which was in the running clown's hand as he closed on Ryan.

The glance at the other clown's approach cost the boy. Something twisted Ryan's foot and he winced in pain as he went down hard, face-first into the gravel next to the train tracks. He felt thick, strong hands grab him by the collarbone and wrench him to his feet.

"No! No! Help!" Ryan screamed, his voice echoing through the jungle and this time he did feel the hot gush of the urine come. He was dead, he was about to die. His mom, Granny, Nevada, the guys, they all shot through his mind like a train through a tunnel. He clawed madly at the gravel, the pain in his palms, in his face from the fall were a distant impulse in this moment of cascading fear, thudding adrenaline. His finger settled on something cool and hard and he grasped it frantically.

"Up," the giant sun clown said. His voice was a booming, bass monotone. Ryan screamed at the pain in his back and shoulder. The huge man was hauling him off the ground through his one-handed viselike grip on Ryan's shoulder bones. Ryan dangled two feet off the ground. The pain was dizzying, cutting through even the fear.

The skinny moon clown stood beside his counterpart. They both stared dully at Ryan even as their lips were pulled back in smiles. It occurred to Ryan they almost acted like robots. The ice pick in the moon clown's hand moved close to Ryan's eye.

"Please, I didn't see anything," Ryan croaked, "please let me go, I'll never come back I promise, I'll never come back, please . . ." He was starting to cry, to lose it. After all the horrible things that had happened to him in Baltimore with Kenny, his stepdad, then all the shit with Dickie and his assholes . . . now this? Ryan's brain had tunnel vision, all he could see was this moment, this end to everything. The only emotion that fit in his cramped universe right now was fear. The icepick was a blurry smear in the field of vision of his right eye.

"No, no . . . Mama . . ." he whispered, trembling. The pick was nearly touching his eye.

There was a sound like the crack of a baseball bat hitting a ball and Ryan dropped to the ground at the giant's feet. His legs were rubber and he fell back onto his butt in the grass. The giant was stumbling, partially bent over and clutching at his bleeding head. A third clown stood with a long, heavy ax handle in his hand. The sun clown's blood was dripping from the end of the handle.

The third clown had the same pallid, oily skin as the other two, as well as a fringe of hair, almost like a military crew cut, and the shadow of beard stubble on his face. He was easily as tall and as powerfully built as the sun clown, but his mass was not flabby, he was thick with muscles. He wore a simple, old, frayed flannel shirt of red-and-black-checked pattern, dirty canvas work pants, and scuffed-up black work shoes. His features were unadorned with any type of colorful clown face. The only makeup he wore was a black circle on his forehead with three equidistant spokes. His eyes were dark, like the other two clowns, but his eyes still welled with the human light of emotion, a sadness, a terrible sadness, as opposed to the empty windows of the sun or moon clowns' eyes.

"No," the circle clown said. His voice wasn't as deep or booming as the sun clown's had been but its timbre was powerful, frightening. The moon clown lunged at the circle clown with the ice pick meant for Ryan. Circle clown swung his ax handle but the moon clown was too quick and slipped under it and jammed the steel needle deep into the circle clown's side. Circle grunted and staggered back, the pick still buried in him.

Ryan saw the sun clown right himself and heft his sledgehammer as he shambled toward the circle clown, who was pulling the ice pick out of his side with a grunt. The moon clown licked his painted lips, and slipped two more ice picks free from his bandolier, one for each hand, as he moved to flank Circle. They were going to gang up on him. Outnumbered and wounded, the circle clown wouldn't stand a chance.

The moon clown darted in quickly again, taking advantage of the circle clown's distraction from the pain of his wound, but Circle was feinting and as Moon slipped close, the clown caught a powerful fist square in his gaunt face. Circle grabbed Moon by the wrists and the two struggled as they grappled.

Ryan glanced down at the metal thing he had grabbed as he was hauled to his feet. It was an old railroad spike that had come loose from the rotted wooden track ties, but this spike was strange. It had been sitting out in the hot sun but it was cool, almost cold, to the touch. It looked like it was made of some silver metal and showed no signs of corrosion or wear. Weirdest of all was the thin, fine tracery and etching that covered the spike. In the split second Ryan looked at the spike in his hand, a shimmering blue energy passed through the spike and illuminated the almost invisible symbols.

The sun clown moved closer, getting behind the struggling Circle, ready to smash in the back of his skull with the sledge, while his partner, Moon, kept him occupied.

Ryan didn't pause to think, he didn't have the time or the capacity in this moment. He stabbed the skinny Moon in the thigh with the silver spike as Sun was rearing back to swing at the struggling circle clown. There was a brilliant flash of blue light, like lightning with no thunder, and Ryan swore the old dilapidated tracks flashed for an instant with the same blue fire as the spike buried itself in Moon's greasy flesh.

The moon clown let out a mournful bellow of pain and anger. His pale hand shot out and slapped Ryan hard. Ryan saw a flash of bright light behind his eyelids as the force of the blow sent him flying. He landed on the now smoking old railroad tracks and experienced another burst of pain-light as the back of his head struck the rail, hard. Slipping into darkness, Ryan raised his head feebly and saw the moon clown. The clown was wailing in pain as his body, wreathed in blue fire, crumbled to ash. The after-image of the clown's ghastly screaming face remained with Ryan for a moment in the darkness before he lost all awareness.

. . .

Ryan awoke to music. His head thudded in dull pain and he could feel all his accumulated wounds aching, burning, and throbbing. He felt like his bones were fused solid with pain. It was night outside and an old engineer's lantern shed buttery light on the room he was in. It looked like he was in the caboose car of a train. He was in a bunk under clean cool sheets; a large pillow cradled his pounding head.

The music was coming from a very old record player with a crank on the side. Ryan thought they called them phonographs. The music was scratchy and hollow like it was coming from a well, as it sang out from the phonograph's large metal speaker horn. The record and the song were really old, but sounded familiar to Ryan. Maybe he had heard it on TV? He listened to the words for a moment, the mournful, tinny voice of the singer. His head hurt so bad he was a little afraid to move. The song was "The Wabash Cannonball" and now that he was a little more awake Ryan realized that someone was playing harmonica along to the record. Ryan took the chance and rolled over onto his side. The circle clown sat in a rocking chair next to a small table built into the wall of the caboose. He was playing Nevada's harmonica and playing it well. There was a shuttered window above the table that was open and the cool night air wafted in. The clown had no shirt on and his chest and arms rippled with muscles and were marred by scars. His skin was all the same washed-out ghostly white as his face. It didn't look like it was makeup. He stopped playing when he saw Ryan awake.

"Better?" the clown asked the boy. Ryan nodded and winced.

"Yeah, but my head really hurts."

The clown put the harmonica down and stood. His head nearly scraped the roof of the caboose. He walked to the phonograph and lifted the large needle arm and the music stopped. He turned it off. He picked up a small, black glass jar and knelt on one knee beside Ryan, who slid back in the bunk, closer to the caboose's wall. Circle clown shook his head as he slid a single large finger into the jar.

"I . . . won't . . . hurt," he said. It was if the words, putting them together in a row, getting them out of his mouth, was a tremendous effort. He withdrew his finger from the jar covered in a white, greasy paste. Whatever the junk was, it had a strong chemical smell. "This . . . will . . . help." Ryan was trembling a little as the clown rubbed the stuff on the boy's forehead. It reminded him a little of the smelly goo Mom used to put on his chest when he had a bad cold. The chemical smell was strong and kind of gross but his headache faded almost at once and so did all the pain from his wounds and falls.

"Wow," Ryan said. That's pretty cool. Thanks." The clown lifted the finger he had applied the cream with and nodded at it.

"Just . . . a . . . little. Too . . . much . . . very bad."

"Okay," Ryan said. The clown rubbed the remainder of the cream on his finger on his side wound. The stuff seemed to soak into his skin immediately. "Hey you okay? That guy with the ice pick got you really bad."

The clown nodded and pointed to his wound, which was nothing more than scabbed-over hole now.

"Better . . . now." He said and held up the finger that had been covered in the cream again. "Fixes . . . things." Ryan nodded. As he started to sit up, the clown placed a huge hand on his chest. "Wait."

The clown walked to a dark section of the caboose car and returned with Ryan's jeans, folded. They smelled of soap, not pee. He handed them to Ryan. "Clean," the clown said.

"Thanks," Ryan said slipping his jeans over his now dry underwear and fastening them. He sat up and was surprised again how fully the weird white cream had cured his headache and dizziness.

"Thanks . . . you," the clown said. "You . . . helped . . . me."

"Well, yeah," Ryan said. "Those guys were going to kill me and you jumped in. I couldn't let them do the same to you."

"Thanks," the clown said again. He sealed up the black jar of ointment and placed back on the table. "We're . . . square."

"You, ah, you know what time it is?" Ryan asked. "I'm supposed to be home by dark. I'm probably in a lot of trouble." The clown stared at him for a long moment, then reached over and handed Ryan his sneakers and socks from the floor beneath the bunk. "Thanks," he said and began to struggle into his socks. "These bunks are really little. How, uh, how do you sleep in them?"

"Don't . . . sleep," the clown said, looking out the shuddered window. "Not . . . anymore. Chair . . . fine."

"You don't sleep, ever?" Ryan asked. The clown looked away from the window and nodded. "That's cool!"

The clown shook his head.

"No . . . it's . . . not." He picked up Nevada's harmonica and wiped it clean with a white linen hankie he pulled from the pocket of his pants. He handed the harmonica back to Ryan.

"I'd let you keep it," Ryan said, slipping the harmonica back into his pocket, "but it doesn't belong to me. Those older guys stole it." The clown nodded. He then picked something up off the small table with the hankie and handed it to Ryan as well. It was the silver railroad spike. The spike gleamed with faint blue light for just a second when Ryan took it. "So all that stuff, with the blue light and that clown turning to dust . . . it was real?" The clown nodded and pointed to the spike but didn't touch it.

"Yours," he said to the boy. "Keep . . . you . . . safe." The clown struggled with each word, fighting to pull them out of himself. "He . . . will . . . want . . . revenge . . . for . . . killing . . . one . . . of . . . his . . . Harlequins. He . . . will . . . have . . . to . . . replace."

"Who's he?" Ryan asked, "What's a Harlequin? You mean like Harley Quinn from the comics, and how can this spike do all that stuff it did?"

"He . . . is . . . evil," the clown said. "Old . . . evil. Won't . . . die." He pointed to the spike again. "This . . . of . . . the . . . Rail. Still . . . powerful."

"The Rail?" Ryan said, confused. He slipped the spike in his other pants pocket and finished tying his Chucks. The clown gestured for the boy to follow him. Ryan did. The clown unlocked the caboose's door and led the boy out on the small porch at the back of the car. Ryan saw the shadow of the Ferris wheel in the distance and he realized that the caboose was near the railroad tracks on the opposite side of the jungle from where the other clowns had jumped him. The clown climbed down the iron steps on the side of the car and then held his hands out for Ryan. The boy let the clown lift him effortlessly and place him on the ground.

"Get . . . you . . . home," the clown said. "Walk . . . with . . . you."

They made their way through the dark jungle and up the gentle slope of the hill toward the creek.

"Were you, were you with the old carnival?" Ryan asked. The clown nodded. "Are you a ghost?" The clown stopped walking for a moment.

". . . I'm . . . not . . . sure," he said.

The clown led him through the woods and all the way to the edge of the field. He stopped at the edge of the woods.

"Thanks again," Ryan said. He held out his hand to the clown. "I'm Ryan, Ryan Badel." The clown clasped the boy's tiny hand in his own massive one.

"Emmett," The clown said.

"You're Emmett," Ryan said. Emmett nodded. "You're kinda famous in the park. It's nice to meet you." Emmett nodded and pointed toward the lights of the trailer park on the far side of the field.

"Home," Emmett said. Ryan nodded.

"Yeah, I'm going to get grounded till I'm thirty," he said. "Thanks again. Bye." The clown raised his hand slowly, the palm open. Halfway across the field, Ryan looked back to the woods. Emmett wasn't there.

Since Max's arrival in Coalport she had spent most of her time at the borough's library and at the Coalport Area Coal Museum located in the Community Building on Forrest Street. Lovina had managed to secure Max a room across the hall from her own at the Central Hotel in town. She told Max everything on the drive from the bus terminal, including her suspicions that while Calvin was clearly dangerous, he was not the person they were looking for in this case. The hardest admissions had been about the city and her hallucination of seeing it when she was leaving the trailer park the other night.

"Metropolis-Utopia has always been connected to the viamancers, to road magic," Max had said after listening quietly as they'd driven to Coalport through the bright morning. It was already getting hot and they had the windows down as the Charger hummed along the two-lane country road.

"What do you think Metropolis-Utopia *is,* Max?" Lovina asked, forcing herself to keep her eyes on the road and not on Max.

"There's a theory in physics that time is an illusion, a trick our brains play on us," Max began. "The theory goes that all the events that have occurred, are occurring now, and will occur in the future are happening at the same time, the only time. There's another long-standing theory that matter interacts with other matter based on its location to each other in space. Objects interact with their immediate neighbor. The theory is called locality."

They passed a deep, ugly, barren wound in the land from the strip mining that still continued in the area. It was like someone had dropped an alien landscape, an oasis of desolation, in the lush green of the mountains and forests. Massive, stories-high piles of accumulated waste rock and soil, called spoil in the mining business, stood beyond the edges of the deep pit like watchtowers in Hell.

"So, basically things interact with other things that are close to or immediate to them. That's the short definition of locality," Max concluded. Lovina nodded.

"Haven't lost me so far," the investigator said. Max held up her hands, put her fingers together like pincers, and moved her hands further away from each other.

"Well here's where it starts to make a lot less sense. Quantum mechanics has really messed with the theory of locality. Experiments have been conducted that show that the same particle, the exact same unique particle can exist in two locations at once, that the cause enacted on a particle in one part of the universe can have the same effects on another particle somewhere else. You only see the result of the effect when you view both particles. In other words, our understanding of physics is leading us to the conclusion that the universe is *nonlocal,* that space is not a structure laid down like a fence to separate everything, that it's an illusion, like time, that our brains use to make sense of what we can scarcely comprehend with our limited perceptions."

"So you're saying everything that exists," Lovina said, "exists at the same time, in the same place."

"That's the theory," Max said.

"And we just fool ourselves into thinking it's otherwise?"

"Yes," Max said. "The human mind would be hard taxed to experience everything, everywhere at once without slipping into what we now consider madness."

They were clear of the mine and the slag pits. The sunlight fell once again through the canopy of green leaves, pinpricks of bright light pushing through.

"And you're trying to tell me," Lovina said cautiously, "that this damned city, this Metropolis-Utopia is . . ."

"The place where all of space and time crash together," Max said. "Many mythologies and religions have the belief in an *Axis Mundi,* a center of creation, a halfway point between Heaven and Hell. Purgatory, for example. The K'iche Mayans had a god, *Q'uq'umatz,* who was the center of all the worlds and powers, the mediator and the gate between them. The Egyptians had *Isfet* and *Ma'at.* Some nihilist fringe cults speak of Azathoth, a mindless abomination that squats at the center of all time and space."

"And I'm going crazy . . . because I'm beginning to see past the illusions of space and time?"

"It's just a theory," Max said, shaking her head, seeing the strain play across Lovina's face. "Please don't worry. You're okay, and you're going to keep being okay. I won't . . ." She reached out to take Lovina's hand but then stopped herself. "It's just a theory."

They were both silent for a little while. The radio was playing the Civil Wars' cover of "Disarm." Finally, Lovina said, "Cops and scientists have a few things in common. We both play hunches, but we both need evidence to bring it to court. Thank you, Max, for not bullshitting me." They were both quiet again for a time. "So about this case . . ." Lovina began.

. . .

Max made numerous trips to the county courthouse up in Clearfield and did some digging. She also raided the archives of the old *Coalport Standard* newspaper that had become the *Houtzdale Citizen and Coalport Standard* in 1934.

Meanwhile, Lovina went about doing the legwork all cops had to do sometimes to shake loose a lead. She interviewed residents of the trailer park about Raelyn with the blessing and assistance of the park's manager, Bob Valenti. She also asked about any other strange happenings connected to Coalport and the park and got an earful of local mythology and ghost stories, but little solid information.

Lovina even wandered through the woods behind the park with Valenti as a guide to check out the boxcar jungle. She found nothing there but hot, empty train cars and decaying carnival rides. She did take photos of the strange symbols marking the boxcars, some in spray paint, others in chalk. She had noticed some of them back at the park and took pictures of them too. Valenti said he had no idea what they meant but he thought they were graffiti from the local teens. He'd clean it off and it would show back up a few days later.

"Man," Bob said after they returned from the sweltering and seemingly fruitless exploration of the graveyard of trains and rides. "I hate to say it Lovina, but Raelyn missing might just be, like, one of those, y'know, things that never get solved. It's a bummer, but y'know, it happens."

"I know, Bob, but I'm not ready to quit yet," she said. "There's something up here, something wrong and I'm going to figure it out." Valenti invited her into his tiny silver Airstream trailer for a cold beer, but Lovina declined. She changed tactics and spent the last few days expanding her canvass to cover Coalport itself, but she met with similar results: plenty of stories but few hard facts.

Max had been in Coalport about a week. They were in a booth that had kind of become "their booth" at the Central Hotel. They had ordered steaks, which were excellent, and Lovina had a tall, cold pint of Genesee beer. Max finished off her second can of energy drink as she slipped her files, her tablet, and her notebooks out from her satchel.

"Well," Max began, "I found newspaper articles about the Valentine Traveling Carnival and Sideshow. The carnival traveled all over America in the late twenties, through the Great Depression, and during and after World War II. The carnival fell on some hard times in 1952 and Coalport literally became the end of the line for the carnival's carnies and performers."

"What happened?" Lovina asked.

"Carnivals were dying off all over the country," Max said. "Television killed a lot of them. The Valentine Carnival was going bankrupt and was no longer able to afford to transport the carnival on the rails, or even to pay the performers. They scuttled the carnival's boxcars and rides beside the railroad tracks that are behind the trailer park now.

"When Coalport's spur of the Pennsylvania Railroad's Northwestern division was discontinued due to changes in the railroad and coal industries, those sections of track where the carnival had deposited itself were abandoned too."

"I guess the railroad pretty much was this town," Lovina said. Max nodded.

"The town had a boom at the turn of the twentieth century due to King Coal," Max said. "They brought it in on barges down Clearfield Creek and then it became a rail stop, a home to coal miners and their families. Things changed over the course of decades. By the sixties, Coalport was another American town without an industry. The population shrank decade by decade ever since. Today, only around five hundred people live here, and the majority of them commute to work in other localities or are on public assistance."

"Did the trailer park spring up from the folks left out in the cold when the carnival went bust?" Lovina asked as she swirled a thick steak fry in the A.1. Sauce on her plate. Max retrieved a sheaf of photocopies from a folder and slid one of them across the table to Lovina.

"What's this?" the investigator asked.

"A copy from the courthouse of the deed to the lands the trailer park is on, and the lots behind it abutting the old railroad tracks," Max said. "The county clerk's records state that in 1953 the land was purchased from the borough council by the owner of the carnival, one 'N. Flamel.' The listed purpose for the purchase is to provide cheap housing for the borough and specifically for the former employees of the Valentine Carnival. Apparently there had been some complaints about the living conditions of the carnies. They were living in trailers, shanties, some in tents, others in the old boxcars down by the tracks. That area was becoming a hobo jungle and the borough fathers and the locals were not thrilled with that. So, from that purchase, the Valentine Trailer Park was created."

"Hobos again," Lovina said. "Remember I told you about that hobo nickel that Russ found in Raelyn's car?" Max nodded as she cut and ate a tiny bite of her steak. "I think we've found our ground zero for whatever the hell is going on." Lovina tapped her phone and pulled up the pictures she had taken of the strange chalk symbols all over the trailer park and the jungle. She showed them to Max. "These mean anything to you?"

"Hmm." Max pushed her glasses back on her nose and studied the pictures. "Not magical symbols from any school or tradition that I'm familiar with, but they do look familiar. Could you send them to me?" Lovina did. "There are occult groups and secret societies that have their own languages and secret symbols. I'll run them through the Builders' database and see if anything pops up."

"Anything else on this N. Flamel?"

Max nodded eagerly, snapped her fingers, and pointed to Lovina, like she had just remembered something vitally important. She shuffled folders and papers. "Um, yes . . . um." She plucked one out, like it was a prize. "Born in 1919 in Toledo, Ohio, died in 1959 here in Coalport. The property has remained in his family's possession and is now run by a property management company his family established in 1979, along with numerous other properties all over the country. No relations still live at the park or here in town."

"Do the records say anything about cause of death, Max?"

Max scoured her notes and the paperwork. "Um, yes. Natural causes."

"That's it?" Max nodded. "I guess 'murdered by clowns' would be a bit too much to ask for," Lovina said. She traced her fingernail along the weathered green and white Formica of the tabletop. "Well, asking around here got me a little intel but not much. Folks here don't like to gossip to strangers."

"There were a few deaths back in the fifties on the land the park's on now, back when it was pretty much a hobo jungle. The locals got up in arms about it, a few kids went missing, never showed up again, and a local grocer turned up hacked to death pretty bad and left near the train tracks. Some of the local men went out to the camp and beat and chased off the transients, but they drifted back a few months later. Rough time frame for all that seems to be in the early fifties, right around the time the trailer park was created. I've got a call into Wojick and see if I can get the staties' reports about it."

"Anyone say anything to you about local myths, phenomena?" Max asked. Lovina drained the last of her beer and dabbed her lips with a napkin.

"That everyone seemed to have a story about," she said. "Clown sightings have been happening around Coalport since the early fifties from all over Clearfield and Cambria counties. They seemed to be connected with unsolved disappearances and murders. I have to tell you, Max, the way the folks are repeating the stories it sounds like pure one hundred percent urban myth."

"So you don't think there's credence to the clown phenomena?" Max asked just as the waitress arrived to check on their drinks. She was in her early twenties and her brown hair was in a ponytail. She had mascara wings and a septum piercing.

"Oh, clowns!" the young woman said. "They're so creepy! Yunz know people have seen them around here, right?"

"Really?" Lovina asked, nodding to Max. "You got a story?" The waitress nodded as she refilled Max's beer and placed a fresh can of Monster in front of Max.

"Oh yeah, ask anybody," she said. "There were these two kids from Pennsylvania Community College over there by Altoona. They had some car trouble coming home from a party. They ended up a little ways down 53 from here with their car on the berm, and while the boy was working on it they started hearing this weird singing, like a little kid's voice or something. Anyways, the singing turns into laughter and this clown with a big old machete comes running down the road toward them. They get in the car and lock the doors, but the clown keeps circling them, hit the windows and the windshield and cracks them bad! He's about to get 'em, when another car comes by and the clown just walks away and disappears!" The waitress waited for a response from Lovina and Max and after a moment Max realized this and pretended to jump as if startled.

"Oh!" Max said. "That is . . . uh creepy, right." Lovina laughed and nodded to the girl.

"Scary!" she said. The waitress laughed with them and nodded.

"Yeah, right?" the girl said. "Coalport is famous for having 'em! George Norse's TV show—*Paranormal America*—did a special on the 'Clowns of Clearfield County.' Cool huh?"

"Very cool," Lovina said. The waitress grinned and headed off to another table. Lovina shook her head and nodded after her. "That's what I'm talking about. I heard that story or a variation on it a dozen times last few days. Others too. I checked. That never happened, or if it did it was never reported to anybody. Max, I know what my dream showed me, but thinking some supernatural evil is walking around in big floppy shoes and a big red nose just seems, I don't know, too much."

"It's a global phenomenon," Max replied, cracking open her third can of energy drink.

"You keep drinking those things," Lovina said, "your heart's going to pop like a balloon."

Max gave a dismissive wave. "They, uh keep me, uh . . ."

"Focused?" Lovina offered. Max nodded quickly and pointed to Lovina.

"I've never been one to go for the theory that hallucinations can be some kind of mass viral hysteria," Max said. "Too convenient an answer with too little data to back it up. There is something to these clown sightings, and clearly there is some kind of dangerous phenomenon at work here. Maybe we should look at the why's, not the what's."

"What do you mean?" Lovina asked.

"Why Coalport? Why the trailer park?" Max said. "We have an effect, but the cause is a mystery. I think I need to start taking a look at that."

"Okay," Lovina said. "Sounds good, and I'll see if I can dig anything up on the Flamel family who were involved with the carnival and then the park and check with Russ about . . ." Lovina's phone hummed and she checked the screen. It was Russell Lime. She tapped the screen and put the phone to her head. "Were your ears burning?" she said with a smile.

"Hello, *chère*." Russ's voice was low, and he sounded exhausted.

"Russ, what is it, you okay? Is Treasure all right?"

"I'm afraid not," he said. "We're in the hospital, they just took her back for another surgery. It's . . . not looking good, Lovina."

"Russ, I'm so sorry. I can be down there in—"

"No, darlin'," Russ said. "Work the case. All you'd be doing here is sitting with an old man worrying and frettin'. I can do that all by myself. I wanted to give you the results of the tests on that hobo nickel and the clown white makeup you gave me. I submitted them to the lab myself and the results came back this afternoon, but then I got . . . kinda busy." He made a dry sound attempting to be a chuckle. It made Lovina wince. She could hear the pain in her old friend's voice and wished she could do something, anything, to take it away, or even just ease it.

Russ cleared his throat and sniffed. Lovina imagined him wiping his eyes. "Whatever that makeup is it's a very strange soup of chemicals," he said, back to business now. "There's traces of some form of diluted sulfuric acid, naturally occurring base sulfur with particles of gravel." Lovina gestured to Max and mouthed the words 'pen and paper.' She hastily scribbled down the description as Max folded her small legs under her and leaned over the table to read it upside down.

"The acid could be used as a catalyst in the makeup," Russ said. "There's also sodium carbonate, calcium oxide, more commonly known as lime," Lovina kept writing, "and red mercuric oxide. Rubbing that stuff into your skin for a long enough time is a great way to go stark raving insane, *chère*."

Lovina noticed that Max was silently mouthing the names of the chemicals and it was obvious that her formidable mind was at work unraveling some knot the information had presented her with. Russ continued but Lovina heard someone on his end say "Mr. Lime?"

"There were minute traces of animal fat proteins, possibly for binding," Russ said, his voice a bit more strained and hurried, "and a few compounds the chromatograph blew a fuse trying to figure out. They came up as inconclusive. But one of the mystery compounds bears an odd resemblance to organic N,N-Dimethyltryptamine."

"N, N what, Russ?" Lovina said.

"Hold on, *chère*." Russ was talking to someone and Lovina thought she heard Treasure's name mentioned. The forensic scientist was back, his face next to the phone again. He said thank you to someone on his end, the weariness back in his voice. "It's a powerful hallucinogenic. On the street they call it DMT."

"Everything okay, Russ?" Lovina asked and felt stupid as soon as she did. His wife was dying. Everything was far from okay.

"Just this sweet little nurse checking on me," Russ said, fighting to sound like classic Russ Lime. "I'm fine. I told her I already have a girlfriend, just waiting on her to get back."

"DMT," Lovina said, deciding that changing the subject was probably the best way to go. "That's a club drug, Russ. I thought that was synthetic?"

"Some plants and animals produce it naturally," Russell said. "Human brains actually produce something close to it too. It's released in large doses by our brain just prior to death. There are signs of something like dimethyl sulfoxide, more commonly known as DMSO, in the compound too. That means whatever this stuff does, its chemicals would leach into the wearer's skin and bloodstream. Whoever made this goop, they're a brilliant and eccentric chemist. I checked out the hobo nickel too."

"Please tell me there were prints," Lovina said.

"A partial, but it doesn't show up in IAFIS as-is. Sorry, *chère*."

"It's okay," Lovina said. "Didn't figure it would be that easy. Send the partial back to me anyway."

"Your strange white makeup was on the coin in small traces," Russ said. "Same stuff as from your dream-clown. I'm not even going to try to figure that one out. The coin is authentic, old, and handmade. That's a bit of good luck. These hobo nickels have signature styles that can link them to specific artists that carved them."

"So maybe we can trace this guy through how he came into possession of that particular coin," Lovina said. "That's great, Russ. You know any collectors or art appraisers that might be able to give me hand?"

"I'm afraid I'm not up on the hobo art world, *chère*," Russ said. "Hold on." His face was away from the phone again and Lovina heard several voices talking to Russ. He replied softly and then he was back on the call. "Lovina, darlin' I have to go. Treasure's out of surgery. If I can dig up any—"

"You hush," Lovina said. "You've done plenty. Go take care of your girlfriend, y'hear? Give her my love."

"I will, darlin'," Russ said. He was choking up again. "I'll keep you posted and I'm FedEx'ing you the hobo nickel along with the reports and print."

. . .

The call came in the final dark hours before dawn stirred. Lovina answered her cell on the second ring. "Yes," she said into the receiver, already sliding out of bed.

"Yeah, Lovina, it's Dave Wojick. We found her."

It took them about forty minutes to reach Windber. The spot Wojick directed them to was lit up like beacon of blue and red lights they could see halfway up 219. There was a cluster of first-response vehicles huddled together in the gravel parking lot of a local baseball field. State police and local patrol cruisers were joined by Crime Scene trucks and ambulances. Wojick, looking miserable and tired, greeted them as soon as they pulled up.

"Dave, this is Dr. Max Leher with Georgetown University. She's helping me on the case," Lovina said. "Max, Dave Wojick, Pennsylvania State Police investigator."

"Good to know ya," Wojick said, shaking Max's hand. "I think yunz may have come all that way for nothing. H'okay, hope you brought your comfy shoes. The scene's a ways up in the woods. Everybody and their frickin' mother's wanted to move the body but I told 'em you got first dibs." Wojick snapped on his batonlike Maglite. "'Side's, this scene's a little more involved than most."

"What is it, Dave?" Lovina asked. "A boneyard? This his dumping ground?" Wojick shook his head.

"Nah . . . it's . . . it's fucked up is what it is. Yunz better see it yourself."

"You sure it's my girl?" Lovina said, holding out some strand of hope, already imagining knocking on Malyssa Dunning's door to tell her the wait was over. "They may need to do facial reconstruction or DNA depending on how much the wildlife didn't get to."

"It's her," Wojick said. "I did a facial ID from her photo. We're running prints now to be a hundred percent."

"Her face? Dave, she was abducted over four years ago. You trying to tell me she's been alive?"

"I don't know what I'm trying to tell you," Wojick said. "It's fucking weird."

Max looked to Lovina as they headed deeper into the woods, following Wojick.

"I'm sorry," she said softly. Lovina nodded, tried to give a thin smile, but Max saw the defeat in her eyes, and the simmering anger.

The hike up took a while and it was a bit unpleasant, especially in the dark. The circle of Dave's flashlight bounced and dipped with each step, illuminating skeletal fingerlike branches one moment and the narrow footpath they were following the next.

"The owner of the property has a security guard that checks on the place to keep the kids away, since it's showed up on some internet sites, but the guard says there was nothing when he made his rounds at 3:30, but when he came back at 4:30, there she was. No noise, no headlights, no car tracks. Nothing. They called us, and I called you."

By the time they reached the rise, the sky had lightened to a dim curtain of watery blue mixed with ash. Topping the rise, Lovina and Max saw what lay beyond. Over a dozen old trolley cars in various states of decay huddled against the trees of the forest in the feeble predawn light. Their bodies were rusted hulks with paint leached by weather, sun, and time. The windows of most of the cars were smashed out by growing, gaunt tree branches.

"First the boxcar graveyard at Coalport," Max said, "now a trolley graveyard in Windber. Pennsylvania seems to be the place for old trains to die."

One trolley they passed, painted in cracked and peeling red, white, and blue, had its undercarriage compartment doors swung wide open below the conductor's broken windows and a bulbous red trolley bell. It made the car look like a giant clown's face leering, laughing.

Forensic technicians had created a perimeter of bright lights on tripod stands, illuminating the edges of the scene, a clearing between three of the old cars. They moved about quietly, like hooded, bunny-suited monks attending to and recording the tiniest minutia of atrocity. Lovina entered the circle of light alone. Max paused at the terminator, knowing this was a private moment. One CSI guy began to protest but Wojick shut him up with a hand on his chest and a curt shake of his head.

Lovina looked down. The forest floor, carpeted in layers of brown, decaying leaves cradled the remains of Raelyn Dunning. Raelyn had been savagely cut into two pieces at the waist. Her abdomen and legs were a few feet to the left of her upper body. Raelyn's arms were above her head as if she were raising them in surrender. The girl's mouth had been savagely cut on both sides into a wide, bloody grin. The killer had tucked her entrails under her buttocks. The detail pushed through the sadness and anger filling Lovina's mind and nudged the cop back to the fore. The girl had been mutilated and arranged in the same manner as the ghostly apparition of the black-haired girl Lovina had encountered in the trailer park courtyard that night with the flamingos.

Lovina knelt near the girl's upper body. Raelyn's glassy eyes met the investigator's gaze.

"I'm sorry," she whispered. It was the same thing she had said when she had found her sister's body. It felt as hollow now as then. There was something under a dead brown leaf near Raelyn's head. Lovina picked it up. It was another hobo nickel with the same death's head carved into it as the one Russ had found in Raelyn's car.

"Uh, see what I mean." Wojick was standing behind her now. Lovina could tell the big cop wanted to give her some condolences, but he knew that wasn't how the job worked. You grieved on your own time, not on the clock. She palmed the nickel and slipped it into her jacket pocket. "No signs of decay, or animals eating the body. Either she's been alive all this time or the sick bastard preserved her somehow."

Lovina stood and glanced to where Max still stood in the darkness at the edge of the lights. The professor was circling the scene and chewing on her lip, obviously deep in thought. Lovina looked around the scene as she got her bearings again.

"Can you get the autopsy rushed, Dave?" Lovina asked softly. "Please."

"Yeah, yeah, sure, of course," Wojick said.

"I've seen this before," Lovina said. "Exactly like this." She saw something on one of the trolley cars in the circle. Lovina stepped out of the light and let her eyes adjust to the pale dawn. A series of symbols were drawn in chalk on the snout of the trolley. They looked similar to the ones placed all over the trailer park and the boxcar graveyard. One of them was a rectangle with a dot in its center, just like in her dream of Raelyn being abducted.

Max was beside her, her tablet in her small hands. She held the screen up so Lovina could see. The image was a grainy black-and-white photo of a dark-haired woman's body, cut and arranged almost exactly the same as Raelyn, lying in the grass.

"That's the woman, the ghost, whatever it was, I saw at the trailer park, Max," Lovina said. "Who is she?

"They call her the Black Dahlia," Max said.

Jimmie was in Elizabeth's kitchen in Lenoir with Layla and Elizabeth, cooking his wife and hostess breakfast when his cell phone went off. He struggled to fish the ringing phone out of his jeans pocket while trying to keep the bacon and pancakes from burning. "Baby?" he said, juggling the sizzling pan of bacon as he struggled with his phone. Layla got up from her coffee.

"What, you can save the universe from cosmic destruction by some big horned guy, but you can't juggle a phone call and a stove?" Jimmie scowled. "Okaaaay," she said with mock weariness and a grin. She took his place at the stove and gave Jimmie a peck on the cheek.

"Thanks," Jimmie said, kissing her back. He answered the phone and walked into the living room for some privacy.

"Lovina? Yeah, go ahead."

"You two remind me of me and Ale back in the day," Elizabeth said to Layla. "My heart would jump up into my throat every time the damn phone would ring or an MC member showed up at our door." Layla nodded as she flipped a finished pancake and placed it on a stack on a plate next to the stove.

"Am I that obvious?" Layla asked. "I thought I covered pretty good."

"You do," Elizabeth said. "He didn't have a clue, but you can't BS a BS'er."

Layla laughed and placed some strips of crunchy bacon on a layer of paper towels on a platter. "Yeah," she said. "I guess not. It's bad enough when he's out on the road just working, but when he's out for the Brotherhood it's a hundred times worse."

Elizabeth nodded. "It was harder when Heck was little."

Layla poured the batter for another pancake and flipped some hissing bacon. "I try really hard to keep my peace, to not let him know how much it scares me. The last thing he needs out there on the road with all the crazies and the monsters is to be fretting about me and the kids. I do worry about JJ growing up with only photographs and secondhand memories of his father. I tell myself I'm overreacting, but, goddamn, Elizabeth, he's just a man, and the things he sees and fights against out there . . . and I know he keeps the worst of it away from me."

"One night, when Heck was maybe . . . six," Elizabeth said, "I heard noise downstairs. Ale was off with the Jocks on a hunt for . . . something. I got my gun and I went downstairs and there was Ale, sitting at this very kitchen table. He was bleeding hard, and his face looked like it had been rearranged with a hammer. He was sitting there with a bottle of Jack and a pair of pliers, pulling these foot-long . . . spine-things out of his side. He said the thing had shot them from its body. It killed Marty Corrigan—I don't know if you'd remember him—when he caught one of them in his throat."

"Jesus," Layla said.

"So there was my old man, bleeding like a stuck pig all over my kitchen at four in the morning after he had been out all night chasing some fucking porcupine-monster-thing. I lost it. I told him I couldn't do this anymore, that it had to stop or I was taking Heck and leaving.

"Layla, I never thought those words would come out of my mouth. Ale was the most decent man I've ever known. He went through hell for me. He couldn't have loved Heck any more if he had been his own flesh and blood, and he was out there in the night fighting to keep strangers safe, to help our little boy grow up in a safer world . . . but I just couldn't bear seeing him like that, knowing he might have been the one to die that night, not Marty, and wondering what night he would die."

"What did he do when you said that?" Layla asked.

"The son of a bitch told me that the only thing that kept him alive out there was knowing he was coming home to us," Elizabeth said. "He said he could make me a bunch of bullshit promises about quitting the Jocks, about not going on the hunts, but that when push came to shove, he couldn't do that, couldn't let other men take the risks, let their families take the risks he wouldn't. And he said he'd understand it I had to go and take Heck with me."

"Did you leave?" Layla asked, but she already knew the answer. Elizabeth smiled and shook her head.

"Couldn't do it," she said. "I've known old ladies who have. But it wasn't for me. He was my man, and he needed me. So I stayed, and looking back now, I don't regret it."

"The things that make them who we love are the same things that can get them killed," Layla said. "It's enough to make you scream sometimes, but I wouldn't trade him for anything, for all the gold in this world." She scooped up a pile of bacon and placed in on the plate. "Goddamn it." They both laughed.

"If it makes you feel any better, we can eat his share of the bacon before he gets off the phone," Elizabeth offered. Layla smiled and popped a piece of bacon into her mouth.

. . .

"It sounds like you were right about chasing down this case," Jimmie said to Lovina as he sat in Ale's old easy chair and looked out the window into Elizabeth's front yard. His view was of two Blue Jocks leaning against their bikes, parked at the curb. The guards smoked cigarettes, scanning the street for trouble. "Now that you've found the girl's body, you're going to stick at it, right?"

"Damn straight," Lovina said. "We've been digging deep in Coalport and the trailer park the last few days and, now suddenly, after all these years, the killer decides to dump the body? I don't buy it's coincidence. Whoever, or whatever, it is, they were hoping we'd pack up and head home once they gave us Raelyn."

"You've got somebody nervous," Jimmie said. "So Max is telling you Raelyn is related to the Black Dahlia case from, how long ago exactly?"

"Nineteen forties," Lovina said. "In Los Angeles. Yeah, she says the staging of the crime scene is a copycat of the original. Killer was never caught." There was a pause on the line.

"It was bad," Jimmie said.

"Yeah," Lovina said after a hard swallow. "It was. He cut her up, set her out for display."

"I'm sorry," he said. He almost asked the stupidest question in the universe, *are you okay?* but he knew better. You could never be really okay after seeing things like that. Why make her lie for your benefit? Instead he shifted gears. "Does the Black Dahlia track with your original theory about I-80?"

"No," Lovina said, "it doesn't. I-80 ends in California, but nowhere near L.A. Max is looking into any mutilation murders along I-80 that might match the MO. I only looked at disappearances. I never thought to check into the highway being a dumping ground too. I should have."

"That's why you brought Max in on the case," Jimmie said. "Can't think of everything, but Max sure as hell can. Tell her I'll reach out to Cecil Dann, see if he's willing to help with the information about body dumps on I-80 that match Raelyn."

"Thanks. Actually, Jimmie," Lovina said, "I was wondering if you knew anyone who might be able to shed some light on a very weird piece of evidence we've run into. You know any Brethren that know anything about hobo nickels?"

Jimmie leaned back on the couch. "Hobos? Yeah, actually I do."

"Of course you do," Lovina said. "You know Elvis for chrissake." Jimmie chuckled.

"There's a guy, more like a kid—he's pretty young—but he's good people and damn smart. He's a nomad, kind of a modern-day version of the hobos, and a scholar and historian about that whole culture. If anyone could help you or point you in the right direction, it would be him."

"How do you know this guy?" Lovina asked.

"His uncle and I are good friends," Jimmie said. "He's a trucker, and member of the Brotherhood. He brought his nephew into the order."

"How do I reach out to this wandering scholar?"

"I'll make a few calls," Jimmie said. "See if he's checked in with the network. His name is Dustin Acosta. His traveling moniker is Bang! Pow! Boom!"

"Are you kidding me? I thought 'Bandit Two' was bad."

"Be nice," the trucker said, "he's Brethren."

"How are things there?" she asked.

Jimmie sighed. "Heck's declared himself president of the MC and he's got himself into a two-front war. It's a mess. I think I know who's behind it, and he makes Cherokee Mike look like a Boy Scout."

"You need us?" Lovina asked. "Max and I can—"

"No," Jimmie said. "Whatever you're into sounds like bad news and Brethren bad news at that. Stick at it. We got this."

"Tell Heck I said hello," Lovina said.

"I will," Jimmie said, "as soon as he gets back from his date with the werewolf."

There was a pause on the phone line. "What?" Lovina said.

. . .

Heck's and Ana Mae's bikes cruised along I-40 skirting the edges of the Nantahala National Forest, heading southwest. The day was clear and warm, perfect for a long ride and Heck had to admit he was enjoying himself in spite of the reason for his mission today and his company on the ride.

Ana Mae rode a 2016 Harley Softail and Heck had to admit the president and war chieftain of the Bitches of Selene rode it well. Once they got out on the open highway, away from the city traffic, Heck had opened up his Blackie and taken off like a rocket launched from Hell. Ana Mae caught up to him and passed him in the wrong lane on a narrow blind curve of highway hugging a mountain. Heck smiled behind his demon mask and accelerated after her and the chase was on.

The two riders darted back and forth, one taking the lead, then the other, as they slipped between the safe and the oncoming side of the two-lane. They were right beside each other when a pickup appeared around the curve and headed straight toward them, its horn blaring. Neither one peeled off and the truck rushed forward, the driver struggling to brake in time. The driver swerved, straddling both lanes long enough for Heck to go around one side of the truck and Ana Mae the other. The truck's driver laid on his horn and screamed at the two bikers as he swerved back into his lane and vanished off in the distance. Heck and Ana Mae continued on for about a mile or two before pulling off onto a gravel shoulder. They both pulled off their helmets, laughing.

"You are as crazy a son of a bitch as they said you were," Ana Mae said, wiping the sweat from her eyes. "I wipe out, I come back eventually, unless the grille's silver, but you they sponge up and pour into a bucket." Heck laughed.

"I'm too fucking pretty to die," Heck said, pushing his sweat-drenched hair back, away from his face.

"You're not that pretty," she said, shaking her head. "We close to Cherokee Mike's lab?" Heck nodded.

"Yeah." He checked the GPS on his phone mounted on the bike's instrument panel. "About another thirty minutes and we're there. Roadkill and his crew should be in position by then too."

"And your buddy, Hume, the were-possum, is hitting another of Mike's labs here in Swain at the same time we are?" Ana asked as she climbed off her bike. Heck couldn't help but be impressed by how lithely, how effortlessly, she made every movement. His eyes moved over her body. She glanced back at him and he looked away quickly.

"That's the plan," Heck said, nodding as he slid a Lucky Strike from the pack to his lips and lit it. "Roadkill's and Bobby-Ray's boys will hit that lab first. Your girl, Yogi, and her crew hit the second lab a few minutes later, then we give it a few minutes for Mike and the boys to get wind of it all, and then we move in after they take off."

"So we get to snoop around a little before we blow the place up," Ana Mae nodded. "Nice, Sinclair." Heck offered her a cigarette. Ana Mae shook her head curtly. "Pass," she said, looking him over. "They won't fuck me up, but you might want to consider quitting."

Heck shrugged. "Something to do," he said.

"Still, it will catch up to you and slow your ass down when you need to be haulin' it."

"I'm pretty sure if I live long enough for cigarettes to kill me, I'll be damned lucky," he said, dropping the butt at his feet and crushing it out with his boot.

"A lot better ways to kill yourself," she said, her eyes roaming over him for a moment. It was obvious she didn't give a shit if he knew she was giving him a once-over. He arched an eyebrow, a weird half-smile played at his lips. She laughed. "You couldn't keep up, chew toy." They donned their helmets and rode on.

. . .

The meth labs were a quartet of double-wide trailers two miles back on a private, rutted, dirt service road within spitting distance of the Tennessee state line. Roadkill had told Heck that the site had been used for generations by some gold ole boys from Swain to cook mash. Apparently Cherokee Mike had muscled in on the moonshiners and taken over their business and their solitary cook site. He'd done the same to a pot farmer and a rival meth cooker and took their land too.

Heck and Ana Mae ditched their bikes at the fringe of the woods and hiked in. Once they were in the deep woods Ana Mae took point, padding silently as a poisonous thought, scanning the path ahead, avoiding twigs and dry leaves. Heck followed at a distance, shadowing her steps. The lady knew what she was doing, so he let her be and maintained rear guard.

A half-mile from the trailers they ran into the first of the mines. Ana Mae sniffed the warm, still air and raised a hand to signal Heck to hold. She knelt carefully on the sun-dappled forest floor to show Heck the taunt tripwire spread between a tree and large dead stump. Heck nodded and they moved around the trap, very slowly, very carefully. It took a few more close calls to figure out the safe path through the maze of claymore antipersonnel mines, but the two bikers were successful.

"You do a tour someplace?" Heck whispered, knowing Ana Mae's ears would pick it up. She gave him a curt shake of the head, keeping her eyes on the path before her.

"Been on my own since I was fifteen," she said softly. "Thought I was nuts until the first change. Got tired of being in mental hospitals, doped out of my mind, so I took off. I spent a lot of time in the woods."

"You'd make a hell of a Force Recon Marine," he said.

"Shit," was all she said.

It was late afternoon by the time they reached a ridge about a quarter-mile from the perimeter of the lab complex. They were late and he knew Roadkill and his people were probably chafing at the bit to go in. Heck slid Ale's huge blade off his back and then retrieved his binoculars from his tactical web harness. Looking down on the trailers with the binoculars, Heck could see there was a courtyard of sorts between the labs that contained a rotten old picnic table and a few folding metal chairs, all occupied by Blue Jocks Heck didn't know right offhand and all with scoped rifles and shotguns. They were drinking beers and talking quietly. One guy sitting on top of the picnic table was eating a Subway sandwich and cradling an AK-47.

"I make seven assholes," Heck muttered.

"Nine," Ana Mae corrected. She had no binoculars. Two more Jocks, assault rifles slung, wandered into Heck's view from the other side of one of the trailers.

"Nobody likes a smartass," Heck said, looking at the BoS's president.

"I do," she said.

There was a large dog pen set up between a stand of bare trees about ten yards off from the trailers. Heck made out three squat, sleek pit bulls pacing in the pen. "I need to staydownwind of the doggos," Ana Mae said. "Dogs get spooked by us." By the gate to the entrance of the access road a dozen motorcycles were clustered next to an old Ford pickup with FARM USE ONLY spray-painted on the rusting tailgate. There was an ATV parked nearby, an Igloo cooler bungee-corded to the back of it.

"Probably two or three more to each trailer," Heck said. Ana Mae nodded. Heck slipped his phone free from his harness and texted Roadkill, *We're in position.*

About damn time, the response came back almost immediately. *What did you guys do, fuck in the woods?*

"Nice," Heck muttered.

"What?" Ana Mae asked as she typed into her own phone.

"Nothing," Heck said. "My best friend is an asshole." He typed back, *Ready?*

Roadkill replied they were. Heck glanced down the ridge to see if anything had changed. It hadn't. He looked over to Ana Mae, who was busy texting her team as well. "Your people set?"

She nodded.

"They'll hit the third lab thirty minutes after Roadkill hits his," she said.

"And we'll be long the fuck gone before they realize we're going for the hat trick," Heck said. He messaged Roadkill, *Go get 'em man.* They waited silently, Heck scanning with his binoculars, Ana Mae with her extraordinary sight.

After about five minutes, Cherokee Mike burst out of the central trailer, shouting into his phone as he hustled down the two-by-four steps. It looked like he was trying to not look angry. He wasn't doing a very good job. The Jocks sitting around drinking in the courtyard jumped up and Mike alternated between shouting orders to them and to whoever he was talking to on his phone. The gunmen sprinted toward their bikes, while several more Blue Jocks exited the other trailers and hustled toward the motorcycles and the pickup.

"Beautiful," Heck said, "fucking beautiful."

A big guy with long red hair, sideburns, and a handlebar mustache walked out the same trailer Mike had been in. He wasn't in a hurry and he wore no Blue Jock colors on his back. He had an amused smirk on his face. There was something in his gait, his smartass smile that gave Heck an uneasy feeling. Mike calmed down and talked respectfully to the red-hair giant. The giant said a few words, the smirk never leaving his face, and Mike paled visibly.

"You catch any of that?" Heck asked. Ana Mae shook her head.

"Should have been able to catch at least a few words of it," she said, "but it's like someone hit the mute button. I got nothing. Who's the big Lemmy-looking motherfucker? I haven't seen him around."

"Fuck if I know," Heck said but something twisted inside him, a feeling like a toothache in his gut. He did know. Down the ridge, Mike nodded. The redhead slapped Mike on the back and glanced up the ridge in the direction of where Ana Mae and Heck were hidden. Red ambled toward the bikes like he didn't have a care in the world, while the Jocks raced past him to head out and defend the other lab Jethro was hitting right now. There was a roar of engines and the troop set off down the access road, led by the redheaded giant. Only Mike's cycle remained. Mike moved to an isolated spot in the camp where the remaining Jocks couldn't see him. He took something out from under his leather jacket. It was a little over a foot long, narrow and crooked. It looked like it was made of black wrought iron.

"What the fuck is that?" Ana Mae asked. Heck shook his head. Mike gestured with the iron wand and a halo of indigo light swirled around its tip. The light trailed around the biker as he performed an intricate series of widdershins movements with the wand. An unseasonable cold wind rose through the forest, violently shaking the leaves and the branches of trees. The dogs in the pen howled, a bloodcurdling chorus. Dark, brooding clouds muscled in and devoured the sun. The shadows lengthened around Mike and seemed to slither along the ground on their own accord.

Mike finished the movements and lowered the iron wand. The violet light faded. The chill wind and the dark clouds abated and the biker slipped the wand back under his coat. He ran to his bike and within a few moments he joined his men in riding off down the road to intercept Roadkill's raiders.

"Cherokee Mike is a wizard?" Ana Mae said, arching an eyebrow. "When I was barely eighteen I hooked up with a wizard for a while. He was a narcissistic asshole from West Virginia, but, Jesus, he had some real power. And that," she gestured down the ridge to where Mike had been a few moments earlier, "looked and felt like real power."

"Mike's no fucking wizard," Heck said. "I've known him since I was kid. If he'd had any real power of his own, first, he wouldn't have been able to keep his big mouth shut about it . . . and he'd have used it to clean up his pizza-face acne, and second, he'd have tried taking over the MC a long time ago. No, someone gave him that wand and that's where all this new mojo and all his monster backup is coming from."

"Let's go," Ana Mae said. "We ain't got long until Yogi and her crew hit their target, all hell breaks loose, and all those assholes come back. Yogi, the sergeant at arms of the Bitches of Selene, was a 360-pound MTF transgender woman who also happened to be a werebear. They started down the ridge, still moving quietly, carefully, in case Mike had left a sniper behind to guard the compound.

"Be careful," Heck said. "That was some kind of working he was doing with the wand-thingie. He may have been leaving us a surprise."

It took a few minutes to reach the forest floor. Ana Mae and Heck split up so that she could stay downwind of the dogs. The clearing had a weird chemical smell—a cross between rotten eggs and cat piss—which Heck knew was a by-product of the drug production. He unslung one of his MP9s and then thought better of it. Guns and meth labs didn't mix very well.

He slid his combat knife out of its gravity sheath on his harness and carefully made his way to the door of the trailer Mike and the redheaded giant had come out of. It was locked. Heck checked the flimsy door for any wires using the knife's blade along the seal. He tried to recall his demolition training from Afghanistan, but he had never been an EOD guy, never had the patience or enough self-preservation instinct. He jerked the door open with his considerable strength. There was small, metallic "tink" sound as the lock gave and the door flew open. Nothing went boom. The chemical stench was stronger inside. Heck stepped in. The lights were off but there was enough sunlight pouring in the open door for him to make out the interior. The interior walls had mostly been removed. Over half the trailer was the lab. There were several folding plastic tables covered in flasks, beakers, and Bunsen burners. Several propane tanks were clustered together on the floor. Looping coils of clear plastic tubing ran like an artificial circulatory system between the flasks. Some of the network of tubes ran down to a large plastic paint bucket on the floor.

Baggies of iodine crystals and a glass jar marked RED PHOSPHOROUS on a piece of masking tape were on one cluttered table along with a cardboard box holding hundreds of small plastic baggies of finished product, a couple of handguns, and a Big Gulp soda cup next to a half-eaten KFC meal still in the open red and white box. Someone had left the radio up on a shelf on and it was playing Whitey Morgan and the 78's "Waitin' 'Round to Die."

Heck thought he saw something on the baggies of meth. He walked over and picked one up. A tiny slip of paper inside the baggie had the sword and knotwork circle of the Blue Jocks stamped on it as the maker's mark.

"You motherfucker," Heck said, crushing the bag and the crystal inside and dropping it back into the box.

The other half of the trailer was a poorly maintained office. There was another plastic table with a laptop on it and a few cardboard boxes full of scraps of paper. A leather address book and a calendar were on the table next to the laptop. Several USB drives were clustered next to an ashtray overflowing with butts and a plastic bottle of gin. Heck gathered up the laptop and the drives into an empty satchel he had brought along.

He turned and something struck the side of his head with the force of a speeding car. There was the strobe of impact-light behind his eyes, terrible pressure and pain, and then he was slumped against a tree a few yards from a jagged hole in the wall of the trailer he had been inside. It was hard to stay awake, to think clearly. He was wet from bloody cuts all over his body. The dogs were barking.

Heck struggled to his feet. He had no idea where his knife had gotten to. Standing at the edge of the demolished wall swaddled in the darkness of the trailer was a man-shaped thing. It skin was smooth and the color of moonless night. Its face was empty—no eyes, no mouth, no features at all—and curved horns, like a ram's, spiraled away from the sides of its head.

An old memory shook itself loose from the rubble of Heck's concussed thoughts, *shit, it's a Nightgaunt*. It had been a hunt he was on with the Jocks when he was fourteen, fifteen? Nightgaunts were silent nocturnal predators, one of the bizarre creatures that slipped into our world at the frayed fringes of the highways, of the Road. One Nightgaunt had killed seven people, two of them kids, before the Blue Jocks had hunted it down. Two Jocks died in the process of dropping the damn thing.

The Nightgaunt launched itself silently from the hole in the wall toward Heck on tattered, batlike wings. This was wrong. It was daylight and Nightgaunts never, *never* went out in the light. The creature reached out for Heck's cut face and throat with shadowy talons. Instinct saved him. Heck clumsily tumbled away from the tree he was against. The Nightgaunt's claws splintered the two-foot-diameter trunk of the tree and it crashed down. Heck came up out of the tumble into a crouch to its left and opened up on it with the fire-belching MP9. The Nightgaunt appeared untouched, unchanged by the spray of bullets. It strode toward Heck as the biker ceased fire.

There was a snarl from the pit bulls and a second Nightgaunt appeared, flying low above the roofs of the trailers. Ana Mae was grappling with the winged shadow. Heck could see her form growing, flowing as she traded clawed slashes with it.

"Get ready to ditch!" Heck shouted to her as he pulled the pin on a grenade from his harness. He tossed the grenade towards the trailer the flying Nightgaunt was over. The monster he had tried to shoot drove a powerful punch into Heck's jaw, and Heck flew off the ground crashing through more trees, rocks, and bushes before hitting the ground.

For a second he thought he heard Ana Mae shouting, "Are you fucking kidding m . . ." At his back he felt a sucking vacuum, then the universe exploded in brilliant fire and a sound that swallowed thought and made his bones ache. The trailer exploded, lifting into the air and then crumpling like a crushed beer can. The volatile chemicals inside went off a second later, creating a second and even more powerful explosion. The blast engulfed the Nightgaunt wrestling in the air with Ana Mae and the one fighting with Heck in a roiling ball of fire.

Ana Mae felt the force of the pressure wave coming and used it to kick herself and the shadowy creature apart, both tumbling out of the sky. She crashed down, her skin and hair burning, into a thicket of brush on the side of the ridge. The fire felt cold on her dying nerve endings and blackening flesh, then the thudding drumbeat of her heart drowned out the screaming, petty, human pain. Her heart jumped and raced in 2-2 time, replacing pain with a crystalline rage and an antediluvian joy. The monster swallowed her whole and she laughed, embraced it, as it did.

Heck groaned and climbed to his feet. His ears felt like they were stuffed with wool. There was another hollow "whoomp" and a flare of heat on his face as another trailer went up. Fire was everywhere. He hurt all over and he knew he was bruised head to toe from the force of the explosion. Then he saw a Nightgaunt rising out of the popping, cracking flames. About fifty feet away, the other one climbed to its feet. If either of the creatures had been injured by the explosion, they showed no sign of it.

Heck began to reach for his machine guns when he recalled how they had finally killed the Nightgaunt on that hunt so many years ago. It had been Ale, one of the last hunts Ale had gone on before he started to get sick, before they had fought and parted so poorly. Gunfire hadn't done it, fire didn't mark the creature. It had been Ale's sword that finally laid it low.

"The blade," Ale told him. "It's old, as old as the Sinclair Clan, older even. It was a Templar treasure, won from a Fae knight with armor like stained glass and a voice like cold rain. It's laced with secrets and glamours of this world and so many others." Ale had held the Claymore up, the gaunt's oily blood reflecting on it, a wet mirror. Ale took a cloth to the blade.

"A good family's like a good blade, son," Ale had told him. "They both make you stronger and stand with you when you're weak." Ale wiped the blade clean. "You tend 'em, and they'll tend to you too."

Heck licked the blood from his split lip and took up the stance with the Claymore he had practiced over and over again so long ago with Gordon and Ale. His head spun and his insides felt like wet concrete from the explosions. "C'mon, then," he snarled at the silent, faceless killers.

When he was a kid practicing with a teak *bokken,* a wooden practice sword, Heck would pretend he was a knight battling the monsters his grandfather and stepfather told him about. The Nightgaunts closed and split ranks to try to flank him. Heck pivoted, shifting his back leg to keep them both in sight as best he could.

"I got something for you, you fucking hell-mimes!" The fire danced in his chest and whispered in his ear. The blood was like wine in his mouth. "Come and get it." A Nightgaunt flew straight at him, its claws ready to open his throat. Heck dropped to a single knee at the last instant and braced the sword, holding it at the dull quillons. He let the monster impale itself at full velocity on the blade. The creature jerked and twitched as the ancient steel pierced its smooth chest and exploded out its back between its wings. Smoke poured from the wounds instead of blood, and the Nightgaunt thrashed wordlessly. Heck stood, using leverage to jam the Claymore deeper up into the creature's chest. It slumped on the blade and was still.

Heck spun, with the body still on his sword, trying to smash it into the other Nightgaunt behind him, but he felt the hot talons of the other monster rip deeply into his back and spine with the same ferocious strength it had used to fell the tree. Heck gasped at the depth of pain. He felt his arms and legs going numb as he fell to the ground. The fire reached another trailer and a third explosion tore through blazing forest, sending splintered trees and jagged metal everywhere. The dogs were whining in their pen and Heck wished he could set them loose before everything became char and ash. It was the last thought Heck summoned before the world fell away to darkness.

The Nightgaunt reared back to drive its claws into the motionless, bleeding biker a second time. As its arms came down to end Heck's life a howl pealed across the burning ridge. A beast, almost seven feet tall, whip-thin with red-gold fur and flaring yellow eyes, erupted from a crackling stand of burning trees. Ana Mae cleared the twenty yards between herself and the Nightgaunt in a single bound and checked the monster before it could finish off Heck, grabbing its arm in mid-swing.

They staggered back. Ana Mae's claws flashed out and tore at the Nightgaunt. Smoke poured from the wound. The winged monster struck back with its own claws spraying blood and fur in its wake. The two stood toe-to-toe, neither giving ground, and traded claws while the final trailer exploded and fire rained down around them.

The Nightgaunt sank its talons low into Ana Mae's stomach. The werewolf grabbed its arm before the Nightgaunt could draw its claws free of her flesh and held it in a clinch as her free hand slashed with all her strength over and over at the monster's featureless face and neck. The Nightgaunt's head tore free of its neck and evaporated into smoke in midair. The body slumped to the ground, and Ana Mae staggered backward gushing blood from her gut wound. She fell to the ground near Heck, unmoving.

Heck's hand clawed across the ash-covered ground and took hers. Together, they struggled to their feet. Heck used Ale's sword like a cane to help hold him up. They leaned on each other, holding each other up. Ana Mae's form was shifting back to human but her wounds kept bleeding.

"We . . . gotta . . . go," she mumbled. "Up the ridge." Heck tried to nod, he almost blacked out. "Wait!" he said and they both lurched to a halt, almost falling over. "The dogs," he said as earnestly as a child. "We . . . got to get them." Ana Mae was human again, naked and covered in blood and ash. She was shuddering, fighting going into shock from blood loss. She looked at Heck and realized he was serious. She tried to smile.

"Okay," she said, "okay. You are fucking crazy. Let's go get the puppers."

They staggered into the inferno, toward the pleading cries of the dogs and were lost in the smoke and haze, their laughter echoing down the dying ridge.

TWENTY-TWO

CLEVELAND, OHIO
August 5, 1940

Detective Peter Merylo scanned the haggard faces of the men surrounding the crackling cook fire and wondered for the millionth time which one of them might be the Butcher. He knew he could trust the young man to his left with a fringe of a beard and dirty, greasy hair since that young hobo was an undercover policeman like himself, Frank Vorell of the Cleveland PD. The other men sharing the circle around the fire this hot summer night, feasting on a meal of beans and a bottle of bourbon, Merylo was far less sure about. One of them could be the murdering maniac he had been pursuing for almost four years.

The bottle of hooch was being passed right, the small pot of beans left. As was tradition, part of the Code of the Road, since Merylo and Vorell had been the guys to acquire the cans of beans, they had gotten the first mouthfuls of the food that had been simmering over a left-behind cook pot for a while over the fire. Having not eaten much since they had arrived back in Cleveland last night on a rail, Merylo was ashamed to admit it, but the beans tasted better than his wife's pot roast dinner with all the trimmings.

The other men, his fellow "knights of the road" as they jokingly called each other, were equally grateful for the night's bounty. Some of them Merylo and Vorell knew from hopping freight cars between eastern Ohio and western Pennsylvania the last few months. As was part of the Code of the Road, each man obscured his true name and identity behind a road name, a moniker. Merylo knew many of the faces by heart now, having traveled, broken bread, and lived with these men in ramshackle hobo jungles across two states, but he knew next to nothing about who they really were or if one of more of them were involved in the horrific slayings he had been investigating.

"Good chow, Cleveland Pete," one of the older men, a factory worker from Youngstown who called himself "Stickball," said to Merylo. "Much obliged. How'd you cop it?"

"Me and Patchy," Merylo began, jabbing a thumb to Vorell as he mentioned his traveling name. Vorell hated the nickname he had been stuck with due to the scraggly nature of his thin beard, "we tumbled to a coop that had been marked with sign an angel lived there. The sweet old broad lived up to her rep and she gave us three cans of torpedoes." The men around the fire grunted in approval and kept shoveling the beans into their mouths.

Stickball nodded and smiled. "Thanks, Pete." Merylo raised the bottle of bourbon that had reached him in salute and took a long drag on the bottle before handing it to the big man on his right known as "Wall." The Wall's real name, Merylo had been able to suss out, was Emmett Wally. The broad, tall Wally had a plain, sad face and prominent ears sticking out below short cropped hair. He had been a farmer somewhere out west until the Dust Bowl had devoured his livelihood about five years ago. He been hopping the rails ever since, looking for any work he could find to send money home to his wife and kids. Merylo liked the Wall, even if he figured he'd heard about maybe ten words out of the guy's mug since they had been riding the same route. That made it even harder to suspect Wally as his butcher but the detective inside him felt something was screwy with the quiet farmer.

A colored hobo by the handle of "Candy Rappaport" got out his mouth harp and played some songs as dinner winded down. His renditions of "Take Me Back to Tulsa" by Bob Wills and the Texas Playboys and Roy Acuff's "Wabash Cannonball" brightened the mood as the beans were devoured and the booze continued it rounds. Another hobo began to play the spoons while several other men sang along.

Merylo took a few more pulls off the bottle before excusing himself from the circle. He was a pious, fastidious man, devoted to his God, to his family, and to the law. It had taken more from him than to grow out his whiskers and don some shabby clothes to blend into the world of the hobo. This secret society was full of stern, distrustful men who did not share easily with outsiders. It had taken over a month to gain entrance into their dominion of secret codes left on houses and barns, their lingo and their mythology. Merylo had drunk and swore more in the past few months than in several years combined. He had worked "songs and dances"—con jobs and sob stories—on townsfolk to elicit food, money, and shelter. These were things Merylo had thought he was incapable of doing, but he did them to survive in this secret culture and to track down the madman he had sworn he'd bring to justice. While he had met many individuals that he looked upon with more than a little judgment and disgust in this shadowy world, he'd also met men who were as good and decent as any he had met in his church or on the police force.

The Wall, as usual, had passed on the bourbon and left the circle silently a short time earlier. Merylo had waited, noting the direction Wally headed and then took off, nodding to Vorell to keep an eye on the others. The encampment was at the base of Jackass Hill, near the Nickel Plate and Shaker Heights Railroad tracks. The neighborhood was known as Kingsbury Run and Merylo recalled how this area had once been the home to a sprawling hobo jungle. That had come to an end with the killings.

Merylo saw Wally up ahead. The big man had a distinctive gait, powerful and patient. He was headed for the Erie Railroad tracks. Merylo followed at a discreet distance. Of all the hobos, tramps, marijuana pushers, prostitutes, and railroad bulls he had encountered, he kept coming back to Emmett Wally as his best suspect for being the Butcher of Kingsbury Run.

The murder investigation had begun on September 5, 1934, with the discovery near Lake Erie of a woman's rotting torso. It had been the first grisly discovery but it wouldn't be the last. By the late summer of 1936, when Merylo was assigned full-time to the case by the chief of police, there were five dismembered victims of the killer the press was calling the "Mad Butcher of Kingsbury Run."

In each case, the victim was cut up with almost surgical precision. There was seldom a lot of blood at the scene and the victims were always beheaded, the head often recovered some distance away or never recovered at all. One of the victims, the pathologist determined, had been alive when he was decapitated. Another victim had some unknown chemicals applied to him that turned his skin red and leathery. Most of the victims had not been identified, anonymous John and Jane Does. Merylo and other detectives believed some lunatic was wandering among the faceless bums, whores, and hobos of Kingsbury Run and using them for guinea pigs in some mad experiment.

Merylo lost sight of the Wall. The summer night was sticky and dark as pitch. A dry wind rasped through the corridors of abandoned freight cars. Charred, brittle wood crunched under the detective's feet, reminders of the old hobo jungle that had once thrived here. Merylo slid his hand under his coat and felt the butt of his .38 nestled in a shoulder holster. Peter Merylo wasn't a big man and life on the rail had made him skinnier. He didn't relish the idea of going up against a hulk like Emmett Wally but this killer had to be stopped, the things he was doing to these people, it had to stop. Merylo slid his revolver free of its concealed holster and stepped into the shadows of the maze of abandoned cars.

Near the beginning of the killings a new public safety director had come on board in Cleveland and promised to bring the killer to ground. His name was Eliot Ness, the famous lawman who had got Al Capone. As the murders had continued they had become what everything in Cleveland eventually becomes—political. The Butcher turned out to be harder to get a handle on than the gangs of Chicago, and Ness had been feeling the heat to close the case and bring in a suspect.

In the late summer of 1938, Ness, no closer to an arrest, decided to eliminate the symptom if he couldn't cure the disease. The director personally oversaw a massive roust of all the hobos and other transients in the hobo jungles of Kingsbury Run and ordered the Cleveland Fire Department to burn the whole encampment to the ground. Ness figured that if he deprived the Butcher of his "test subjects" then the killer would either stop or move on.

For a time, it seemed that perhaps Ness's action had stopped the murders; however, at the end of the year a local newspaper received a letter, supposedly from the killer, addressed to the Cleveland police chief. In it he claimed to be doing God's work to advance the cause of science, that he had already continued his experiments with new victims. The Butcher also said he had departed Ohio to sunny California to wait out the harsh winter.

After that, Ness began to lose favor with the public and the politicians. Cops like Merylo were given less and less time and resources to chase down leads on the case. Even with the permanent jungle destroyed, hobos, tramps, and other displaced people still came in on the trains, still needed a place to flop away from the eyes of polite society, and they still found their way to Kingsbury Run.

Even as the case grew colder and resources toward it sparse, knowing the Butcher was still out there drove Merylo to keep searching, keep hunting. Merylo was a God-fearing man. He believed in the Lord and he believed in the Devil and he knew that the Butcher was the Devil's agent on this earth. After years of trying to convince the chief to let him go undercover among the hobos, Merylo finally got permission and he convinced young Vorell to descend into the underworld with him. They had been living among the knights of the road for almost three months now. And in all that time, Emmett Wally was the veteran cop's best suspect.

Wally was always sneaking around the jungle, snooping. Merylo had noted that whenever there was a body found, Wally was never too far away. Emmett Wally carried himself like a hunter and he was looking for more than a job and a place to flop.

In the gloom between the abandoned freight cars, Merylo heard something up ahead, it sounded like a struggle. He sprinted toward the noises and turned the corner. A truly bizarre sight greeted him. Emmett Wally was in a brutal struggle with an equally large man in a dirty pair of bib overalls. The two men were were grappling, circling each other while attempting to gain some advantage over the other. Scattered on the trash-and wood-littered ground before them was the dismembered and headless remains of a man's decaying body. Merylo stepped out and raised his pistol.

"Police!" the detective cried out. "Hands up, both of ya! Reach!" The two men paused in their fighting and looked over at the slender, balding policeman. Merylo was surprised to see that the man who the Wall was tussling with was wearing makeup—clown-white—a pale face, crimson triangles above and below his dull eyes, and a wide, painted-on, scarlet smile. A large black dot and two smaller black dots covered the clown's forehead.

"The hell?" the cop said. "You run away from the circus, bub?" The clown said nothing.

"Shoot him!" the Wall shouted and tackled the clown. "Just shoot him!" The two men rolled around in the dust and debris, punching each other. It was looking like the Wall was getting the short end of the stick in the brawl. The big clown seemed stronger and more resilient. The clown drove punch after punch into the big hobo and Merylo saw the Wall's head loll limply from the blows.

This was nuts. Merylo fired the pistol off to his left and the retort rumbled like thunder through the rail yard. "Knock it off!" he shouted. The clown scrambled to his feet. Wally slumped to the ground and didn't move. The clown moved menacingly toward the policeman. "Freeze!" Merylo growled. "Any closer and I'll plug ya!" The words and the pointed gun didn't slow the clown's advance. Merylo heard distant shouts and panicked voices.

"Over here! It came from over here!" It sounded like Vorell. The clown kept coming.

"We're going to have company in a second," Merylo said, his pistol unwavering, even if his nerve was. "Stop. You're not getting away this time."

"I'm . . . going . . . to . . . kill you," the clown said, advancing. "Take . . . your . . . corpse . . . to . . . him and let him . . ."

Merylo didn't wait to hear any more. The clown was less than ten feet away and the Cleveland cop opened fire. A .38 bullet ripped through the man's massive chest. The clown staggered but didn't go down. The clown paused for a second, then moved toward Merylo faster. The dead eyes now held madness and anger. *Blood,* the thought flashed through the detective's mind like a match striking, *he should be bleeding like a stuck pig . . . where's all the blood?* Merylo fired again and a second bullet burned its way through the giant's chest before it blew out the back. The clown kept coming, a sneer of pain and anger on its painted face. Massive pasty-white hands grabbed the detective by the frayed lapels of his coat and lifted him off the ground. Merylo was raising the .38 to the clown's forehead when the large man hurled him a good thirty feet and he smashed into the rusted steel body of a railcar.

The detective tried to rise, to find his dropped pistol even as the clown strode toward him to finish him. Thoughts of his little girl, his sweet wife tumbled through his pain-fogged brain. Merylo said a silent prayer.

There was a roar like an angry bear and the Wall crashed into the clown, knocking them both to the ground again. The big hobo drove punch after punch into the clown's face, but no blood came from its broken nose and split lips. The clown drove a strong right into Wally's jaw; the force of it sent him flying several feet up and back. The clown began to stand again, looking at both fallen men with undiluted hatred in his glassy eyes. Bobbing lights and a jumble of voices came around the corner of distant train car.

"There!" Vorell's voice called, echoing at the head of the mob. "There they are! Pete? Pete, you okay?"

The clown and the cop locked eyes for an endless second, then Merylo looked down and grabbed his gun from the ground. He brought it back up, but there was nothing to shoot. The clown was gone, vanished into the oven-hot night.

"Damn," Merylo muttered as he struggled to his feet. He was helping Wally get up by the time his partner, the rail yard's police—known as bulls—and the assembled hobos and vagrants reached them.

"Thank you," Merylo said to Wally.

"Figured you for a flatfoot," Wally grunted. "You're too damn prissy 'bout being clean." Both men laughed. "Here," Wally said, handing something to Merylo. It was a carved Buffalo nickel. Merylo held up the hobo nickel and saw the carved death's-head skull on its face side leer up at him. "He dropped that near the body," the Wall said. "Looks like he meant to do it." Merylo was about to ask the big hobo something but then the mob, the cops, and Vorell descended upon them and it all got lost in the noise and the confusion.

▪ ▪ ▪

Cleveland Public Safety Director Eliot Ness looked serious, but he pretty much always did. Ness had a reputation for fastidiousness and no-nonsense. In his brief time in Cleveland he had undertaken to clean up a police department rife with corruption, and to make the streets of the city safer. He brought his lunch in a brown bag every day, usually eating it in his office alone. The retired treasury agent seldom joked or engaged in small talk with his subordinates. Ness had sworn to clean up Cleveland just as he had cleaned up Chicago in the bloodiest days of Prohibition and it was clear to anyone who spent more than five minutes with him that Ness was a man of his word. "So the Butcher of Kingsbury Run, the murderer we've been chasing for years, isn't a doctor, or some mad scientist . . . he's some bug house goon dressed up like Pierrot? Is that what you're telling me, detective?"

Ness's attire was always immaculate and he looked with more than a little disdain on Merylo's appearance after three months out on the road. The director held up Merylo's report and shook his head slowly. Merylo had no idea who the heck Pierrot was, but he figured it wasn't good. George Mantowitz, Cleveland's chief of police and Merylo's boss, sat beside his detective but remained silent.

"Tell me Detective Merylo, what am I supposed to do with all this?"

"Sir," Merylo began, "you saw the body. There's no doubt this man is the Butcher. He's using the rails to hunt. We may have dislodged him by burning down the hobo jungle in the Run, but we didn't stop him." Chief Mantowitz saw the color come to the director's face at the mention of the razing of the hobo camp Ness had ordered a few years earlier. It was sore spot for Ness. Its failure to stop the killer had galled him and he silently hoped Merylo would get off the subject quick. "In fact," Merylo continued, "I've been looking into similar killings near the rail lines in Pennsylvania. A place called New Castle." Ness began to shake his head, he waved Merylo's report in his hands dismissively. "There have been multiple killings, same treatment of the bodies, same methods—"

"I am not the director of public safety in Pennsylvania, Detective Merylo," Ness interrupted. "And you are paid by the people of this city to investigate crimes committed here. *Here*. Am I clear on this?"

Merylo began to continue, but a quick glace to Mantowitz told him to clam up. "Yes, sir, Mr. Ness," he said instead.

Ness flipped through the report, shaking his head as he did so. "Besides being dressed like a fool, your suspect also apparently took two bullets in the chest and didn't bleed or drop," Ness said. "You state that in your report also, detective. Do you have any idea how insane that sounds?"

"I do," Merylo said. "However, insane or not, sir, it's the truth."

"I understand wanting to find this man," Ness said. "I do. I've been hunting down leads, chasing suspects for years, just like you. I believe in your desire to see justice done, Merylo, and your record as a cop speaks for itself. However, we can't move forward on this report, detective. Do you understand?" Ness opened one of the drawers of his desk.

"Sir!" Merylo said.

"Your only collaborating witness to any of this is that hobo you said helped you. And he hopped a rail out of town five minutes after we cut him loose. No name, no ties to the community. We can't—"

"You mean you won't," Merylo said. "You've been burned by the press after you executed all those warrantless searches on the buildings and homes in Kingsbury Run, and now you're afraid of what they'll say about you in the papers if you tell them the truth. That thing—whatever it is—it's still out there, still harvesting people for someone! You're worried more about your constituency than the people he's slaughtering down there. Most of them don't fucking vote, right, Mr. Ness!"

"Pete . . . Detective Merylo!" Mantowitz shouted. "That's enough!"

"No," Ness said. The director sighed and rubbed his eyes. "He's right." All three men were silent for a time. Ness placed Merylo's report in the open drawer. "Keep on it, detective. I know I will be. You can count on that. Dismissed, gentlemen."

Merylo and Mantowitz stood and headed for the door. "Detective," Ness said. Merylo turned back. "That hobo nickel you found. I need that too please." Merylo sighed, took the odd coin from this coat pocket, and handed it to Ness. "We can't just . . . we need more . . ." Ness let the thought drift into silence. The two men locked stares. "That will be all, detective. Thank you."

As the Chief and Merylo departed his office, Ness examined the skull-faced nickel and then placed it in an evidence envelope in the drawer next to Merylo's report. There were two other identical nickels already in the envelope. Ness shut the drawer.

Merylo retired in 1943 from the Cleveland PD. The last few years of his career were working unrelated cases, and in his spare time and on his own dime, chasing down any clues he could discover on the Butcher. He never took his daughter to the circus again. Much to his wife's concern he continued to covertly hops rails and try to gather any scraps of information on the Butcher, what it truly was and its mysterious master.

Merylo never saw or heard anything else from the giant hobo, Emmett Wally, the Wall, in all his train-hopping excursions. Then in the early days of 1947, he received a terse letter from Wally with no return address. Accompanying the letter was a newspaper clipping from the *Los Angeles Examiner*. Merylo read the letter and the clipping multiple times that day, and then at dinner told his wife and daughter he had to go to L.A.

A few days later, Merylo was standing on the cracked sidewalk of South Norton Avenue in the Leimert Park neighborhood of Los Angeles, looking into a grass-and-weed-choked vacant lot.

"This is where we found her, Pete," LAPD Detective Ralph Asdel told Merylo. Asdel was probably half Merylo's age and was burly and broad-chested, to the older man's slight build. "Lady who lives in the neighborhood was walking with her three-year-old. At first she thought someone had dumped the pieces of a department store mannequin. She called us when she realized what it was."

Merylo walked out into the desolate lot in the middle of what looked like an average, working-class neighborhood. Back in Ohio it was snowing. Here the sky was gray and the wind blustery but he didn't need his overcoat.

"Her name was Elizabeth Short," Asdel said, flipping open his small notebook. "Came to the city to become an actress last year. Shame what he did to her. She was a looker."

"She was cut up, dismembered?" Merylo asked. "Very little blood at the scene?" the Cleveland detective asked, already knowing in his gut the answer. The lot reeked, screamed of the same evil Merylo had encountered again and again and again. Asdel nodded.

"Yeah," the young detective said. "Drained of blood, cut in two at the waist. All probably done someplace else. He hacked off her nipples, the freak, and he cut up her mouth to give her that big, wide, bloody grin. Ear-to-ear, like a clown or something, y'know." Merylo felt cold gravel in his guts. He nodded, but said nothing. Asdel continued. "So, Pete, what's got you out here from Cleveland about this? It relate to an ongoing? C'mon, I showed you mine, now show me yours."

"The Torso Killings." Merylo walked back to the curb. "Someone tipped me off to this and it sounded like our man." Asdel whistled.

"Yeah, I hear that nut's been giving you guys hell for years now," Asdel said. "Jesus, I hope you're wrong. No offense, it's just we already have all kinds of wild theories going around about this since the papers started with that 'Black Dahlia' shit. 'She was killed because she was blackmailing some movie producer,' 'she was killed by some secret cult.' All we need is 'she was killed by the Cleveland Torso Killer.' Swell."

"If it makes you feel any better," Merylo said, "I'm here as a private citizen, not on behalf of the department. I got this tip from . . . a snitch."

By the end of the day, Merylo had a general overview of the case and had seen enough evidence to satisfy him. It was the Butcher. He sat in a diner off of Olympic Boulevard drinking coffee and making notes.

"May I . . . join you?" Merylo looked up. Emmett Wally was standing there. The Wall was dressed in a frayed trench coat, fedora, shabby work shirt, and pants. His broad face was unusually pale. Merylo stood and the two men shook hands. Wally's grip was like a bone vise.

"Good to see you," the old detective said. "Let me buy you a cup of joe." Wally just looked at him for moment, like he was trying to understand the words. The big hobo shook his head.

"Thank you," Wally said. "But I . . . can't. You spoke with the police? You know . . . it's him, don't you?"

"Yes," Merylo said. "I think he's been busy in Pennsylvania too. He's using the rail." Emmett nodded.

"He is. I wanted you to know you were on the right track. You deserved to know that, Peter," Wally said. "I'm going to find him. I wanted to . . . warn you . . . before he . . . did to you what he did to me." Merylo looked closer at the hobo. His face and neck were pasty, almost greasy, as if he were wearing cold cream or some other pale makeup.

"What did the bastard do to you, Wall?" Merylo asked. "Are you okay?"

"No," Wally said, his eyes unfocused as if he were seeing someplace other than the empty diner. "I'm . . . not. I was working when you met me, Pete. I was tracking him, just like you were."

"Working?" Merylo said, confused. "You a cop, Emmett?"

"No," the hobo said, "not exactly. He found out I was . . . tracking him.

He . . . killed my wife, my children." The big man's eyes focused again in pain, and rage. "He cut them up, like the others . . . left their . . . heads . . . on our mantel for me to find. Don't let him do that to you, Pete. Please. Go home. I'll find him . . . I have . . . nothing else now."

Merylo was silent. Emmett nodded to the Cleveland cop. "Go home. While you still have one." He walked out into the L.A. night without another word.

Peter Merylo returned to Cleveland, to his wife and daughter. He never rode the rails again, never made another attempt to find the Butcher of Kingsbury Run. He never saw or heard from Emmett Wally, or the monstrous, slaughtering clown they had confronted that night, ever again, except in troubling dreams that followed him until the day he died.

Cherokee Mike Locklear had learned from decades in a cell how to control his anger. Anger made you stupid, anger usually made you make the wrong choice, say the wrong thing. Anger was for the weak. So when Mike's sergeant at arms, his old cellmate, Vincent "Vinnie" Wiseman, told him about the raids the Blue Jocks and the Bitches of Selene had made on the meth labs, he kept his cool. What Mike didn't know was that he was really, really bad at "keeping his cool." His face grew red as Vince gave him the news.

"All the labs?" Mike said. Vinnie nodded. "All blown to shit?" Vinnie nodded again. "Do you have any idea how much fucking money those stupid bastards just cost us?" Vinnie nodded again.

"We've already got calls from customers," Vinnie said. "They paid in advance because you sweet-talked them into doing it, and now we can't deliver. Mike, we're fucked. We're going to have motherfuckers popping out of the fucking wallpaper to whack us!"

Mike's face was the color of a beet but he forced a smile and reached for a bottle of Tums on his desk. "No worries, no worries. Tell them once we have this little personnel problem with the other Jocks under control, the MC can ramp back up production to twice what it is now. They'll get their goods. Not . . . a . . . problem." Mike glanced at his silent redheaded ally sitting on the couch in the corner, his massive snake-tattoo-covered arms crossed, that annoying smile on his rugged face.

"Mike," Vince said, "I don't think they are going to go for 'the check is in the mail, brother.'" Mike tossed the bottle of antacid across the room and chalky, multicolored tablets flew everywhere.

"You think I don't fucking know that!" Mike screamed, the muscles in his neck taut. He caught himself and breathed deeply and looked down at the desktop. He looked back up and tried to plant his fake smile on again.

"Okay, okay. I need a minute. Get out." Vinnie looked at his old friend and started to say something and thought better of it. He walked out of the small office in the back of a strip club that Mike owned controlling interest in and used as a money-laundering front. The door closed behind him with a click.

Mike looked over to the redhead. The giant chuckled a little and shook his head. "Well, you're BOHICA'ed," he said.

"BOHICA?" Mike asked

"'Bend over, here it comes again,'" the huge biker known as Viper said and laughed his dry, rasping cough of a laugh.

"Great," Mike said, reaching down and opening the saddle bags he had propped against his desk. "Fucking Tony Robbins with the inspiration, man." He withdrew a black iron rod from the bags. It was crooked like a switch from a tree branch might be, a little over a foot long, thirteen inches to be exact, and it had small sharp iron thorns jutting irregularly over its surface. The wand ended in an uneven two-tine fork, like horns. "You told me this was all I needed to conquer Heck and Elizabeth and take control of the Jocks. What the fuck, Viper?"

"It is," Viper said. "But it still requires some semblance of competency on your part, Mike. You know Heck. You honestly figured he'd just keep letting you hit him without hitting back? You should have seen this coming."

"I did!" Mike said, his voice rising. "I had like three times the men on each lab." He brandished the iron wand. "I had the fucking Nightgaunts there, at all three sites as backup. I did everything I could!"

"Obviously not," Viper said with a smile. Mike's face was magenta, a vein throbbed visibly in his temple. "You need to smoke a little weed, take a Valium, bro," Viper said. "You're about to pop a gasket."

"It's those goddamn Bitches of Selene," Mike said, pacing now, still holding the wand. "They provide the occult firepower the Jocks don't have to deal with the things I'm summoning up. The way I set everything up . . ."

"You?" Viper asked, a sliver of ice in his deep voice.

"Us," Mike corrected. "They should be at the Jocks' throats right now and vice versa. That would leave them both too weak to keep us from coming in, mopping them up, and getting on with business. Why aren't they killing each other, Viper? Why are they working together?" He held up the wand again. "And why the fuck doesn't this thing work on them?"

"I told you," Viper said, nodding at the wand, "the Key of Thorne only gives you influence over the Nightborne breeds who agreed to the Compact of Accord. The shapeshifters never did, they refused. That was why I said you needed to get rid of the Bitches, as you'll recall."

Mike stopped pacing and started to punch a wall then stopped himself, thinking better of it. He struggled to put his smile back on his face. Viper shook his head. "As to why they aren't killing each other, your plans didn't take into account the influence one Jessie James Aussapile has had on Heck."

"Aussapile, that old fat trucker?" Mike said. "He used to run with the Jocks back in the day. He and Ale were tight. Ancient history. What's he have to do with any of this now?"

"That old fat trucker is more dangerous than you know," Viper said, the smile finally sliding from his face. "He's one of the last of a dying breed, he's a genuinely decent man. They're becoming extinct, hell, they should put him a zoo. He's the one keeping Heck's head on straight, urging him to not fly off the handle, giving him a compass to try to follow. You remove Jimmie Aussapile, and I guarantee you, you'll see Heck completely out of control."

Mike looked at Viper and wondered again at how he had partnered up with the mysterious biker. Mike had made his first attempt to get the Jocks into the drug trade back in the late nineties. He had a handful of Jocks loyal to him wanting to make bank, acting as mules and muscle for low-level deals.

Glen Hume and Ale had discovered his business and Mike had come damn close to dying at Ale Mckee's hands. Mike set up another Jock as the fall guy for his scheme, and played the stupid dupe. The deception had worked, along with pointing out that his mom was dying in a nursing home in Charlotte all alone. Ale took pity. Mike was granted nomad status in the Jocks, never belonging to a chapter again, but wandering between them. Ale also told him that if he ever pulled any more stupid shit like that with a Blue Jocks' cut on his back, Ale would take it away before he blew Mike's brains out.

Mike rode to visit his dying mother for about three days and then left after he stole about a grand and a bunch of her pain meds from her. She died alone two months later. By then Mike was on to his next scheme, his next scam. He hated Ale and he knew sooner or later he'd get the chance to step up and make the Jocks into the badass organization it was meant to be. Then he got busted for possession with intent to distribute and got fifteen years. That was how he met Viper.

In prison, he saw the redhead working out with massive weights in the yard. Eventually they struck up a conversation, at first about weight lifting, then bikes, but then later about Mike's desire to take over the MC. Turns out

Viper had had few run-ins with the Jocks too. Mike recalled hearing Gordon and Ale and a few of the other originals mention the name Viper a few times. They never said it like he was a friend.

After a few months, Viper was no longer in the yard or the mess hall. Mike figured he had been released. When he asked Vinnie about Viper's fate, his cellmate looked at him weird. "Who the fuck you talking about, Mike?" he said, and swore he had never seen Viper in the prison population.

About a year later, Viper began to show up to visit Mike, not in the visitor's hall, but in his cell in the dead of night.

"You're not fucking real," Mike had whispered to the huge man squatting on his haunches next to his bunk. "You are just some kind of hallucination." Viper slapped him hard. It stung, it felt real.

"That feel like a hallucination, asshole? Now shut up and listen, and I'm going to tell you how to get out of here early and how I'm going to help you take over the Jocks."

So Mike did, and Viper was true to his word. After he got out, Viper took him to the Road to Nowhere, the site the Jocks used for initiations and important meetings. Viper disappeared into the tunnel for a time and when he returned he held the iron wand called the Key of Thorne. Viper told him it would give him control over the monsters the Jocks hunted.

Mike walked over to the door to his office and opened it. He gestured to Vinnie and his lieutenant approached. "Get me a crew together," Mike said. "I want Aussapile dead by sundown tomorrow." Viper smiled and leaned back on the couch.

"Good plan, Mikie," he said. "Brilliant."

. . .

Jimmie and Layla were camped out in Elizabeth's guest room. Jimmie entered and found his wife lying on the bed reading a paperback by Sharyn McCrumb. The radio alarm clock was playing the Marshall Tucker Band's "Heard It in a Love Song."

"Anything?" Layla asked, sitting up. "Any word?"

"Nothing," Jimmie said. "Jethro called in. All three raids were a success. Mike's meth labs have been blown back to Hell, but not a word on Heck or Ana Mae Wade."

He sat down on her side of the bed, shrugged his boots off, and slipped his arm behind her back. She scooched closer to him. Layla smelled of clean soap and shampoo. "I should have gone along with them."

Layla gave him a tight hug.

"I'm glad you didn't," she said. "Jimmie, all these people dying, all these guns and drugs and police . . . baby, I understand how much Ale meant to you, how much Heck means to you now, but your family needs you. *I* need you. Alive, not dead, not in prison."

Jimmie pulled Layla to him tight and held her. She fit perfectly against him, they always had. "It's okay, baby," he said and his voice rumbled through her skin, through the core of her and she felt herself relaxing, breathing deeper. "I really do understand. It's bad enough to have to deal with the freaks and the monsters and the criminals on the road, right?" She nodded against his shoulder. His flannel shirt smelled of wood smoke and faintly of grease.

"You're in a war, Jimmie," she said, "a gang war. I want to help Elizabeth and Heck as much as you do but, baby, this is not what you or me or the kids ever signed on for. This is not your MC, it's not your fight, and I'm scared I'm going to lose you in this." Jimmie kissed the crown of her head, and held her as tight as his big arms would let him.

"Yeah," he said. "I'm scared too, baby. There's a reason I walked away from this life, walked straight to you."

"Then let's go home," she said, "before some stray bullet hits you and takes you away from JJ, from Peyton, from your mom and dad. Time . . . time always catches up, you can't cheat it, can't outrun it. We have so little time to fill up with so much good, so much happiness . . . please, let's go home." She felt so right against him and he lowered his unshaven face and found her against his chest. He kissed her like this was the only kiss he'd ever have. Finally the spell broke. Time pulled them and their lips parted.

"I . . . I can't do that, baby," Jimmie said. "I want to, believe me, but I can't just yet."

"Why?" she asked. There was no anger, no recrimination in her tone, just a need to understand.

"There's a man . . . we'll call him a man, anyway. He's evil and he's cunning and he caused a lot of trouble a long time ago, back before Heck was even born, back before I was with you."

"Is it that Viper guy you and Elizabeth were talking about?" Layla asked. Jimmie nodded. They still held each other.

"That's the son of a bitch," he said. "He's back and he's either working with Mike or he's using Mike to get to Elizabeth and Heck. Either way I can't leave them to deal with him alone. Ale would want me here, doing all I could to stop him."

"Have you talked to Heck about any of this?" she asked.

"I . . . can't," Jimmie said. "We . . . we all took a vow, an oath, a long time ago, me and Ale, Elizabeth, the other originals, everyone involved. We all took an oath in a place where oaths hold tight. We all swore we wouldn't drag Heck into the middle of this, wouldn't make him have to deal with . . . it. He was . . . he was just a baby." Jimmie's voice drifted and Layla saw her husband's eyes peering through time.

"He's not a baby anymore, hon," Layla said. "If this man is threatening Heck's future, his present, he ought to know." Jimmie nodded.

"He should, but I can't tell him, neither can Elizabeth. We're just about the only ones left who even know the whole story."

Layla looked up into Jimmie's kind green eyes. "Can you tell me, baby?" Jimmie seemed to weigh some invisible burden in his mind. Layla ran her hands over his head. "Tell me the whole story, please." Jimmie sighed.

"You ain't gonna believe this," he said, and then he told her.

Layla was quiet for a long time after. Jimmie could see her trying to grapple with it, trying to wrap her mind around it. The radio was playing the Dead South's "In Hell I'll Be in Good Company."

"God, Jimmie," she almost whispered. "How do you . . . how have you stayed . . . such a good man, a good person when you've been through that, seen that . . . I mean . . ." She lost her words in the middle and just held Jimmie tight. Jimmie wished he hadn't told her now.

"I try not to think about it," he said. "Most of the time it's like a bad dream, another life, like a lot of the stuff from over there, in Iraq, and I have you and the kids. You have no idea how much you've helped me. Kept me straight. But do you understand why I have to help Heck, why I can't leave him now, why he can never know." Layla nodded.

"Baby," she said, "someday he's going to know. The truth's like a splinter, it either works itself out or it turns into poison." Jimmie made the face Layla knew he made when there was no good solution to a problem. His normal response was to soldier through whatever it was.

"Someday," he said. "Not today, not now, not in the middle of all this shit. I just hope he gets the truth from Elizabeth. He should hear it from her, I think."

Layla held him tight and they were quiet. The radio played "Stay" by Sugarland.

"I love you," Layla whispered in his ear.

"I love you," he said and they held each other, and listened to the radio and eventually they slept, never letting go of one another, holding tight, even in dream.

. . .

Heck opened his eyes and coughed, his first two mistakes. His throat was raw, like it had been clawed with razor blades. Bright sunlight stabbed his eyes. "Fuuuuck," he croaked.

"Watch your fucking mouth, highland boy," the voice was Ana Mae's, "you're in my mama's house." Heck rolled over, away from the sun streaming in the window and toward her voice. Did he hear music? Ana Mae was near the bed, rummaging through a dresser drawer. The Sinclair family Claymore was propped against the wall next to the dresser. The sword was secure in its blackened and singed leather scabbard. Her cell phone was sitting on top of the dresser next to a small, spherical Bluetooth speaker. Music drifted out of the little globe. It took Heck a moment to process what it was. It was "Dreaming My Dreams with You" by Waylon Jennings. Heck remembered Ale and his mom taking him to see Waylon Jennings once when he was a kid. The guy had seemed dangerous and Heck loved him.

Ana Mae wore only a man's blue work shirt that fell to her thighs and black and purple socks that stretched up to meet the shirt so only a slender strip of pale skin was exposed. Her hair was tied back into a simple ponytail. She had cuts and bruises on her face and hands but they were nearly healed. She pulled a pair of dark sweat pants out of the drawer, unfolded them, and held them up to examine.

"How long?" Heck asked.

"Two days," Ana Mae said, nodding in approval at the sweats. "I just woke up this morning myself. You slept in. You snore." Heck looked around at the four-poster bed he was lying in. The sheets were covered in dried blood, tufts of charred fur, and bits of blackened skin. He looked down at his bruised and cut arms and his chest. The Ouija board tattoo that was on his chest was covered in green, blue. and purple shadows, but he knew the bruises looked better than they had a day ago. "You also don't burn, you know that, right?"

Heck nodded. "Yeah."

Ana Mae moved to another drawer and sifted through folded shirts. "You wear a medium, right?" Heck nodded again. "So what's the story with the not burning? You're strong, and faster than most, you heal damn quick and you're fireproof. You sure you ain't got some of the blood in you?"

"Well, I haven't felt an urge to lick my balls recently," Heck said, grunting as he sat up and swung his legs over the bed. It was only then he realized he was naked. The cuts and bruises that mapped his skin were already sore memories for the most part. "So, I'm going to say no."

Ana Mae grinned and glanced back. "Well, with balls like that, I don't blame you, sugar." Heck laughed and that started a coughing fit.

"Nice. You save my smokes?"

"'Cause that is exactly what you need right now, charcoal in your lungs." She held up an old faded olive drab T-shirt. She seemed to approve of it.

Heck grunted. "C'mon, Little Mary Sunshine, I fucking need my breakfast."

Ana Mae sighed and placed the shirt and sweats on top of the dresser. She left the bedroom and returned shortly with a crushed and partly charred pack of Lucky Strikes, his chain wallet, Zippo lighter, and his denim MC club cut. They all reeked of wood smoke. She tossed them to him. "The rest of your clothes I ditched, but I figured you'd want these. I was going to wash the cut."

"Thanks," Heck said. There was a clicking on the wood floors in the hallway outside the bedroom and the three pit bulls from the drug lab encampment trotted into the room. One of the dogs was reddish brown, another was black with white patches, and the third was pure black. All three launched themselves at Heck like wheezing, slobbering missiles and tackled him back onto the bed, covering his face in messy, wet licks. "Jesus," Heck mumbled, buried under the onslaught, "get off me, you meatheads! No, don't eat the fucking cigarettes!" Ana Mae smiled broadly.

"You guys bonded, don't you remember? When we got here they insisted on curling up in the bed with us and guarding us. They've decided I'm their mama."

"What does that make me?" Heck struggled back to the surface and looked over at the MC leader.

"Little brother," she said, "of course. The stupid one."

Heck shook his head and rummaged around under the churning pack for his Luckies. "It was kind of your mom to take me and the boys in," he said.

"She's not home at present," Ana Mae said, walking over to him with the clothes she had gathered in her hands. "Mom teaches classes on nature and Fae magic. She travels a lot. I think she's at some festival or other right now. She lets me use the place whenever I need. I didn't think anyone would look for us here."

"Your mom sounds pretty cool."

"She is." Ana Mae handed him the sweats and the shirt, and sat on the edge of the bed. "I wish I could have grown up with her."

"You didn't?"

"No. My brother and I got put in foster care after my dad went to prison and Mom . . . well, Mom is great but she comes off flaky as hell, so the court sent us into foster care."

"That sucks," Ale said said, lighting a crooked Lucky. Ana Mae pinched the cherry tip out with her fingers.

"No smoking inside," she said. "Mom's rule." Heck put the cigarette and lighter away. "Foster care wouldn't have been so bad but Mom and Dad hadn't told me and Scottie about our . . . heritage. Mom had been waiting for a good time, it's pretty heavy to drop shit like 'your from a family with werewolf blood' on a kid, y'know?" Heck nodded.

"Yeah, I can see that," he said. "So you didn't know what you were. Man, that would be scary as hell."

"It was," she said, looking at her bare feet, not him. "Dad went nuts one day and killed a guy in a bar fight, nearly tore him to pieces. He got sent away in 1991. He killed a bunch of guards a year later in prison and took off. No clue where he is but Mom's pretty sure it was the blood in him that made him go crazy like that. It usually wakes up in puberty . . . but not always. It did for me. They locked me up in some mental hospitals. Told me I schizophrenic, dangerously psychotic. They gave me a fucking shit-ton of pills. Didn't take. I took off on my own at fifteen. I finally met some other werefolk and they helped me figure out who and what I was. I've never looked back."

Ana Mae finally looked at Heck. "I have no fucking clue why I'm spilling all this to you. You know more about me than most of my MC, Sinclair. Why is that?"

"Maybe 'cause you know we're alike," Heck said. "I felt outcast my whole life, like everyone but me knew why I was different, why I had these thoughts, these desires. It felt like everyone around me was tiptoeing around some big secret, all of them afraid to speak the truth. I've felt this . . . force in my blood, inside me, since I was a kid. It's like a pressure, or a fire that just seems to build and build until I feel it hot behind my eyes, until my guts are humming and I can taste blood in my mouth. It comes screaming out of me, rides me, I've never met anyone or anything it couldn't destroy. But I can't control it. It burns everything, my friends, my family, everything but me. It's my greatest strength, I use it all the time like fuel, like nitrous, but it's also the thing that fucks everything else up." He looked up to see Ana Mae's beautiful blue eyes burning into his. She nodded slightly. "I'm afraid to keep it, for what it will cost me, and I'm even more afraid of what I'd do without it."

"'Wolf Like Me,'" she finally said.

"What?" Heck asked, drawing closer to her. She smelled of sandalwood and wildflowers.

"It's a song," she said, leaning up toward him. "That feeling in your blood, dizzy, angry, needing . . . hungry. Out of control." Heck reached out and took her by her thick reddish brown hair at the base of her ponytail.

"Come here," he said, a hoarse growl.

Ana Mae took him by his tousled red hair, gripped a hunk of it tight, and pulled him in. "You come here," she said with a whispered snarl.

The kiss burned. There was need behind it, a desperate ache to devour each other that could not be defined, could not be contained in a cage of rationality. It spoke to the primordial mind, a language of scent, muscles fluttering, skin and teeth. It annihilated reason like a fire gobbling up oxygen.

Heck pulled Ana Mae onto him as he fell back on the bed. The dogs scampered off the bed for fear of being trampled. "Cadillac Dust" by Elliott Brood was playing now but neither Heck nor Ana Mae heard anything but the song of their blood. She grazed Heck's nipple with her teeth, her long hair hiding her face. Heck gasped at the sensation, and pulled her up to his face. They kissed again as he tore at her shirt, buttons flying. She sunk her teeth deep into his shoulder and he returned the favor by kissing and nipping at her throat.

Heck flipped Ana Mae onto her back and was above her in an instant, one hand clutching her throat while the other explored and teased her body. Ana Mae's legs wrapped around his waist, she released her grip on Heck's hair. She raked her nails with both hands down his back, leaving glistening dark ribbons in her wake. Her eyes rolled back in her head at his touch.

Heck hissed at the pain and thrust his hips forward, entering her. Ana Mae's legs, scissored around him, pulled him deeper into her as they both cried out in pleasure. Heck's hands pushed her shoulders firmly against the bed, bruising her pale skin, pinning her even as she used her legs to meet his thrusts, her arms ringing his neck, grabbing his hair, clawing his skin.

Heck blinked for a second, holding the slavering, hungry thing inside him at bay. He looked down at Ana Mae. Her eyes were stars, blue fire. He tried to say something. His voice was lost, words were bullshit. There was only her face, those eyes, swimming between glittering sapphire and the color of the baleful moon as she fought to control the change.

"Give ... me ... ," he croaked the fire rising, the monster ascendant in him. "All ... of ... you. I can ... take it."

"Talk ... too fucking much ... chew toy," Ana Mae moaned as they pulled together tight, kissing, clutching, nails sunk in deep, joined, lost in something older than words, older than reason.

They stayed in bed most of the day, occasionally dozing, or going into the kitchen to raid the fridge, gobbling down most of a platter of cold roast beef and a loaf of homemade bread Ana Mae found in the breadbox. They stood in the kitchen naked and tossed food to the dogs, who wandered around. Heck let them run outside for a while. They washed down the food with iced tea and a few cold PBRs. Then they went back to bed and got lost in each other again, and again. The sheets stayed damp with sweat and blood, but they both healed quickly during their naps.

"This is the first time in my life I've never had to hold anything back," Ana Mae said as they lay next to each other. The day was a washed-out ribbon of melon-colored light through the lace curtains of the window. The dogs barked and played outside in the dwindling light.

"Me too," Heck said. "It felt ... really good."

"Yeah," Ana Mae said. "It did."

"You mean even like with other werewolves?" Heck asked. Ana Mae nodded.

"Even with them."

A wide smile grew on his unshaven face. "Cool."

Heck pulled out a Lucky and lit it. He put it to his lips and Ana Mae plucked it away. "I told you already," she said, taking the lit cigarette and grinding its cherry tip into the pale, smooth swell of her breast, "no smoking in Mama's house." Heck could smell the bitter tang of the charred flesh. He and Ana Mae kept looking at each other and he saw a twinge of pain and then a well of desire flash across her eyes. "Besides there are so many more enjoyable ways to kill yourself, Sinclair. You need to up your vice game." She tossed the now crushed cigarette onto the floor and pulled Heck closer. Heck let her.

"You know," he said, inches from her lips, "tomorrow ... ."

"Yeah," she nodded, "we've got to go back. Tomorrow."

"Tomorrow," Heck said, and kissed her like it was the first time again.

Dusty Acosta was on the couch cuddled up next to his friend and current roommate, Moxie Dolittle. They were sharing a bowl of Fruity Pebbles and watching Svengoolie's old-time monster movies on TV. Tonight it was *Killer Klowns from Outer Space.*

Moxie was a few years older than Dusty. She was about five foot three and carried a little extra weight, but she carried it very well. Her pigtailed hair was currently dyed aquamarine and she wore horn-rimmed glasses. Moxie had about a dozen tattoos strategically placed all over her body.

Dusty met Moxie on the road a few years back. They had hit it off and spent the spring exploring the California coast before parting ways in Seattle. When Dusty had sent out feelers through the online nomad community that he was headed back to Philly, he was overjoyed to learn that Moxie was wintering there and had a place where he was more than welcome to crash.

Moxie had even been great when she ended up having to pick Dusty up at the police station when he had first got into Philly. The cops had leaned on him as long and hard as they could but eventually they had to cut him loose, only charging him with a misdemeanor for trespassing in the rail yard. It had been a few weeks and Dusty was working his contract IT job and enjoying the city, but he had also reached out to try to find out all he could about the mutilation murder by the tracks.

"Look," Moxie had said one night as they met for an after-work drink at the Tattooed Mom, "I understand that you were, y'know, right in the middle of it at the start, but Dust, don't you think that might be a really good reason to not poke around in it? The cops wanted to pin it on you real bad. Why give them any help with that?"

Dusty shook his head as he took another sip of his beer.

"I kinda need to look into it a little, Mox," he said. "It's . . . it's kind of my . . . responsibility." She rolled her eyes.

"Whatever," she said, "but just so you know, I am not bailing you out, Encyclopedia Brown."

The doorbell buzzed at a particularly scary spot in the movie and Dusty and Moxie both jumped, almost upsetting their cereal bowl. Dusty caught it and they both laughed.

"Jesus," Moxie gasped. "Who's buzzing this late?" She walked to her apartment door in her fleece PJs, which were adorned with various dinosaurs. "Yeah?" she called through the door. "Who is it?"

"Police," a woman's voice replied, muffled through the door. "I need to talk with Dustin Acosta." There was a pause. "Bang! Pow! Boom!" Dusty had joined Moxie once he heard his name spoken. Moxie glanced over to him

"She knows your road name," she said. "I guess I should let her in?"

"Yeah," Dustin said, nodding, "I guess."

Moxie unlocked the half-dozen locks and deadbolts she had on the door of her shitty South Philly apartment. When the door opened into the dark hall, a tall, pretty black woman stood there. She had long straight hair that reminded Moxie of a fifties pinup, like Betty Page or something. She wore a black leather jacket, jeans, and a yellow blouse. There was an accordion-style file folder tucked under her arm. The woman raised her hand and showed her badge and ID, which were in a small leather wallet.

"My name is Lovina Marcou," she said. "I'm a state police investigator. May I come in?"

"ID says Louisiana State Police," Moxie said, narrowing her eyes. "I think you missed your exit."

"I'm in Philadelphia following up on an investigation with the cooperation of the Pennsylvania State Police, the Philadelphia PD, and the FBI," the woman said.

"FBI, huh?" Moxie said. "Okay, come on in, then."

"Hey," Dusty said as Lovina entered. "What can I do for you, officer?"

"I need your help," Lovina said, walking into the living room. She sat on the edge of an easy chair that faced the coffee table in front of the sofa. She pushed aside the bowl of now soggy Fruity Pebbles and began to open her file folder. "On a case, several cases, actually."

"Whoa, hold it, hold it!" Dusty said. "Look, I just blundered into that field and found that woman's body." He sat on the couch near Lovina's chair. "If this is some backdoor way of trying to interrogate me again about that killing, or to try to implicate me in some others—"

"I'm not trying to do any of that, Dustin," Lovina said, cutting him off. "I was told you could help me. Imagine my surprise when I go looking for you only to find you up to your neck in a similar case to the one I'm working. I need your expertise. I was told you were the man with the answers I'm looking for."

"What?" Moxie said, sitting down next to Dustin. "Lady, Dusty's just a computer nerd. He doesn't even like watching serial killer documentaries with me."

"I don't see how I could be any help to you, Officer Marcou," Dusty said. Lovina placed the hobo nickel with the skull motif on it on the table in front of the young nomad.

"The wheel turns," she said. Dusty looked up in surprise from the nickel to her face. He answered almost automatically.

"The wheel turns. Oh, wow. Are you here because of the call I made to the automated number?" Lovina shook her head.

"Not exactly, but that was how I found you."

"What the fuck does 'the wheel turns' mean?" Moxie asked. "That an old Buck Owens song?"

"It's a road secret, Mox," Dusty said, looking at his friend. "I can't tell you about it, I'm sorry, but she's legit. Can you give us a few?" Moxie looked over at Lovina and screwed up her face.

"Okaaaay," she said, switching off the TV. "Fine. I'll let you have your secret pow-wow, in my apartment. Late at night. Cool beans. Nice meeting you, 'Officer Tall, Dark, and Mysterious.'"

"Moxie," Dusty said as she retreated to her bedroom and shut the door. *"Mierda!"* he said, gesturing with his hands toward the bedroom door. "I hate it when she gets like that!"

"Sorry if my timing is bad," Lovina said, "especially in relation to your girlfriend."

"It's okay," Dusty said. "Moxie comes off like that sometimes. 'Moxie Dolittle' isn't even her real name, it's her road handle."

"Like yours is Bang! Pow! Boom!" Lovina said. He nodded and saw the questioning look on Lovina's face.

"It's from an ICP album," he said. "Insane Clown Posse? You into that?"

"Not my thing," Lovina said.

"You should check them out, change your life. What's your road name, anyway?" Dustin asked.

"Apparently 'Bandit Two,'" Lovina said with a sigh. Dusty gave her an odd look. "I'm working on it."

"Anyway, Mox and I met on the Rail, she knows there's weird shit out there, and she knows I kind of research it, catalogue it. She doesn't like being cut out of it. She'll get over it. She not my girlfriend, by the way. We're just really good friends, that's all."

Lovina gave him an incredulous look.

"Well I hope you're more of an expert on weird stuff than you are on women, kid," Lovina said, "because that girl is claiming you, even if you're the last one to know." She paused for a moment as if her mind had just tripped up over something. "Wait, did you just say you'd run into weirdness on the *Rail*? You mean the Road, right?"

Dusty shook his head, "No, the Rail. The railroad lines that run across America, they have the same problems the highways do, they seem to attract monsters . . . things from other places, attract damaged, twisted personalities close to them. No one's sure why, any more than they know why the roads do it."

"So, did a damaged personality have anything to do with this?" Lovina asked. She placed the hobo nickel on the coffee table before Dustin, its carved skull face leering up at him.

"Wha . . . Oh yeah, hobo nickels," Dusty said. He picked up the carved nickel and examined its skull-face details and then its other side with the odd markings, the sideways teardrop with the small cross under its tail on one side. "Yeah, yeah, this one's consistent with the story," he finally said. "Even the weird symbol on the back."

"Consistent?" Lovina asked.

"This came from a crime scene, right? Shit! Did it come from the one I wandered into? Damn it, I knew something about the way that woman was cut up seemed familiar . . ."

"Slow down, Dustin," Lovina said, raising her hands as if the young man's enthusiasm would run her over physically. It reminded her of how Max got when she was on a tear, and Lovina smiled at the thought. "Okay, obviously I came to the right place. Jimmie Aussaplie sent me. Do you know him?" Dusty shook his head. "He's an old friend of your uncle's."

"Uncle Tomás?" Dusty said. "Oh, wait, Aussapile? That the guy Uncle

Tomás said helped him out when they had to stop that Cegua thing in New Mexico from killing people?"

"I guess," Lovina said. "He didn't give me a lot of background, other than he was good friends with your uncle and that he brought you into the Brethren."

"Yeah," Dusty said. "My uncle told me all these stories about the stuff he saw out on the Road as a trucker. It inspired me to get out there too and the Road led me to the Rail. I've been a train hopper ever since. My parents kind of hate it, think I'm wasting my life being a bum, but I got no regrets."

"So you recognize the coin? Its style?" Lovina asked. "I was told these kinds of coins are individual to the hobo artists, that right?" Dusty nodded, looking closer at the coin's details. Lovina slid a series of photocopies out of her folder and laid them on the table. They were all of the same skull-faced hobo nickel.

"Mmhmm," he muttered as he tried to read the script at the edges of the coin. "Yeah, yeah. Each artist has his own style and it's bad form to cop someone's style, just like graffiti taggers. This one," he held up the coin to the investigator, "this one looks legit. It matches the ones in the old stories."

"What stories?"

"Well, Officer Marcou," he began.

"Just call me Lovina."

"Okay, Lovina. There is the history in the history books you read in school and then there is the history and the legends of the Road. Two different things, two different worlds, both as real as the other. This nickel, ones exactly like it, they weigh heavy in an old hobo story goes back over eighty years ago. You ever hear of the Butcher of Kingsbury Run?" Lovina shook her head. "Guy was like a ghost. He murdered twelve people we know of in Cleveland starting in the early 1930s, cut them up, decapitated them, cut off arms and legs, cut them in two at the waist."

"MO sounds familiar," Lovina said.

"The guy was never caught," Dusty said. "The cops hunted him for years. Nothing. He preyed on the inhabitants of the hobo jungle in Kingsbury Run in Cleveland, near the railroad yards. The story goes he was some kind of mad scientist, experimenting on human beings. He hunted hobos, the homeless, junkies, and prostitutes, faceless, nameless people. All the people no one really gives a damn about."

Lovina was silent. In her mind she was kneeling by her sister again, cut and torn, used and discarded. Dusty frowned. "You okay?"

"Yeah," she said. "Go on."

"That coin, that particular style of coin, supposedly showed up at all the Cleveland murder scenes. The cops collected some of them, hobos who got to the scene collected a few more. No one ever went public with them."

"Why?" Lovina asked.

"For pretty much the same reason," Dusty said. "If it got out that a hobo token was found near the bodies, it would have become open season on the homeless, on train hoppers. So everyone kept it quiet. After a few years of killings, the Cleveland safety director ordered the hobo jungle at Kingsbury Run demolished, the hobos chased away or arrested. The official reason given for the demolition was to not give the Butcher more victims. The real story goes that it was to chase away the hobo who was carving these nickels and was, most likely, the Butcher. The killings seemed to stop after the jungle was burned down, but the hobo myth says that the Butcher just moved on, to another city, another jungle and kept on killing."

Lovina slid a series of photocopies out of her folder and laid them on the table. They were all of the same skull-faced hobo nickel. "Could you tell if these are all from the same guy or a copycat?"

Dusty examined the detail on each of the photocopies. After about ten minutes he handed them back to Lovina.

"All carved by the same hand," he said. "He leaves a little divot in the same spot by the date stamped on the nickel. It's his maker's mark."

"This," Lovina said, placing an identical coin on the table next to the first hobo nickel, "is from a crime scene in Windber, Pennsylvania," she said. "Found near the body of a mutilated woman who had been missing for over four years. Her name was Raelyn Dunning. The coin you examined was found in her car on the side Interstate 80 back in 2014." She laid a photocopy on the table. "This one is from the crime scene you ran into here in Philadelphia—"

"Alice," Dusty interrupted.

"What?"

"The dead lady by the rail yard, the crime scene here, her name was Alice."

"How do you know that?" Lovina asked.

"I listened to the rails, they told me." Lovina nodded, she didn't know what to say to that, so she said nothing. She placed another photocopy of the hobo nickel on the table.

"This one," she said, "is from an apparent body dump of a mutilated woman, in Fogelsville, around the same time we found Raelyn."

"*Mierda*," Dusty said, shaking his head. "It can't be the same guy as did the torso murders, he'd be like, over a hundred years old."

"That's not as far-fetched as you might think," Lovina said.

"Maybe a cult or a gang?" Dusty offered.

"Would a group of people have exactly the same MO, down to the placement of the body parts? "Some . . . evil things go on a lot longer than they should. They duck the justice of time, hide in the cracks of it, like roaches."

"Well, I guess it could be one guy. He supposedly gets around. There are theories that the Butcher may have been responsible for more killings in Ohio and here in Pennsylvania too. Maybe even in California."

"The Black Dahlia murder?" Lovina added. Dusty gave her a surprised look and nodded.

"Yeah, that's one theory. The story goes, the Cleveland killer sent a letter saying he was vacationing in California. The timing would be right for the mutilation murder of Elizabeth Short to be one of the Butcher's."

"For a guy who doesn't like serial killer documentaries, you sure got your stuff down," Lovina said.

"It's all part of the mythology of the Road and the Rail," he replied. "They've both got a pretty bloody history." They were both silent for moment. Dusty picked up one of the hobo nickels. "Maybe I can help you find whoever this is, but the way I do it may seem kind of crazy. You open to crazy?"

"These last few years? More than you can possibly imagine," she said with a sad smile.

"Okay, let me grab my stuff," he said and left the living room.

Lovina checked her smartphone to see if there had been any word from Cecil Dann. The FBI assistant agent in charge was in Philadelphia chasing down some physical evidence they had uncovered at Raelyn's crime scene, fingerprints. Apparently, someone—maybe two people—had leaned against the old trolley car Raelyn had been placed in front of.

The PPD's state-of-the-art Forensic Science Center was running the prints right now and Cecil had promised Lovina he would share the results with her, off the record, of course, when they came back. She doubted they'd get lucky enough with a print to end this. Everything Dusty Acosta had told her made sense in an insane way. This killer had been abducting people for medical experiments for almost a century, riding the rails, using them to find fresh victims, and elude old pursuers. Why the killer was doing these experiments was still a question that burned in her but the cop in her knew that why was usually the last question to get answered, if it ever did. Sometimes the why was because the criminal was simply insane.

Dusty returned from the kitchen with an armful of plastic Faygo soda bottles. The bottles had candles melted over their mouths that were the same color as the soda in the bottle. Dusty meticulously arranged the bottles in large circle, adjusting the direction of each bottle slightly. "We need to try to be quiet," he said. "I don't want to wake up Moxie."

"You do magic?" Lovina said, standing. "You're a road witch?" Dusty shook his head as he adjusted the bottles.

"No, I know a few minor tricks, like reading the rails. A lot of the old hobos knew that stuff." Dusty entered the circle with an old worn leather satchel. He lit the candles in the bottles carefully with a purple Bic lighter, lighting them left to right. He closed his eyes for a moment and seemed to be sensing for something. He turned in the circle of bottles several time and then, apparently satisfied, sat down cross-legged. He popped the tube on a large container of white makeup he took from the satchel and used a small hand mirror he retrieved to apply it to his face evenly. "My magic style is pretty unique, not too many practitioners." He used a tube of black makeup to draw designs around his mouth and eyes. He filled in the lines of the eye designs with the black paint, and filled in his mouth with another stick of makeup that was cherry red. He pulled his hair back to keep it from covering part of his face.

"What are you doing?" Lovina asked, the clown makeup making her a little bit nervous.

"My magic is tied to the Dark Carnival," he said. "I walk through its many rooms. We all do. The Dark Carnival is where souls await judgment." Dusty pulled his T-shirt off and tossed on the couch outside the circle. His chest was covered in numerous brightly colored tattoos and symbols. Prominent on the center of his chest was a tattoo of a skull-like face in the center of what seemed a jagged representation of a cartoon explosion. Lovina noticed one of the tattoos on Dusty's arm was the silhouette of a cartoonish figure running with what looked like a meat cleaver in his hand.

"Is . . . is your magic based off of . . . Insane Clown Posse?" Dusty nodded, taking several items out of his satchel. "You do magic based off the rap equivalent to Kiss?"

"Hey, watch that now," Dustin said. "ICP are the best! What I do is closer to Voodoo than anything. The six joker card entries mentioned in the ICP albums are representation of universal forces, the way earlier Voodoo practitioners hid worshipping their gods behind veneration to the Catholic saints. The six jokers are like the loa."

"The what? Look, I know a little bit about Voodoo," Lovina said. "It runs in my family. It's an ancient practice, grounded in the venerable religions of several peoples. This . . . is . . . not Voodoo."

"All things have to adapt," Dustin said, arranging his phone, a small Bluetooth speaker cube, and another bottle of Faygo soda next to him, "or they fade away. Magic is like water flowing. It finds cracks in the stone to move through, and it carves the stone, alters it, as it moves through. What I do is a new kind of magic. I just said its *roots* are in Voodoo, maybe a little Santería too. Those practices changed to adapt to the new world. And like those practices, what I do is lifted by the faith of the believers, and the practitioners."

"That symbol on your chest?" Lovina asked, pointing to the tattoo.

"That," Dusty said, "is my totem, Bang! Pow! Boom! He is the seventh joker. He blasts evil souls out of the Dark Carnival and into Hell. Kind of a karmic hand grenade."

Lovina sighed. "Okay, if you say so."

"Hand me the two hobo nickels," Dustin asked. Lovina handed them to him. He placed them on the floor in front of him one directly above the other. One skull-face side up the other facing the side with the strange teardrop symbol.

"It turns out rap, hip-hop, many other forms of modern music are perfect for incantation and shaping and directing energy," Dusty said. "They evoke emotion, can produce trance states, and unlock primal parts of the mind, freeing them. It's really cool. You'll see."

"And this will find the guy who made the nickels?" Lovina said, setting back in the chair. Dusty shrugged.

"If we're lucky and the six jokers will it," he said. He searched through the menu screen on his phone until he found what he wanted. He tapped a few times on the screen and music began to throb from the small Bluetooth speaker. It was "Miracles" by ICP. He kept the volume low, still wanting to avoid the wrath of Moxie.

Dusty closed his eyes for a moment and swayed to the music. He slowly raised a crumpled joint and lit it. Lovina raised an eyebrow but remained silent. He continued to vibe to the music, taking a deep draw on the joint. He held the smoke and then raised his bottle of Faygo Moon Mist soda to his lips. He blew the thick pot smoke into the bottle and then took a drink, the smoke trailing at the corners of his mouth.

Lovina saw the similarities to Voodoo, but she was still pretty skeptical that this was anything that was going to help her find the killer. Then she glanced down at the hobo nickels. They were moving inside the circle of candles. The coins were sliding along the wooden floor like two moons orbiting Dusty. The coins were in oppositional orbits, one sliding left, the other right. Dusty blew more smoke into the bottle and this time muttered something Lovina couldn't quite catch. He crushed out the smoldering tip of the joint and then screwed the white plastic cap back on the soda. The smoke swirled inside, trapped, seemingly growing thicker. Dusty muttered something again and the coins stopped moving. The soda in the candle bottles began to light up, to glow as if they were phosphorescent, in brilliant reds, oranges, and blues.

The Moon Mist soda in the bottle Dusty was holding flared to life too, a brilliant electric green. Dusty held the bottle close to his face and whispered to it, gesturing with his fingers as if he were coaxing it. Lovina stepped closer as she saw the smoke begin to shift, swirl, and take the shape of a face. The face formed and Lovina audibly gasped when she saw it. The smoke had created the face of a clown, *the* clown. The clown that haunted Lovina's dreams, that had taken Raelyn from her car on the side of the road. The face in the bottle was animated, it blinked, facial muscles tightened. It had the large circle and the two smaller dots painted on its forehead. The clown glared at Lovina with dead eyes made of smoke.

"His name . . . is . . . Altair," Dusty said in a voice that was almost not his. "Like the star. It's not his birth name . . . but he's almost forgotten that now. He's so hollow inside, eaten up by the white. Dutch. . . . his old name was Dutch. He's old and he's been killing for him for a long time now."

"Who?" Lovina asked, watching Dusty now shimmering in sweat, fighting to dredge up the knowledge from a distant alien place. "Who's he killing for?"

"Altair . . . doesn't know his real name . . . he's changed it so many times over the ages . . ." The contents of the candle bottles that encircled Dusty were bubbling now as if they were boiling. Dusty's eyes opened, they were rolled back in his skull. "I can see him . . . he . . . used to own part of the Dark Carnival . . . embraced it, fed it souls, but kept so many for himself, for the spagyric . . . the distilling . . ." Dusty's sightless face turned to Lovina. "He's diluting them, stealing their dreams, the seat of their soul—the soul that is born on the forty-ninth day—he uses the spagyric to make the fluid, he needs them for his fluid, for the Azoth! The Azoth!"

"Dustin, his name, what is his name?"

"The Cooker . . . Valentine . . ." Dustin began. Lovina saw he was convulsing, shivering. She could feel the heat coming off his skin in waves. Many of his brightly painted tattoos were glowing, giving off sparks of light. His voice was louder now as he fought through the fog of the trance. "Flamel . . . Abraham the Jew. So far back . . . so many people . . . harvested . . . A road of corpses he's walked upon through endless ages. A king of death. Murder that stretches . . . back in time. Sci . . . scion of Locusta . . . Locusta!"

The door to the bedroom flew open and Moxie stood there, still in her jammies. "What the hell are you doing out here!" she shouted. The candles all flared then went out, slender snakes of smoke from their wicks slithering toward the ceiling. The bottles and Dustin's tattoos all stopped glowing as well. The smoky face of Altair the clown swirled and melted, dissolving into nothing. Dusty slumped forward and Lovina caught him.

"He needs a blanket and some water!" Lovina said, helping Dusty over the circle of smoking candles and onto the couch.

"Listen, lady, I don't care if you're a cop or not," Moxie began. "I step out here because I thought I heard shouting, and I find you with Dusty, his shirt off, all sweaty, and the room smells of weed. So don't start bossing me around in my own place, Officer Pinup!"

"Mox," Dusty croaked, "it's okay. I did a magic thing. It kind of wiped me out. Nothing else, Scout's honor."

"Magic?" Moxie said. "Since when do you do magic, Dusty."

"Could you just please grab a blanket and some water for him," Lovina said. Moxie screwed up her face, reentered the bedroom, and returned with a thick *Star Wars*–themed comforter and helped Lovina tuck it over and around the shivering Dusty.

"I had to entreat and placate all six of the jokers to get his name," Dusty said, still panting. "I've never gone that deep before. This guy you're looking for, his boss has got some heavy-duty juice. He's not in Philly, by the way. Look at the nickels." Lovina glanced over to the dark circle. The coins in their parallel orbits had stopped at two different locations. "Looks to me like he's west of here."

"Coalport," she said. "The trailer park."

Moxie returned from the kitchen with a bottle of water. Dusty chugged it down. "Okay so this wasn't some freaky tantric-orgy kind of magic was it?" Moxie asked, looking from Dusty to Lovina. "You know, fucking for enlightenment?"

"Oh, no," Lovina said, shaking her head. "Hell, no."

"Just trying to help," Dusty said to his roommate, coming up for air from the water bottle. "Just being a good citizen, Mox." Dusty looked over to Lovina, "Was that any help to you, Lovina?"

Lovina nodded. "Yes it was. I recognized at least one of those names. You were a big help, Dustin." Lovina's phone chirped. It was Cecil Dann. She answered it. "Yes, Cecil. Any good news?"

"I think you'll like this," the FBI agent said from the other end of the line. "We got a hit off the prints and PPD has already picked one of the guys. Name's Angelo Potts. He's got a record, gang-affiliated. Lovina, I think we may have your clown killer."

It was late in the afternoon when Max gave up putting the theory out of her mind and decided to revisit the boxcar jungle behind the trailer park. A storm of ideas, theories, and conjectures had been tumbling again and again in her head since she had spoken with Lovina in Philadelphia late the night before.

Lovina told Max she was on her way to the police station to help interrogate a man the FBI and the PPD had picked up based on his fingerprint being at Raelyn's crime scene. He looked like a good fit for the killer, but Lovina had some doubts based on what Dusty Acosta had told her after performing his divination ritual.

"Wait, hold on," Max had said as she grabbed her tablet from the bedside table. "That's a fascinating variation on magic your Brethren friend has there. I'd love to discuss it with him in greater detail."

"He's with me now," Lovina said. "You can pick his brain later. Right now I need you to check out the names he . . ." The connection was lost and there was only a staticy warble of Lovina's voice for a moment.

"I lost you," Max said. "What did you say?"

The phone connection solidified to Lovina but was still fuzzy and the investigator was obviously in a moving car. "I said he gave us a bunch of names of who's behind the killings, and the clowns. I wanted to see if you could research them."

"Go ahead," Max had said, sitting on the side of the bed now, ready to tap the information into her tablet.

"He said the names 'Valentine'—"

"Like the trailer park!" Max said as she typed frantically on her tablet's screen.

"Yes," Lovina said. "Here's another one that should sound familiar, 'Flamel.'"

"Flamel!" Max exclaimed. "The name of the family who purchased the land the trailer park is on now, back in 1953."

"Yeah, then he said some other stuff that didn't make any sense to me. I hope you can chase it down."

"I'll try," Max said.

"He also mentioned 'scion of Locusta.' Then, something called a spagyric? Said he was using that to make an Azoth out of the people he's abducting."

"Azoth," Max asked, "and spagyric? You are sure, Lovina?"

"Yeah, do those mean anything to you?"

"Those names sound very familiar."

"Let me know what you can find," Lovina said. "Thanks, Max."

Max stayed up until after dawn running the strange names and terms through the Builder database and across the internet. The results were fascinating and pointed to a common source but there was data missing and the only way she could fill in those pieces was to go out to the park.

When she eventually crashed, the itch of a possible connection to the trailer park made sleep difficult. Max tried to push it away but to no avail. She awoke late in the afternoon and gathered up her gear and stuffed it in her satchel. She left a message for Lovina with the folks downstairs in the restaurant and headed down Main toward the trailer park.

The weather was not too hot. The small borough was quiet and lights were starting to come on along the street by the time she passed the Coalport 5&10 Store. She saw the Minit Mart's sign stutter to life as she approached it. For someone who grew up in big cities her whole, life, Max found places like Coalport refreshing. She had little doubt her colleagues would be disparaging everything here from the lack of a real hotel to the sacrilege of no Starbucks or Whole Foods. Max loved it for exactly those reasons. It didn't look like every other malltopia she had lived in. The buildings along Main were old, not cookie-cutter. The storefronts for the most part were old homes repurposed to become businesses. Coalport felt more real to Max than Washington or New York or Boston because of what it didn't have.

By the time she reached the trailer park's entrance most of the sky was a purple bruise and daylight was an orange scar along the horizon. She walked straight down the access road through the trailers toward the field behind the park. Max felt the eyes on her as she walked by. She kept her head down and began to wonder if perhaps it would have been more prudent to wait until morning to verify her troubling rash of an idea. If she was right, it would clarify the tumble of facts and figures in her mind—Raelyn Duning's crime scene, Lovina's troubling dreams, the disappearances and murders along I-80, the railroad jungle. Max hated an incomplete picture. When she worked puzzles she always worked them to completion. No, the sooner she could verify her thoughts, the sooner they could stop these horrible acts.

That was the excuse, and Max had half-convinced herself that was why she was running out here at this hour, but the real reason had less to do with the murders and disappearances. Max wanted to go because something had struck her while she had been researching Coalport, a notion that would expand and validate her own theories and her own work significantly. It may also explain the mysteries Lovina was determined to unravel, but if she was honest with herself, Max was being selfish.

She reached the edge of the road, and began to cross into the grass at the edge of the gently sloping hill that took you down into the field. A voice called out to her in the deepening darkness.

"Uh, excuse me, ma'am," it was a boy's voice, "where you going? It's almost dark." Max turned and regarded the boy. His face was illuminated in yellow from the light above the door to the trailer. He was on a small stoop, leaning against the rail. He was twelve at most, and had a mop of curly hair. He wore a shirt with a Captain America logo on it. "It's not safe to go back into the woods at night," he said, looking at her with big, wise dark eyes. Max paused a second and then walked over to the boy, She looked up at him from his perch on the stoop.

"Hi," she said and waved. "I'm Max."

"Ryan," the boy replied and waved back. "You are one of those people working with that state police lady, aren't you? You came here the other day with her."

"I guess I am helping," Max said as if the notion just occurred to her. "I'm a scientist. I'm helping Investigator Marcou with a case she's working and that brought us here."

"You were trying to find out who grabbed that girl who used to live here," Ryan said.

"I . . . I really don't think I should discuss an ongoing case with anyone, Ryan," Max said.

"Well I heard they found her body the other day," Ryan said. "You know lots of people go missing around here, not just that one girl."

"I do." Max gestured to the iron stairs of the stoop. "May I?" Ryan shrugged and Max took a seat on the stairs. "I can tell you Investigator Marcou doesn't just want to catch who did that to Raelyn Dunning. She wants to stop it for good . . . and so do I. What do you know about the people who go missing here, Ryan?"

"If I told you, you'd think I was crazy," Ryan said.

"I am actually pretty flexible on the whole crazy thing," Max said. "I won't laugh."

"I've seen some things in the park in just the little time I've been here. I haven't been here too long," the boy said. "My mom and I came from Baltimore at the beginning of summer to kind of start over with my grandma here."

"Start over from what?" Max asked, looking back at Ryan. He had taken a seat on the topmost stair. She could tell the boy felt uncomfortable talking about whatever had happened, so she changed the subject. She nodded toward his shirt. "You like Captain America?" Ryan nodded. "Me too," Max said. "I wasn't thrilled with that whole 'Cosmic Cube turning him into a Nazi' business but it's better now."

Rayn's eyes lit up as he realized a grown-up actually kept up with stuff like that.

"Marvel or DC?" Ryan asked.

"Image," Max replied.

"Exactly!" Ryan said. "You know who Jack Kirby is?"

"The king of comic artists?" Max said. "Are you serious?"

Ryan offered his small hand for a fist bump and Max tried to give him five at the same time. It was awkward and they both withdrew their hands and laughed. "Max, you seem cool. Look, you really don't want to go into that forest at night."

"I have to go into it to get to the boxcar jungle," she said. "I need to test a theory and verify something I think I saw in there. It's important to solving what's happening."

"By yourself?" Ryan said, obviously anxious about her safety. Max smiled.

"Lovi . . . Investigator Marcou is in Philadelphia running down some other leads, and you don't have any local police. So I guess it's just me."

"Aren't you scared?" Ryan asked.

"Well, to be honest, I am more so now than I was a few moments ago," she said. "But my grandfather, his name was Max too, he told me you can't let fear gobble up your reason. Reason is the enemy of fear."

"I'm pretty much scared of everything," Ryan said. "I hate it. A lot." Max took off her glasses and polished the lenses on her coat sleeve.

"I think you're not giving yourself enough credit," Max said. "There was a time, not too long ago, that I couldn't just say hello to a stranger, let alone talk to them. I would get way too nervous, too anxious, to do it. It was even hard for me to talk to people I knew well. I used to lecture my classes with my head down. So from where I am sitting, you are pretty brave, Ryan."

"How did you get over being frightened like that?" Ryan asked. Max looked up at the spill of brilliant stars overhead now.

"I met someone," she said. "A . . . friend. Somehow they made me believe I could do anything, and I got stronger, braver." She looked back at Ryan. "At first I thought I did it for them," she said. "Then I realized I really did it for me. They encouraged me to be a stronger me. That probably makes no sense at all."

"No, Ryan said, looking over at Nevada and Joe's trailer, at the light he knew was on in Nevada's room. "No, I understand."

"So," Max said. "I think I need to get on my way before it gets much later, don't you?" She stood and held out a fist, offering it to Ryan. He stood as well. "It's nice to meet you, Ryan." This time they did accomplish the bump.

"Wait a second!" Ryan said as Max stepped off the stoop. "Just wait, I need to get something inside. Don't go nowhere!" Within five minutes Ryan was back. He had on a maroon windbreaker over his T-shirt, a Baltimore Orioles baseball cap, and now wore sneakers. He held something wrapped in a hand-kerchief in his hand.

Before Max could say anything a group of children appeared from the shadows of the trailer park. Two of them, a dark-haired, serious-looking boy and girl, probably in her early teens with pink and blue hair, came from a trailer off to Max's right. The group of kids surrounded Max and stood quietly, shuffling, nervously.

"You, ah, you kids don't have black eyes do you?" Max asked.

"Huh?" Joe asked.

"I got a black eye once from not watching where I was going and walking smack-dab into the Oscar Meyer Wienermobile," David offered.

"Ignore him," Sam said to Max. "Ryan called us, said you wanted to go to the jungle. So you're a cop?"

"Not . . . not exactly," Max said.

"You got a gun?" Joe asked.

"Uh, no," Max said. "I don't like guns. I like brains instead."

"She's a scientist," Ryan said, walking down the stairs to join the others. "She's helping the staties solve that missing girl's murder. She's got to go into the jungle . . . and we're going to help her."

"Tonight?" Sam said. "Uh, why not wait till the morning? Or we could go get Karl . . ."

"Karl's chasing down alligator men in Pensacola," Ryan said. "It's just us."

"Look, guys," Max began, raising her hands, "I really appreciate the offer but you are all minors and I can't have you to go in there with me. Your folks . . ."

"I'm already grounded," Ryan said, "but Mom's working and Granny always falls asleep watching *America's Got Talent.*"

"Our dad's on third shift this week," Patrick said, gesturing to David, "so we're good."

"Listen, doctor—you are a doctor, right?" Nevada asked. Max nodded. "We're all scared of going in there. We've all seen what lives in those woods, in the boxcar jungle. But we also know that a lot of our friends and a lot of good people who don't deserve it have all gone missing. It's been happening around here for years." She glanced over to Ryan for a second. "If you can help stop it, stop the monsters, then we want to help you, scared or not."

"We're like a secret club," David blurted out. "Oh, I wasn't supposed to say that, was I?" Joe punched David in the arm, giving him "a frog." David winced. Max grinned in spite of herself.

"Secret club, huh?" Max said. "I happen to be in one of those too. Does your club have a secret phrase you use to identify members, like 'the temple restored'?"

"Um, 'run faster'? Sam offered.

"I like it," Max said. "Short, sweet, and to the point."

"So, can we go with you?" Nevada asked. "We promise we won't get in your way."

"And if anything scary pops up, we promise we'll run," Sam added, nodding vigorously.

Max looked around her at the earnest faces. She knew what Jimmie or Lovina would tell them, it was too dangerous and send them home. Her grandfather, Big Max, came to her then, the first adult to treat her like she wasn't an idiot.

"Okay," Max said. "Let's, uh, go. Everyone stick together."

Flashlights and cell phone flashlight apps were brandished and the company headed down the slope toward the field and the dark mantle of the woods off in the distance.

"It's like we're the Fellowship of the Ring," David said, "or the dwarf company in *The Hobbit.*"

"I don't like the *Hobbit* movies," Max said. "Let's be the Fellowship."

"See," Ryan said to the others, "I told you she was cool."

The passage through the woods went quicker than Max had expected. Ryan and his friends guided her along the proper trails to get there swiftly while avoiding "bad spots." Joe, Nevada's brother, wanted to lead the way, but Max insisted on walking along beside him.

"You don't seem like a cop," Joe said as they moved through the forest of shadows.

"Really?" Max said. "What do I seem like?"

"You're more like this hippie substitute we had in fifth grade. She kept sneaking into the crafts closet to sniff the glue."

"Oh," Max said. "Um . . . okay."

"Hey shut up you guys!" Patrick hissed. "I hear something."

"That's the creek, numbnuts," Sam whispered. "We're almost to it."

"No," Patrick said. "Something else, like voices."

Everyone was still and quiet, and after a moment Max did hear voices from up ahead.

"I think you kids need to head back now," Max whispered.

"Come on!" Patrick said, trying to keep the excitement out of his voice and speak softly. "Look, if anyone spots us, we'll run, you can believe that."

"Oh yeah," Sam said.

"Please?" Ryan said. "We really do want to help."

"Just a little further and then you kids have got to go home," Max said. "Flashlights off. Now try to be quiet moving through the trees." She walked forward pushing branches aside. Max's heart was fist punching her chest, trying to fly out. What was she doing? This was the kind of stuff Jimmie or Heck or Lovina did. She was a Builder, an analyst, not a field person. She didn't even know how to shoot a gun or fight a monster. The memory of the Carriage Ghoul came back to her, and she took a deep breath and steadied herself.

They crossed the creek on slippery stones, only the moon and the stars to light their steps. Sam stepped on a rock that was wobbly and for an infinite second, floundered as if he was about to fall in the water with a loud splash. Nevada and David caught and righted him, helping him reach the other side of the creek, dry and relatively quiet.

The party stopped at the point where the treeline thinned and peered out onto the boxcar jungle. The voices were coming from a clearing near the base of the steep incline that led down to the jungle. There was a blazing fire contained in an old metal trash can there. A metal grill had been placed over the mouth of the can and a half-dozen people were circling the fire, apparently cooking their dinner on it. A few small dome tents had been erected near the fire and some of the people were sitting in folding camping chairs near the makeshift grill.

"Looks like a bunch of homeless folks," Nevada whispered.

"Bums," Joe said. Nevada gave her brother a dirty look.

"Well, they seem harmless enough," Max said. "No big rubber noses, so that's good. I think I'm going down to, uh, say hello. You kids stay put."

"Be careful!" Ryan said.

"Yeah, my dad says these bums can be pretty sketchy," Joe said.

"Just because people are down on their luck, doesn't make them bad people," Max said as she broke the treeline.

"Doesn't make them good either," Joe muttered.

Max carefully navigated the steep incline, almost falling on her butt a few times, but finally made it down. She waved to the group of campers as they saw her descend.

"Hi," Max said. "Smells good! Mind if I join you?"

There were four men and two women. The oldest looked to be in his forties. Most of them were in their twenties.

"Howdy," the forty-ish man said, waving back. He had a full, thick, gray beard. "Always welcome around the fire. The more the merrier." He offered his hand to Max and she shook it. "Ben Grimes, nice to know you."

"I'm Max," she said as several of the others around the fire walked over to her and Ben. "Max Leher. Pleased to meet you." Ben made quick introductions to the others, who all seemed friendly and at ease.

"So, Max, you on the road too? " Ben asked. "Hobo, or as these kids say, 'nomad'?"

"Actually I'm a professor," Max said. "I've been studying these odd markings that are all over the boxcars and rides back here. They appear in the trailer park as well."

"You mean the code?" one of the young women asked. Ben had said her name was Harmony. She had a mop of red hair and freckles dotted her nose and cheeks. "I know some of them. They're old-school hobo codes."

Ben nodded in agreement.

"In the old days the knights of the road—that's one of the names hobos called themselves—left messages for their comrades who might be passing through after them. Stuff like, 'they will feed you at this house,' or 'the rail yard bulls will rough you up here.' Things like that." He looked at Harmony and smiled. "These new kids, the nomads, some of them do it too, messages like, 'open WiFi network here' or 'your GPS won't work here.'" He laughed. "Some things change, but people are always going to have that lust to wander, to pick up and go, to say 'to hell with sitting in one place until I rot.'"

"So you understand the symbols," Max said. "Could you, uh, translate for me please?" Harmony smiled and they headed over to the nearest boxcar, covered in graffiti and the odd ubiquitous symbols. Max took out her phone, noticed she had no signal here at all, and switched the phone over to camera mode. She took pictures of the symbols in the considerably strong light of the nearby fire. Ryan, Nevada, Patrick, and Joe, seeing that Max was not being set upon, left the treeline and began to descend.

"What are you morons doing?" Sam hissed.

"It's lit," Joe said, continuing to descend, "don't be a wuss."

David stood and began to follow his brother. "I'm no wuss!" he said. Sam let out an exasperated huff and then realized he was alone in the trees and hurried to follow the others down.

"This one," Harmony said to Max, pointing at the crosshatching symbol, "means, 'unsafe place.'"

"These kids belong to you?" Ben asked as the group of children entered the camp.

"What? Kids? Me?" Max stammered. "I . . . well, no . . . yes, actually, but not like in biological sense . . . I . . . they're not mine . . . but they are with me. Yes."

David had found his way to the grill. He peered over at the cobs of corn roasting and the pot bubbling with mulligan stew. He sniffed and then smiled over the flames at the cook, a stocky nomad named Eddy. "Hi," the boy said. Eddy grunted a welcome. "That sure smells good." Eddy rolled his eyes.

"You hungry kid?" the nomad asked. David smiled bigger.

"Pretty much all the time," David replied.

"You got anything to add to the pot?"

David fumbled in his jeans pocket. "I got a half-eaten Fruit Roll-Up in here somewhere."

"Keep it," Eddie said, shaking his head. "First bowl's on the house. Welcome to the jungle."

Ryan and Nevada had joined Max, Harmony, and Ben by the boxcar.

"How about this one?" Max said, pointing to the diamond with a line projecting from the apex of the diamond.

"Another warning," Harmony said. "This one means 'be ready to defend yourself.'"

"Sounds like someone was trying to warn nomads off from camping here," Max said. Ryan and Nevada looked at each other, as the same idea popped into their heads. "Why did you all stay if you understood the warnings?"

Ben chuckled. "Well, a few of us have camped here before. Never had a lick of trouble. We figured maybe some other hobos or local homeless folks were being trolls and trying to scare folks away from their spot. Those abandoned railroad tracks back there can carry you east quite a ways too. Almost all the way down to where that abandoned stretch of the Pennsylvania Turnpike is near I-70. It's a safe route and a prettier view than walking the roads or the highway. Less hassle too."

"This one," Harmony said pointing to the sideways teardrop with the cross near the tail," I don't have a clue. Never seen that one before, anywhere." Max noticed the symbol was drawn in different color chalk and clearly by a different hand than the other two. Something about it was troubling her. She had seen this before in her studies. Then she recalled the names Lovina had given her to research and everything slid into place.

"I don't think this one is hobo code," she said, the jumping firelight in the lenses of her glasses. "It's alchemical."

"Huh?" Harmony, Ryan, and Nevada all said.

"The great and secret work," Max muttered more to herself than the others. She took a picture of the teardrop symbol.

"Maybe those hobo symbols was Emmett trying to warn people away," Ryan said. "Warn them about the bad clowns."

"Emmett?" Max asked, looking at the boy.

"He's, uh, a ghost clown," Nevada said. "He lives in an old caboose here in the jungle. He helped Ryan get my grandfather's harmonica back to me. People in the trailer park have been talking about him forever."

"I see," Max said. "A . . . ghost clown."

"You don't believe us?" Ryan said, obviously hurt. Max shook her head vigorously.

"Oh, no, no! That's not it at all," Max said. "I do believe you. My friend, the police investigator—Lovina—she's been looking for a clown for quite some time."

"Emmett, the killer ghost clown?" Ben Grimes said, nodding. "Heard the story in these parts, as far away as in Philly, but in all the times camping here

I've never seen any clowns, good, bad, or otherwise. Heard some weird noises further back in the jungle at night a few times, but never seen anything."

"He's real and he's not a bad guy," Ryan said, pulling the object he had carefully wrapped in a hankie out of his pants pocket. He unfolded the hankie and held the silver rail spike out of his pocket. The tiny glyphs and runes etched into it appeared clearly as the spike seemed to drink in the firelight and reflect an almost acetylene blue glow. Max's eyebrows went up at the spike.

"Ryan," she said, "this clown Emmett gave this to you?"

"Well, he told me to hang on to it," Ryan said. "I found it back by the train tracks. I used it to help him fight the bad clowns that were trying to get me. It kinda disintegrated one of them."

"Disintegrated? Like a phaser!" Sam said. "Holy crap! Why didn't you tell us about this?" Sam asked. Patrick and Joe nodded.

"I told Nevada," Ryan said in his defense. "I figured you guys would give me crap about it."

"Well, sure," Sam said, "but still . . ."

There was a terrible wrenching noise from back in the deep darkness of the boxcar jungle. It sounded like the groan of metal grinding to a stop, almost like the sound of a train breaking.

"What the fuck was that!" Joe shouted.

David dropped his Solo cup of stew and some of it flew out of his mouth. "That was bad, real bad! Time to go, Patrick!" he gurgled.

"What was that?" Ben asked, trying to peer into the deep shadows. Male voices, a lot of them, laughing, jostling were coming out of the darkness into the firelight. The nomads all got to their feet, some slipped pocketknives out and opened the blades. Others had cans of pepper spray. A few knelt down looking for a rock or a piece of wood to use if need be.

"Everyone be cool," Ben cautioned as the shadow shapes began to gain form in the jumping firelight. Max made out seven or eight figures. Fear coiled in her stomach like a snake made of ice and grease. She looked at the kids.

"Run," she said. "Up the hill, back home. Go!" The kids were frozen for a moment and Max heard a voice come out of her mouth she didn't recognize, it was strong, almost fierce. "Run! Now!"

The kids started to sprint up the incline. Max turned back to see the men coming out of the darkness and immediately wanted to join the fleeing children.

There were a half-dozen men, closer to teenage boys, Max thought. They were all armed, wielding hatchets, axes, a crow bar, and an aluminum baseball bat. One of them had a cheap samurai sword, the kind you'd buy at a flea market. All of them were in street clothing and their faces were painted like ghoulish clowns.

In the midst of the procession, leading them, were two giants. Both wore greasy clown-white, covering their skin, both had eyes like a corpse. The one with a black sun painted on his forehead hefted a sledgehammer. The other, with a large black dot on his forehead, with two smaller dots beside the large one, carried a machete in one hand, a butcher's meat cleaver in the other.

The teen clowns were laughing and leering as they approached the nomads. The two giants were silent, plodding.

Ben, holding his walking stick like a cudgel, stepped toward the invaders. "We're not looking for any trouble here, fellas. We'll move along."

"No you won't," one of the bigger boys, carrying a piece of rebar, said. "It's harvesting time, Grandpa."

Ryan was almost to the treeline stopped when he heard the clown's voice. He looked back.

"Dickie?" he said. Nevada and Joe had stopped as well.

"It is Dickie," Nevada said.

"And that's his whole asshole crew," Joe added, pointing to the other clowns. "Who are those two big guys?"

"They're bad," Ryan muttered, "real bad."

"Harvest," the huge clown with the three dark circles on his forehead croaked to Dickie and his crew. The teens whooped and howled, charging into the crowd of nomads.

"Don't . . . injure . . . the heads," the black sun clown rumbled.

Ben shoulder checked the snarling clown racing toward Max, and the two began to struggle. Max stumbled back toward the train car and frantically tried to use her phone to call 911. The phone display reminded her she had no service here. She looked around frantically for a weapon, anything she could use to defend herself. If she were Heck, she'd be covered in guns, but she wasn't, so she grabbed a handful of dirt instead. A clown's ghostly face jumped out of the darkness at Max, its tongue darting in and out of its mouth.

"C'mere bitch!" the clown said, spit flying from his mouth. He had an awful smell, a weird stench, like chemical toilet combined with the acrid odor of cheap cigarette smoke. "I'm going to saw your head off for the Cooker and then I'm going have fun with your body!"

Max staggered backward and tried to swing her heavy leather satchel at the clown. It partly connected but her attacker kept coming. Everywhere it was chaos. Max heard screams and grunts all around her. She saw Harmony, the smiling girl who had helped her only moments ago, lying on the trash-covered ground, her eyes lifeless, blood gushing from her hacked and muti-lated neck. One of the giant clowns backhanded Ben and there was a grisly sound like a chicken bone snapping as he flew back several yards and lay still.

Max's attacker grabbed her by the shoulder and spun her around, raising a large kitchen knife to drive it into her chest. She threw the dirt she had man-aged to grab while searching for a weapon into the face of the clown. He cursed and let his grip loosen on her throbbing shoulder. Max drove her heel as hard as she could into his instep and felt something give beneath her foot. The blinded clown howled in pain and fell. Max ran.

She reached the base of steep hill back toward the forest and then turned. Only a few nomads remained standing and fewer of the clowns lay on the ground beside them. She couldn't just leave these people to be slaughtered, no, not slaughtered. What was the word the clown had said, harvested? Why did they not want the heads of their victims injured?

She raced back toward the fray. She grabbed the handle of the pot of bub-bling stew on the trash can grill and splashed its boiling contents into the face of one of the clowns struggling with a woman nomad. The clown howled in pain and staggered a few steps back and fell, writhing in pain.

"Go, Go!" Max shouted to the woman. Max turned to find herself facing another clown, this one with a straight razor. Max froze for a second. It was all the time the clown needed. He began to slash at her throat with the blade, when there was a flash of motion and sound. Two of the children from the trailer park—Sam and Patrick—tackled the clown and took him off his feet. The three wrestled and struggled on the ground.

"No, no!" Max shouted. "You kids have to get out of here now!" She saw the boy named Joe close on the clown who had spoken, the one with the piece of rebar. Joe ducked under the clown's first swing, still catching the edge of the steel bar to his cheek and jaw, but following through with a nasty upper-cut driven by what Max could only assume was fierce rage. The kids were doubling up on the clowns, focusing on helping the surviving nomads. Max winced when she saw the boy David fly several feet to crash into the side of a train car, struck by a glancing blow from the black sun clown. She had no idea where Ryan was. She staggered to her feet and tried to help Patrick and Sam with their assailant. Sam let out a little yelp, almost like a puppy, Max thought. He staggered back looking at her with terror in his fluttering eyes. He had been cut deep with the razor in his neck.

"Oh no, no!" Max shouted and rushed to his crumpled form. She examined the wound; it had nicked his carotid artery but not fully opened it. But he was losing a lot of blood and had passed out in shock.

A shadow fell over her and Sam. She looked up to see the giant clown with the three black circles on his forehead standing over her, his blades ready to finish her and the wounded child. When the machete came down toward Sam, Max threw herself at the legs of the giant in hopes of knocking him off balance. Something thick struck the back of her head and neck. She saw a pulse of brilliant white light behind her eyes and fell face forward and everything became dark. Max thought she heard the sounds of the battle at a great distance away. She also thought she heard a deep, powerful voice near her utter a single word, "No."

Everything went away then, sound, time, awareness. Then there were hands pulling her up, voices talking to her. Max blinked her eyes a few times and breathed in fresh air. She opened her eyes. She was on the ground near the trash can fire. Ryan, with a bloody nose and scrapes on both cheeks and his forehead, was kneeling down beside her. Nevada was beside him as was Patrick. Someone was saying she had been out for almost ten minutes.

"What happened?" she asked, the words feeling weird and jagged in her mouth.

"They took off," Ryan said. "We got reinforcements." Max looked up and saw a third giant of a clown. Max kicked and struggled to scoot back, away from the clown, then stopped when she saw his oddly sweet, but sad face. Max was reminded of a hound dog when she looked at him. An odd symbol was on his forehead—a three-spoked ring. It was a symbol Max had known since childhood. It was the symbol of the three orders. Max struggled to her feet. The sad-looking clown was close to two feet taller than her.

"This is my friend Emmett," Ryan said. "He saved us, chased them off."

"They took some of the nomads," Nevada said. Her eyes were red and wet. "They took Joe."

"And David," Patrick said glumly.

"And Sam," Ryan said. "They took off on some of those little railroad handcar things, headed away from Coalport."

Max, still groggy and fairly certain she had a concussion, looked up at Emmett, at the symbol on his forehead.

"The temple restored," Max said.

"The . . . wheel . . . turns," the clown replied.

TWENTY-SIX

"10-34"

Where Dock and South Water Street bump into each other in Cape Fear, there was a waterfront bar and grill named for the infamous female pirate Anne Bonny. The place had become a favorite of Ale and Elizabeth's when they were young and they had spent many years at the tables looking out over the river. Tonight, Elizabeth, Heck, Jimmie, Jethro, and about a dozen other Blue Jocks had taken over Anne Bonny's awning-covered waterfront porch. Layla had volunteered to stay home at Elizabeth's still guarded safe house in case any new news came in about Cherokee Mike and his people. It was not exactly a victory celebration, but it came in the wake of the raids on Mike's meth labs and Heck's and Ana Mae's safe return.

"To the free enterprise system," Heck said, hoisting his fifth beer, "may it give old Mike everything he deserves!" A cheer went up among the bikers and many glasses were drained.

"Word on the street is that Mike's caught by the short and curlies," Road-kill said, popping another fried shrimp in his mouth. He chased it with a shot of tequila. Heck had noticed his oldest friend had been drinking more than was usual even for him since his dad's death. Heck knew the crash would come eventually, and he wanted to be there to help Jethro back up, the way he'd helped Heck after Ale passed. For now, though, Roadkill was putting everything he still had into the war. "All the customers he lined up by sweet-talking them on quantity and delivery, well, they're putting word out now that they want him for a little sit-down," Roadkill said. "His people are starting to make themselves scarce. We've even had a few ask if they can come home."

"Fuck 'em!" Galen North, one of the Jocks who had gone on a meth lab raid, said. "They had a chance to do the right thing and be loyal, they fucked it up. We don't want the bastards back."

"We'll take it one at a time," Heck said. "On an individual basis."

"You serious, Heck?" Galen asked.

Elizabeth looked at her son across the table, raised an eyebrow, and then smiled at him. Heck gave her a slight nod. "Yeah," he said. "Galen, these guys are our brothers. Some of them were being blackmailed by Mike, their families threatened. Others got bullshitted. You're right, most of them we don't want back, but we're kin, so we'll take a look at them one by one." Galen nodded, shrugged, and raised his glass to Heck.

"You're the prez, Heck. Thy will be done."

Heck raised his bottle back and doffed it to Galen. Everyone else used the exchange as an excuse for another toast and more drinking and a general toast, "to Heck, to the president!"

Jimmie, sitting beside Elizabeth, toasted as well, then as the conversation fragmented off into numerous tangents between the tables he leaned close to Heck. "Hail to the chief," the trucker said.

"You gonna bust my chops some more about the squire thing?" Heck asked. Jimmie dragged a crinkle cut French fry through a lake of ketchup on his plate and shook his head as he ate it.

"Nope," he said, chasing the fry with a swig of his draft beer. "That dog don't hunt, clearly. I have to say, you've done good, Heck. You held the truce with the Bitches of Selene, hell, you even strengthened it."

"I guess strengthen is as good a word as any," Heck said. "The Jocks and the Bitches are solid."

"That Ana Mae, she's a hell of girl," Elizabeth said. "I don't have to even have to tell you to treat her right, now do I, Hector?" Heck, Elizabeth, and Jimmie laughed.

"I figured that one out on my own," Heck said. "Besides we're not like 'together,' together, Mom. We just enjoying hanging out and chilling together."

"Mmhm," Elizabeth said. "Sure. You just mind yourself, Hector, or she'll make sure you don't have anything left 'hanging out.'" They laughed again. Elizabeth looked past Heck's shoulder and excused herself when she saw an old friend of Ale's at the bar.

"So where is lady president?" Jimmie asked.

"Ana Mae? She had some MC presidential business to take care of. She wanted to come. She lost good people in this shit too. They need time to scab up, to heal, just like us."

"You know it ain't over, right?" Jimmie said. "Mike's wanted this too long. He's wounded, but he can still hit back and he will." Heck nodded, gesturing at his empty bottle to the waitress, who was taking an order from a few of the Jocks a few tables down. She nodded and he gave one in return.

"You're right," Heck said. "Sooner or later, I'm going to have to put Mike in the ground to get this behind the MC. I'm figuring that right now he's lying low to avoid getting hit by one of his unhappy customers. His troops will follow suit, get out of state if they can, or try to come home to us. Whichever it is, they'll be too busy ducking and dodging to give us much trouble."

"A wise assessment," Jimmie said. "Just remember some bastards are never more ornery than when they're bleeding and cornered." He nodded toward Heck. "I know a few like that personally."

Heck looked at Jimmie for a moment.

"What?" Jimmie asked.

"I just . . ." Heck seemed to be at a loss for words. "Jimmie, am I through it, am I a knight now, a Brother?"

"I told you, when you're ready, you'll know it," Jimmie said. "You won't need me to say a damned thing. Do you feel ready?" Heck drained his bottle and examined it for a moment before he met the trucker's gaze.

"I . . . still don't know," he finally said.

"And there you go," Jimmie said, taking another sip of his beer. He saw the exasperated look on his young squire's face. "You kept your head when Mike was pushing you to do something foolish. You stepped up to lead these men when they needed you the most. You made your own choices, kept your own counsel instead of doing what me and Elizabeth wanted you to do. You've done good, Heck. Ale would be proud of you." Elizabeth returned with another glass of wine from the bar and paused by her son long enough to kiss the top of his head.

"You have, Hector," she said. "He would be proud."

As the party headed out of Anne Bonny's Elizabeth slid up next to her son and hooked her arm in his. "Ale would be proud of you," she said, "and, it goes without saying, I am too." Heck smiled over to her and put his arm around her.

"You're drunk, mother of mine," he said. "In your cups."

"I could still whup your narrow little behind," Elizabeth said and Heck laughed. "And sober or not, I love you, son."

The group poured through the doors of the bar to the narrow, crowded parking lot. Roadkill sidled up to Jimmie, who was carrying a Styrofoam to-go box with dinner for Layla. "I hear tell you're the only man to ever drink Ale Mckee under the table?" Jimmie laughed.

"I was on the floor with him about two seconds later," the trucker said. "Now I may be the only *man* to out-drink Ale, but I saw Elizabeth put him down a time or two." They both laughed as they followed the rest out into the parking lot. Jimmie was about to tell Jethro a story about his dad when he saw the side door on a work van idling in the street at the edge of parking lot fly open. A man in a stocking mask was behind a mounted .50 machine gun, like a door gunner on a military chopper.

"Down!" Jimmie shouted, diving for cover. Roadkill had seen it too; he was groping to draw his pistol from his waistband as Jimmie pushed him to the ground. "Heck, everyone, down!"

Jimmie's voice was drowned out by the harsh rattle of the big gun. A couple walking to their car were cut in two by the initial burst and sparks and broken window glass flew everywhere. The glass windows of the bar erupted as they were hit by stray fire.

Heck heard one of the Jocks off to his left, a guy he knew by the handle of Griller, get hit and die as he was slammed against a now bullet-riddled car. Heck pulled Elizabeth low behind a car, about where the engine block would be. Elizabeth was fumbling with her purse to find her gun.

Heck pulled his H&K .45 pistol from his shoulder ring under his jacket as he ran, staying low, behind an adjacent SUV. He popped up and returned fire on the van. He could see that the door gunner had on head-to-toe ballistic armor, the kind of shit the cops and the military had. There were now four more masked men in sight. They were on foot, fanning out from the other side of the street, near the van. They were carrying guns, one had a clip-fed 12-gauge shotgun, two were armed with pistols, and the last was packing an AK-74 rifle that he was spraying on full auto to cover their advance into the parking lot. Heck popped off a few more rounds and then ducked as the guy with the AK sprayed bullets in his direction.

Drunk or not, the remaining Blue Jocks had drawn their weapons now and were sprinting between cars in the lot, ducking and even belly crawling to avoid the withering fire from the van and the advancing assassins. Jimmie had managed to make it over to the poor couple that had got hit in the initial volley. The man was dead, the woman would be soon if she didn't get medical assistance. Jimmie flipped open his cell phone and called for help.

The Jocks who had been with the club for a while knew how to handle themselves in a firefight. The four of them still on their feet split into two two-man groups and cut right and left, leapfrogging forward by covering the other group's advance with gunfire. The left team took out two of the masked gunmen, but one of theirs was hit and went down.

The van's gun kept going, clattering without pause. Jimmie and Heck both figured the .50 cal was belt-fed and God only knew how much ammo they had tucked away in that van. Heck took the lead with the Jocks and moved up the right side of the parking lot, ducking, firing, advancing, ducking again as more and more cars were reduced to mangled junk. Heck heard a scream behind him as another civilian, a woman who had been huddled by her car since the shooting started, was hit by stray rounds.

There was a lull in the gunfire as different combatants reloaded, but some sounds remained constant, the thudding of the .50 mowing the parking lot and a child's crying, shrill above the relentless tattoo of death. Jimmie saw the little girl, about nine, huddled near her dead mother—the woman who had just been hit. The third sound came from far off, but it was getting closer—sirens.

"Heck!" Jimmie shouted, "lay down some fire! Cover me!" Heck and his boys opened up on the masked gunmen, who were now moving among the cars in the parking lot. Under the Jocks' withering fire the masked men ducked for cover. Jimmie took the few seconds to sprint over to the little girl, scoop her up, and carry her toward safety. A whining rain of bullets from the van's big gun clawed at the ground around Jimmie and the girl as the big trucker tried to shield the child with his body as he ran.

"It's Aussapile!" one of the masked gunners shouted. "Take him out!" The remaining gunmen concentrated their fire on Jimmie, but they had to switch focus as six Wilmington police cars screeched into view from both ends of South Water Street, choking off the road. The cops fell out of the cars with pistols and shotguns at the ready.

"This is the police," a cop bellowed over his car's bullhorn. "Everyone place your weapons on the ground and lie down on your stomach. Do it, now!"

"Fuck you!" one of the masked gunmen, the one with the shotgun, shouted as he spun and opened fire on the closest police car. The blast of the 12-gauge crumpled the door to the police cruiser and shattered the window. Heck and his boys, one of them wounded now but still fighting, opened up on the shotgun wielder about the same time the cops did. The masked man spun from the lethal crossfire, staggered back, and fell dead.

Jimmie held the sobbing little girl, "It's all right now, darlin'," he whispered. "It's okay." He looked up to see the last gunman about five feet from him and the girl. Jimmie thought of Layla and Taylor and his baby boy. "It's going to be okay," he said, his voice steady as he tensed, awaiting the shot. The masked man leveled his pistol at Jimmie's face and began to squeeze the trigger.

A boom of gunfire swallowed Jimmie's ears but he didn't feel the burning freight train of pressure from the bullet. He opened his eyes to see Elizabeth standing up from behind her cover, her pistol smoking. The dying gunman twisted away from Jimmie and fired at his attacker.

"No!" Jimmie shouted, lurching to tackle the man, but it was too late. Elizabeth fell to the gravel floor of the parking lot and did not move.

"Mom?" Heck said, seeing her fire and then fall. He stood even as the deadly hail of machine gun bullets tore the cars around him. "No!" He screamed and vaulted the car headed for the van's open door. Something burned his cheek and leg. Normally he would have stumbled in the middle of the road, fallen from the pain, but the pain was a puny thing in the furnace of his rage. All sound was like he was underwater, muted, distorted. He didn't need his ears. All he needed was his hands.

The look on the door gunner's face under the bulletproof mask was one of awed fear. Heck cleared the doors of the van, swinging himself in. He put a bullet in the head of the gunner and drove his boot into the face of the driver with such force that the man was knocked halfway through the shattering driversside window and hung limp. Heck came to rest, pivoted to his left, and put two bullets in the masked man who had been feeding ammunition to the machine gun. The man smashed into the back doors of the work van, slid to the floor, and died. Everything was silent except for the sirens and the crashing river of Heck's blood in his ears.

Cops were at the door, shouting cop things, "Hands up! Drop the gun!" Heck barely heard them over his blood. He handed the pistol butt first to the nearest cop. Heck's mouth was moving, words were falling out.

"My mother's been shot, get her an ambulance right now . . . please."

*   *   *

In the hospital waiting room again. Heck knew this room was prepared for him in Hell. This time Heck sat alone, without his mother at his side. The MC's lawyer had managed to get Heck out of custody due to his mother's condition, but several of the surviving Jocks who had been in the firefight were stuck in jail on firearms charges. Jethro was with him in the waiting room,

Jimmie, a few others. So few of them left these days. The Blue Jocks were becoming extinct in front of his eyes. The river of human events moved around him, but he hardly noticed. He was alone in a room full of people.

First had come the chaos of the arrival, multiple gunshot wound victims, blood and shouting, IVs, rushed surgical teams. Then the glacial waiting, like time had been choked off. Minutes that were years of endless pain and fear. At the end of it, the surgeon came out, Mom's blood still on his scrubs. He said the words that Heck had already known, that the ambulance team, and the nurses, and the doctors had all known.

"I'm sorry," the doctor said. "She's gone."

Then was the grieving, the anger, the desperate need to comfort and re-assure. Jethro, crying, had hugged him, said something to him Heck couldn't even comprehend, or remember. Ana Mae had been there too; he almost lost himself in the soft, warm comfort of her embrace, but he was too far away for her to reach him. Jimmie had been the last to leave, of course. Jimmie sat with him, saying nothing, just trying to hold up a little bit of the mountain of pain that had been dropped on Heck.

He couldn't recall when Jimmie had finally left. Heck was pretty sure he had asked him to go, but had let him know he appreciated his effort most of all. Jimmie understood. There are colors in the human palette, subtle, dark, that corresponded to no word, no act. They could not be described adequately, or muted. They could only be endured.

There was the heavy thump of boots on tile and a shadow fell across him. It was the redheaded biker, the one he had seen at the meth lab. The one his mom and Jimmie had called Viper.

"They took my gun," Heck said after a long time, "but I'll kill you with my bare hands. Just give me a minute."

"I came," Viper said, "to pay my respects. Your mom, she was a hell of a woman."

"She told me you were a right bastard."

"I am." Viper sat down next to Heck. "I am a murdering, thieving, rap-ing son of a bitch . . . and I loved your mother more than the night loves the stars."

"You've got a fucking sick way of showing it," Heck said. He felt nothing. His rage was gone and without it he was an empty shell. "You're in bed with Cherokee Mike. You've been helping him all along. Those were Mike's boys out there today. One of them was Vinnie Wiseman, Mike's personal-ass puppet. So why are you here, really?"

"I did love Elizabeth," Viper said. "I never wanted her to get hurt in this. My end of this was just business, I wanted a taste of the profits in exchange for my help. Just business, nothing personal. Mike sent those guys out there to hit Jimmie Aussapile. He wanted to get you good and pissed and out of control, so you'd fuck up and be easy pickings. He's in deep shit and he needs to consolidate the Jocks under his control pretty damn quick, or he's past tense. It was a desperation play. I told him not to do it, but . . . well, you know Mike, he thinks he's smarter than he really is."

"That wand thing he's got," Heck said, fumbling for his cigarettes, "the one that lets him summon and control monsters, he get that from you?" Viper sat and offered Heck a pack of Lucky Strikes. Heck took one and Viper did too, lighting both with a matte black Zippo.

"Excuse me," a scowling nurse called out. He was well-muscled and shaved his head. "You guys can't smoke in here." Without missing a beat, Viper snapped the Zippo shut with a clank. The nurse suddenly clutched his chest, and grew very pale.

"Yes, we can," Viper said as smoke streamed from his mouth. "Fuck off." The nurse, his eyes damp with fear, turned back to other business at the admission station. Viper turned back to Heck. "It's called the Key of Thorne. It was the binding focus the vanquished Nightborne clans swore upon at the end of the War of the Iron Gate. The Nightborne swore allegiance to the commander of thirty-six of Hell's legions, the Great Duke, Flauros, who had vanquished them in battle."

"Okay . . ." Heck said.

"The wand is indestructible, as is the pact the clans swore to," Viper said. "The wand and the pact can only be broken by an infernal force of terrible fury, no power of this world can harm it. It was locked away for time out of time in a vault in Hell's darkest bowels. Somehow it made it to earth and into Mike's hands."

"So . . . it's a magic wand from Hell that controls things that go suck in the night?" Heck said. "Am I getting the gist of this?"

"The gist of, if not the spirit," Viper said. "It lets Mike summon and command supernatural creatures. Not all of them, like the shapeshifters of the Bitches of Selene, but a lot."

"How the fuck did he get it?" Heck said.

"Devil if I know," Viper said, blowing some smoke in the direction of an old woman on oxygen who was being wheeled past him.

"You some kind of magician or something?" Heck asked.

"A dabbler," Viper said. "I like getting laid more than I like books. I heard Mike had the wand and offered to help him go into business. I wanted to get a closer look at the Key and see if I could figure out how he got it, maybe get it away from him for myself."

"Your business cost my mother her life," Heck said. Viper was silent for a moment. He crushed out his cigarette on the small table next to the row of plastic chairs and stood.

"It did, and I hate the smarmy little bastard as much for that as you do."

"I doubt that," Heck said. "I want him."

"This needs to end," Viper said. "I can give him to you. It's all I can do. I know it don't mean shit now that she's gone, but it's all I got."

"Where, when?" Heck said.

"Tomorrow night," Viper said. "You familiar with Bear Creek? State Route 902? You take I-40 and get off along—"

"Route 421," Heck said. "Yeah." He remembered finding himself there after his meeting at the mall with Mike. "The Devil's Tramping Ground."

"Exactly," Viper said. "I think Mike's looking to try to call up some of the big boys to help him now. Like I said he's desperate. He's going to be bringing the remnants of his army, about twenty-five strong, riding down 902, heading north onto State Road 1100 to the Tramping Ground. There's nothing out there for miles but woods and dark. He should be heading there around 2:30 in the morning. He wants to be in the Devil's circle by 3:00." Viper walked toward the waiting room's exit. "I don't give a fuck what you think, kid. Your mother was a good woman, the best. She didn't deserve this, and I'm sorry. It's your move now." The sliding glass doors parted for the big biker, and he dispersed into the parking lot. Heck was alone again.

He crushed out the cigarette in his palm, oblivious to the looks a horrified patient nearby gave him. He sat for a little while longer. Time still seemed stretched like taffy. Eventually he took out his cell phone and called Roadkill. "Hey, it's me. Get everyone in, yeah, everyone. Call Ana Mae too. I want everyone strapped, everyone. The biggest guns we got left, everything. We got one last ride."

TWENTY-SEVEN

Angelo Potts sat in an interrogation room at the 17th District police station in South Philadelphia. His face and arms were smeared in white makeup and his spray clown face hadn't worn off yet. He was humming to himself and keeping the beat by pounding loudly on the tabletop in front of him. Occasionally, he'd grin over at the dirty and cracked two-way mirror on one wall of the room, and wave.

"That is one twisted piece of fuck, right there," precinct captain Butch Lind said. Lind was a small, compact man in his late fifties, wiry and smelling of Old Spice. He looked back to the other law enforcement agents sharing the cramped observation room with him. "So we've been on this punk for hours and so far he's given us squat. Any of youse want to take a crack?

Besides Captain Lind, Dave Wojick of the Pennsylvania State Police, FBI Assistant Special Agent in Charge Cecil Dann, and Lovina Marcou were huddled in the small room. Dusty Acosta was sitting in the hall outside the cramped room.

"We have his print at the Dunning girl's crime scene, on several stolen and abandoned cars," Dann said, "and on a trash can at the park in Fogelsville at the scene of a copycat body dump and attempted arson."

"Anything on that other print you found at Raelyn's scene?" Lovina asked. Dann shook his head.

"We do have numerous patrons at a restaurant just off the I-78 exit in Fogelsville that can attest to Mr. Subtle being in there the night of the body dump and the fire. Someone picked him up from there. We're going on the assumption it was an accomplice and the owner of our mystery print."

"He hasn't lawyered up yet?" Lovina asked.

"Nope," the captain said. "Look at him, he's enjoying himself. Not a care in the world. He wants to talk. Hell, I think he wants to gloat, just not to my people."

"I could get on the horn to my people," Cecil said. "Try to get someone from Behavioral Science at Quantico out here, or least see if they can give us some direction about how to talk to him."

"I've never put much stock into all that profiling crap," the captain said. "No offense."

Lovina looked at Angie through the glass, his clown makeup smudged and partly wiped off. He looked like a chalk drawing running in the rain. "I have another idea," she said, turning to the other cops. "Let my guy in the hall take a run at him."

"The kid with the backpack?" Captain Lind said.

"He's not sworn law enforcement personnel, Lovina," Cecil Dann added.

"We don't want to give Angie's lawyer anything to use to get a confession thrown out," the captain said, "especially in a high-profile case like this."

"I'll go in with him," Lovina said. "Make sure he doesn't cross any lines."

Dave Wojick had been quiet until now. "I say, we go for it," Wojick said, looking at Lovina. "Lovina's made more progress on this case than any of us had. Hell, she's pretty much lead on it. She's got good instincts. She thinks the Acosta boy can help get Potts talking, I say we give it a shot. He craps out, we can still try something else, right?" Lovina gave Wojick a quick smile. Cecil nodded in agreement, as did the captain.

"What the hell," the captain. "You're up."

Angie was getting hungry when the door to the interrogation room opened. This tall, hot, black bitch walked in dressed in a fancy-looking pants suit and blouse. She had cop ID and a badge dangling on a lanyard between her nice tits—a little small for Angie's taste, but not bad. He ran his eyes over her like she was a piece of prime rib. She looked at him like he was something somebody forgot to flush. She was followed into the room by some Hispanic guy, a few years younger than Angie. Long hair, tied in a man-bun, jeans and hiking boots, flannel shirt open with a T-shirt under it bearing the logo of something called "the National Hobo Museum" in Britt, Iowa. Lovina sat down opposite Angie at the scarred old table, which was pockmarked with blackened cigarette craters.

"Mr. Potts," Lovina began, "I'm Investigator Marcou. This is Mr. Acosta. We'd like to talk to you about how you ended up here. First, you have been advised of your rights, correct?"

"About a hundred times now, Investigator Tits," Angie said. He laughed at his own joke. "What say you get Pancho here to fuck off and we play strip interrogation? For every question you ask and I answer, you take something off." Potts laughed again.

"As much as I'd like to get the fuck out of your air, Angie," Dusty said, taking off his flannel shirt and draping it over the back of his chair, "the cops say I gotta stay." He sat down next to Lovina. "Lucky me. I think they're just picking up anybody even remotely connected to this clusterfuck. They don't know shit."

Potts began to say something to that when he glanced down and saw Dusty's Hatchetman tattoo. "ICP," he said. "All right, all right, all right!"

"What's the word, my ninja?" Dusty said. Angie replied with a loud "whoop-whoop." Lovina would have laughed at the exchange, then she remembered that this man across the table from her had been present at the site where Raelyn's mutilated body had been scattered like garbage. She remained stone-faced and silent and let Dusty do his work.

"You're a Juggalo," Angie said. "Cool. Still feel the music, bro, but Lunatic Clown Squad is next-level shit. You should check LCS out."

Dusty frowned a little.

"LCS?" he said, shaking his head, "I . . . I don't know them, man. Tell me."

In the observation room, Dave Wojick shook his head as well. "What the hell is a Lunatic Clown Squad?"

"They're an ultra-violent offshoot of the Juggalo culture," Dann said. "It's a rip-off music group. Their music incites a hell of a lot more violent action than Insane Clown Posse. They recruit at ICP concerts and gatherings. Their followers—they call themselves 'Harlequins'—have been connected with arson, rapes, assaults, and murders in twenty-eight different states. They're a small group but they're growing. Our Philly office has reported a lot more of LCS activity in the last few years."

In the interrogation room, Angie Potts was elaborating on the musical superiority of LCS to ICP. Dusty was offering some counterpoint and getting Angie to agree on some the musical pros of ICP music. Lovina couldn't tell if the young nomad was working Potts with all this or had genuinely forgotten their goal and was just enjoying talking about his favorite music group.

"So you on a mission for the Squad?" Dusty suddenly asked, smoothly slipping it into the pattern of the back-and-forth conversation. "You know so much about them, I figure you for being a big-ass Harlequin all up in their business." Lovina was impressed. Angie didn't turn cold, instead he kept talking as if nothing had happened.

"Shit, yeah, my ninja," Angie said. "You looking at a soon-to-be High Harlequin, bitch." Angie laughed and Dusty laughed with him, bumping fists from across the table.

"What's that mean exactly?" Dusty asked.

"It means the Cooker's making me one of his boys, up close and personal. I'll be in on the major shit going down. It means I'll never die and I'll party forever!" Angie let out another "whoop-whoop."

"The Cooker?" Dusty asked.

Angie started to reply, then he caught himself. He looked over at Lovina and smiled and leaned back in his chair. "Nice try, officer. I've said all I got to say."

Lovina looked over to Dusty. "It's okay, I told you this guy was a pissant. He doesn't know anything we need." Lovina gestured toward Angie. "He probably doesn't even know about the toxic chemicals in the clown-white makeup he's wearing, the poor stupid bastard." She stood and walked toward the door. Dusty followed her lead. "I'll see if they can get you a Happy Meal or something, I'm sure you're hungry."

"Hey!" Angie said, standing as well. "What about the makeup? Toxic chemicals? What are you talking about, bitch?" Lovina opened the door and paused to look back at the obviously rattled Harlequin. "Yeah, that crap you're rubbing all over your face and body is like a toxic waste dump in a jar. Don't tell me you don't feel the difference. I hope you haven't been wearing that sludge too long, Angie, because they'll wash it off you in lock-up and hopefully your face won't rot off."

"Rot off?" Angie's voice sounded like a frightened child. Lovina gave him a smile and followed Dusty out into the hallway, shutting the door behind her.

"Hey, hey!" Angie shouted, his voice swallowed by the closing door. Lovina motioned for Dusty to wait in the hallway.

"What was all that makeup stuff all about?" Dusty asked. "I didn't know what you were talking about. I tried to play it cool, but you threw me as much as you did that *gilipollas*."

"You did good. I found out that the clown makeup that turned up at a few of the crime scenes has some really weird chemical compounds in it," Lovina said. "From the way our boy is reacting, he knows that too. Let's give him a second to baste and then we'll go back in."

Angie was still standing and shouting at the observation mirror when Lovina and Dusty reentered the room.

"What do you know about my face?" he said, moving toward the investigator and the nomad.

"Sit your ass down, Angelo," Lovina said, standing her ground. The hulking Harlequin obeyed and resumed his seat. Lovina and Dusty reclaimed theirs. "Now, about the Cooker, he's the one who gave you this messed-up paint?"

"Yeah," Angie said. "Well, he makes it and his people, his High Harlequins, they distribute it to us. All the Harlequins wear it. Now tell me what the fuck it's doing to me."

"Not done yet," Lovina said. "Who is the Cooker? Where do we find him and what does he have to do with these people going missing, getting killed, chopped up, and dumped?"

"I tell you anything," Angie said, "they'll kill me."

"And you think that shit on your face isn't?" Dusty said. "Wise up, my ninja. This lady is trying to save your life, Angie."

"There is an FBI agent behind that mirror," Lovina said. "I can't speak for him or for the D.A. or the U.S. attorney, but you help us, Angie, I'm sure they'll help you."

Maybe it was how long he had been made to sit here, or maybe it was how much of the paint the cops had washed off when they took his mug shot, but Angelo wrestled with what to do now. The tingling over his skin had started, like tiny ants with needles for legs crawling all over his body. Angie knew that tingling would soon turn to cold fire burning as his nerves screamed and called out for more of the paint. The memory of how it had been when he had forgotten to put on his paint made the decision for him.

"You got to promise to keep me alive," Angie said, the panic creeping into his voice, "to help me with this shit. I need doctors, and Witness Protection. You got to give me that, these mutherfuckers are everywhere."

Lovina shrugged.

"Depends on what you give us," she said. "But that all sounds reasonable with your full cooperation."

"The Cooker," Dusty said.

"Yeah, yeah," Angie said. "Okay, he's an old white guy, really old—gray hair, gray beard, wears a hoodie, so you can't always get a good look at him. He makes the paint, a bunch of other drugs too. He tests them out on us, on the Harlequins. You serve him well, bring him . . . people, help dump their bodies later, do the rituals and stuff he tells you to when you dump them, you eventually get to become a High Harlequin and live forever."

"Ritual?" Dusty asked. Angelo nodded.

"You got to put the bodies in a certain position," he said, "and read these gobbledygook words off a little card. Sound like Harry Potter shit."

"Latin?" Dusty said, "The words are in Latin? You recall any of it, Angie?"

"I don't know, ninja," Angie said. "We just read the shit."

"Excuse me." Dusty stood and left the room, almost running.

The missing people," Lovina said, leaning closer to Angie, "what's he do with them?"

"He's got Harlequins, High Harlequins, all over the country, maybe the world. All those stories you hear about clowns wandering around towns and streets in the dead of the night, chasing people? That's us. We prowl, we hunt for people for him, grab them, hang on to them until a summoning, and then we bring them to him. Alive, he always tells us to bring them to him alive. I . . . I don't know what he does with them after that."

"I said full cooperation," Lovina said, her voice held a knife's edge of anger. "What's he do with them?"

"I don't know exactly," Angie said, "but he does some kind of . . . experiments on them. I think it kills them. We get calls to pick up . . . the pieces he doesn't use and dump them, all over the country, but always close to highways, interstates." Angelo paused, digging through his memory for any scrap he could offer her. "Harvest . . . he calls what he does harvesting. That's all I got, I swear."

"No, it's not. Where?" Lovina said. "Where did you and the others take the people, for picking up the remains? Different place every time?"

"No," Angie said. "Same place, every time. I got a text saying to deliver anybody we had picked up there tomorrow night a few hours before the cops kicked in my door. It's on a stretch of the old turnpike, the abandoned part, near Breezewood. I can draw you a map."

Lovina slid a pen and paper over to Angie as she stood. "Do that." She walked toward the door.

"Hey," Angie said, "what about my face?" Lovina shut the door.

Around the corner, near the open door to the observation room there was a flurry of activity. Dann was on his cell phone talking quickly and quietly. Captain Lind and Wojick were engaged in a heated conversation. Dusty Acosta met her as she rounded the corner.

"I got it," Dusty said. "I asked the captain to put me in touch with the detective tossing Potts's place. He found one of those index cards with the Latin phonetically written out. Potts used it to wad up some chewing gum."

"Gross," Lovina said. "What's it say? Why'd you get so excited?"

"It's part of a hermetic incantation talking about massacre to drawn down the moon and feed the sun. I think I remember that being part of something attributed to Nicolas Flamel, but don't quote me on that."

"Flamel?" Lovina said. "I'm hearing that name a lot. It was one of the ones you mentioned when you did the ritual with the hobo nickels. Who the hell is he?"

"Supposedly he was a fifteenth-century scribe and alchemist," Dusty said. "Five hundred years after his reported death he was attributed as the author of a series of seminal alchemical texts and papers. The name may have just been a pseudonym for other alchemists. No one knows for sure. He supposedly discovered the secrets of immortality and the Philosopher's Stone. About all I can tell you. I got bored by Hermeticism about three minutes after I started studying it. It didn't even click with me until the cops read me the incantation on the card."

"What would this incantation do exactly?" Lovina asked.

"Not a hundred percent, but it sounds like a final seal to preserve something stolen from the murdered person, maybe their life force or soul."

"Harvesting," Lovina said as she saw Cecil Dann had finished his phone call and was walking her way. "Angie said he was harvesting . . . something."

"Theoretically," Dusty said, "a person murdered under these conditions, under this spell, wouldn't be able to rest and their spirits would be anchored to their murderer, trapped between death and what's beyond, chained to him forever."

"I have tactical units in the air on their way from Quantico," Cecil said as he walked up. "Captain Lind and your pal Wojick are getting the Philly PD and Pennsylvania State Police tac units up to speed and ready to roll too. We're crashing their party tomorrow night."

"We have an invite to the party, right, Cecil?" Lovina asked. Dann snorted and shook his head.

"Like it would change a damn thing if I said no," the FBI special agent said. Lovina smiled.

"You're getting to know me, Cecil, you're getting to know me." Dann handed Lovina a yellow Post-it note.

"Your colleague, Dr. Leher, called in while you were in interrogation. She sounded a little rattled if you ask me. She said to make sure a thorough autopsy was done of the heads of all the recovered victims."

Lovina took the note and checked her silenced phone. She had missed six calls from Max.

"Cecil, can you ask the local medical examiner to do that please? Check the heads extra carefully."

"I called the ME as soon as I got the message," Dann said. "They told me they were getting ready to call the lead investigator here anyway. They found something missing, Lovina, in every head recovered."

"What?" Lovina and Dusty asked in near unison.

"The pineal gland," Dann said. "In every victim, the pineal gland had been removed apparently through the base of the skull and with amazing surgical precision. The ME almost missed the point of entry on the base of the skulls altogether.

"Someone stole their pineal glands?" Dusty said.

"That's why the heads are not recovered in some of the mutilation killings. I think we just found out what he's been harvesting," Lovina said, dialing her phone to call Max back. "I'm not so sure I want to know the why."

TWENTY-EIGHT  "10-52"

The Valentine Trailer Park was washed in the blue lights of Pennsylvania State Police cruisers. The flashing blue lights were punctuated with the blood-red lights of ambulances.

Max sat on one of the iron steps of Ryan's grandmother's trailer. Ryan sat beside her. They had gone through endless questioning from the summoned police. The parents of the missing kids had all been summoned from sleep or from jobs. Frantic for any word on their missing kids, they walked past Max, giving her burning looks of anger.

"They damn well better find my boy okay," Joe's father growled to Max, "or I'll make sure you pay for it, *doctor*." Nevada took her father by the hand, and tried to pull him away. Max could smell the beer on his breath, feel the warmth of his hate.

"C'mon, Daddy," Nevada said. "It ain't her fault, it ain't." They walked away, Nevada looking back mournfully at Ryan.

"It's not your fault," Ryan said. "Really, it's mine. I got us all psyched up to go help you."

"You were just trying to help," Max said. I should have never let you and your friends . . . I . . . I hope they're okay. I'm really sorry, Ryan."

"It felt good to not be so afraid," Ryan said. "I mean, I was scared but it wasn't like it's been since, well since before we came to Coalport."

"What happened before here?" Max asked, watching the parade of cops and EMS flow by.

"I . . . I killed my dad . . . my stepdad," Ryan said. Max glanced over to the boy. Ryan was quiet for a moment, then he continued. "You know, on TV or the movies, you kill the bad guy and it's all cool. You're fine, you might even make a joke or something. They just . . . fall down. Kenny . . . he, he didn't fall down, he . . . rolled around . . . he screamed, and it was this bubbling kind of scream. With every scream more blood just gushed out of his neck." Max looked back to Ryan, his eyes dry, his voice trembling.

"I . . . cut his throat with the knife he was going to use on Mom. I grabbed it when he was hitting her and I stabbed him in the leg—I was aiming for his ass—and he left her alone and chased me. He was drunk . . . he had trouble with the stairs. I had a fort in my closet, stupid I know to think that would keep me safe. He crashed into it and I . . . I stabbed up again and again and then his blood was spilling on me, squirting. I sat in the closet and peeked out and held the knife until he . . . stopped making noises, until the blood stopped."

Max put her arm around Ryan's shoulder. "I'm so sorry," she said, forgetting her own failure, her own grief. The boy looked down at his shoes.

"He was going to kill Mom and me. He was a butthole . . . but sometimes I feel so bad for what I did. I feel sorry for Kenny. When he was sober, he wasn't a bad guy, a bad dad." They were quiet. Max felt so petty for indulging her guilt and her regrets when this little boy was wrestling with so much more.

"Since then," Ryan said, "I've . . . I've been afraid of everything, like I told you when we met . . . everything. Every noise, dreams, everything. I peed my pants so many damn times." Max nodded. "And you told me you found someone that helped you to not be afraid. I did too. When we got here, me and Mom, I met people who liked me, welcomed me. I've never had friends like them in my life.

"Here, in this shitty, scary trailer park, I've met the best people I've ever known. We . . . I, I couldn't just sit there and let those . . . assholes . . . hurt those people, hurt you. And as scared as I was running down that hill toward all those big, scary guys, it felt a million times better than sitting there safe."

Ryan looked over at Max, looked her in her tired, red, swollen eyes. "A really smart old guy told me if you see something bad happening and you don't try to stop it, you're as bad as the guys who did it. That's what's helped me get over being so afraid. I would have, my friends would have, run down that hill to help if you'd been there or not, Max. I just wanted you to know that. It's not your fault."

Ryan's mom called him inside the trailer. He gave Max a weak smile before he went in. Taylor Badel lingered a moment at the door.

"Ryan told me you're a professor or something," Tay said. "I don't know much. I dropped out of school at seventeen, but I know my boy, and he rushed in to save me without one thought to his own life. It sounds like he did the same for you. He's got a strong heart, a tender one."

"Yes," Max said, "he does." She looked over to Tay. "I imagine he got that from you." Tay snorted.

"I hope that's all he got from me. The world's hard on tenderhearted people." She looked at Max, into Max for a long second. "I tell Ryan all the time not to help the world beat him up. It's good advice, even from a drop-out."

"Thank you," Max said, her voice so low Tay could hardly hear it even a few feet away. "It's good advice, wise advice."

"I just wanted to thank you for getting him back to me, safe and sound," Taylor said. "Good night." She closed the door.

It was less than an hour before dawn when Dave Wojick, Dusty Acosta, and Lovina Marcou arrived in Coalport from Philadelphia. They weaved their way through the chaos of park residents, state troopers, investigators, and EMTs. A few staties nodded to Wojick, called him by name. The investigator split off to confer with the other state police and then caught back up with Lovina and Dusty.

"Your pal Dr. Leher isn't being charged with anything," Wojick said. "She's pretty broke up over those kids being abducted, though. We got positive IDs on a few of the bodies of those clowns, local teens, live right here. What a freaking mess, right?"

The media trucks were being kept at the edge of the access road that led to the trailer park entrance. The field and the forest were alight with flashlights as the dead and injured of the attack in the railroad jungle were transferred to ambulances and the crime scene was processed and searched.

Lovina saw Max sitting alone at an old wooden picnic table in a grassy courtyard not far from the field of plastic flamingos. "Dave, give me a minute," Lovina said. Wojick nodded and he moved on.

"I'm going to go check out that hobo jungle you told me about," Dusty said. Lovina was only half-listening.

"You have any trouble tell them you're with Dave and me," Lovina said, walking away toward the picnic table. Max hadn't looked up from the splintered, rotted wood of the table, obviously lost in thought.

Lovina noticed a strange look on the faces of many of the park's residents as she approached Max. She had seen it before on the job in New Orleans, in the most poverty-stricken and violent neighborhoods. It was a stoic fear in most, the look of a people used to terror and death in their backyard, yet still unbowed, proud of their homes, of their community.

Max had a large bandage on the right side of her forehead and the beginning of a black eye below it and a few smaller cuts on her nose and cheeks. Max's whole face brightened when she looked up and saw Lovina.

"You okay?" Lovina asked.

"Hey," Max said, her voice low and trembling. "Yeah . . . I mean no . . . no I'm not. I . . . I messed up really bad, Lovina." Lovina walked over to her and gently placed her hand on Max's shoulder. The professor was trembling like it was bitter winter instead of the last decaying days of summer. Max took the hand on her shoulder, held it tight. "People . . . children got hurt, abducted, maybe killed." Max fought back tears. "Because of me."

Lovina knelt and hugged Max tightly, Max fell into the embrace and began to cry, quiet little sobs, barely audible. Lovina hugged her as tight as Max was holding her.

"It's okay," she whispered. "It's okay."

The sun was a scarlet incision in the east by the time Max and Lovina released each other from the embrace. Max, eyes puffy but dry now, told Lovina everything that had happened.

The park was still bustling with police activity but a lot of the vehicles had departed. The cops were canvassing now, trying to fill in details. A stray thought sprang up in Lovina's mind—*God help the poor flatfoot that knocks on the door to Calvin's trailer.* Max and Lovina sat side by side at the picnic table away from the flow of activity.

"I was so stupid," Max said.

"From the sound of it, these kids knew the territory and they knew the risk," Lovina said. "They were safe away from the action until they decided to run in and help. Brave kids. They could have run, they didn't. Granted, taking them along might not be the call everyone would have made . . ."

"You wouldn't have," Max said. "Jimmie wouldn't have."

"I can't say that for certain any more than you can, Max. You were here, on the scene. You made the call and you can't eat yourself up by second-guessing. I worked with a cop in New Orleans. One of my training officers. Great cop, good man. His first and only shoot in sixteen years of police work turned out to be a fourteen-year-old offender. He near killed himself with grief, blame, doubt. He quit the force two years later. It ate him up and he couldn't let it go."

Max sighed. "I get that," she said. "I really do."

"He was good cop. In a split second he made a choice. No one on this earth has the right to second-guess him on that. What we do is dangerous work, Max, it's risky and people die sometimes, kids die sometimes. I know you, I know the kind of person you are. You did everything you could given the situation at that time. I know that, and you need to know that, too."

"I . . ." Max said, shaking her head. "The things I do aren't dangerous, the world I come from is not . . . like this . . . I'm not like you or Heck or Jimmie, I should never have come out . . ."

"You've saved lives, Max, mine and the others included, more than once. If you hadn't been there, none of us would be here now, and right now I need you. I need you to help me. There's still time to save those kids and a lot of other people too, but I need your brain back in the game."

"Okay," Max said. "Okay, I'll try." They were quiet for a moment, the only sounds the occasional squawk of a police radio and the chirping of birds.

"You came here to follow up on the information Dusty gave us, right?" Lovina finally said. Max nodded less energetically than she usually did.

"Yes. Our killer is an alchemist," Max said, rubbing her face. "He's extracting something from the heads of his victims, that's why so few heads turn up at the body dumps."

"He's taking the pineal glands," Lovina said. "The autopsies of the heads recovered at the Raelyn Dunning scene and the Jane Doe dropped at that park in Fogelsville are both missing pineal glands removed with the skill of a surgeon. Hardly a mark on them."

"The pineal?" Max said. Lovina could already see Max's mind tumbling through permutations of the data. It was amazing to watch, and sometimes a little scary. "The pineal . . ."

"What is it Max?"

"DMT," Max said. "The hallucinogen? Remember Russell Lime told us that the clown-white makeup you found had, among other compounds, some kind of organic form of DMT in it?"

"Yes," Lovina said.

"The pineal gland can, theoretically, produce DMT. In some research, the pineal floods the body with DMT at the moments leading up to death. It's one of the theories for the so-called near-death experiences many people have."

"Max, there are a lot easier ways to get DMT, and a lot less risky, too."

"He's after more than just the drug. It's a means to an end. Lovina, the pineal gland is believed to be the seat of the 'third eye'—the organ that, if properly opened, allows sight beyond mundane human comprehension. The philosopher Descartes thought it was the seat of the human soul. In Buddhism, they believe that after death the soul reincarnates into a new body on the forty-ninth day, which just so happens to be the day that a human fetus's pineal gland matures after conception." ·

"Hold, it, hold it," Lovina said. "You mean our killer, this alchemist, is stealing people's souls?"

"Regardless of where you stand on the theories," Max said, "I'd say the killer believes it and is acting accordingly."

"What would an alchemist do, exactly, with the essence of a human soul?"

"I can make an educated guess," Max said. "Your Mr. Acosta said a few words while he was deep in trance during his ritual: *spagyric*, and *Azoth*. Both are alchemical terms. A spagyric is a potion or elixir created by an alchemist from the distillation of minerals and plants.

"I came here last night because I wanted to get a better look at the symbols all over the park and the boxcar jungle . . ." Max paused for a moment and Lovina saw the steam go out of her as she stumbled over the horrific memories of last night. "I had an idea of what an alchemist might be up to, especially after Acosta said the word Azoth." Max was holding back something.

"Max," Lovina said softly. "The symbols?"

Max shook her head trying to clear it and seemed to dispel the awful memories.

"Yes, right, the symbols. One of the symbols around the trailer park and the jungle is an ancient alchemical code. I finally located it and its meaning. The teardrop shape with the small cross that's covering the park, the jungle, and is on the back of the hobo coins you and Russ discovered . . . It means, roughly 'the one who receives.'" I think this alchemist has been using this whole trailer park and the jungle to surreptitiously steal and distill life force from the people who live here, using them as his spagyric, if you will."

"That sounds more like magic than alchemy, Max. I didn't think alchemists could do stuff like that?"

"Normally I'd agree with your premise," Max said, picking up the evidence baggie holding the hobo nickels. "However I think this alchemist has been using the rather unique nature of the Valentine Trailer Park and its nearby environs to his advantage, to drain and receive life force from the inhabitants for decades." Again, Lovina felt the professor hold back, and fall into herself a little. "It was the stray thought nagging at me, the one that made me come out here last night. The thought that caused all this trouble and death."

"Max, what is so special about this place?" Lovina asked.

"All the odd occurrences here," Max said, leaning closer, almost whispering, "recognized for decades, talked of as local legends and urban myths, pretty much ignored as much as possible by the authorities and locals. Strange creatures, unexplained deaths, supernatural activity, demented personalities, like that Calvin fellow, it's all the same kind of phenomena you'd encounter on the Road, isn't it? All right here. Those hauntings, like the ones you encountered, they're residual fragments of souls stolen by this killer, held trapped here on this land by the binding he's invoked, the power he's tapped into."

"What power is that?" Lovina asked, gesturing to the park around her. "There isn't a major highway near Coalport. Doesn't that kind of invalidate your theory about the highways being so strange because they are running along ley lines of magical energy."

"No, Lovina," Max said. "I came last night to find out if my theory was still valid and it is. I was so . . . damned determined to be right, I endangered myself and those poor nomads . . . and even those children." Max's voice rose, louder than Lovina could ever recall hearing the shy scientist speak. Her eyes were rimmed with tears again, and her voice trembled, quavering as she grew angry. "What kind of monster would do that? Tell me. You tell me!"

Lovina was silent. Max started to cry again, then denied herself the release of it. She sniffled and coughed a little, then wiped her eyes and went on. "The abandoned rail line back at the edge of the boxcar jungle . . ."

"Max . . ." Lovina began. Max ignored her and went on, like she was lecturing a class.

"The railroad track . . . it was set up along a ley line, a conduit of supernatural energy. The alchemist is using it, using the power, to siphon life from these poor people. He's been at this as long as the trailer park has been here, longer than that. The deed to this land is from 1953, remember? It said the town sold the land to the former owner of the Valentine Carnival, one 'N. Flamel.'"

"Nicolas Flamel," Lovina nodded. "The alias of various alchemists in the fifteenth century."

"Or maybe one of the aliases of our killer," Max said. "He used the carnival to travel along the rail lines, tap their power."

"Dustin Acosta told me about what he and some other nomads, hobos, call 'the Rail,'" Lovina said. "He said it has the same basic properties s as the Road does."

Max nodded.

"Yes," she said, "It makes sense. Many of the routes used by major highways and interstates are very similar to the routes of the old railroad lines that crisscrossed the nation close to a century before the highways were even envisioned. Same routes, same ley lines."

"Max, that still means this was all planned by somebody and now you're back into the 1800s for whoever developed this idea. None of the orders of the Templars seem to have their shit together to have pulled this off, so who then? I mean, no offense, but you didn't have any proof of your theory before when it was just the highways, and now you're talking about the railro . . ."

Max stopped her by placing the odd silver rail spike Ryan had found on the picnic table.

"That enough proof for you?" Max said, with perhaps a little anger in her tired voice. "It is conducting ley line energy, raw magical force through it." Lovina picked up the spike and felt a tingle like static electricity move across her fingers and hand. "The runes carved on it are a mystery to me so far, but it's hard tangible proof of my theory. One of the kids, Ryan, found it and let me hang on to it. He said he destroyed an evil clown with it."

"I'm sorry," Lovina said. "I shouldn't have poo-pooed your theory like that out of hand."

"It's okay," Max said with a ghost of smile. "I'm kind of used to it."

Lovina sighed.

"I remember when no one believed me about what was done to my sister," she said. I ought to know better." She looked at Max's battered face and her sad, weary eyes. The professor was exhausted and mantled with so much guilt. Lovina took her hand and held it. "I really am sorry." Max squeezed her hand tightly and neither of them wanted to let go. Finally they did, as Lovina shoved some businesslike conversation into the silence between them. "This punk we arrested, Angie Potts, he says our alchemist calls himself the Cooker. He's got some kind of a base of operations in a tunnel on an old abandoned section of the Pennsylvania Turnpike."

"Makes sense," Max said. "Even if it's in poor shape, that section of highway would still have power due to the ley lines under it."

"The feds, state, and local cops are raiding the place tonight, after midnight. Angie said the Cooker's got some kind of ritual going on there with the kidnapped people. He's set up a kind of cult around this horrorcore band and its fans. Angie says the Cooker promised to make them all immortal if he did his dirty work.

"That all dovetails with what Emmett told me," Max said. "This cult has been around a lot longer than a bunch of band groupies, Lovina."

"Who's Emmett?" Lovina asked, and for the first time Max's old Cheshire cat smile returned.

"I think you should meet him yourself," Max said.

. . .

It was late morning when Lovina and Max made their way down the steep incline at the edge of the forest. The last of the cops had headed out of the park about a half-hour ago. Below were the remnants of their work: crime scenes, marked off with stakes and yellow plastic tape, islands of frozen carnage. Small yellow cones with numbers marked where individual pieces of evidence had been photographed, measured, and recovered. The cops and forensic techs were gone now, having collected all they could from the site. Max froze when she saw the dried blood on the grass where the nomads had died. She saw the stain that marked the spot where the old man, Ben, had been killed, trying to defend his charges. She saw the spot where the young nomad, Harmony, had fallen, the life draining from her eyes as her blood stained the earth.

"Max." Lovina took her arm gently. "Come on, it's okay." They reached the edge of the jungle as Dusty Acosta came into view. The young nomad waved. He had his jacket and T-shirt off and was carrying tangled bars of steel on his shoulder.

"Max," Lovina said, "Dustin."

"Dusty," he said, offering Max his free hand. They shook. "Please to meet you, Dr. Leher. Lovina said you wanted to talk about my Juggalo JuJu?"

"I do," Max said. "It sounds fascinating."

"First things first, though," Dusty said. "Emmett and I are trying to get one of the old railroad handcars lying around here up and working by tonight."

"So you met him?" Max said. Dusty laughed.

"Yeah," Dusty said. "He scared the piss out of me at first, but then we talked. He's a living hobo archive."

"Okay," Lovina said, "everyone seems to have met this guy but . . ."

Emmett strode into view. His face, arms, and bare chest were a washed-out white from the same greasy makeup Lovina had seen the clowns in her dreams wear, but Emmett had no decorations on his broad, plain face, save a painted black ring with three spokes on his forehead, and a shadow of a beard on his face. He was wearing old steel-riveted jeans and work boots. His work shirt had been discarded as Dusty had done. Emmett was carrying one of the old six-hundred-pound handcars over his head with both hands, easily.

". . . me," Lovina said, and looked to Max and to Dusty, who were both smiling.

"Emmett," Max called out, "I'd like you to meet someone, please." The big man lowered the handcar to the ground and walked over. "Emmett Wally, this is Lovina Marcou, she's of the same order as you and Dusty."

"Hello," Emmett said, his voice softer than Lovina had expected, but still with a deep timbre. He offered his massive hand to Lovina and she shook it. His skin was very cold. "The . . . wheel . . . turns."

"The wheel turns," Lovina replied. She looked over to Max.

"Emmett has been living here in the boxcar jungle since the fifties," Dusty said. "He's been tracking our killer since the thirties."

"How have the cops not found you out?" Lovina asked. "How did they miss you today?"

"I . . . have . . . a lot of . . . experience . . . ducking rail yard bulls . . . and cops," Emmett said.

"He surprised the hell out of me today," Dusty added. "Emmett started riding the rails in 1930, looking for a job to send money home to his wife and children. He joined the Brethren in 1932. I've heard of Emmett 'the Wall' Wally and his hunt for the Cleveland Butcher—it's part of hobo and Brethren legend. I just didn't know he was a real guy, until today."

"You know about the Cooker, Flamel . . . whatever this alchemist's name is?" Lovina asked Emmett. The giant stared at her for a moment, like he was still processing the question. Lovina looked at Max again.

"When . . . I . . . discovered . . . his crimes, he called himself . . . Valentine, Basil Valentine, owner of the Valentine Carnival," Emmett finally said, as if he were fighting for each word. "He . . . abducted . . . and killed . . . people . . . who lived and worked . . . near the rails. He used one of his men, his clowns . . . a lunatic named . . . Dutch Holt to commit . . . many of his crimes. Holt . . . came . . . to be known . . . as the Butcher of Kingsbury Run. Today, he goes by . . . the name given to him . . . by his master. He's called Altair . . . and he's still . . . killing . . . for Valentine."

Lovina and Dusty looked at each other as another name from Dusty's vision was uttered.

"Altair is here, nearby," Max added. "Emmett said he was one of the Harlequins that attacked the nomads camping here."

Lovina removed one of the hobo nickels from the evidence baggie. She handed it to Emmett. "This is Dutch Holt's work?" Emmett nodded after a moment of staring at the nickel, turning it over in his massive hands.

"Yes," Emmett said. "He . . . leaves them behind . . . to sign his work, and to consecrate each death . . . to his master."

"You've been chasing Altair and this alchemist all this time, for over eighty years?" Lovina said. Emmett stood silent for a moment and then nodded again.

"Emmett, tell Lovina about the makeup, the clown-white," Max said. The big clown was quiet again for a time as if he were marshaling his strength to do as Max had asked.

"The makeup is . . . one of Valentine's early attempts at . . . immortality," Emmett said. "If you apply it . . . to your skin . . . it will make you stronger, bigger . . . it heals any illness or wound . . . and it does stop your aging . . . as long as you keep using it."

Lovina looked at Emmett and already she was seeing the horrible truth of what he was saying. She recalled the terror in Angie Potts's eyes at the prospect of not having his makeup in prison. "As long as you keep using it," she repeated.

Emmett nodded.

"Exactly . . ." he said, dragging the words, the thoughts, out of him with terrible effort. "After a time . . . the cream stops soaking . . . into your skin. You must apply . . . more of it, the older you get, to still . . . receive its effects. It eats away . . . at your mind, almost calcifying . . . your thoughts. It . . . hollows you out . . . inside . . . and all you can . . . think of . . . is what Valentine orders you to do."

"So you were one of his men, his Harlequins?" Lovina asked. Emmett's face twisted into a sneering mask, as if he had smelled something foul.

"No, never," he rumbled. "I hunted them. Valentine has his Harlequins . . . scattered across the county . . . hiding, waiting, hunting . . . waiting in the shadows of so many small towns. I tried . . . to stop them. Altair . . . he found my wife . . . and my children . . . murdered them, mutilated them as a warning to me . . . a warning to stop destroying . . . Valentine's agents. Bad decision, because after that . . . I had no reason to ever stop. I kept raiding the Harlequin cult gatherings, began using the makeup they used to let me continue my hunt. It's . . . changed me, emptied me, but . . . I . . . fight . . . every day to remember who I was, who I am, and what they did to . . . the people I love. My family . . . keeps a little spark of me alive, sane."

"This has to be the same stuff the Cooker is giving to the Lunatic Clown Squad fanboys, like Angie," Dusty said. "Unbelievable, he just moves along, era to era, recruiting followers to abduct people, harvesting what he needs from them and then dumping them like garbage."

"Preying on small towns like Coalport," Max said, "all across America, maybe even across the world. He leaves his agents, his Harlequins—ageless, silent—in his wake, to hunt among the population, harvesting more and more victims for his 'great work.'"

"We're still a little a shaky on the why of all this," Lovina said. "What's his endgame or does he have one? Does he just wander along through time, a parasite, living off the life of others?"

"I believe the alchemist is using the power he's tapping into from the ley lines to create one of the greatest alchemical treasures in the long history of that art," Max said. "Dusty's ritual gave us the name of what he's trying to make. He's trying to create the Azoth."

"Azoth?" Dusty said. "I know it's an alchemical term but I still have no clue what it's got to do with people being abducted and butchered."

"The Azoth," Max said, "is a legend among alchemists. It's a universal antidote to any illness. It makes the one who drinks it truly and completely immortal and indestructible. If the pineal is in some way linked to the spiritual energy of a human, then our killer may have figured out a way to create the Azoth from the . . . secretions of the pineal. It's morbid, but it makes sense."

"So the Azoth will make him immortal and impossible to kill," Lovina muttered. "Swell."

"It's worse than that," Max said. "The Azoth is also supposed to show the one who drinks it the mind of God," Max said. "To make them as God is, all-knowing, all-powerful. I can think of few things more awful than a serial-killing lunatic with the power of a god."

"We've got to stop this evil fucker," Dusty said. "Right here, right now."

"Yes," Emmett said. "Tonight."

"Tonight," Lovina said, nodding. "We shut him down."

As they began to plan, none of them noticed Ryan Badel hidden at the edge of the treeline in the forest, listening to their plans, terrified for his new friends and the fate awaiting them at the hands of this monster. Ryan nodded too.

"Tonight," he whispered.

Cherokee Mike led his remaining soldiers off I-64, onto the old U.S Highway 64 and then south onto Route 1100, Mike's motorcycle at the spear tip of the formation of thirty bikes. The sun was a memory and the swollen moon glared down at the earth whispering madness and night secrets to those who listened to her. The warm summer night was heavy and still along the scar of a road winding through deep, untamed forests.

Mike knew he had to turn this around and fast or he'd lose all his support. Viper had told him the ritual in the Devil's circle at the Tramping Ground would bring him many powerful new allies from the unseen worlds. Enough firepower to end Heck Sinclair and solidify his grip on the MC. While most men would be planning an exit strategy from this clusterfuck, Mike prided himself on not being like most men. He would still get everything he wanted. He would still win this.

A shadowy mass appeared on the road ahead, blocking Mike's procession. Bright, single headlights created a halogen wall before a large group of motorcycles blocking the road. At the head of the blockade sat Heck on his T5 Blackie, his demon mask hanging by its leather straps around his neck, his battle harness of guns and grenades tight against his chest. The Sinclair family Claymore was strapped to his back. Mike felt a cold shiver in his guts but slowed and stopped about one hundred yards from Heck's men. He raised a leather-gloved hand for the bikers behind him to stop as well and they obeyed. Mike counted about roughly twenty to twenty-five bikers with Heck and he smiled his most charming smile.

"That all you got left, Heck?" he called out, his voice echoed in the vast dark woods. "You come to join up?" Some of Mike's men laughed, but only a few. Heck's face was as set as the steel demon face on his mask.

"Listen, all of you," Heck began. "If you drop your guns, take off, and leave your colors, you can ride back the way you came. Don't stop riding until you're out of North Carolina and don't you ever come back. This is the only chance you get and it's gone at the count of three."

Mike tried to summon up a veneer of confidence; at the very least he didn't want to sound scared. "You and your boys are the ones leaving, Sinclair. You fucked up this club, you and your senile old grandfather . . ."

"One . . ." Heck called out, reaching for his steel mask. The riders behind Heck blipped their engines, the growl rolling through the ancient forests.

"Your whoring sot of a stepdad . . ."

"Two"

"And your manipulative bitch of a mother."

Mike heard the screech of bike tires behind him and the stench of burnt rubber. He glanced back to see a half-dozen of his bikers roaring away back up Route 1100, their MC vests and a pile of guns left in their wake.

Heck slipped the grinning demon face over his own grim facade. "Three," he said, his voice muffled but heard. "*Bráithreachas!*" Heck bellowed out over the thunder of the bikes.

His men replied, brandishing their weapons. "*Bráithreachas!*" Heck and his men tore down the road, barreling toward Mike's column.

"Go, go!" Mike shouted to his remaining men, and they roared forward to meet the incoming horde. Mike stayed put and withdrew the iron wand, the Key of Thorne. He closed his eyes and shouted out into the darkness, demanding aid and allegiance.

The bands of bikers merged into a single mass. Chains, spiked bats, fighting sticks, flexible retracting steel batons, pistols, machetes, and in one case a massive Scottish Claymore were brought to bear on opposing riders as they passed within inches of one another. In the cramped space of the press, Heck heard the crack of gunfire, screams of pain, the shriek of tearing, tumbling metal, and howls of berserker fury. Blood splattered his mask and chest from the blow he struck to one of Mike's men.

He came clear of the press and jammed his leg down as he downshifted, decelerated, and turned the bike to make another run. Heck heard the boom of a shotgun and saw one of Mike's men fly off his bike and tumble into a ditch by the side of the road, his bike skidding and sparking its way off onto the other side of the road. Jimmie Aussapile came clear of the crush, a nasty cut on his arm and his sawed-off shotgun smoking as he looped wide to come up beside Heck.

"You okay?" Jimmie asked as he loaded two more cartridges of birdshot into his shotgun.

"Mike's holding back," Heck said under his mask. "Fucking around with that magic pig-sticker of his. I'm going to him."

"I'll cover you best I can," Jimmie said and the two of them launched back toward the fray. Heck cut to the fringes of one side of the fighting, banking low and fast, his Claymore resting on his handlebars throwing sparks as it scraped the road in the bank. Jimmie ran blocker between the melee and Heck. He blasted another of Mike's men with the shotgun, and saw the man fly free from his bike and the motorcycle tumble and crash into another biker.

As the bikers clashed, turned, and reengaged, the number up and still fighting dwindled. Roadkill aimed his motorcycle at two of Mike's boys, one of them his righthand man, Vinnie Wiseman, and gunned the engine, Vinnie decided to play chicken, the other rider lost his nerve and tried to peel at the last second but it was too late and he was too close.

"It ain't chicken, asshole," Roadkill muttered. "It's possum." He let the change take him. On a full moon it was more of an effort not to change. The possum launched himself from his bike an instant before the three bikes collided in an eruption of tangled metal and ripping flesh. Roadkill bounced along the road and then scampered to the berm.

Heck righted his bike out of the bank and barreled down on Mike. His hand wrapped around the hilt of his blade and he lifted it one-handed, ready to strike as he passed. Dark shapes, at first glance perhaps clouds, suddenly dived toward the road and the battle below. Massive owl-like luminous eyes opened, burning with an unnatural light. They had no arms, only massive wings and legs with foot-long talons. The things let out a mournful screech as they descended and began to attack Heck's men. One of the creatures swooped down and grabbed Heck by his sword arm as he was preparing to close on Cherokee Mike. The bladelike claws sunk deep into Heck's arm and began to pull him from his speeding bike. Jimmie swung the shotgun up, clutching it by the action and chambering a new round with one hand. He fired it across his chest, blasting the creature between its two glowing saucerlike eyes. The bird-thing wailed and released Heck as it fluttered out of control and crashed into the dark forest. Heck flew in one direction, his bike tumbled and crashed not too far away from him and Jimmie pulled over to help his squire to his feet.

"What the hell are those things?" Heck asked as he staggered to his feet.

"Mothmen, I think," Jimmie said.

"Moth*men*?" Heck said incredulously as he opened fired on another of the creatures with one of his MP9s. "I thought it was Moth*man*, and that it was in West Virginia."

"That's just the famous one," Jimmie said, shucking the empty shell from the shotgun and chambering a fresh one. "They're all over."

"Fun fact," Heck said. "When I get my hands on Mike I'm going to stick that fucking wand up his ass sideways."

From his vantage point on the sidelines, Roadkill could see the Mothmen were making short work of his fellow Jocks. He was about to scamper over to a pistol discarded on the side of the road, when he heard a slight sound to his back and felt a familiar ache in his belly and balls that could only mean silver was near. He reflexively dived forward and missed being skewered on a silver spear point. He glanced back to see his attacker and wished he hadn't.

Coming out of the woods in large numbers were manlike creatures. They were about five foot tall, with long, white, dirty, tangled beards that almost fell to their feet. Their skin was the color and brilliance of the full moon, their eyes huge, empty, and dark, as though their eyes had been scooped out, leaving only craters. They carried crude wooden spears, the tips apparently dipped into silver that had dried partly down the haft of the weapons. They wore no clothing, their beards and long wild white hair concealing much of their bodies. Jethro remembered his dad and grandfather talk about the old tall tales of the Moon-Eyed Men, monsters of the North Carolina wilderness who long ago preyed upon and warred with the Cherokee, and who hated any light, even the light from the moon and stars. *Goddamn you Mike and that fucking magic wand of yours,* Jethro thought. *You even got these bastards out of bed and fighting when they hate the full moon and its light.*

The Moon-Eyed Men advanced on Heck's people, many of who were down and wounded among the bloody wreckage of the first few passes. Some were dead or passed out but the others were trying to fight on as best they could. The Moon-Eyed Men ignored Mike's wounded as they crept closer to finish off Heck's wounded, many of whom struggled to get up and find a weapon as they saw the creatures advance. Jim Gilraine, not long out of the hospital but who had insisted on coming tonight, slipped a backup .380 pistol from an ankle holster and began to fire on the glowing creatures. The gun pop-popped and several of the Moon-Eyed Men fell.

"Shit, these guys glow in the dark for you," Jim shouted to his comrades. "Who needs tracer rounds? Light 'em up, boys!"

Jimmie spotted the advancing creatures coming out of the woods on either side of the road—at least thirty strong total—as Heck climbed back onto this bike. "We got more trouble," the trucker said. He looked over to Heck. "I think it's time." Heck keyed his throat microphone as he kicked the Blackie back to life with a fog of gas vapors and an angry snarl from the engine.

"This is Red to Big Bad," Heck said. "C'mon in, darlin', both barrels. We need you."

Ana Mae's voice was in his ear and it made the pain, the rage ease a little for just a second. "On our way, chew toy. Looking forward to it."

"Be advised some of the things Mike conjured up have silver-tipped spears."

"Shit," Ana Mae said, stretching the word out for added contempt. "That junk only works if you can hit us with it."

Heck and Jimmie heard the bikes coming in the distance, further south down 1100 in the direction Mike and his boys had been headed. The original plan had been to choke them off between the two MCs with nowhere to go on the road, but as with all tactical plans it had not survived contact with the enemy. The bikers still battling on the road heard the rumble of a pack of bikes and the howls of hunting animals as the headlights of the Bitches of Selene came into view.

Half of Ana Mae's number had already given themselves to the passion of the silently burning moon. They loped along beside the speeding bikes, some on all-fours, others on two feet. Some of them took to the woods, crashing through the brush, closing to flank the Moon-Eyed Men on both sides of the road.

One of the Mothmen silently circled in the air and then gave off a mournful cry as it dived straight for Ana Mae's bikers. As it came closer to the front of the column of advancing bikes, there was a *whoosh* from the edges of the battle and the Mothman was ripped to pieces in a massive explosion. Heck and Jimmie glanced across the fray to see Heck's brother biker, Bobby-Ray, who had led one of the raids on Mike's meth labs, let out a Rebel yell as he tossed an empty LAW rocket launcher aside and one of his crew handed him a fresh one. "I'm really glad Bobby-Ray's on our side," Heck said.

"I think he just likes blowing shit up," Jimmie said.

The flaming remains of the Mothman fell down around the Bitches of Selene as they rode through the burning rain and into the thick of the battle with blood-curdling screams.

"I'm really, really glad she's on our side," Jimmie said.

"I'll take Mike, you corral any strays," Heck said. Jimmie nodded and the two rode off in different directions, Jimmie back toward the fighting and Heck toward Mike, who sat alone, distant from the fight. Mike saw Heck coming, the steel demon face of his mask reflecting the moonlight. Mike hefted his AR-15 rifle and began to fire on the advancing Heck.

Only a few Mothmen remained thanks to Bobby Ray's steady aim and coordinated fire. The few still in the air swooped down to slash and impale Heck's men on their claws. Roadkill, still a possum, scuttled over to a fallen Jock; he wasn't sure who it was or on which side, since his head had been torn off. Jethro struggled and hefted a hand grenade from the dead man's vest and scampered off with it.

The possum dodged the legs and feet of the Moon-Eyed Men as they struggled with the newly arrived werewolves. Jethro saw one of the Mothmen pulling up out of an attack, the bloody remains of a man's torso lodged on its claws. Jethro ran as fast as his tiny legs would carry him. Just as the creature was rising back into the night sky, Jethro shifted back to his naked human form, pulled the pin, and lobbed the grenade ahead of the rising Mothman. The grenade exploded with a terse thump and the Mothman, its face charred and half-gone, tumbled and crashed into a cluster of the Moon-Eyed Men, crushing them as it died.

Jethro let out a victory whoop, which ended quickly as he felt a horrible, sick pain in his side. One of the Moon-Eyed Men had stabbed him above his hip with a silver spear. Roadkill punched the sneering creature hard in the jaw and as the Moon-Eyed Man spun and began to fall, Jethro shifted back into his possum form, landed on his falling attacker's face, and began to rip, bite, and shred.

Ana Mae drove her bike deep into the chaotic fray, clearing a path for her people. She brought the bike down, skidding, sparking, into a swarm of Mike's men and the strange Moon-Eyed Men, sending them flying as the eight hundred pounds of metal knocked into their legs and knees. Ana Mae launched herself free from the crash and drew a long-barreled .357. She put a silver round into the forehead of one of Mike's men and then a second bullet into one of the Moon-Eyed Men. They both fell before Ana Mae's boots hit the ground.

Two bullets ripped through Ana Mae's leather jacket and her chest, in and out, taking bloody chunks of flesh with them. She winced at the pain, and coughed up some blood, but didn't fall. She turned to see that her attacker was one of Mike's boys, brandishing a 9mm pistol. Ana Mae grinned at the stunned gunman, a red smile, as she began to twist, grow larger, and change, heeding mother moon's silent song in her blood. She tossed the .357 to the ground

"You are one stupid son of a bitch," Ana Mae snarled to the shooter, who was frantically pumping bullets into her, "to bring lead bullets to a werewolf fight." The man's screams were lost in the chorus of battle, the lyric of death.

Jimmie was out of shotgun shells, so he had grabbed a discarded crowbar from a dead man's hand as he rode by. The battle was going their way, thanks to the Bitches of Selene's appearance. He watched in awe as one of the BoS, a transgender woman, whose club name was Yogi, lumbered out of the dark forest in all of her werebear fury, a half-dozen silver spears hanging ownerless from her flesh as she slaughtered droves of the Moon-Eyed Men.

With a second in the clear, Yogi ripped a large tree out of the ground by its roots and hurled it at the last of the Mothmen as it flew overhead. The tree smashed into the flying creature and sent it crashing to the ground with a horrible shriek to move no more. "Damn," was all Jimmie could muster. He saw one of Mike's guys limping away, heading for the woods. Jimmie accelerated and swung the bike around in front of the deserter. The limping man stopped. Jimmie hefted the heavy iron bar. "Okay, slick, on the ground, on your belly, right after you take off that cut you're disgracing." The man was figuring his odds, doing the quick calculations of risk and reward. "I'll bash your goddamned brains in and stop on the way home for a Dairy Queen Blizzard. Now do it."

The deserter took off his bloody cut and handed it to Jimmie. He lay down on the road like he'd been told. Jimmie nodded. "You fucking try to crawl away, you do anything but sit your ass here and wait for the cops to collect you, and I'll be eating my Blizzard out of your fucking skull. You hear me, boy?"

"Yes, sir," the man said, his voice quavering with fear. Jimmie rode off. He didn't like killing. He didn't like the way it left him feeling, but Heck and Mike had left no other choices available. Heck, and Mike, *and Viper.* He knew that son of bitch was close by, pleased as punch with all the suffering and bloodshed he'd fomented.

Layla was at Elizabeth's house, trying to make funeral arrangements, a loaded .38 by her side. He'd wanted her to head back to Lenoir, but she refused unless he came with them. After what had happened to Elizabeth, he couldn't leave Heck to face all this alone.

It was more than that, though. The truth, his truth, was buried, but not deep enough to hide from, was that he wanted Mike and his men to pay for what they had done to his friend Ale's dream, and most of all to pay for taking such a wonderful person as Elizabeth Sinclair out of this world. Jimmie clenched the crowbar tighter and prayed, not entirely sure to who, for the wisdom to keep his anger in check.

Mike's clip was empty and Heck was making another pass at him. He had a nasty wound in one of his shoulders from Sinclair's sword. *Fuck this,* he thought. Mike gunned his bike and sped due south, skirting the edges of the fight, dodging the debris of dead bodies, cast-off weapons, and motorcycles, racing pass Aussapile, who swung a crowbar at him and missed by inches.

Mike knew his only hope now was to make it to the Devil's Tramping Ground, to begin the ritual and hope his new allies were strong enough to crush all his opposition. His men who had remained loyally to fight in his name saw their leader fly past them, running away.

Jimmie watched Mike speed by and narrowly miss his swing. A moment later Heck blasted by, chasing after Mike, the lights of their bikes disappearing past the horizon of the dark, empty road. Jimmie knew where they were headed. He looked over his shoulder. This fight was as good as won. He dropped the crowbar and took off down the road, after his squire.

THIRTY

Darkness fell and the time for the raid on the Cooker and his Harlequins drew near. Dave Wojick informed Lovina that a daytime search of the abandoned railroad tracks and the now dilapidated section of the turnpike turned up no signs of the abducted nomads and children, and no unusual activity near the crumbling turnpike tunnel.

"Hikers walk the old highway in the warm months, right?" Wojick said. "So nothing weird there. We asked the Park Service to make sure they clear any hikers out quietly by nightfall. Philly PD, Bedford County PD, us, and the feds, we're all ready to roll."

Lovina and Wojick prepared to head for the raid site. Lovina was not surprised but a little disappointed when Max decided to stay in Coalport.

"I'm not a police officer or a soldier, Lovina," Max said. "I don't want to be the cause of anyone else dying or getting hurt."

"Max, you didn't do anything wrong," Lovina said. "I need your help in case I run into something this Cooker guy pulls out of his hat that I have no clue about."

"I'll be by my phone," Max said. "Please try to understand."

"I do, but the best thing for you is to get back up on the horse and—"

"I'm terrified of horses," Max said. "I do understand the sentiment, I just . . . I don't want to be the cause of anything happening to you. I can't be."

They were quiet for time. "You have your vest?" Max asked. Lovina thumped her chest against it. "I'm going to take another look at the rail system in the jungle, and check on Ryan and his friends, to make sure they are okay. Please keep your mind on your business, not me."

"That's really hard to do," Lovina said, smiling. "I'll be okay. You be safe."

■ ■ ■

Lovina was quiet for a long time on the ride down Interstate 99 toward Breeze-wood.

"It's none of my, yunz know, business," Wojick said, "but you and the professor, yunz guys got like a thing?"

"Damn if I know, Dave," Lovina said with a sigh. Wojick nodded and smiled.

"Yeah, it was like that with Cindy, my wife. I was the last one to fucking know." They both laughed.

"You're all right, Dave," Lovina said.

"Well, shit, somebody inform Cindy about that," Wojick said. Lovina laughed again.

■ ■ ■

Dusty Acosta pulled and tugged at the bulletproof vest Lovina Marcou had insisted he wear if he was taking part in the plan they had formed for the raid tonight. It was heavy and stiff and it made him feel like he was carrying a manhole cover on his chest. It beat getting shot, though, so he'd live with it.

The plan was that he and Emmett Wally were to take the repaired hand-cart and ride the rail down to the woods near the abandoned turnpike. Their only job during the raid was to try to locate the abducted and get as many of them clear as they could.

"You ready, partner?" Dusty asked Emmett. The big clown appeared from his caboose home and nodded. The two walked back to the tracks where they had left their repaired transportation. As they approached the moon cleared the trees and brightened the night.

"Uh, Emmett," Dusty said looking at the empty tracks, "where's our ride?" Emmett looked at the place where the handcar should be for a while. Finally he turned and looked at Dusty.

"Ryan," the clown said.

■ ■ ■

Many miles down the track, Ryan and Patrick pumped the handcar's handles while Nevada pointed a flashlight along the hurtling dark track to give them some idea of what was ahead of them. She looked down at her smartphone GPS. "Keep going," she said. "It's still a ways to go."

"When we get close we've got to kill the light," Ryan said.

"I know," Nevada said, a little testily. "You've told me that ten times already."

"Sorry," Ryan said. "Just, you know." Nevada nodded.

"I know. Me too."

. . .

The party started around midnight along the southern tip of the thirteen miles of broken and cracked abandoned highway near Breezewood. Weeds jutted out of the scars in the road and the paint that had once delineated lanes was faded. There was a tunnel that straddled the dead highway, cut through a section of mountain. Lights on aluminum poles and tripod stands illuminated the crowd of Harlequins gathered at the mouth of the tunnel. They were close to a hundred strong.

Most of the Harlequins were young men, with a smattering of women. They all wore street clothing and had their faces smeared in the greasy white paste provided by the Cooker and adorned with red, blue, yellow, and orange face paint in a variety of patterns. They were armed with an assortment of guns, clubs, knives, and chains. They had gathered from across the country at their master's summons and many had not come empty-handed. The Harlequins gathered the huddled group of bound-and-gagged abductees to the southern side of the tunnel mouth.

From their vantage point on the northern side of the highway, the assembled teams of law enforcement personnel were able to set up in the thick forests. The booming hip-hop music—something by the Cooker's proxies, the Lunatic Clown Squad—coming from a boombox near the mouth of the tunnel helped mask their movements. The Harlequins had sentries posted at strategic areas in the woods, but between the FBI's hostage rescue teams and the state and local tactical units, the sentries were taken out with no chance to raise a warning.

Lovina counted about thirty hostages huddled together in fear. Some of them looked emaciated, their clothing filthy and tattered. Many seemed nearly oblivious to their surroundings, most likely drugged.

"Cecil, some of them look out of it," Lovina said to the FBI assistant special agent in charge, who was next to her also scanning the surreal scene with a pair of night-vision binoculars. "It may be rough getting them moving and out of there. Can we give my team some smoke for cover?"

"I'm not crazy about you having a couple of civilians trying to rescue another bunch of civilians—some of them kids. The only reason the locals even went along with this was I said they were confidential informants for you on the inside of the case."

"And why did you go along with it?" Lovina asked.

"Because I know your little secret Triple-A club would send them in regardless, so at least this way, we can keep from getting them shot by our people, hopefully."

"Thanks," Lovina muttered. Dann shrugged.

"Okay it's almost show time," Dann said into his walkie-talkie. All units in position." He looked over to Lovina. "Your people good?"

Lovina keyed her throat microphone. "Dustin, You in position?"

"Yeah, about that," Dusty replied. "We're haulin' ass. We ran into a little snag but me and Max worked it out. We may be a little late to the party, but go ahead and start without us, chief."

Lovina looked back to Cecil. "We're all go," she said, keeping her face calm. Dann looked at her oddly for a second and then nodded. The music stopped, and the crowd of Harlequins began to howl and cheer and clap. Two of the largest clowns stood in a row near the entrance to the tunnel. "Right there, those," Lovina said to Dann, pointing at the row, "those are the High Harlequins, the Cooker's oldest and most loyal servants. Trouble." Lovina recognized one of the stone-faced clowns from her dream, the one Angelo and Emmett had called Altair. "Big trouble."

Smoke was drifting out of the tunnel's mouth now, and the Harlequins became even more agitated. They reminded Lovina of rowdy kids at a rock concert. In a lot of ways, she thought, they were. Stepping out of the smoke and into the lights was a man. He was dressed in jeans and dark-hooded jacket, the hood on the jacket obscured most of his face, but Lovina could tell he was Caucasian and clean-shaven.

"There's the man of the hour," Cecil said. He keyed the microphone on his walkie-talkie. "All units, stand by."

The Cooker raised his hands to the sky and his followers went wild with hoots and cheers. The hooded man's voice carried over the excitement of his Harlequins. "As always, my loyal soldiers, you haven't disappointed me," the Cooker said. "You will be rewarded with eternal life, eternal youth. When your parents, your teachers, who try to control you, keep you down, when the police, the politicians, who persecute you are nothing but dust you will still be striding this world under my banner!" The crowd cheered again, louder.

"H'boy," Wojick muttered. "This guy's a fruit loop all right."

"Now, bring your tribute, the fruit of your harvest, unto me," the Cooker said.

"Jesus," Dann said. "All units, stand by," he said into the mic.

. . .

In the woods near the hostages, Nevada, Patrick, and Ryan moved silently forward. "There," Patrick whispered, pointing. "It's them." The three saw Joe, David, and Sam, bound at the wrists, elbows, and knees with orange duct tape. Sam looked pale. The orange tape, caked in dried blood, was covering his neck wound. Other strips of tape covered their mouths and eyes. David and Sam were still, but Joe was still squirming, thrashing about. That ended when Dickie Dennis, still wearing the bloody clothes of the night before and the clown-white on his face, savagely kicked Joe until he groaned and stopped fighting. Nevada began to bolt toward her brother, her face twisted in anger. Ryan and Patrick grabbed her arms.

"Wait!" Ryan said. "Nevada, as soon as the cops bust these guys we run out and get them. You can spray that whole can of pepper spray in Dickie's stupid face then. Okay? But we have to wait and we have got to be quiet."

Nevada stopped struggling.

"Okay," she said, "but I'm going burn that asshole's eyes out." Nevada had taken the pepper spray from her dad's closet. Patrick had brought a heavy pipe wrench from his dad's truck, and Ryan wished he'd had time to get his rail spike back from Max. He had settled for a nasty-looking kitchen knife he stuck in the back of his belt. It wasn't much compared to the machine guns and machetes of the army of Harlequins but it would have to do. They were getting their friends out of here, no matter what.

. . .

Emmett carried another broken handcart to the tracks and set it down on them. Dusty and Max had been conferring since Dusty had called her to come to the jungle. "We've got to get there and fast!" Dusty said to the professor. "Those kids are walking into a buzzsaw, Max!"

"Can you two get another cart up and running?" Max asked. Dusty looked over to Emmett. The clown shook his head.

"I'm thinking we try some rail magic," Dusty said. "Lovina mentioned to me you're kind of an expert in that."

"I'm not a viamancer," Max said, "but I have worked out an incantation program that managed to mirror the effect of viamancy once, about a year ago."

"Well, I'm not a viamancer either but I know a few rail charms, maybe between us we can get us there in time to help those kids and do the job we were supposed to be doing."

It took a few moments to prepare. Max took out the rune-covered rail spike and studied it again. She hadn't had much time to do that since Ryan had given it to her. She had already noted a single symbol that seemed to be repeated in the same location on all the sides of the spike. They quickly drew the symbol on the four sides of the rotting wood base of the cart with a Sharpie marker that Dusty had in his pack. Max was already tumbling rushed formulas through her head to figure where on the rusty, long-abandoned rails she needed to apply the spike, while Dusty carefully drew the single master symbol on the crumbling metal wheels of the handcar.

"There's no guarantee this will do anything," Max said. "I'm making huge assumptions about the formulas used and their application. I'm assuming the creators of this system are the same ones who undertook the highway system's magical circuit. I'm retro-engineering this all based on that premise. I could be wrong."

"You're all we got, Max," Dusty said, checking his watch as he climbed aboard the cart. Emmett stood ready at the slightly twisted hand pump.

"This . . . cart . . . won't hold together . . . very long . . . on these tracks," the big clown said.

"Hopefully, it won't have to," Max said. "Dusty, you focus on that symbol you just marked the cart with. Hold it in your mind, feel the edges of it, the parts, and the totality. You've had magic training, you understand creative visualization. I also need you to focus on your destination, you must believe in your mind you are only a few moments away from it. Emmett, you start pumping as fast as you can when I say the word. Good luck."

"Thanks, Max," Dusty said and closed his eyes. He was sitting cross-legged on the front edge of the handcart.

"Emmett, go!" Max called out as she walked down the weed-tangled tracks. The giant began to pump, his broad, muscled arms raising and lowering the handle. Max turned away, hearing the old, corroded metal groan in protest as the car began to move wobbly down the tracks. She estimated the distance needed for a connecting anchor like the spike in the overall design of the tracks. A stray thought crossed her lines that the designers may have incorporated some magically acoustical elements to the steel used in the rails. She pushed the notion aside and focused on the symbol, its purpose, to close and perpetuate a circuit.

She stood on what her best guess told her was the correct spot. Max knelt and touched the tip of the rail spike, which was now dancing with blue magical fire, the symbols easily seen, to the decaying steel of the track. She didn't care about the rightness of her theory or proving it to anyone. She thought of Ryan Badel and his brave battle against the fear, to do the right thing.

Metal touched metal and the rails were awash with acetylene blue fire. Max felt the charge run up through her body. It hurt, it burned. All the pain she'd ever felt was squared, cubed, to the fourth power, the eighth . . . and more. She was pain and she found insight in this, understanding. She held the spike still despite the screeching command of a billion nerves. It felt like burning gasoline was pumping through her body, pooling behind her eyes, blackening her brain. In the moment of the fire, Max saw, felt the vast distances covered by the Road, the Rail, felt all that energy pooling far away, in a place built to hold magical energy for its masters.

The rickety rail cart blasted away, shot down the tracks faster than any petty shackle of the physical would could hinder. In a flash it was gone. Max raised the tip of the spike, breaking the connection. The fire vanished and Max collapsed back onto the warm, humming steel of the track. Blue sparks danced along the now dark metal, all around Max, and the spike retained its azure glow. Max, reeling with a cosmic hangover, managed to smile and silently mouth the word "yes."

A group of Harlequins moved toward the huddled hostages to bring them to the Cooker. Dann looked to Lovina and then spoke into his radio. "All units, go, go! Move in now!" Lovina began to move deeper into the woods.

"I'm going for the Cooker," she said. "See you in the middle!" Dann drew his own gun, said a silent prayer for his wife and daughter, and followed the federal Hostage Rescue Team as they rushed out of the woods and onto the cracked asphalt of the old highway.

Overhead a state police helicopter zoomed into view, bathing the dark corners of the highway near the tunnel. A booming voice called out from the heavens through a speaker on the copter, "This is the police. You are all under arrest. Put down your weapons and lie on the ground."

The staties and the Philly cops came out of the woods in a pincer formation with the feds at the center. Wojick, wearing a bulletproof vest, led a group of SWAT team members toward the mass of armed Harlequins. A clown with a knife rushed the investigator. Wojick took the punk down with a shoulder tackle, flipped him on his stomach, and buried his knee hard in the Harlequin's lower back. He was halfway to cuffing him when another clown advanced and took bead on him with a pistol. Wojick shot him in the chest and the clown fell, never getting off a shot.

A few of the clowns did as instructed, lying down and being cuffed and detained by the advancing cops, but the majority opened fire on the police or charged them, brandishing their assorted weapons. Gunfire began to punctuate the night, the pops of pistol fire, the occasional jabbering of a fully automatic weapon.

Ryan, Nevada, and Patrick darted free of the treeline when the cops made their presence known and made straight for hostages about fifty yards in from the trees. Most of the Harlequins were focused on the advance line of police, so the three kids made it to their bound friends with no trouble. Ryan began to cut Sam, Joe, and David free. That was when Dickie Dennis turned and saw them.

"You little bastards!" Dickie said behind his painted face. The makeup the clowns in the jungle had given him and his crew made him feel like Superman with a hard-on. He was a high-as-fuck demigod. He lunged for Ryan, who was just finishing freeing Joe. The blood-caked piece of rebar in Dickie's hand was poised to crack the boy's skull. There was the flash of an arm past Ryan's head and the hiss of an aerosol can. Dickie howled as his eyes were coated with pepper spray. He stumbled back and fell on his ass, clawing at his eyes and face, gasping in pain. Nevada kept going, walking past Ryan and the others, intending to empty the can into their tormentor's burned face.

"How you like that, Dickie?" Nevada said as the can dribbled the last of its contents. "That's for all the times you scared us, chased us, beat us up."

Ryan completed his work and Sam, Joe, and David were free. Joe blinked as he pulled the painful duct tape off his eyes and saw his sister picking up the rebar Dickie had dropped in his pain. She brought the steel down in an awkward, unbalanced strike against Dickie's undefended stomach. Dickie groaned at the hit and moved a hand from his swollen, wet face to cover his stomach. He tried to curl up into a shrimplike fetal position to defend more of his body. Nevada brought the rebar down on his side again and again.

"And this is for telling all your stupid squad that I did it with you! Dream on micro-dick!" Nevada shouted, rearing back and striking him again. "And this is for kicking my brother, you piece of shit!"

Dickie groaned. He was bleeding, blind, and in pain. Joe walked up next to his sister. Nevada handed him the rebar and hugged him. Joe hugged her back.

"Come on," Joe said. "Let's get the fuck out of here."

Sam stood with Ryan's help. He had been crying under the tape and Ryan noticed Sam's pants were damp, stained and reeked of ammonia. Sam looked down, ashamed. Ryan gave his friend a pat on the shoulder and tilted his head to meet his eyes. "It's no big deal," Ryan said. "Come on, let go!"

All around them was loud, bright, shifting chaos. The cops were pinning down the Harlequins who hadn't been shot or surrendered already. A ground of body-armored FBI agents in full military gear were weaving their way toward the cluster of hostages. The six friends turned to head back to the forest and the path to the train tracks. The massive clown, the one that had chased Ryan his first night in the trailer park—the one with the black sun— was blocking their way back to the forest. The clown had his sledgehammer. It dripped with fresh blood.

"No," the clown said, raising his hammer.

"Yes," a soft but powerful voice said from the edge of the treeline. Emmett and Dusty emerged onto the highway. "Let . . . them . . . be."

Dusty sprinted forward to put himself between Helios and the kids. "It's okay, guys," Dusty said. "I'm a friend of Max's. Come with me, we're going to get you all out of here and back to the tracks. C'mon." Helios turned to face Emmett, forgetting the children for now.

"You've . . . tried all . . . these years to kill us . . . in the boxcar jungle . . . for what Altair did . . . to your family," Helios said, stepping closer to Emmett. "You've . . . always failed . . . always ran . . . away." Emmett stepped closer too. "What . . . makes you think . . . it will . . . be different . . . this time?"

"Your master . . . is finished," Emmett said. The two began to circle each other, crouching, looking for an opening. "I . . . had to live," Emmett said, ". . . until his scheme . . . was ruined, the killings . . . ended." Helios shifted. He cocked his arm, ready to swing, to pulverize with the sledgehammer. "The Harlequins . . . had to be . . . ended . . . forever," Emmett said. "I had to stay alive. I was the only one . . . to know . . . to try to stop him . . . stop you. I had to stay alive . . ." Some anger, some fire, came into Emmett's tired, struggling voice, "even though . . . I hated . . . every . . . second . . . of having . . . to live . . . like one of you . . . walking corpses. And . . . besides . . ."

Helios swung the sledgehammer aimed at Emmett's head and neck. Emmett caught the head of the sledge in mid-swing one-handed and stopped the blow cold. Helios looked at his opponent, some awe and fear trickling into the Harlequin's lifeless eyes. "You . . . never . . . had the guts . . . to fight me . . . one-on-one," Emmett said.

Emmett drove his fist into Helios's face with the power of ten sledgehammers. The Harlequin's nose crumpled like paper and blood smeared his false, painted face. Emmett advanced, decades of anger denied driving him forward, powering each blow.

Lovina broke the cover of trees near the lip of the tunnel. The smoke from the Cooker's theatrical appearance was her ally, letting her move unnoticed past swarms of Harlequins battling the advancing police. The smoke irritated her eyes, but she got clear of the worst of it by entering the tunnel and stepping over the oddly cobbled together devices at the tunnel entrance to produce the smoke. Lovina knelt down to examine the devices and heard a scuffling near the other edge of the tunnel. The Cooker, his face still obscured by his jacket's hoodie, ran into the tunnel and began to head deeper into the darkness.

"Police! Hold it right there!" Lovina called out, her voice echoing through the tunnel. She leveled her Glock .40 and a flashlight at the hooded alchemist. The Cooker looked in her direction for a second before sprinting deeper into the darkness. Lovina ran after him, keeping him pinned in her flashlight beam. "Cooker . . . Nicolas Flamel, Basil Valentine," Lovina shouted as she ran, "whatever your name is, you're done here. You know that."

The Cooker stopped roughly twenty yards ahead of her. For an instant, Lovina thought he might be going for a gun, but instead he pushed on the walls of the tunnel. Lovina heard a click and the rumble of stone against stone. A section of the tunnel wall slid away to reveal a doorway. The Cooker slipped inside and the door began closing behind him. Lovina pushed herself, ran harder, and reached the hidden door just as it was sliding shut. Without thinking, she jammed the barrel of her pistol into the disappearing crevice of the closing door. There was a grinding sound and the door stopped closing, wedged open by her now stuck pistol.

Lovina paused for a second to catch her breath. Massive, pale, white hands came out of the darkness behind her and began to strangle her. Lovina tried to flip her unseen opponent over her but he was too massive to be budged. The strangler's breath was cold and it smelled of wet dead places. In desperation, as she began to feel light-headed, she smashed the heavy police Maglite's aluminum frame into the temple of her attacker and heard a satisfying crunch of bone for the frantic effort. The flashlight tumbled to the asphalt floor of the dark tunnel, creating a dingy island of light. Lovina staggered away from her attacker, who stood motionless.

It was the clown from her dreams, the one called Altair, the one who had abducted Raelyn Dunning. He looked at Lovina and cocked his head slightly. Blood gushed from his crushed temple, looking like the night was bleeding out of him, but Altair didn't seem to even notice the wound. His eyes were void, and in the tunnel's darkness his sockets seemed to be windows to the lightless pitch all around Lovina.

She looked back to her gun holding the secret door open. Could she pull it free before he reached her again? Shoot him and hope bullets worked on this walking, breathing nightmare. And what of the Cooker, even now retreating deeper into his mountain lair? Every minute dealing with this monster meant its master got further away. Lovina rubbed at her neck and kept her eyes on the unmoving clown.

Something was tossed out of the darkness. A bloody sledgehammer clattered to the floor, the sound echoing in the darkness. Emmett, bloodied and torn, stepped from the infinite darkness into the feeble light. He was off to Lovina's left. Altair's eyes flicked down to the hammer.

"Helios . . . says . . . hello," Emmett said. He and Altair locked eyes. "Pick it up," Emmett said.

"Finally . . . enough nerve . . . to try to . . . avenge your family?" Altair said. Emmett looked over at Lovina briefly.

"Go . . . get . . . Valentine," Emmett said. "Stop Valentine. I'll take care of him. I owe him something." Lovina reached her pistol and began to use the barrel like a short pry bar to open the hidden door. The carbon fiber frame of the gun was virtually unbreakable. She grunted and the door squeezed open a few more inches. Lovina began to slide through the opening. She looked back to Emmett, whose eyes were fixed on Altair. The hammer on the ground between them in the circle of light.

"The wheel turns," Lovina said.

"The wheel turns," Emmett said. Lovina slipped through the door and pulled her gun free. It clicked completely closed behind her.

"Would you like to know . . . how . . . they died?" Altair asked.

Emmett took a step forward, nodded to the sledgehammer. "Pick it up . . . or die empty-handed," he said.

Altair charged at Emmett, a meat cleaver suddenly in his hand. Emmett met the charge, and drove a powerful punch into the side of Altair's head as the cleaver sank deep into Emmett's shoulder, almost severing the arm. Emmett followed up the punch with a head butt that knocked Altair back and off his feet, as it did Emmett.

The two big men climbed to their feet. The wound in Emmett's shoulder bled but not the amount of blood such a wound would cause in a normal man. Emmett pulled the cleaver from his shoulder and tossed it on the ground next to the sledgehammer. "Try . . . again," Emmett said. Altair let out a growl and lunged forward, Emmett met his snarl and his charge and the two collided. They grappled, looking for any weakness, any opening.

"You . . . people . . . are so . . . afraid of dying . . ." Emmett said, teeth gritted as he and Altair struggled. "You . . . sold your soul to that . . . snake-oil peddler . . . a little bit . . . at a time . . . for this mockery of life . . . to . . . be . . . his . . . slaves."

"Shut . . . your . . . mouth . . . widower," Altair hissed. He slipped one of his hands free and drove it into Emmett's shoulder wound. Emmett winced. His knees almost buckled, but his beautiful wife, his sweet little girl, and happy little boy were there to hold him up, to keep him on his feet.

"The sad . . . part . . . is," Emmett groaned as his free hand shot out and took Altair by the throat, ". . . none of you . . . ever really . . . lived. Too much fear."

Emmett's grip on Altair's throat tightened. He lifted the big man off the ground with one arm. Altair gurgled and struggled, punching Emmett's wounded shoulder again and again. There was a sound like dry twigs snapping and Altair went limp in Emmett's grip. Emmett dropped the dead Harlequin and let his arms fall to his side. He hurt so bad and he was so weary.

He felt his children's hands take his own massive hands. He looked down at the body of Altair. "Some . . . things . . . are . . . worth more . . . than taking another breath," he said. Emmett staggered in the darkness, his wife's lips touching his own. Their presence led him out of the darkness and guided him all the way home.

. . .

On the other side of the secret door, Lovina found a narrow fissure in the heart of the mountain the tunnel had been blasted out from. She swept every inch, checked each shadow as she moved down the narrow hall. The hall ended in carved stone stairs that went up a few feet and opened into a larger cavern filled with hanging lights and bizarre scientific equipment. Everywhere there were coffinlike capsules of glass and steel filled with corpses, or parts of corpses. Many of the bodies and parts were in some kind of pale green liquid and they all seemed to be perfectly preserved. There were hundreds of capsules, of bodies. One wall was stacked from floor to ceiling with preserved severed heads, all staring blankly at Lovina. She swept the room with her pistol before her, trying not to think of the hundreds of dead eyes looking at the back of her head.

Lovina saw no way out of the room, but she did see strange symbols, including the teardrop-cross symbol that had been drawn all over the Valentine Trailer Park. Small tubes covered with symbols ran up the wall, across the ceilings and out of the cavern.

Four man-sized tubes lay at an angle to Lovina's left. Three of them contained a man, apparently the same man at various stages of development. The men had no hair whatsoever and no navels. They all looked to be in their thirties and Lovina had the strangest feeling she knew the single face all the men in the tubes shared. The fourth tube was empty and open.

There were large, well-lit operating tables orbited by trays of bizarre and disturbing surgical equipment. The operating table had thick leather arm and leg restraints, as well as a device to immobilize the head and neck. There were saws, clamps, scalpels, and various suction devices. A mechanized hoist and net contraption mounted to the ceiling looked capable of hauling bodies on and off the table. Lovina saw nothing that resembled anesthesia equipment anywhere, which only made her skin crawl even more. There was a desk covered in antique books and scrolls as well as a laptop. Lovina opened a book at random. It was filled with cramped scrawl-like writing in a language she suspected was Latin. Detail anatomical drawing of humans accompanied most of the entries.

There was a crash in one of the recessed shadowy alcoves on the far side of the room. The Cooker appeared, smashing and destroying a complex-looking series of pipes, pumps, and tubes that all fed into a cylindrical device mounted on the wall near the alcove that strangely reminded Lovina of a barista's espresso machine.

"They'll have none of it, without me!" the Cooker said, smashing another series of pipes and tubes with a crash. "My genius will die with me. I won't let them steal it, copy it." Lovina kept the gun leveled at the man's chest as she advanced.

"You can tell them all about your genius when we have you in a nice, safe rubber room," she said. "Put your damn hands up and be still."

"You won't shoot me, Investigator Marcou," the Cooker said, walking to meet her in the center of the room. "As much as you loathe me, you want to understand, understand my work."

"You want to test that theory?" Lovina said.

"You could have shot me in the tunnel, but you didn't. You are curious about all this." He gesticulated to encompass the whole laboratory. "How I have slowly milked the undeserved life from the ignorant peasants and trash that inhabit the Valentine Trailer Park. How I've gathered so many subjects for my work. What I have done is so great, so sweeping, it baffles you, and you demand explanation." The Cooker looked satisfied with himself. Lovina realized that his face matched those of the men in the tube. She glanced over to the tubes and the Cooker chuckled as he came closer to her, navigating the stainless steel maze of surgical trays.

"I see you are admiring my homunculi," he said. "I believe today the crude scientific term for them would be clones. Your science has no heart, no poetry."

"You find beauty in abducting, torturing, and mutilating innocent men, women, and children?"

"That, no, no," the Cooker said. "It is simply necessary to the process. My raw material. It is what I do with them, their parts, their essence. That, my dear investigator Marcou, is wherein lies the poetry."

The Cooker was close now, a few yards away. "Stop moving," Lovina said. "I don't want to kill you, but I will if I have to."

"I think your mind is already turning to the things I could help you with," the Cooker said. "I have conquered death, conquered disease. With my imbibing of the Azoth, I will be a god among mortals. You want to be part of my ascension, don't you? The things I can accomplish now, the things I can do to this planet once I am truly unending. Once know the mind of the universe.

"The girl you sought . . ."

"Raelyn Dunning," Lovina said. The Cooker gave a dismissive wave.

"Yes, yes. When I saw how close you were getting, I couldn't allow you to interfere with my work, not when I was so near to fruition. So I gave you her body back, I even gave you a ready-made villain in Angelo Potts to heap the blame upon. But you were smarter than I gave you credit for, more determined. You wanted the puppeteer, not the puppets, and here I am."

The Cooker was in front of her now. "You can consign me to a prison or some lunatic asylum, but you will be damning this world and the human race to the loss of all the fruits of my labor. I can do miracles now, think what I'll do when I'm God? I'm betting all that means more to you, investigator, than one forgotten, anonymous tramp from a trailer park."

Lovina's eyes flicked away, lost in thought for an instant. The Cooker's hand came up, a scalpel hidden in it. He flicked his hand out to open her jugular. The retort of the Glock thundered through the cave. The Cooker stumbled backward, knocking trays of instruments to the floor in a clattering steel rain. He fell back onto one of his tables, and died upon it, his eyes open, but no longer seeing.

"You lost that bet," Lovina said. "I saw you palm the knife." She walked over to his body, looked into his dead eyes. "Her name was Raelyn," she said, "and even one of her is too goddamned high a price."

Heck found Cherokee Mike's bike beside the road, near the path that led into the forest. He parked his bike beside Mike's, drew his Claymore, and sprinted into the forest clearing. Mike was already in the circle at the Devil's Tramping Ground. A fire was burning in the circle where no fire was ever supposed to burn. It crackled with green flames. Mike held the Key of Thorne and was walking around the circle counterclockwise, or widdershins as it was known in witchcraft. Off to one side of the circle stood Viper, his arms crossed, his face devoid of any emotion. When he saw Heck his face broke into a wide smile.

"You're too late, Sinclair," Mike sneered, his face illuminated in jumping green light. "Once I've begun the ritual, no man may enter the circle."

Heck stepped into the circle on the opposite side of the fire from Mike. He held his blade before him with both hands.

"I ain't just any man."

Mike froze. He looked over to Viper. The big redheaded biker shrugged. "Well, that's what I was told, Mike. Sorry." Mike held the iron wand by one end, with both hands, trying to avoid the metal thorns that covered it. Heck began to move around the circle toward Mike. Mike moved too, trying to keep Heck opposite him.

"All your mischief," Heck said, "all your lies and deceit ends now, Mikey. You end now."

Mike held his ground as Heck came closer. Mike kicked some dirt up with his boot and caught Heck in the face with it. He lunged in to smash Heck with the wand, but Heck, even partially blinded, parried to the strike. Green sparks flew off both weapons as they clashed. Heck advanced again swinging the huge blade in a wide arc. Mike ducked it and came up inside of it, striking Heck with the Key of Thorne on the hip and leg. The hit sent Heck stumbling back, falling out of the circle, but a powerful wind pushed him the other way, keeping him in the circle. Mike took advantage of Heck's disorientation and rammed the key like a mace into Heck's stomach. Heck managed to slam the pommel of the Claymore into the top of Mike's lowered head. Both men staggered back, wounded in the exchange.

Jimmie arrived and hurried into the clearing, still carrying his now empty shotgun. He took up a position on the opposite side of the circle from Viper, closer to Heck. He kept his eyes more on Viper than on the fight going on inside the Devil's circle. Viper locked gazes with the trucker. The smile dropped away from his lips.

Mike, bent over and groaning from the blow to his skull, slipped something out of his boot. Heck, bleeding from his face and stomach, began to advance again on Mike, who raised a small .22 pistol and opened fire on Heck from only a few feet away. The first bullet hit Heck but was slowed by ripping through his leather riding jacket. It then burned its way through Heck's right lung and exited his body, blowing out just below his right shoulder blade.

Heck kept coming, causing Mike to flinch and miss with the second round. Heck slapped the gun from Mike's hand as the third bullet was flying off wildly into the woods. Heck raised his left arm and brought the Claymore down in an angry one-handed strike. Mike stumbled backward and fell on his ass. He brought the Key of Thorne up to block Heck's blow, the green sparks flying once again as the two weapons clashed. Heck snarled in frustration and advanced another step, bringing the sword up again, using both hands now. Mike pushed backward with his legs, trying to get an opening, get some space to get back on his feet again, but Heck would have none of it.

The blade whistled down aimed for Mike's head. Mike shouted in fear and brought the Key up again, holding it with a hand on each side, both hands bleeding from the thick thorns of the wand. The Key stopped the sword mostly, but Mike's arms gave a little and he now had a nasty cut from his forehead to the severed tip of his nose. With the blade bound up with the Key, Mike drove a nasty kick into Heck's already injured leg with a steel-toed boot. Heck gasped at the pain and went down to one knee. Mike kicked him again in the face, breaking Heck's nose and crushing part of his cheek. Heck went down onto his back as Mike struggled to his knees and swung the Key down hard onto Heck's chest. Heck couldn't get the big Claymore up in time to block the hit so he rolled onto his side to absorb it with his shoulder and arm. There was an ugly cracking sound as the iron wand broke something in Heck's right arm. Heck howled like a wounded animal and lashed out at Mike with his injured leg. The kick didn't have much power behind it, but it got Mike off him long enough for Heck to stumble to his feet, now wielding the big blade with only his left arm. Mike was on his feet as well now, and both men began to circle each other again, barely able to keep standing.

"How long you plan to keep this up?" Mike said, blood spitting from his mouth with his words. "I'm going to have help from Hell in a little bit, and you, you will be my first human sacrifice to the lord of the pit. My new boss."

Heck shook his head. That was a mistake, because everything tumbled and dipped for a second. He kept his cool and kept circling Mike, the green fire surging and roaring between them. Heck strained with every muscle still under his command and kept the Claymore high above his head swinging it in faster and faster circles. His one good eye locked on Mike. "If I'm to be the Devil's meal, I guaran-fucking-tee I'll stick in his craw," Heck said, blood flying from his lips too, "and give him the shits for a hundred years. I'm spicy, motherfucker."

Mike was holding the Key of Thorne like a club, trying to find his opening. Blood drip-drip-dripped from the blunt missing tip of his nose. Heck winced a little, apparently from the bullet wound and Mike took to the opening like a shark sniffing blood. He swung the Key with all his remaining might at Heck's momentarily vulnerable neck.

And Heck closed the feint he had left for Mike, howling with all the burning rage in the world as he did. The sword of his father and his father before him whistled down striking the Key in mid-blow. Again there was green sparks but they vanished as the ancient Claymore sliced the supposedly indestructible Key in two. One half flew out the circle into the dark woods. The other half stabbed deeply into Mike's fingers and palm from the force of the blow. The sword's blade ended the arc buried deep in the bloody soil of the circle. Panting, Heck stood, barely. Mike was on his knees trying to pull the remains of the wand out of his torn and bleeding flesh.

Heck grabbed Mike by his hair with his bad arm and drove a powerful punch to his face with his one good arm. Teeth and blood flew and Mike made a gurgling sound. Heck yanked Mike's drooping head back up and hit him again. Viper hooted and clapped.

"Yes," Viper said. "Fucking A!" Jimmie circled again, watching Viper and then watching Heck. Heck let go of Mike's hair and let him slump to the now blood-soaked ground.

Heck staggered over and grabbed his sword. He pulled it from the earth with his good left hand and walked over to the stuporous Cherokee Mike. The green fire leapt and flared as he stood over Mike.

"Mhhfh," Mike uttered, looking up at Heck. "Don't . . . please . . . I'll, I'll run away. You'll never see me again, Heck . . . I promise."

"You know how good his promises are, right?" Viper said, now close to Heck on the other side of the circle. "Lying sack of shit. Lying to you from the start."

Heck's face was bathed in green light. Jimmie saw the cold rage that lived behind his squire's one good eye. He moved to Heck's side as well, getting closer to Viper than he cared to.

"He killed your friends," Viper continued. "He made your brothers turn on each other. He's nearly wrecked the dream your grandfather and Ale had, pissed on its hot ashes. He killed Jethro's dad . . . killed Glen. Glen had been like a dad to you, hadn't he? He killed Elizabeth, he murdered your mother. You know what he deserves, you know what you have to do to end this don't you?"

Heck brought the sword up to his good shoulder. His breathing was as even as it could be with one lung filling up with blood. Mike was half-dead already. He couldn't stand, couldn't even crawl away. He looked up a Heck and he trembled with fear, the wounded deer facing the wolf.

"He needs to go into the ground," Heck said, echoing his words to Jimmie a million lifetimes ago. Viper smiled. He looked to Jimmie and the smile widened.

"Hell, yeah," Viper said in agreement.

Heck winced at the exertion but he raised the sword, ready to deliver the final blow. He looked down into the sloppy, bloody mess that remained of Cherokee Mike Lochlear's face. His eyes were wet with tears, filmed in fear. That just made Heck hate him more for not even having the balls to go out like a man. He raised his family blade, a blade that had already done the impossible once today. The green flame roared, casting more emerald light. In his mind the fire laughed and whispered awful things to him, awful, but true.

"Heck . . . son." It was Jimmie's voice close to his ear. Even quiet, like his voice was now, Heck could hear it over the flames, over the blood racing in his veins, in his ears. Heck paused, and looked over to Aussapile. "I know you want to kill him. Hell, I've wanted to kill him for all the pain and suffering he's caused you, caused Elizabeth. He deserves to die and go straight to Hell.

"But Heck," Jimmie said, looking over to Viper, "I know him, I've known him since before you were born. He's sided with Mike this whole time, played him, then when you were vulnerable, at your weakest, he played you too."

Heck looked from Jimmie's somber face to Viper. The grin was gone now, the jaw set, the eyes told you nothing about what was going on behind them.

"I told you I was a bad man," Viper said, "back at the hospital. I told you the truth. Your mother was a fine woman and she didn't deserve to be killed by a scrub piece of shit like Cherokee Mike. Now you got him, dead bang. Kill him and you can start over. Let him live and you'll be looking over your shoulder the rest of your life, waiting for him to put a bullet in your back."

"Heck," Jimmie said. "I know you want to kill him. I know you have every right to kill him, but please, please believe me if Viper wants you to do it right here and right now, it's because he set this up to happen. I don't know how, I don't know why, but I know him and he's as bad, as crooked, as they come. You killing Mike, it benefits Viper, and nobody but Viper. Walk away, son."

Mike made a burbling sound. It was pathetic. Heck looked down at him. The sword trembled as his arm began to lose its strength. The green fire was a chant now, an ancient language that slithered and coiled in his mind, singing of other places, alien cities crumbling, older than time. He closed his eyes and still the green flames were there. He pushed them out of his mind and waited for a moment in stillness, darkness. He opened his eyes.

Heck lowered the sword to the ground. He looked at Jimmie. "I'm ready," he said, his voice a dry growl. A hot wind swirled around the circle and the green fire was snuffed out.

Jimmie smiled and nodded. "That you are, knight, that you are."

Heck looked over to Viper. He was no longer next to the circle but further back, near the treeline of the clearing.

In Viper's place, all around the circle now were every manner of nightmare creature. The Moon-Eyed Men, the Mothmen, the snarling wolflike Cu Sith, the Nightgaunts, and others, legion. One of their number, a creature with the body of a woman, garbed in black tatters of silk, and the dry, yellowed skull of crocodile for a head, held in her hands the warped and severed piece of the Key of Thorne that had flown out of the circle.

"The Key has been broken," the crocodile skull hissed. "Our bond of slavery to Hell has been broken. The Treaty of Thorne is no more, our time of service is no more." Heck limped to the edge of the circle and stared down the crocodile skull. He saw tiny, chittering, moving things skittering about inside, behind, the bone face.

"You're welcome," Heck said, and hawked up some blood and spit at the foot of the crocodile woman. He turned in the circle staring straight into the monstrosities that surrounded him, barely able to stand. "All of you stay the fuck out of North Carolina if you know what's good for you. You see the Blue Jocks' colors, I promise, we're coming for you." He turned back to the crocodile woman, "Now get the fuck out of my way." Heck stepped out of the Devil's circle and the army of monsters moved back, stepped aside, to accommodate him. A corridor opened in the ranks and Heck, the family Claymore over his shoulder, walked down it, head held high, no hesitation in his step, telling the pain to shut up.

Heck heard whispers in the ranks of the army of the night. They sounded like rats chewing in the walls, "Sinnnnnclair . . ."

"The last of the line . . ."

"The blade . . . the Fae."

"If we can't have him, we will have our tormentor, our fallen master . . ."

Waiting at the end of the corridor was Jimmie, looking one part worried to three parts proud. He clapped Heck on the back, and then righted the young knight of the Brethren when he almost fell.

"I got you, son," Jimmie said. "I got you."

There was a sound like bone scraping on slate and both men turned to see the circle had closed. There was a weak cry from within the circle. It sounded human, it sounded like Cherokee Mike. The assembled horrors fell into the circle then, devouring, ripping, slashing everything inside. The frightened human sound became a gurgling scream for a moment, then it was gone, devoured too.

Jimmie and Heck walked away from the clearing, toward their bikes, toward the brilliant, bloated moon, and the road. Heck glanced back for one second to the spot Viper had been standing in near the trees. He was gone.

"Come on," Heck said. "Let's go home."

Max walked through the quiet field, the trees of the forest at her back. She was still feeling random muscles spasm a bit from the connection of the spike to the railroad tracks. Now in her jacket pocket, the spike itself still jumped and flashed with blue energy, apparently charged from the contact.

She looked up at the stars and the full, blazing moon. She wished Big Max was still alive and could be beside her now. Her grandfather would have lain down in the still warm summer grass and pointed out constellations to her, told her stories about the humans and the gods immortalized in the night sky. Max had loved doing that with her grandfather as a girl. Now she just wished he was here to help her to deal with her persistent thoughts of failure.

It had made her feel better to help Dusty and Emmett Wally reach the others, hopefully in time. Now there wasn't anything to do but wait and worry. She topped the gently sloping grassy hill and found herself near the curve of the access road around the park. Ryan Badel's trailer was to her right. She saw the door of the park manager's small silver Airstream trailer open.

Bob Valenti climbed out the door, wrestling a duffle bag out behind him. The old hippie's face lit up when he saw Max. "Hey, hey! Dr. Max! How are you? Glad all that commotion settled down, I'll bet."

"Hi, Bob," Max said with a weary wave. Valenti had helped Max and Lovina in every part of their investigation, even the parts he figured were nuts. "Yes," she said. "It's finally hitting me. I'm beat. I'm going to head back to the hotel."

Bob nodded.

"Yeah more pigs around here than at a student protest! Hey, you wanna cup of tea for the road? I'm buying."

Max smiled. "I don't want to keep you from whatever you were about."

Bob snorted.

"Laundry," he said, hefting the duffle bag up again and tossing it back in the trailer. "You'd be doing me a favor."

"Sure," Max said. Bob held the door open for her and then followed her in. The interior of Bob's cramped trailer was a testament to hoarding and organization. There were clipboards on one side of the door related to various bits of administration for the park, a large dry-erase monthly calendar on the other side with various milestones and deadlines to be met, including when everyone owed rent. A note scrawled on the margin of the calendar struck Max's eye, REMIND CALVIN TO DO SOMETHING ABOUT THE GOD-DAMNED GOAT CARCASSES!!!

There was a small table with two benches under the window on the opposite side of the door. Bob had various books and yellow legal pads covering the desktop. He gestured for Max to have a seat, and she did. The back part of the camper where a chemical smell made Max think the cramped bathroom must be was obscured by a wall of rainbow-colored beads. The small galley kitchen was in the front and Bob went to work on a hot pot of water with a very beautiful, ornate, antique tea pot.

"That's lovely," Max said, nodding to the pot. Bob held it up for inspection before he put it back on the eye of his hotplate.

"Thanks, I got it in India back in '73. It had belonged to a colonial governor in the uh . . . 1800s, I think. Poor shmuck got poisoned by Thugees. It ended up on a peddler's cart and I traded him two big Thai sticks for it. Best deal I ever made."

Bob chuckled and Max settled into her seat, looking around at all the birds Bob had in his tiny home. There were bird figurines and tchotchkes tucked away on small shelves and display cases everywhere. There were ravens, swans, peacocks, pelicans, and finally a few examples of carved wood or porcelain figurines of the phoenix—the bird arising from the ashes of its own death. Something about the birds tickled a thought in Max's vast memory.

"Here you go." Bob placed a mug in front of Max. He had a little silver caddy full of different types of tea he placed between them. He cleared the table between them and set the steaming tea kettle on top of a book long enough to get himself situated across from her and then lifted the kettle and poured her a cup of hot water. He poured himself a cup of water while Max picked through the selection and felt yet another tremor from her muscles from the exposure to the energy of the Rail. She held an envelope up and Bob took it. "Ah, green Darjeeling," Bob said with a smile. "An excellent choice."

He slipped open the envelope and dropped it into Max's mug. He selected an Irish tea for himself and did the same.

"Thank you, Bob," Max said. "I . . . I was going a little crazy waiting for word from . . . well, everybody."

"I hear ya," Bob said, sniffing his steeping tea and smiling in appreciation of the aroma. "I do freakin' everything for people around here. Their toilet backs up, I hear about it, power line on the fritz, guy in the lot over growing weed, I hear all that, but I'm the one they forget to tell anything else to, births, deaths in the family, new jobs, kids graduating." He chuckled. "I get zip."

Max laughed.

Once steeped to their satisfaction, Bob and Max removed the tea bags. The tea caddy had side holders for honey, sugar, and powdered cream. Max loaded hers up with sugar. Bob added a bit of honey to his and raised his mug. "To those who stand and wait," he said. Max laughed and lifted her mug. They both drank and Max made a yummy sound, and licked her lips as she set the mug down.

"Delicious," she said. "Best tea I've had in ages. Thank you." Bob shrugged and took another sip of his. "I was admiring your birds," she said, taking another sip.

"Really? Thanks!" Bob said. "I just picked them up here and there, y'know."

"Mmmhm," Max said. There was a strange metallic taste in the back of her throat. She took another sip of the tea to dispel it, but it persisted. Her jaw was feeling very tight too.

"When I was young," Bob said, "my mother had birds of all kinds all over her home. Birds like these, but alive. I loved them, loved to watch them soar through the heavens, but it wasn't until I was older that she explained their meaning to me."

Bob's voice had begun to lose much of its middle Pennsylvanian by way of California accent. Max felt a thrill of terror fill her as she realized she couldn't move her hands, her arms, anything. The tea mug hung at an odd angle in her stiffening fingers. Bob reached over and pried it from her hands and sat it aside. "There we go," he said. Max's eyes still worked and she looked at Bob with terrified eyes. "I know," he said, "it's scary. The drug's a paralytic, I made it myself. It will start working on your lungs and heart in a little bit. I could lie to you and tell you it's a painless way to die, but I think you deserve the truth, Max, from one scholar to another. The search for truth can be painful. Usually, the greater the secret, the greater the pain. I know you'd agree if you could."

Max couldn't talk, couldn't move. Bob moved her arm from her face where the mug had been and brought both her arms down to her lap. She felt a shudder of movement in her leg as another muscle jumped as a result of the energy from the tracks.

"Where were we," Bob asked. "Oh, yes, the birds. You asked about them. My mother taught me of them. She wasn't my real mother, you see, but I apprenticed myself to her and never saw my other family again, or cared to for that matter. I grew up in a beautiful estate within sight of Rome. Max, I wish I could describe the glory of Rome to you then. It wasn't a city of half-decayed corpses as it is today. It was the bustling, vital heart of the greatest empire to ever exist upon this planet. It was magnificent." Bob's eyes were looking into memory and they sparkled as he brought forth the dead.

"My mother, my teacher, was named Locusta. I once looked her up on this amusement you call the internet. Quite a narrow and biased vision of so many things, and yet your people claim it the sum of all human knowledge, all wisdom. Ridiculous! Limited, I must say, but then it seems human beings today have the attention span of a gnat, so I supposed knowledge must be fed to them in a dropper. My mother, Locusta, was the founder of the alchemical arts, the creator of chemical and mystical miracles, and yet all she is remembered for is that she is the first recorded 'serial killer.' What utter drivel."

Max recognized the name now that it was put into context. Locusta was a poisoner, one of the greatest of her time. She worked for at least two emperors, and freelanced to the Roman aristocracy. She was eventually found to be a political liability and was arrested and put to death in a most horrific spectacle by the Emperor Galba. Bob nodded.

"I can see by your eyes you know of her. Good. That saves some time in the telling, since you have such little time left. I must also congratulate you on your mind and your will, Max. I have seen grown men, warriors, in this very situation, and their minds turned inward, they went mad with fear and panic. But not you, you are exceptional. I salute you."

Bob got up from the table and began to rummage for something on one of his overflowing shelves. "Now where did I put that? You must think me a fool to let such a treasure out of my grasp, but you and your friends have been keeping me very busy, Max, very busy. Disrupting my Harlequins' harvest, sniffing around the boxcar jungle. Interfering with an operation that has run smoothly for almost a century? I simply could not have it. That's why you are going to die, Max, why I invited you in. I want Lovina Marcou to find your cold lifeless body and feel the depths to which she has failed to stop me."

Max was finding it very hard to swallow and a tightness was grasping her chest, her diaphragm. There was another spasm, this time in her back. The energy from the Rail seemed to be more powerful than the paralytic poison. But it was completely random. She had no way . . . to . . . focus. The spike in her pocket!

"Ah," Bob said. "Here it is!"

Bob slid back into his seat and took another sip of his tea. "I'm certain my homunculus has given Investigator Marcou the details of how I attempted to get you two off my trail, just as I was preparing to culminate almost two thousand years of research and experimentation. But you were not as easily diverted as most agents of order I have encountered over the years."

Bob placed a tiny brown bottle on the table between them. It had a small sliver of cork for a stopper. "I wanted you to know what you were dying for, I wanted you to see it, before your eyes fail you. He picked up the bottle and held it near her face. "For this tiny distillation, these pitiful few drops, I have slaughtered millions, tens of millions across the gulf of time. From their deaths has come my enlightenment in this teeny, tiny bottle."

Bob uncorked it with a tiny pop, and held it under Max's nose. "Can you still smell? I hope you can. You deserve to know, to understand that all that death came to something, that it was not only worth it, but that it was a cheap price to pay for the Azoth, for godhood. The only being in the universe who has murdered as many as I is God himself. A fitting irony, don't you think, Max?"

Max's eyesight was getting bad and it was agony to pull another breath from her lungs. She closed her eyes and focused her brain on the symbol on the spike, the conducting symbol. She felt its every curve, every line. She could smell the Azoth under her nose, it smelled like the ocean, like tears.

"Oh, Max," Bob said, "shutting down, turning inward? I had hoped you would remain unafraid until the end, how glorious would that have been. You still need to know the secret of the birds. Each bird represents a different stage of the alchemist's journey, each step he must take to reach the ultimate goal of the phoenix—enlightenment through rebirth. I wanted you with me, one scholar to another, one seeker of ultimate truth to another, here at your end and my beginning." He placed the small stopper on the table and held the tiny bottle to his face. Max was beginning to wheeze, her face was very red.

"I, Valens Locustus, Born AD 37 by the reckoning of the Fisher's calendar do die this day and be reborn as God incarnate, divinity within flesh.

My last victim as a mortal, witness to my ascent." He lifted the tiny brown bottle to his lips.

"Waaaaaait," Max gasped, her eyes open again. Valens stopped, shocked.

"I've . . . I've never seen anyone fight the poison as hard as you, Max. Remarkable." He placed the tiny bottle on the table and slipped off his bench to move beside her. "Tell me your last words. I'll carry them with me throughout all eternity. Tell me." He leaned close to Max's lips, listened to her struggle to breathe.

"G . . . g . . ." Max struggled.

"Yes, yes," Valens said, "you can do it. Are you trying to say 'god,' are you trying to pray to me?" Valens leaned closer to Max's mouth.

"G . . . g . . . gotcha," Max uttered as she drove the crackling railroad spike into Valens's chest with all the strength her spasming muscles would give her. The force of her stabbing shook the table and the tiny bottle tipped over, a single drop of silvery liquid, sheened with blue power, dribbled out onto the table. Valens fell back, off Max's bench and onto the floor, blood and blue lightning gushing from his chest wound. Max forced her aching muscles to lurch her over the tabletop, and with her lips and tongue she managed to lap up the drop of the Azoth. At once she felt the death grip on her lungs and chest lessen, her eyesight returned, and she began to breathe again, be able to move again. She took the small bottle and corked it up again. Max stood and looked down at the almost two-thousand-year-old murderer, who was struggling, fighting for breath as his life blood pooled around him.

"Very good," Valens mumbled. "I should have expected that from one of my own fraternity."

"We're nothing alike," Max said, trembling. "You used science, knowledge that could have helped the whole world to help yourself, to create an army of soulless creatures to obey your every command. You could have lived forever as a healer, a scientist. Your legacy would have been the lives you saved. You don't deserve to call yourself a man of science."

Valens gasped and sputtered. The spike was burning him, turning his blood to steam. "And who do you think helped me all these long years with my great work? Who taught me the secret of the Rail, of the ley lines? Who do you think my patrons were, you foolish, naive child?" Valens began to convulse, the light already dying behind his eyes.

"The . . . temple . . . restored . . ." he hissed with his last breath, and then escaped the justice of this world for the judgment of whatever waits beyond the black.

The month of funerals felt like a year. Heck attended the services for all the dead Blue Jocks, regardless of whose side they had been on. He made sure the MC's lawyers and accountants set up trusts for every child who lost a daddy in this asinine war.

He attended the funerals and rituals held deep in the forests for all of the fallen Bitches of Selene. He went to the funerals of the civilians who had been caught in the crossfire of the civil war. He didn't wear colors, he wore a dark suit, his hair tied back. He always sat apart, alone. Only twice did the families recognize him and ask him to leave. He made sure every family, every orphan, got a check, just the same.

He stood beside his best friend as Jethro said good-bye to his father. Jethro spoke the words at the service remembering Glen. They carried the coffin together with the others who were so honored, like Jimmie. At the end, when Jethro stood by the grave and finally allowed himself the luxury of tears, Heck put his arm around him and stood silent sentinel until the final tear had been shed.

Ana Mae came to as many of the funerals with Heck as she could. The last one, she asked if he wanted her to go, and Heck kissed her and told her no.

After so much death, if felt good to ride again. Not into battle, but just to breathe the air, feel the acceleration in the darkness. He made his way up U.S. 74, into South Carolina, and finally on to I-26 into the cool darkness of the woods.

As he made the final turn, he saw the blackened scar on the ridge where fires had burned during the Jocks' battle with the monstrous Cu Sith. Faded yellow plastic police tape, shredded by the wind, was tangled in a few trees still, the only monument to the men who fell here battling Cherokee Mike's summoned evil. He flipped down the kickstand on the Blackie and killed the engine, but he left the headlight on. Its light was swallowed up by the tunnel that marked the end of the Road to Nowhere.

They had put her ashes in a beautiful silver cask, marked with the sun and the moon and stars. Heck had wrapped her favorite scarf around it. He took the Claymore, scabbarded on his back, and carried Elizabeth's ashes in one hand and a bottle of her favorite wine in the other into the tunnel.

On the other side he found a nice spot near the water, where they had cast Ale's ashes a few years back. As he sat on a rock, he lit up a joint and uncorked the wine.

"I keep thinking how much I missed of everything you tried to tell me," he said to the night, exhaling the smoke and taking a long pull on the wine bottle. "I wonder how frustrating that was to you. If it was, you never let me in on it. Not once." He looked across the water, the moon and stars mirrored in the darkness. "You taught me to think, to question, and to cherish. I got so lucky to have you as my mother. You deserve an honor guard, an audience, guns and pipes, and I damn well know you'd have insisted on a proper wake." He raised the wine bottle high. "But I wanted you to myself, Mom." Heck took another long drag on the bottle, chased it with the weed. "I can't really imagine a world without you in it." The forest night hummed with the song of summer ending and Heck sat and smoked and drank and talked to his mom.

Finally, when the weed and the wine were gone, he stood up and began to scatter her ashes, mingling them with the water, the trees, the rocks, and most of all, her beloved Ale. The forest grew silent for a moment, the waters still. The cask was empty. Heck nodded and closed the box. "Well, that's it, then," he said. "Good night. I love you."

He walked back to the tunnel, to his bike, and rode home, listening to the sound of the motor and the road. Elizabeth's scarf fluttered in the warm August night, wrapped around his handlebar, a token and a reminder.

. . .

A few weeks remained until school started again. The weather was still hot, the days long. It had taken over a month for everything to blow over from the fight in the boxcar jungle, for wounds to be mended and healed, for everyone's parents to relax a little, and for threats of being grounded for life to be forgotten.

Ryan, Nevada, and the rest were now part of the myths, the tall tales, that other kids who lived in the Valentine Trailer Park would grow up hearing about. The bogyman had begun to change too. Emmett the ghost clown was slowly replaced by the madman Dickie Dennis and his pack of monster clowns. Dickie himself was in prison, for murder, assault, and kidnapping. He'd be getting out in his fifties.

The forest belonged to all the kids again and as the ones who had stood up to Dickie and the other older boys, Ryan and the others came to be looked up to by the younger kids in the park. It was a weird sensation for most of them, having been picked on and ignored most of their lives. Sam took to it like a pro, and even took it upon himself to spread and embellish their tales as much as he could get away with. For his part, Ryan went back and forth in his mind between becoming a scientist, like Max, or a hobo, like Emmett. He eventually decided he could be both.

This evening, they had all met up back at the boxcar jungle to say goodbye to Emmett. The ancient clown was leaving his home in the jungle, taking to the rails with Dusty.

"I don't see why he doesn't just stay," David said. "He kicked all the bad clowns out. Now he could really gentrify this living space."

Joe looked over at Dave as if he had just grown a second head, then to Patrick. "He's really into HGTV right now," Patrick said. "It beats his Guy Fieri phase."

"He only stayed here to try to stop the alchemist and keep the Harlequins from hurting anyone," Ryan said. "He's a hobo, he wants to see the world."

"I still can't believe old hippie Bob was the psycho," Sam said. "I would have laid money on it being Calvin."

"Speaking of money, Sam," Joe said, "You still owe three bucks for the poker game on Tuesday."

"Three cigarettes do it?" Sam asked. Joe nodded.

"You're too young to . . . smoke, kid," Emmett said, coming into view, "or gamble." Some color had returned to Emmett's face since he had stopped using the clown-white makeup, but so had deep furrowed wrinkles, making him look decades older. Emmett told no one about the horrible withdrawal from the drugs in the makeup. He was still experiencing it although close to a month had passed. Some nights he wondered if he'd feel like this until he died. If he did, it was still worth it.

Emmett still had stubble of hair on his head and his face. He wore an old work shirt, work pants, and boots. He was carrying a canvas bag. He smiled at the assembled children. "I have a few things for you . . . before I go." He withdrew a chain from around his neck. He dangled it up for the kids to see. On the chain was an old key, it was wide and made of well-worn brass. Emmett handed the chain and the key to Nevada. "It's the key to the caboose. It belongs to all of you now."

"Holy crap," David said, "we just got a secret hideout upgrade!"

"Don't be doing . . . anything in there . . . you shouldn't be doing," Emmett said, looking at Joe and Sam, "like smoking or gambling."

"Furthest thought from my mind," Sam said.

"Suck-up," Joe muttered.

"All my books . . . my music, it's all yours now," Emmett said. "If you meet . . . someone . . . a decent person down on their luck . . . let them sleep over in the caboose. It will do you and them a world of good."

"We will," Nevada said.

"One hobo hotel coming up," Sam said.

"Come on," Patrick said, "let's go check it out!"

"Why do you get to keep the key, 'Vada?" Joe shouted as Nevada took off.

"Because I can kick all your little asses," she said, laughing.

The kids headed off in the direction of the caboose near the old tracks. As they ran by, they waved and shouted farewells and 'thank yous' to Emmett. Only Ryan remained behind.

"You . . . get lost?" Emmett said.

"No," Ryan said. "I just wanted to tell you thank you, for, well, saving my life, helping to stop crazy Mr. Valenti . . . I think . . . your family would have been really proud of you and what you did." Emmett smiled. His eyes shimmered a little.

"First time in over eighty years I think I might be able to cry," he said and chuckled. It was a deep rumbling sound. "Thank you, Ryan." They shook hands. "You saved me too, remember?"

"Oh, come on," Ryan said. Emmett shook his head.

"No, you did. Honest. I have something I want to give you." He slipped his hand into his pants pocket and pulled out a small penknife. He handed it to Ryan. "This . . . belonged to my boy. He gave it to me when I went on the road, for luck."

"Emmett, I can't take that," Ryan said.

"I've . . . held on to it . . . long enough," Emmett said. "It's given me plenty of luck. It's your turn now." The folded knife looked so small in Emmett's massive hand. He offered it to Ryan, who took it.

"Thanks," Ryan said. The man and the boy stood in the silence of the jungle, rusting time all around them. The cicada choir sang a song of the Sun and the Earth.

"The one part of living on the Rail . . . I've never gotten the hang of," Emmett finally said, "is parting ways with the people you meet and care for."

"My mom always says, nothing ever ends," Ryan said, tucking the knife in his pocket and offering the giant his hand again. "She says 'good-bye for now.'"

Emmett shook Ryan's hand. "Good-bye for now," he said.

"Yo, Ryan!" It was David's voice, squeaking a bit at the high end. "Get over here, this is soooo cool!"

"Go," Emmett said. Ryan nodded and ran across the debris-littered field toward the rails. He paused to look back at Emmett, but he was already gone.

"Ryaaaaaan!" It was Nevada this time. Ryan smiled and quickened his pace. He didn't look back again.

▪ ▪ ▪

In the heart of Manhattan's Financial District there is a fortress of mirrored glass and steel. At 1,776 feet in height, it towers over the New York skyline and is a bastion for international commerce. Thousands of people work there every day for various companies, agencies, banks, and brokerage houses. Many of the workers labor well into the night in the bleary-eyed pursuit of the American Dream: wealth, power, and unlimited personal freedom. None of them really have a clue who they actually work for, or that they all actually work for the same cadre, the same bosses.

Information moves through the very air of the fortress, summoned from across the globe, tabulating, assessing, judging, and executing the fiscal fate of billions of men, women, and children, every minute, of every hour, of every day.

Today the people who actually know what's going on are meeting in a completely nondescript conference room hidden away on the supposedly un-inhabited physical plant of the ninety-first floor. The attendees look like Wall Street bankers, lawyers, college professors, college presidents, men of means, and men of letters.

The room has been sealed, and not just electronically, by the best counterintelligence capabilities of the world's most powerful spymasters, but magically as well, by some of the world's most powerful masters. What is said in this room does not leave, does not exist beyond these walls. Today they discuss little people who have no clue the attention they have garnered.

"It's contained," the scholarly-looking black man with a salt-and-pepper beard and steel-rimmed glasses says, looking up from his tablet. "I say doing anything . . . actionable at this point would only create a greater vulnerability, a higher threat of exposure."

"Dr. Leher's continued inquiry is already increasing the likelihood of exposure," said a heavyset white man, a partial ring of white hair still clinging to his liver-spotted head. He is in his sixties and wearing an Alexander Amosu suit that costs more than most families in the United States make in three years' time. "She has her teeth into this, obviously," the liver-spotted man continued, "and now, thanks to this lunatic, the late Valens Locustus, she has physical proof of the Rail's existence and construction and how that naturally leads into her theories about the highway plan. Why are we simply not killing this girl?"

"This 'girl,' as you so rashly put it," said an older woman in her mid-sixties, dressed in a conservative, expensive, and slightly dated suit, "is one of the foremost experts in her field. Her death, even now, even if executed as an apparent accident would attract attention, investigation. It would leave us with the same problem of exposure and leave our order with one fewer very valuable asset. I think not." The scholarly man with the salt-and-pepper beard nodded in agreement.

"Not every problem can be handled like a line item on a balance sheet," he said, looking across the table at the liver-spotted man.

"Enough of this," said one of the men at the end of the table. He was white, painfully so, with snow-white hair and eyes the color of bright sunlight on ice. He was old, in his late eighties perhaps, and somewhat shriveled and stooped. Unlike the others at the table he made no pretense in regards to his dress, wearing a shirt and a sweater vest, old khakis, and well-worn loafers. His voice was enough to silence everyone at the table. "Bickering between the orders here will do nothing but make us less capable of acting decisively. Wouldn't you agree?" he asked his counterpart at the other end of the conference table, an elderly woman also in her eighties. She wore a sweater over a simple blouse, along with a skirt, and sensible shoes that gave her the appearance of a retired college professor or librarian, but the strand of pearls at her throat would have paid for a multimillion-dollar mansion anywhere in the world.

The woman nodded, and scanned the faces around the table. "I do. We knew going into this project the risks and the rewards. Now is not the time for a fracturing of the compact. We have a problem. We must seek an equitable solution to it."

"My apologies, Grandmaster," the scholarly man said to the old woman. "The temple restored." The old woman gave a slight nod in acceptance of the apology.

"Apologies, Grandmaster," the liver-spotted man said to the old man at the opposite end of the table. "The invisible hand." The old man gave no acknowledgment of the contrition.

"For now," the old woman said, "we will watch Dr. Leher closely. We shall make sure she is far too busy to go running off into the field again."

"But what about the contamination," the liver-spotted man asked the assembled at the table, "the reason we gathered today? Dr. Leher has shared these theories with the Brethren cell that she has been working with. They know her thoughts on the Road and its origins.

"James Aussapile has spread the information to his father, Donald Aussapile, and the senior has now made the Grandmaster of the Brethren aware of it. Grandmasters, if the Brethren discover the nature of the project, discover who is involved, the wheel will crack and split, we will have a civil war on our hands."

"Yes," the old man they called Grandmaster said, "you're correct. They cannot be allowed, at any cost to learn of the project, of the coming convergence. If the Aussapile family continues to take an interest in our business, then we will simply have to give them things closer to home to occupy their time."

. . .

It was night, Russell Lime knew that much. Sitting next to his dying wife in the hospital the days had smeared into one another. For a man who had made a career out of accuracy and details, it only made the whole experience with Treasure seem even more unreal.

Treasure was asleep right now, wheezing. Even the machines huddled around her, connected to her, couldn't mask the sound of her labored breathing. Russell had lived long enough, seen enough friends pass, to know that breathing meant Treasure's time was near.

The thought tumbled and grappled in his mind. She had suffered so much, he wanted her to have peace, release. But the thought of his life continuing without her made him want to cry again, but his tears no longer came. He took her hand, it was cool and dry, and he squeezed it three times like they had done since they had first met. Each squeeze was a word: I love you. Treasure would then squeeze back the same reply. Now, here, her hand made a feeble attempt at a squeeze, nothing more.

There was a knock on the open door on the other side of the blue privacy curtain. "Hello?" Lovina stepped around the curtain. Russ stood. He tried to summon his best face but it was a pretty shoddy attempt.

"The triumphant Amazon returns," Russ said. He shuffled over and hugged Lovina. She hugged him back.

"How is she?" Lovina asked.

"Sleeping," Russ replied. "She's hardly been awake the last few days."

"I'm sorry, Russ. I wish I had been here sooner."

"Don't matter," Russ said. "You're here now." Lovina walked over to the side of the bed.

"Russ," she began. "I have something that will help her, save her." Lovina held up a tiny brown glass bottle with a sliver of cork for a stopper. "There are only a few drops of it in here. Enough for you and her."

"Me?" Russ said. "What is it? Where did it come from?"

"It's born out of unimaginable evil and suffering," Lovina said. "It was made to do even worse, but we stopped that. You helped me do that." She looked down at Treasure. "If I can salvage one good, decent thing from this mess, I want to." Russ joined Lovina at the bedside. "One drop on her lips and she'll heal, she'll be fine, and she'll live a long, healthy life. A drop for you too, so you'll be there to live it with her."

"Lovina," Russell said, his voice cracking a little. "There have got to be other people, in this very building, in the world, more in need of that than my bride and I. We've had our run, *chère*."

"Whenever I don't think I can take one more atrocity, one more abomination, one more wound," she said, "I think of you and Treasure, and it reminds me that there is good in this world and that there are human beings who aren't dipped in evil. You two are my faith." The tears were hot on her cheeks, racing to fall into gravity's embrace. "Please, let me help you. You both deserve a happy ending and this awful world seems built to never give them. Please"—she held up the bottle—"one little miracle?"

Russ was crying now too, his tears returning. He nodded and mouthed the words "thank you," his voice gone. Lovina uncapped the bottle and dripped a tiny bead of the Azoth onto Treasure's tongue. Still sleeping, she licked her lips and swallowed. Lovina turned to Russ.

"You once sat at Daddy's bedside," Lovina said, "and I saw in your eyes that you would have taken his place, if you could have. I love you, Russ." She handed him the tiny open bottle. He held it up to examine.

"I don't deserve this," he said. "Treasure alive, healthy, that's my magic potion, that's my Avalon."

"Russ . . ." Lovina began.

"There's a little boy up on Twelve. I saw him in the elevator a few days ago," Russ said. "He's dying. Give it to him, *chère*. Please."

Lovina hugged him tight, kissed his cheek. He handed her the bottle back and she sealed it again. "I'll be by to see you all as soon as I get Max back home," she said. "A few days." Russ nodded, and smiled.

"Best get going," Russ said, wiping away Lovina's tears. "You know how Treasure gets about all my girlfriends." Lovina laughed and she saw the light back behind Russ's eyes once again. She gave him one more hug and headed for the door.

"Twelfth floor," Russ said. "Thank you, *chère*."

Russ stood by his bride's bed for a long time after that. He wrestled down his fear, the gnawing regret that hung at the edges of him. Eventually, his legs got tired and he sat again. He took Treasure's hand. It was warmer now. He gave it three squeezes, the second squeeze the strongest. Russell smiled when Treasure, still slumbering, replied with three squeezes back.

. . .

Lovina climbed back into the Charger. It was parked in the hospital's underground parking deck. Max sat in the passenger seat, her window down. The car radio was playing "Stay" by Zedd and Alessia Cara off a fuzzy FM station. Lovina could tell Max had been crying.

"I want to run to Baton Rouge before I take you home," Lovina said. "Malyssa Dunning deserves to hear Raelyn's story in person. You okay going there first?"

"Yes," Max said quietly. Lovina handed Max the brown glass bottle. "Here," she said. "There's a little residue still in there. Probably enough for the Builders to analyze it."

Max looked at the bottle for a second and threw it out her open window. They both heard the glass shatter as it hit the floor. "It's better lost," Max said quietly. "The things people would do to have it . . . no, it's better lost."

"Max, what going on?" Lovina asked, taking Max's hand. Max shook her head and tried not to start crying again.

376 · R. S. BELCHER

"I . . . honestly . . . don't know anymore," she said. "I don't know . . . I can't trust . . ." She sighed and turned to Lovina. "The only thing I know I can trust," she said, "is you." Max leaned forward and shyly, slowly, waited for Lovina to pull back. She didn't. They could feel the tickle of each other's breath, feel the warmth of each other's skin, so close but still apart. Max brushed Lovina's lips with her own. Lovina surprised herself in her response. She pulled Max closer, felt the lines between them melt and gave herself to the kiss in a way she had never done before. They finally parted and looked into each other's eyes.

"What was that?" Max whispered, like her voice would break a spell.

"It was real," Lovina said. "I know that."

"Can you please take the long way back to D.C.?" Max asked. "Please?"

"Yes," Lovina said, starting the car. "As long as you need."

. . .

It was night at the Devil's Tramping Ground. The state police, the cops, and the ambulances had been gone for weeks, everything was quiet again. A massive turkey vulture fluttered and then plopped into the clearing with a croak. The wounded, waning moon bled its stolen light onto the clearing. The vulture had something in its beak, and it spit it out at the edge of the Devil's circle. The sound of boots crushing old dead leaves came to the clearing, as Viper walked toward the vulture and its prize. Viper knelt and petted the bird's skull-like scarlet head.

"Good girl," Viper whispered. "Go on now, piss off." The bird groaned like a squeeze box and took flight into the night. Viper picked up what had been in the vulture's mouth, a chipped piece of Cherokee Mike Lochlear's skull, a decaying flap of putrefying skin still attached to it, and the jellied remains of an eyeball pooled in the one socket on the piece of bone.

Viper knelt, still holding his prize, and with his free hand picked up a handful of soil from the circle and let it spill slowly back to the earth as he whispered something old and terrible to the scrap of bone. Mike's decaying eye came to life, looking about frantically.

"Hiya, sport," Viper said with a grin. "Hardest time you'll ever do, pardner, I guarantee it." Viper stood and walked the edges of the circle, counterclockwise. A tiny noise came from the bone, it sounded like it was whispering "help me."

"Well, I know none of this ended up the way we'd have liked, Mike," Viper said.

The tiny voice wheezed, "Please."

"If Heck had killed you here . . . well, I know a lot of folks who'd be pleased as punch right now. But he didn't. There are a few upsides though. And as you know from your time in stir, you have to keep that little spark of hope guarded, tend it, so it doesn't go out, right?"

The scrap of bone sounded like it was sobbing. Viper held it up so it could see the moon and stars. The weeping increased.

"Bright side number one," Viper said. "Elizabeth is dead, and while I may have mixed feelings about that personally, in the grand scheme of things that's one less anchor Heck has to cling to in a storm, one more wound to make him bleed. I also learned that Heck trusts Jimmie Aussapile more than anyone alive on this dingy little spinning rock. That means when I arrange for Jimmie's betrayal of Heck, it will hollow out a nice big chunk of what's left of young Hector's crunchy little blackened heart."

Viper stopped at the six o'clock position on the Devil's circle. He looked back into Mike's remaining eye. Ants were chewing on its viscous pulp.

"Bright side number two. Heck destroyed the Key of Thorne. I didn't know the boy had it in him. Blood will tell, huh? With the Key gone, the dukes and presidents and barons, all the infernally entitled lose so much of their armies, so much of their control here in the lands of light. The established order of Hell will be in chaos now, and another name for chaos is opportunity."

Viper looked down at the chip of bone, the puzzle piece of Mike's face. "I want to thank you for your part in all this, Mike. I really couldn't have done it without you. Well, actually I could have but you made it all so much easier. You took the brunt of every consequence, bore the reaction to every action, and you were stupid enough to do it all willingly." He leaned in close to the glaring, melting eye. "Thanks."

Viper crushed the bone in his bare hands. He could hear the screams of "No" diminishing as the last part of Cherokee Mike upon the earth was reduced to dust. Viper let the bone dust spill inside the circle. "*Adios,* pardner," Viper said as the dust fell. "See you around."

As the last particles of the dust fell, the clearing was empty and silent once again, with only the dying moon as witness to the deed.

. . .

Jimmie pulled up into Elizabeth's driveway and parked his bike. There was an old oil spot on the driveway Jimmie remembered from helping Ale with his bike . . . over thirty years ago? Time played tricks on you.

It was late in the evening and the house was dark. Heck's T5 Blackie was parked in the driveway too. He had backed it into the drive, just like Jimmie did. Jimmie touched the engine of Heck's bike, it was cold.

Jimmie walked around the house to the backyard and opened the gate to the chain link fence. A large pit bull trotted up to Jimmie and made a loud "gromph" sound. Jimmie let the dog smell his hand and then petted him. The dog trotted over to the picnic table in the center of the backyard. Heck was sitting on it. He was surrounded by empty beer cans and liquor bottles. The pit bull made its "gromphing" sound again as if he were announcing Jimmie and then plopped itself under the table.

"A fine fucking guard dog you'll make," Heck said. He nodded to Jimmie. "Hey."

"Hey. Thought I'd see what you were up to."

Heck snapped open a fresh beer can, handed it to Jimmie. He took a long drink and handed it back to Heck.

"This is pretty much it," Heck said. "Mom'd be pissed at the mess the kitchen is in." Heck smiled and took a swig off a bottle of Bushmills. He offered it to Jimmie. Jimmie groaned a little as he sat on top of the table next to Heck and took the bottle. He took a long drink and handed back to Heck.

"Oh, I made an executive decision as the president of the fucking club," Heck said and burped a little. "I told Jethro everything, all about the fucking Brethren. Ana Mae too. If that means I don't get my fucking decoder ring or whatever, I don't give a shit."

"It's okay," Jimmie said. "They're good people. They'll keep your secrets. Not a problem." Heck looked over at Jimmie and narrowed his eyes.

"You already drunk?" Heck asked. Jimmie laughed and shook his head.

"Thought you were headed back to Lenoir?"

I did," Jimmie said. "Few days back. I figured I'd come on down and see how you were?"

"Breathing," Heck said. "Good and truly pished."

"Understandable," Jimmie said. "I'd be worried if you weren't getting a little fucked up, to be honest."

"I'm still shoveling up Mike's bullshit," Heck said. "Royal Elkins, the cop? He came by, paid his respects about Mom, and then gave me a very polite, very decent-of-him warning that the cops are looking at me and some of the Jocks for the murders that took place during the war."

"A good guy, that Royal," Jimmie said, sipping his beer.

"The best," Heck said, taking another pull of the bottle, "for a cop anyway. Well, come what may, I got this. I'm a full Brethren, president of a practically nonexistent, mostly broke MC with a shaky rep. I'll get it sorted out."

"I know you will," Jimmie said. "Anyone who knows you knows you will. You don't give up on anything, ever. I just wanted to remind you, you're not alone in this."

"I'm not a squire anymore," Heck said, "Not your squire. I should—"

"I took money from my folks to make the mortgage this month," Jimmie said. "I don't think a week goes by I don't ask my dad for advice about something. You never outgrow family, Heck. Even in the times you feel most alone, you're not."

Heck looked over to him and handed him the bottle again. Jimmie took it, drank, and handed it back. They passed the bottle back and forth for a while. Eventually it was empty, and Heck added it to the bench full of dead soldiers. Jimmie's mind slipped to a terrible thought. He was the only one left, the only one to tell Heck the truth about Viper. It felt like a dull knife in his guts.

"What?" Heck said. Jimmie blinked. "You look like you had something to say."

Jimmie shook his head. "It'll keep," he said. "Hey, I got a run to make. Atlanta, day after tomorrow."

"Cool," Heck said. "See, you'll be outta money trouble in no time, man." Jimmie laughed.

"Shit," he said, "but it's a job. I was thinking maybe you could ride along with me, give me a hand?"

"Jimmie," Heck said, "I'm okay, really."

"Well, there may be another . . . job to look into on the way," Jimmie said. "I could use your help, Heck, one knight to another."

Heck grinned. It was the first time Jimmie had seen that smile in a while. "Okay," he said. "Sure. One condition, though." Heck pointed to the dog slobbering on a chew bone at the foot of the table. "He comes too."

"What?" Jimmie said. "Are you serious?" Heck held up his hands.

"Hey man, I had to make a fucking case to get to keep one of the three we rescued. Ana Mae said she bet Drooly ended up taking care of me . . . it has, but that's not the point. If Ana Mae got wind I left him here, she'd tan my hide." Jimmie laughed.

"Okay," he said, "but you clean up after him, you hear?"

Heck nodded.

"Can't be worse than cleaning up after me," he said.

"Good point. Okay, we'll head back to Lenoir tomorrow, pick up the rig. Layla said to come for dinner, whatever you'd like."

"Well damn, why didn't you open with that?" Heck said. "I'm going!"

"You good if I crash on your couch tonight?" Jimmie asked, crushing an empty beer can.

"Couch is his." Heck nodded at the dog. "I'm sure you two will work that out."

They laughed and it felt good and real again, like some dark bird made of pain was freed from its cage in their chests. They drank and they talked. They remembered the lost, brought them back to life with stories, honored them with laughter, and toasts, and tears. In time, the sky lightened and they made their way inside, to sleep.

"Thanks Jimmie," Heck said.

"We're family, son," the trucker said. "It's not the wheel part that matters, it's the brotherhood part that means something. Some wise old fart told me that."

"Figured that," Heck said. "Sounded too deep to come from you."

Jimmie sighed.

"Let's get some shut-eye," he said.

The patio door closed but Jimmie's voice carried through it. "I just hope that dog doesn't hog the damn blankets."

. . .

The rattle of the train was a heartbeat. Dusty Acosta and Emmett Wally stood at opposite ends of the boxcar's open door watching as endless fields of golden wheat flew by.

"'One more train to ride,'" Dusty said. Emmett nodded, but kept watching the farmland roll past him. It hadn't changed, not really, not in the ways that counted. It was the same glorious view he recalled from eighty-odd years ago. It still made him feel young, made the world a place full of promise. He knew, could feel, he was dying. He wasn't sure how long he had but this view, that sky, it was worth whatever came next.

He knew he was headed in the direction of home for a spell, long enough to visit his wife and children, tend their graves. Indulge the luxury of the tears he now had once again. After that . . . well, this was the only life he'd ever known and it did give him joy, the feeling of being connected to all of life, the dirty, smelly, petty bits and the glimpses into paradise. The clouds parted and rays of sunshine caressed the swaying field of gold.

"Hey, big guy," Moxie said, "what do ya think?" She was sitting cross-legged opposite the car's open door. She was wearing a Grateful Dead T-shirt and bib jeans overall. Her turquoise hair was up in a ponytail held tight by a hair tie adorned with a little pink troll doll. She had been carving on a nickel with a very sharp little pocketknife. Emmett walked over and Moxie held up the coin proudly. She was carving the three-spoked symbol of the Brotherhood on the coin's face.

"Very good," Emmett said. "I never could . . . get the hang of that."

"Let me see, Mox," Dusty said, kneeling beside her. She showed him the coin.

"It's for your secret club," she said and made a production of putting her finger over her mouth and making shushing sounds. Dusty laughed.

"Okay, okay. Keep it on the DL, will you? Else I'll have to merder ya, see."

"I can't believe you sweet-talked me into this," she said and grabbed one of his ears and played at twisting it. "I was almost settled in, you goon."

"Well then I showed up in the nick of time," Dusty said, tweaking her nose. They both stuck their tongues out at each other in mock indignation.

Emmett enjoyed the sounds of young lovers laughing, the light, and the warmth on his skin after lifetimes of perpetual cold. Everything from here on out would be gravy, every day, every moment. The immortal he had known as Basil Valentine was dead. The monster who had killed his family and so many others had faced final justice. The alchemist's followers were dead, in jail or scattered, hiding in old abandoned buildings, back-road towns, slowly decaying under their carnival paint. He wondered how many were still out there, still hiding, still hunting.

"Hey, Emmett, you okay, man?" Dusty asked. "You looked kind of worried there for a second." Emmett looked over to the young hobo and shook his head.

"Probably . . . nothing," Emmett said. "It will . . . take care of itself . . . in time. If not, you and I and those like us . . . will deal with it as we always have." Dusty smiled, slapped his fellow Brethren on his broad shoulder, and returned to Moxie.

Emmett had forgotten so much in the darkness. The sky, the sun, they were a promise, another day, another breath, another chance. Life's engine clattering under your feet and pumping in your blood, shaking you, reminding you to live and to best be getting to it. Emmett smiled and let the sun kiss his face, like meeting back up with an old, dear friend. Whatever time he had remaining he would spend it living on the rail, on the roads. We all end up in the same place, so best enjoy the way you take to get there.

Emmett glanced away from the boxcar's open door for a moment, and in that moment the view of the sea of gold racing by was split by something else for a second, like a frame of another film spliced in for a flickering flash of an instant. A looming figure alone near a barn, an isolated farmhouse—a flash of garish colors, reds, blues, yellows . . . and white. A figure standing, staring, waiting. Then it was gone, lost to the thunder and velocity of the rails. Perhaps it was a scarecrow.

END

ACKNOWLEDGMENTS

Thank you to the various members of the outlaw MCs, long-haul truckers, hobo, nomad, and Juggalo communities that reached out to me by email or in person and answered my dumb-ass questions.

Thanks to Greg Pizzino, for pointing me to some excellent resources for research, and Patty Templeton, for great resources on the modern nomad movement.

Thank you to my brother, Dave Lystlund, for my amazing Hobo Nickel, and a lifetime love of useless trivia facts that are like gold.

To Gina Matthews of Little Engine Productions, for all the kindness, enthusiasm, and unwavering belief in the Brotherhood of the Wheel.

Heartfelt appreciation to my peerless agent, Lucienne Diver, of the Knight Agency, and the wonderful folks at Tor I have the privilege of working with, Christopher Morgan, Desirae Friesen, and my always-amazing Editor, Greg Cox. Thank you all.

Finally, to you, the readers, for your time, supportive words, and kindness. You are the fuel that keeps the wheel turning. Thank you so much.